"*They Will Be Coming for Us* offers both quality writing and an irresistible story—a winning combination all around."

— BLUEINK REVIEW (STARRED REVIEW)

"Well-constructed science fiction with an admirable heroine and a chilling premise."

— KIRKUS REVIEWS

"Kim Catanzarite's *They Will Be Coming for Us* slowly and stealthily sweeps you away with its stellar writing and thrilling plot twists. What starts out as a seemingly simple story of young love becomes a complex tale of deception and duplicity. ... I dare you to put this book down. I read it in two nights because it is just that good.

— JORDAN ROSENFELD, AUTHOR OF *WOMEN IN RED* AND *HOW TO WRITE A PAGE TURNER*

"Kim Catanzarite's *They Will Be Coming for Us* is a cross-genre novel that skillfully blends thriller, sci-fi, and romance to create a wonderful and haunting storyline. I could not stop turning the pages. "

— VALERIE JOAN CONNORS, AUTHOR OF *A BETTER TRUTH* AND *IN HER KEEPING*

THEY WILL BE COMING FOR US

KIM CATANZARITE

forster
publishing

A LUCY H SOCIETY BOOK

Copyright © 2021 by Kim Catanzarite

All rights reserved.

No part of this book may be reproduced, or stored in a retrieval system, or transmitted in any form or by any means, electronic, mechanical, photocopying, recording, or otherwise, without express written permission of the publisher.

ISBN 978-1-7359522-1-5 (paperback)

ISBN 978-1-7359522-0-8 (ebook)

Printed in the United States of America

1 3 5 7 9 10 8 6 4 2

Published by Lucy H Society Books, an imprint of Forster Publishing, United States of America. Distributed by Ingram Book Group, www.ingramcontent.com.

Proofreading by Rachel Randall

Cover design by Damonza

For my husband, who has been very patient

Where, like a pillow on a bed
    A pregnant bank swell'd up to rest
    The violet's reclining head,
    Sat we two, one another's best.

—John Donne

Well we all shine on
    Like the moon and the stars and the sun.

—John Lennon

THEY
WILL BE
COMING
FOR US

I chase my sister, Helena, across the soccer field, threatening to "get her" like some big bad American boogie man (or maybe I should say "woman," considering I am female). We both find that word *boogie* so strange and gross, and that's why Helena runs from me. "I'm going to get you," I shout with the delight of a child, though I'm far from it at the age of twenty-three.

Helena kicks the heads of daisies and rips leaves from the low-hanging branches of trees. She turns partway around and yells, "You'll never catch me. I'm too fast for you, fatso!"

"How dare you?" I feign insult.

You would think we were drunk. And perhaps we are, or at least *I* am—on happiness, on life, on the fact that it is Friday evening and we have finished work at the ice cream shop for the week.

Nonetheless, we are too old to play games of chase like little girls. Helena is only six months younger than I am. Our parents boarded a plane to India this morning and will be gone for ... I cannot remember how long. Months. They're gone more than they're here. Saving the world one family at a time, as my humanitarian father likes to say. They're good people, my adoptive parents, and I love them.

When you grew up in an orphanage like Helena and I did, the fact that you live in America in a house with a mother and father is reason enough to be happy—and grateful— every day of your life.

I catch up to her at the front door of our parents' house —*our* house (I must always remind myself even after seven years of living here). She's doubled over and panting; her asthmatic lungs can't handle her own vivaciousness, and she's wheezing. "You better get a breath of your inhaler when you get inside." I pull up my keys from the bottom of my purse. She doesn't answer, so I nudge her. "Did you hear me, little sister?"

The "little sister" thing is something she both loves and hates, the way every little sister does: the plight of the younger sister is the same whether the sisters are blood related or not—and we are not.

"Shut up, boogie man," she mutters. Then she springs up and pushes me out of the way, bursting through the door I have unlocked. She runs into the family room and dives onto the couch. "You really do look like a monster. Or an alien. Yes, you and those big eyes and pale Russian skin of yours. Has anyone ever told you?"

I make a smirk of my lips and try to think of a good comeback. I happen to know Helena finds me beautiful. When she's not joking this way, she tells me all the time. *Sveta, your legs are like a pageant queen's. Sveta, your face is like Oil of Olay. Sveta, if I could have a few ounces of your beauty, I might be average.* (She's as cute as a button, as my American mother says, though a bit on the glass-is-half-empty side.)

"If I'm an alien, you are the alien's crazy adopted sister," I say, winking at her.

Then I head into her bedroom and find her inhaler on her night table, where she always keeps it.

I toss it to her. She misses, and it bounces off her stomach, making us both laugh once again.

It's been seven years since this house in Kirksberg, Pennsylvania, became our home. Seven years since we left Miss Sonja at the orphanage at Petranko, since we've eaten the gruel that passes for food in institutions across the Russian Federation. Seven years since we slept two to a bunk under dirty blankets riddled with holes in rooms fifty degrees and sometimes colder. I miss Miss Sonja, who made our American adoption possible. Miss Sonja, who told me the truth about my birth parents when no one else would. I send her a letter every six months or so. She never returns them, and that is as it has to be according to Russian law. I would send her some money as well, but that would only get her into trouble. Instead my parents make an annual donation to the orphanage each December.

I've been staring into nothingness the way I do whenever I think of Russia, or my past, or my birth parents and Miss Sonja—and Helena has noticed.

"You are thinking of going back?" she says.

Her words hit me like a snowball in the face. "To Russia? *No.*" I cross my arms over my chest. "Never."

She shakes the inhaler, brings it to her mouth, and squeezes so that the small blast of medicine is released. With a noisy exhale, she says, "I sometimes do," and looks away from me. "Lately, more than usual."

I drop onto the couch pillow next to her, my weight making an angry bounce. "No, you don't." As if this is enough to change her mind.

"I *have* thought about it."

Her dark eyes have something strong like black coffee brewing in them.

"You would leave me?" I say. "But your family is here. Where will you go? You have no family in Russia, Helena. No home."

Her brow crumples the way it does whenever I tell it like it is. I know she wants to shout, *Duh, I know that.* Instead she says, "I miss Russia because I'm Russian. I want to speak Russian, to hear Russians, to smell Russian food, to be surrounded by Russian people. People like *me.*" Her anger makes a stone of her face. "Too many smiling Americans here."

"So what if they smile all the time? It's not their fault. You would too if you grew up here. We're lucky to be here, lucky to have a mother and father, to be a family. All I've ever wanted was a family."

"Right. We have parents who are never here and—" She stops. Looks me in the eye. "They never wanted children. I don't know why you don't see that. They saved us from the streets—the sex trade, as they say. All they want is to save the world with their Heifer International and their Habitat for Humanities and Doctors at the Borders. You and I are just two pieces of the plan."

For a second I feel like I might cry. But this is so Helena. Never-happy-for-long Helena. "You know they care about us," I say. "You know they *love* us."

She makes a sputtering sound that mocks my words. "They spend ten days a year with us. This trip they're on, how long will they be gone?"

Like every annoying little sister, she can be so stubborn. I've been saving her from her stubborn self since our days at the orphanage when she was six years old and thought it a good idea to sneak away in the middle of the night and find a cave to live in.

"They will be gone for months, and so what? I'm grateful

to them, and I like the weeks we spend together each year. And you do, too. You just don't want to admit it."

Helena shakes her head. "Not true."

"Besides, we're not little babies who need our hands held." My face is getting red. I can feel it. "And when we were younger, they were here for most of the year. They took turns going away, remember?"

Her next words are so warm, so gentle, they break my heart: "You may love them, but it's not *real* love. And they're not a family the way you and I are family."

I'd rather she growl at me than speak to me in this tone.

"But it can be," I say, "if you stop being so ..."

She raises her dark brows in wait of what comes next.

"... *you*," I say.

Her chin dips into a reluctant nod, accepting my opinion while she pushes the inhaler into her pocket. "I've been saving my money, and one day I will go back."

An insulting bit of a laugh escapes my mouth. "How much can you save when you make nine dollars an hour at an ice cream shop?"

She says nothing.

"Do you have some other job I don't know about? How many secrets do you keep from me, little sister?"

No answer. She won't go anywhere. She can't. "So you're leaving forever? Or only for a visit?"

She presses her lips together, hesitates. "Maybe forever."

"I see." I take in an angry breath and withhold the other words I would like to say.

"I'm not asking you to come with me. I know you won't."

"You're right," I say without pause. "I won't."

My answer seems to have slapped her face. Her mouth droops with sadness. And I'm glad. Because I'm angry. I don't appreciate these threats of leaving.

"You love to complain," I say with a sigh. "Whoever your mother was, she gave you the genes for complaints."

"So you always say."

I wonder if it is possible that Helena has saved enough money for a plane ticket. Taxis? Food? A place to stay when she gets there? Even if she's been frugal, which she hasn't— she loves video games far too much to be frugal—I doubt she has enough. When our parents decided we would have to pay for our own cell phones, Helena couldn't come up with the necessary amount each month. That's why we've been sharing a phone ... and driving our parents' car and living at home (no reason to rent when we're on our own so much of the time anyway). So this is Helena being dramatic. Helena wanting me to cry, "Please don't go."

Instead I say, "So you're saving your money then?"

She places her hand on my shoulder. "Yes. And one day I *will* go."

Our American hometown of Kirksberg, Pennsylvania, population 15,500 or so, is well-known for one thing: a UFO sighting that occurred in 1965. Can you believe it? Helena and I always laugh about how we came from another world and landed in Kirksberg just like the aliens did. It's a big deal, this UFO stuff. *Unsolved Enigmas*, the television show, put together a special episode about what happened in the woods of Kirksberg. My parents know some of the people they interviewed.

But if you ask me, it is not much of a mystery. Thousands of people saw a spaceship fall from the sky. The people said it was nothing like an airplane or a helicopter. It emitted a green streak of light and took precise turns before it crashed into a ravine. And people even saw the crash site. They saw the spaceship up close and said that it had strange writing on it like Egyptian hieroglyphs.

So, where is the mystery?

The logical explanation is that a spaceship crashed in our town. What's the harm in saying so? Americans are known for overthinking, and that is why the debate continues decades later. It's not like space creatures have invaded the country—or even visited again.

Oh, but wait, that's not true. Kirksberg gets invaded every August during the annual UFO Festival. You should see the oddballs that roll out of the woods that day. The town becomes a gathering place for costumed extraterrestrials and their oversize skulls, ET, Martians, Yoda, Spock. The festival draws a huge crowd and makes very much money. It's great for tips, especially for people like Helena and me, who are in the ice cream business. Aliens, like humans, love ice cream in the summer.

"That's why they're so fat," Helena says, as we discuss Americans and their habits (her favorite subject) while lugging five-gallon buckets of Fifty Chilly Flavors into the store from the refrigerated truck that's parked in the loading zone.

Michael, our boss (and grown son of our parents' closest friends), places the orders when he comes in on Mondays, and Helena and I drag five-gallon containers into the store every Wednesday when they arrive. Once they're inside, we have to move them into the walk-in freezer—making sure the door is propped open so we don't get trapped inside, something I have nightmares about.

The festival is this weekend, so we are dealing with three times the normal delivery. We can hardly fit it all into the chaotic mess of a freezer, and of course Michael isn't around to tell us what to put where, so we stack the buckets at random.

"You think Russians aren't fat?" I say, my words coming in icy puffs as I heft a Chilly's Best Buttery Scotchy to the top shelf. "Do you not remember Miss Sonja and her voluptuous behind? What about Miss Victoria? Arms like tree trunks. And, well, Miss Darya, with a face like a chipmunk and the body of a scarecrow." I puff my cheeks. "Still. No one would mistake her for skinny."

"Okay, okay,'" Helena says with a laugh. "I suppose everyone packs on the pounds soon enough. Except for you. You're too perfect for that." She sticks out her tongue, and I give her a playful push out of the freezer.

"But you don't see me eating ice cream, do you?"

She takes a sample spoon and dips into the new bucket of Fudge Brownie Swirly we opened. It's her favorite. "This is true. I do a lot more sampling than you do, but only because I never eat a big enough lunch."

"Don't let Michael catch you."

She juts her chin and raises her voice as she says, "Free samples to the public," while thrusting her fist in the air.

The door opens to the sound of tinkling bells, and Helena drops her plastic spoon. I laugh because I can see that for a second she thought it might be Michael. Of course it's someone else. Someone who wants to buy ice cream. Someone I have never seen before. And if I'd been holding a plastic spoon when I looked up and saw him, I would have dropped it, too.

It's strange because I don't know him, but for some reason it seems wrong for him to be alone. I expect a pretty girl to come rushing in behind him and say, "Here I am, sweetheart. Sorry I took so long. I was on the phone with Angela, and she wouldn't stop talking," the way people in love always do.

But no. He walks in by himself. The bells jingle, and he lets the door close behind him as he smiles right at me.

Helena bends over to pick up her spoon, and I'm left to gaze at him over the counter. Suddenly I'm nervous. Happy nervous. I smile back and say a shy hello as my pulse speeds through my body and slams into my heart.

Helena unbends and turns her head in my direction—I see her in my peripheral vision. I have never said a shy hello in my life, and it has attracted her like a child to candy. She looks first at me and then at him. And then she laughs out loud. A rude and stupid laugh. Childish.

"I'll take my break now," she says.

I pay her no mind. We never take official breaks, so this is unusual.

"Bathroom break," she says, as if I didn't hear the first time.

I turn toward her, and she points to the corner of the room where the bathroom is, then raises her eyebrows in a teasing way.

"Yes. Of course," I say. "Go."

I'm not a lovestruck kind of girl. I do not have crushes on boys—or men. I get to know a person before I consider dating him. So this is strange behavior for me. Strange feelings for me. I can't look this guy in the eye, and I can't look away. And I'm smiling. Like an American.

He tips his upper body forward and gazes into the cabinet that holds the assortment of frozen yogurts. His hand rests on the top, and his fingers tap as he weighs his options. Mango. Chocolate. Vanilla with cherry chunks. These are what Helena and I call the "mommy treats," because young mommies who want to stay (or become) slender are the only ones who ever order them.

"Can I help you find a flavor? We give free samples."

I am the perfect hostess.

The hand resting on the top of the cabinet points. "Are these the only frozen yogurts?"

"Yes. There are six." I'm sure he can see that for himself.

His face reminds me of a face I've seen before. A name on the tip of my tongue. Whose? I cannot think. Someone on television, maybe? Not that he's like an actor or a model from a commercial I've seen. I've never liked model boys, and he's not one of those. He has no cleft chin, no bulging biceps. He's handsome, though. Ordinary light brown hair. Good-looking. Not fussy. Not a blond dressed in a suit. He's a jeans-and-nice-shirt kind of guy. Possibly someone I knew from college? No. I would remember.

"Do you live around here?" I blush as soon as the words hit the air.

Our eyes connect like a snap on my purse, and we both hunch over into polite, soundless laughter. I'm shaking my head, letting my overgrown bangs fall across my cheeks. "That sounded wrong."

He stands straight and takes a more balanced stance. "Yeah, yeah. It's okay. I do live around here. I've been away for a few years, but it's nice to be back."

"Well, welcome home then." I hope he notices my dimples and not my awkwardness.

He smiles again, and I smile back. And then he says. "Mango looks good."

I reach over for a bright purple sample spoon, dip into the mango bin, and extend it in his direction.

"Oh, you don't have to …"

"Yes, I do. It's my job." I put on my serious business face.

He takes the spoon from me, puts it in his mouth. "Damn, that's good."

"Thank you. I scooped it myself."

He laughs. He has nice teeth. Very straight.

"You have an accent. Where are you from?" he asks.

"Russia. But I've been here for years."

He nods. "Cool."

"Would you like a single or a double?"

"Oh, double, please. How could anyone have just one?"

A little wrinkle forms in the bridge of his nose when he smiles.

Helena rejoins me with the same smirk she left with. "Oh, yes, you have to have two. Having only one would be un-American," she says.

I can see that he's not sure whether she is joking with him or giving him a hard time. He's a thin man, so it's not like she could be making fun of his weight.

"This is my sister, Helena. She scoops ice cream, too."

"So it's a family business."

I don't want to correct him, so I say, "Yes, a family business."

―――

That night, after we have eaten dinner and are about to clean dishes, Helena says, "Do you know where they keep our passports?"

"*They?*" I say, squinting. "You mean that strange man and woman we live with?" She never calls them Mom and Dad anymore.

"Sorry. Do you know where our passports are?"

I look to the ceiling to give me strength. If she wants to leave, I won't help her. "No."

"I thought you knew everything. Where do you *think* they keep them?"

"I don't know. Probably in a drawer somewhere. Use your head."

She snaps her fingers. "In the office. His office."

"You mean *Dad's* office?"

She runs off to the part of the house that contains the

master bedroom and the office and a small gym that neither of my parents ever use.

I don't want to follow her. I'm tired of her games. But I do want to know if she finds the passports, so I go. I stand in the doorway and lean into the doorframe while she squats in front of Dad's desk, the side with the drawer that opens to reveal a short filing cabinet. "Where are you going, anyway?"

"Home." She pulls up a folder and opens it, shuffles through, then replaces it so our father will never know she's been there.

"You realize that you can't return to the orphanage, right? Because I hate to inform you, but you're too old. Miss Sonja won't take you back."

"It turns out I have a relative in Tula," she says without looking at me.

Her boldness stabs my heart. "You've been searching on the internet?"

"Of course I've been on the internet. And I have a cousin. … And he's willing to give me a room."

"You've been in touch with a cousin? He's going to *give* you a room?"

"Yes."

"Sounds like a perfect angel." I grab my forehead. "Is he really a cousin or a pimp trying to trick you?"

She stops what she's doing and glares at me. "You think I'm stupid? I went through that website we found together. The one *you* said was real."

"I said it *looked* real. What do I know? Please don't do this. You said you wouldn't go away so soon."

"Oh my gosh …"

The passports have dropped out of a file onto the carpet. Two navy blue ones, two red ones. She grabs for them, her hands fumbling as she opens each one. "The American ones are good for five more years. And the Russian ones, two more." She stares down at them as if she's found the family diamonds, then extends her arm, passports in hand. "You want yours?"

I feel myself pouting. I want to scream at her, to tell her how stupid she's being, how she's making the biggest mistake of her life. But I can't. Because I know that I want her to stay because *I* want to stay, because the idea of being alone scares me more than anything—except the idea of going back to Russia.

"I can't believe I found them." She looks up, glowing with happiness. It makes me want to hug her, to be happy for her and celebrate with her.

Instead I put a damper on her high spirits. "You said you don't have the money yet."

"If I stay with my cousin, I need only enough to travel. He says he has a big garden, and I'll have to help out with the planting and the harvesting—you know how good I am with plants—"

"So you'll be a farmer then," I say.

"Until I find a job."

"Please stop. It's too good to be true. You know this."

At that, she puts my passports back in the folder and tucks the folder back into the drawer.

"Coming here was too good to be true, and yet here I am."

Her words are loaded with confidence, and suddenly I'm exhausted. I know she's never been happy about leaving Russia. She's never been happy, period. I had always hoped she'd come to love our new home.

"Don't worry," she says. "You'll be fine. You and Mr. Mango Two Scoops are going to hit it off, I can tell."

"Mr. Mango what?" I can't help it, I laugh.

"The guy buying the mommy treat today. The one you drank with your eyes." She flutters her lashes. "You're too pretty not to have a boyfriend."

"Don't be a ridiculous child. This conversation is about you and your plan to run away."

"Yes, Sveta, I know I'm like a younger sister. You've always been the responsible one. You are why I'm here, the reason I didn't rot in the orphanage. I know this. I'm grateful." She pauses. "But I'm grown up now, and I know what I want." She looks away, and I think she may start to cry.

She doesn't.

"I'll always be your sister no matter where I am," she says.

I don't at all agree with this plan. I don't want her to save her money so that she can run away. I don't want her to leave me.

She can read my mind, I have no doubt. She comes up close and wraps me in a hug, whispering, "Don't worry," in my ear.

When we step back, I pretend to look at my wristwatch (even though I don't wear one). "So you go when? After dessert?"

She laughs and bows her head. "I'll keep you posted."

"But not too soon, right? Maybe in the fall?"

She steps around me and enters the hall. "I will let you know."

─────────

When I wake the next morning, my sister's bed is empty, still tucked in at the sides. The inhaler is missing from the night table. The house is quiet. Empty.

Abandoned.

She lied to me.

2

I arrive at the ice cream shop at five minutes before ten, and plenty of people are already milling about Main Street in their silly green-man costumes. I need to hurry up and get the store open. If Michael knew I was this late, he'd have my head—or maybe not. Not after he hears what Helena has done.

It's at least ninety degrees, and I'm slippery with sweat. "Stupid heat wave." I slap the switch to turn on the air-conditioning unit.

With an angry swipe of my hand, I flick on the lights and stomp across the room, barging through the door with the sign that says "Employees Only" and into the back office, no bigger than a walk-in closet. I throw my purse on top of the wooden desk and wipe my stupid nose. I don't have tissues and I don't care. My shirtsleeve does the job just fine.

"Shit," I say. "Why did she ... that idiot."

The tears rain down so thickly I'm gagging on them. I want to pummel something. Michael's desk will do. "Shit, shit ..." My fist comes down upon the wood like a judge's gavel. "Stupid, stupid, why?"

That's when I hear a tap on the office door.

I stand straight as a rocket, adjust my cap, which has fallen sideways on my sorry head. "Uhhh, one second, please."

Whoever it is doesn't barge in. Michael, maybe? Who else would be here before opening? I check the clock. One minute until ten. Can't be him. He thinks Helena is with me. No reason for him to come.

"Yes, coming," I say as pleasantly as I can. Probably an early customer.

I wipe my nose and blink a few times, then pull the door open and ... it's him. Mango Two Scoops. I push the door back again, rifle through my purse for a tissue, and do a better job of wiping my nose. "I'll be right there." Why did I attempt to put makeup on this morning? *Idiot!* I'm pretty sure I couldn't look more ridiculous than I do right now.

But that's okay, right? It's festival day, a day for strange beings of all kinds.

"Take your time," he says.

For a second I want to hug him. Or have him hug me. It's one of those reflexive urges that flashes and dissipates.

I've suffered a trauma this morning. Too bad for how I look.

I pull back the door and try to smile, but my lips don't quite make it there, quivering like wet noodles. "Oh, hi." I look at him for half a second before turning away.

I feel him studying me. Probably thinks I'm a silly immigrant with silly immigrant problems. "Are you all right? I'm sorry to barge in like—"

"Uh-huh." I sniff much louder than I wish I had. "Can I help you?"

Today he's not looking at the yogurt. He doesn't seem to care about the ice cream. He's fixated on my blotchy, nose-running face.

"I was across the street, walking to the coffee shop, and I, uh, saw you. … And, well, it seems like you're not having a very good day. I thought maybe I could help." His words are slow and careful, and they have thrown me for a loop, as my American mother sometimes says.

"I—um …" I pause to clear my throat. "… don't know what you mean."

Then I remember that I haven't switched on the Open sign. The people standing in front of the store are looking at their watches and the unlit sign, and confusion muddies their children's green faces. I hurry through the main part of the shop and reach for the chain that turns on the sign. Then I spin around and find myself right in front of Mr. Two Scoops.

He says, "I'm not joking, I can help you."

The bell rings as a family of four enters. Behind them an even bigger group emerges with several chattering children.

Their presence draws his attention for a moment before he continues: "It's going to be a really busy day, right? And you're already slammed."

I look right and left around myself like a confused bird. I'm a mess. I rub my forehead. The tears are threatening again. "You want to work?"

"Yes," he says with the kind of confidence I wish I had. His eyes are blue-green. And kind. On the large side. "You seem to be all alone here."

I am alone! I press my lips together because I don't want to cry. My history of loss and aloneness flutters through my mind along with my Russian birth parents, my American traveling parents, and now Helena. I nod, hair bouncing in front of my face. I can't speak.

"Your sister isn't coming?"

I shake my head.

"I can stay until you get someone else to come in. I didn't

tell you this the other day, but I used to work here, in this ice cream store, when I was in high school." He puts a hand on my shoulder and leads me to the Employees Only door. "It wasn't the same owner, of course, but I promise you I'm more than qualified to handle the job."

"Really? Oh. Wait—really? And you don't mind? But you'll miss the festival."

He stands behind the ice cream cabinet, pulling a plastic glove from the box. "I'm twenty-eight years old, and I was born in this town. I've been to at least twenty-five of these things. I only came by because I wanted to say hello to you— and find out what your name is."

Bold of him, and my response is not. A blush rises up from my neck and settles into my cheeks, and for this, I hate my face.

"Svetlana," I say. "But friends call me Sveta."

He grins, satisfied, as if I've promised him my heart—and maybe I have. "I'm Andrew."

He turns to the first person in line and says, "What can I get for you?"

———

It's 9 p.m., and the last alien has received his double scoop of ice cream. Andrew switches off the Open sign and says, "That's it. We're getting out of here before anyone else comes. Need food now."

"Me, too," I say, running into the office to grab my purse. "And where is it that we are going, because look at me, I'm a mess."

"Okay, first, even if you were a mess, and I'm not saying you are, you still look better than 90 percent of the rest of the world. And second, where we're going, it doesn't matter. Do you like to dine alfresco?"

I worried that once closing time came, Andrew might run back home to wherever he came from and leave me alone like everyone else has.

"I love alfresco," I say, not knowing what it is. "I eat alfresco all the time. It's how I stay thin."

Then I laugh, and so does he.

He opens the door. "After you, madam." I follow his bowed arm, but then I turn back because I have forgotten to lock up. Michael will be the next to open the shop. Not that he cares so much about it. When I called to tell him what happened, he said he was sorry that Helena left me, and then he said, "But you can still work, right?" It's his store, and he didn't even offer to come in. I might have quit except that Andrew had already offered to stay.

He takes my hand. "You don't mind, do you?" he asks. "I don't want to lose you in this crowd."

I shake my head, muted by a sudden bashfulness. I love that he's holding my hand, and I don't want to lose him in this crowd, either.

The UFOs are out in full force, and by this time, many of them have had one too many Martian-tini's or Cosmos Cosmopolitans at the Brigade Bar or the Holy Shots Sports Pub. Big-eyed strangers clad in black Spandex stroll by singing loud, silly songs. Some are teenagers and some are young parents with preschoolers and elementary school kids. One man says "Where'd we leave the spaceship," as he passes us.

"Where are we going?" I say.

"It's a surprise," Andrew says.

I've had more than enough surprises for one day.

He leads me into a pizza parlor and lets go of my hand. I like pizza, but Helena never wanted to eat it—too American for her tastes—so I haven't had much.

"Do you mind if I do the ordering?" he says.

"Go right ahead. Whatever makes you happy. Be sure to get me an iced tea. I need my caffeine."

A laugh trips over his lips. "Whatever makes *me* happy? I'm trying to cheer *you* up." He orders two cheesesteaks and two iced teas to go.

"Chiz steaks," I say. "What's that? Steaks made of chiz?"

His face opens up with bubbly, wide-eyed surprise. "You've never had cheesesteaks from Cerino's? How long did you say you've lived here?"

"My sister has an aversion to pizza parlors, so—" The word *sister* tightens my throat. I clench my jaw, force myself not to go there.

The apron-clad man behind the counter hands over to-go boxes and drinks with straws sticking out.

Andrew pays. His wallet is thick with bills, and I want to laugh and call him "money bags," but that's not something you do to someone you've just met.

Andrew's smile makes me think he's happy as a lark (as my American father likes to say), and he grabs my hand again and leads me out of the restaurant.

"Where to now?" I say.

"Alfresco."

"Fine, don't tell me."

Together we press through the stream of aliens that line the sidewalks all the way to the end of the street, the crowd thinning as we go, until we reach the darker side of town, away from the stores and porch lights. Finally we arrive at the entrance to the park. It's barricaded with yellow police tape and a sign that says "Park Closed for the Duration of the Festival."

I'm disappointed. "We are not allowed?"

"Technically, no, but as long as you don't call the cops, I think we'll be all right." He forges ahead, ducking under the caution tape. "I want to show you something. I know a park bench."

"You know a park bench? What's his name?"

He turns and does one of those half smiles. I love his face. It's on the round side, and he's a bit wide in the eyes. Imperfect and endearing. Honest.

"You're very funny, you know that? Your dry Russian humor."

"Is there such a thing? I was not aware."

"There it is again," he says.

I like him more than I should for having just met him. And I don't want this day to end. I love that he's holding my hand, keeping this connection between us even though it means he has to balance the drink container on top of the food boxes.

We walk across a swath of grass before rejoining the paved pathway. It's dark, with only the occasional lamp to guide us as we pass under tall, leafy oaks and wide-reaching maples. Finally we make it to this bench that he knows. It's beside a cluster of long-needled pine trees, but the view of the sky is open and the moon is like a friendly bystander at our little party.

"So many stars," I say, gazing at all the bright sparkles overhead.

He grins at the sky. "My old friends."

I don't know what he means, but I don't ask. He's maybe a former Boy Scout like I have seen in black-and-white television shows. Suddenly I grow worried. What will he think when he realizes I grew up in an orphanage?

"I'm starving," he says. "You?"

We sit on the bench. He passes me napkins, a drink, a cardboard container with my steak of cheese. I open it, and it steams at me. The bread is fat as a pillow and the cheese white and gooey like glue.

"Wow," I say. "So this is chiz steak."

He takes a huge bite of his sandwich, and bits of meat drop back into the cardboard container along with blobs of melted cheese. "It's messy," he says with his mouth full.

"Wonderful. I'm already a mess, so what's the difference?"

He's still chewing when he says, "Right."

I take a closer look at my sandwich; I like to know what I am getting myself into. "Oh, I see. The shavings of meat are below the melted chiz."

"Stop studying it and take a bite." He laughs before sticking what looks like half of his sandwich into his mouth at once.

I do the same, on a much smaller scale, and thankfully it tastes much better than it looks. The juice rolls down my chin. "Oh, yes," I say with a laugh. "Delicious American delicacy. And to think I could have been eating one of these every day for the past seven years."

He tries not to spit his food. I like that he finds me hilarious.

"How did you end up in the U.S. anyway?" he says.

I take another bite to delay my answer. Not that I'm the kind who makes up stories.

"If you really want to know, I'll tell you. But I give warning: it's not your American dream story. For mature audiences only," I say, trying to keep it light.

"My family's not the usual either," he says.

"Good. We share that in common." I sip my iced tea to clear my throat. "Helena and I were adopted. She's not my blood-related sister. Dana and John Peterman, who are never home, are our parents."

"I know them. They do a lot of work for nonprofits, don't they?"

"Yes, that's right. That Dana and John. They took us in to save us from Russia's streets—the sex slave trade—and to give us a chance at a decent life. I'm sorry to bring up so serious a thing during our lovely alfresco."

He shakes his head. "It's okay. I think that's great. Your adoptive parents are great, I mean, and so is everything they do."

"They truly are good people. Right now they're in India teaching families how to farm and earn their living. Few people adopt teenagers, and I for one will be forever grateful. My sister, on the other hand—" I stop midsentence, not sure I want to continue. "She never liked it here. I'm pretty sure she's flying back to Russia as we speak." My heart beats faster as I say this out loud. "And that's a brand-new injury, so please let's talk of something else."

He puts his arm across my shoulder. "Look up at the sky. You see those stars, that bright cluster to the right of the moon? That's the seven sisters. They're always together, even though they're millions of miles apart."

His kindness feels warm on my face. He's a gem in the rough of the world. "You are familiar with the night sky?" I say.

"It was my major in college *and* grad school. And now it's my job."

"Oh, I didn't know I was in the presence of a grad school boy."

"Just got my master's." He looks down like a modest person would. I wonder if it's genuine or maybe he's playing modest for me.

"Impressive, Mr. … and what is your last name?"

"Jovian."

"Well, that is very nice. Andrew Jovian, astrologer."

"Oh, no. Actually, that's horoscopes. I'm an astrono*mer*. Big difference."

"I'm sorry," I say, annoyed with my dumb self. "Sometimes I get my words confused."

"Not a problem. You speak English a lot better than I could ever speak Russian."

"So you have always found outer space fascinating?" I say. "And aliens?"

"Aliens, yes. Aliens most of all. I'm born and bred in Kirksberg, so it's only natural. My parents' company builds high-powered telescopes. My father started it back in the sixties. Now we work with NASA and other organizations around the world."

"Well, that sounds like an interesting profession. And you are following in your father's footsteps."

"Sort of. We share some interests and not others. What about your birth parents? Do you know anything about them?"

I worried he might ask that question. Some people do, and some people don't. He has, so I will tell: "My parents died when I was four. That's why I was taken from my home of Tula and put in an orphanage in Petranko."

"Oh, wow." He becomes so still that I wonder if this information has stopped his heart.

"Yes, it certainly was difficult. I loved my parents, my home. I actually remember good things about being with them. People wonder how I can remember because I was so young, but I do. Especially my mother. She's the one I clung to, and when she was suddenly gone ..." I feel myself getting warm in the face, so I stop.

"I'm so sorry," he says.

I pause, a familiar ball of cry threatens to roll up my throat. When it eases, I cough a little to make sure my voice won't crack. "My caregiver at the orphanage loved me like her own child, so when I was old enough, ten or eleven, she told me the truth about my parents. They were KGB, though that's not what Russian spies are called anymore."

"FSB, right?"

"Yes. That's what they're called now."

I hope he doesn't assume I'm a spy as well. Then again, how could he when I work at an ice cream store?

"The day they died, they had left me with an older woman who lived in our building. They used to do that every once in a while. She was my babysitter. They didn't return. No explanation. And I was taken to the orphanage soon after."

I wipe my mouth with the napkin. I haven't mentioned my birth parents to anyone since I arrived in this country, and I never thought I'd have reason to mention their connection to Russia's KGB. But I wanted to tell Andrew. I wanted him to know that part of my story. If he didn't like it, better that I find out right away. Somehow I trust him even though I have only known him for one day.

I suppose there are things built into your DNA, things you just know.

"I've been to Russia," he says. "I lived there for six months with a friend of mine from college. We traveled to Europe and ended up in Moscow. It was definitely an interesting place. So cold during the month of January." He shivers even though sweat shines his forehead. "Let's see if I remember. *Privyet* and *dosvedanya.*"

"Hello and goodbye."

"*Gde zdes' vannaya komnata?*" he says with a strange accent.

"That is a handy phrase when you need to relieve yourself."

His shoulders hunch a bit in a sheepish way. "One day you'll teach me some better phrases."

"*Sudovol'stviyem,*" I say with a smile. "It will be my pleasure."

His gaze rests on my face for a moment; I'm pretty sure he's glad to have met me.

"So, did you like your first steak of cheese?" he asks.

"I give it five stars and hope to eat many more." I crumple my napkin and drop it into the cardboard container.

We sit back and take in the silvery beauty of the moon. I don't want this night to end. I don't want to go back to my lonely home. I don't want to be without Andrew just yet.

"I like this bench that you know," I say. "We should stay here all night."

"Yes," he says, and he reaches over and takes my hand.

When we finally leave the park, it's 11 p.m. We duck under the yellow tape like two spirits in the night and float along with the waning crowd of the UFO Festival. Most of the shops and restaurants have closed, but Holy Shots, the busiest bar in town, vibrates with activity. An old couple walks out as we approach, and now they're rushing toward us.

"Andrew," the woman calls. "I was wondering when we'd run into you."

At closer look, they're old but not that old. Older than my parents, but not eighty or ninety. They limp a bit as they catch up to us, and I feel awkward holding Andrew's hand in front of them, so I let go.

The man is frumpy in a disheveled, older-man way, with the tail of his shirt risen from his pants and his thinning hair in a whirl. He shakes Andrew's hand and releases a full-belly laugh. I think he may be drunk. The woman gives Andrew a kiss on the cheek. They both look at me, and Andrew introduces me as Svetlana, no last name. They are Aunt Constant and Uncle Jimmy. I'm pleased to meet them, I say, though I don't know how pleased I really am. I had hoped to continue to have Andrew to myself, to continue this happy night, and I don't want them (or anything else) to change that.

"Did you see it?" Uncle Jimmy's eyes are big and round behind the even bigger, rounder lenses of his glasses. "The launching of the rocket. What a joke."

"I'm guessing it was worse than last year," Andrew says.

His uncle turns his head and spits into the street. "Amateurs. I don't know why they won't ask you to head it up."

"Because it's for the kids. We've been over this."

"Yes, I know, I know, but at least give those kids something to aspire to. A rocket that rises fifty feet in the air is no rocket at all." He looks to me. "Am I right?"

I'm startled by the sudden attention. "Uh—yes. You are," I tell him, wishing I could sound more confident in my answer because I want him to like me. Andrew comes from a family of astronomers, so I assume something like this is important to them.

Then I catch Aunt Constant's eye roll.

"It's the same thing every year, Jimmy," she says. "Same rocket, same complaints."

"Right. You're right. But the thing is we *have* the technology. We've had it for a long time now. Would it be wrong to give the kids a dose of reality once in a while?"

"It's a matter of safety," Aunt Constant says with an air of finality.

Andrew looks up and down the road, perhaps bored with the conversation. "So, you're headed home?" he says.

While his aunt gives him an answer, Uncle Jimmy steps to the side and wavers close to me, thrusting his stubbly older-man head in my direction. For a moment, he stares deep into my eyes, his face hovering in front of my face, demanding my attention. I fear he'll kiss me, but then he reverses direction.

I'm left standing there with my hair like spikes shooting up from my scalp as if I've been shocked with a jolt of electricity. It's a strange sensation, and I comb my fingers through until it goes back to normal.

"Nice eyes," he says to no one in particular. "Blue-gray of the Baltic Sea."

Then he turns to Andrew. "She shows real potential."

"Uncle Jimmy," Andrew says in a fierce whisper. "I beg you."

The words echo in my mind. *I beg you. I beg you.* Why *I beg you?* And in what way do I "show real potential"? What just happened? I suppose Uncle Jimmy drank too many Space Junk shots like the rest of this late-night crowd. The party sounds coming from inside the bar indicate a dance riot going on. I can't imagine Andrew's aunt and uncle would enjoy a place like that, but then again this is a town-wide festival for alien enthusiasts of all ages, so I should expect the unexpected.

"We'll be on our way now," Aunt Constant says, weaving her arm through her husband's and tugging him along. "Nice to see you, Andrew. And nice to meet you, Svetlana. Don't stay out too late."

"A graceful exit, Aunt Constance," Andrew says. "Thank you."

Constance? I thought he said her name was Constant. Me and my bad English.

We watch them head off in the opposite direction. I'm relieved they don't want to hang out with us. "I hope they're not driving," I say.

"They live two blocks off Main Street. The walk will do him good."

Then he takes my hand again, and we continue on our original path toward I have no idea where. "I'd say let's go for ice cream," he says, "but I happen to know the only shop in town is closed."

"Didn't you get enough during the day? You sampled more than Helena ever did. And she was queen of sampling."

"That's true." He rushes forward down the sidewalk,

leading me by the hand into the darkness, through an alley in between two brick buildings.

I'm laughing again. I've been laughing all day; I can't help it. "Where are you taking me? Do you know another bench?"

The alley opens to a colonial-looking building that sells shoes. Next to it is an even smaller shop, a bead store. Both are closed for the night.

There's an urgency in Andrew's rushing steps, like he can't wait to get wherever it is we're going. We reach a little patio area with a wide tree trunk at its center, and he spins around and suddenly my back is pressed against the tree and his smiling face is in front of mine, and I'm looking at him like I love him, because I swear that I already do. It's been twelve hours of knowing him, and I'm in deeper than I've ever been. My heart is full to bursting, and if he doesn't kiss me, I'll die.

He whispers, "Sveta," and leans in. Our lips meet and his arms surround me, and I feel like I'm home. Finally, home. And that I never want to leave my home—or him—again.

———

We're a block from my parents' house, walking side by side, when he tells me he doesn't think it will be appropriate for him to stay too long.

"But my parents aren't home. You could stay the whole night, and I'd be the only one who knows."

"Right. But that's not why it's not a good idea."

At first I think he may be joking, but there's no sign of a smile.

"I'm sorry, Mr. Jovian, but I despise the sound of an empty house, so you're going to have to hang around for a while. I will let you know when you are free to go. Ha ha."

"That's why," he says, pointing at me with his free hand.

"You suffered a traumatic event this morning, and now your house is empty. Your feelings might be mixed up, and tomorrow morning you'll regret ... having me over."

He becomes a light shade of pink; I know because I turn my head at an awkward angle at the right moment to see it. We continue to walk. I'm thinking, *Was it just this morning that Helena left?*

"While it's true, what you say, I don't want you to go. Believe me, I'm not a silly girl who eats alfresco with just anyone."

He doesn't laugh at my joke.

"I don't want this night to end, either," he says.

The words linger in the air between us as we reach the front door.

"So you'll stay." I fish the key from my bag and am about to insert it into the lock. "If for no other reason than I need you to protect me from all of the aliens in town. You know how dangerous Kirksberg can be."

His body goes soft with surrender. "Yes, I'll stay. For a few minutes."

Never was a man so set on *not* staying over. I wonder if I should tell him that I'm not a virgin.

I open the door. I have him by the hand and am walking backward, pulling him through the foyer into the living room.

He's quiet, serious. I'm guessing that he both wants to stay and worries that he should leave. He drops his head. "You're not going to make this easy on me, are you?"

I give him the charming Baltic Sea eyes. "I seriously hope not."

3

In the morning, Andrew groans as his phone rings. As attractive as Helena assures me I am, he slept on the floor of my bedroom, on my area rug, which I haven't vacuumed in some time. It's 8 a.m. He sits up, looking adorably ruffled, and I roll over and stretch. I think about patting his head, but my sterner Russian side rules it a misstep.

"Oh, hi," he says in a whisper. "Everything okay?" The person on the line speaks for a few seconds, sounding like a cartoon character from where I lay. Andrew says, "Yes, I'll be there. ... No. I'm not just saying—yes, Mom, I will. Of course. What? ... Yes. Yes. ... I said I will. ... Yes."

Americans and their yeses. I wish he would hang up already.

"I'll ask her." He looks up at me and winks. "I slept on the floor, not that it's your business. ... Uh-huh. Okay. ... Okay. Do you need me to pick anything up? ... All right. Gotta go, Mom. Bye."

He squints up at me like a loyal canine. His bangs are all aflurry—if that is even a word.

"Your mother is calling at 8 a.m.?" I say. "Must be important."

"To her it is. She's having a day-after party and wants to make sure I'm there. It's actually a fun party. She throws it every year the day after the festival. My father mixes up Bloody Marys and mimosas. They get a band."

"I'm not a morning drinker," I say.

"Well, Mom made me promise to bring you, drinker or not."

It takes a second for that to sink in. I've slept in my clothes, and my brain isn't working yet. "But she doesn't know I exist."

He scratches his scalp, the light brown waves ruffling around. "I'm afraid she does. You'll find Jovian news spreads fast in this town."

I'm glad the shades are down and the light is low. I'm sure I'm puffy and a bit greasy in the hair. I feel a pimple poking up from my chin. ... "News?"

"Uncle Jimmy and Aunt Constance. Last night in front of Holy Shots."

"Ohhhh, Mr. Electric Eyes. I forgot about him."

"Mr. who?"

I laugh a little and then stifle it. "The way he looked me over, it was like he shot electricity into the roots of my hair. It scared me a little, to tell you the truth."

"Electricity? Oh, wow, and I missed that?"

"You were talking with Aunt Constant."

"*Constance*," he says, enunciating.

"Oh, yes, I know. But when you first introduced them, I thought you said 'Constant,' and now it has stuck, I'm afraid. To me, she will be Constant forever."

He laughs. "Okay."

The next I know, he hops onto the bed, jarring the mattress as if it's made of water. He grabs my long hair into a ponytail and lets it drop. "You have some beautiful hair, you know that? So shiny."

"Yes, I am aware," I say, blowing away the strands that have fallen in front of my face.

"And thick."

I shake it back into place. "Stop flattering me, mister. I still have the sandman in my eye, and I'm not in the mood."

He moves in for a kiss, but I'm too quick. "Not before I brush the teeth." I duck my head and roll off the side of the bed.

"Come on, I'm not afraid," he says. "How bad can it be?"

I race to the bathroom across the hall and slam the door behind me, locking it as fast as humanly possible. A thump hits the floor, and I jump.

"What happened? Are you okay?"

"I've fallen and I can't get up," he says, laughing.

I am not fooled by this trick.

"No, I mean it. I've fallen. I am on the ground."

I poke my head out to see and ... he grabs me!

We walk to the party. His parents' neighborhood is about a mile away—on one of the streets with the extra-large houses Helena used to mock. *Extra-large houses for extra-large people and their extra-large children who eat extra-large ice cream sundaes.* Because Helena is an insolent child, but I hope she made it to Russia okay.

If the line of expensive cars in front of his parents' house is any indication, it's going to be an extra-large party of the extra-wealthy sort Helena would despise. There's a row of tall trees that runs parallel to the sidewalk and at first blocks the view of the house, until we reach the driveway. And now I'm standing there blinking like the poor orphan girl from

Russia that I am. *What the hell is he doing with me? He should have a supermodel or sports star for his girlfriend.* I'm pretty sure my mouth is hanging open, and I am feeling lightheaded.

Andrew has grown up in a mansion.

When he sees my reaction, his face goes long with worry. "Look, I know what you're thinking."

"This is your house?" I say, my heart swelling into my ears and Helena's laugh mocking me in my mind.

"It's my parents' house. My *parents',"* he says, turning so he has my full attention. "I don't live here. I live in a second-floor apartment a block away from the post office, like a recent graduate should."

I hope that's true. He seems so normal, though I don't know how he could be if he grew up in a palace like this one. His adamant concern is impressive, though, and it's hard to resist such a face. He's so sweet. It's his large eyes and their wholesome blue-green color. There's nothing mean about them. No sharp edges. He'd have a difficult time looking tough if he wanted to. But I'm still worried about this wealthy family, and my first instinct is to run back where I came from.

"Okay, look," he says, "my father inherited some very old money. Not that he didn't work his whole life, because believe me, he has, but—are you all right? You're pale all of a sudden." He grips my shoulders as if I might topple like an axed tree right in front of him.

I swallow. "What kind of people will be here?"

"What kind?" He gazes across the lawn as if he might find the answer there.

"Chris Hemsworth? President Obama? Princess Kate Middleton?" I don't smoke or vape, but right now I would love something to do with my hands.

"Oh, yeah," he says with a nervous laugh, "there's that Russian humor."

I look down at my yellow sundress, which only moments ago seemed too dressy for a daytime party, and now I'm wondering whether it's not dressy enough. "You should have told me."

"It's just drinks on the lawn with family and close friends," he says. "And you look beautiful; your dress is perfect. I didn't think to say anything because it's not a big deal. I'm sorry. All I wanted was for everyone to see my hot date."

He laughs it off in a shy manner, and that makes me smile. I don't want to smile, but I can't help it. He's cute even if he's one of those wealthy Americans.

"In all honesty, it's rare for me to bring a date to a party. And it's nothing to be nervous about. Just a get-together. Mom calls it a garden party. Very casual. Sundresses and shorts. Nice people, for the most part, most of them hungover and sipping drinks, or pounding them in the case of Uncle Jimmy."

The thought of Uncle Jimmy spikes my nerves. I can't get that electric feeling out of my scalp.

"If we go in, I think you'll have a nice time. I *know* you will."

He said *if*. So he's giving me the option not to go. I like that. That lets some of the air out of the panic I'm feeling.

"You won't leave me alone with Uncle Jimmy, please?" I look to him for some reassurance I can lean on.

"When you meet these knuckleheads, you're going to see how you worried for nothing." He holds out his hand for me to take.

"I've already met Aunt Constant, and she was sweet," I say as we head toward the gate that opens to the backyard. I take another look at the house and notice solar panels on the back side of the roof. So they're rich but conscientious, and conscientious people are usually nice people.

"Right, and you know me," he says, nudging me along. "And my mother already knows you. Sort of. I'll grab a couple of mimosas. We'll down them and get two more. Everything will be fine."

We pass under the gate, which reminds me of pictures I've seen of the Kremlin (it's white and gold and quite tall, though there are no spires to speak of). The music and chatter grow in volume and intensity. The sun shines bright and hot, and there's no getting away from it. But a breeze blows through my hair as if to say, "It's all right."

The Earth is starting to spin. Not in the usual way, but the drunken way. We've been sitting around the table on the patio beside the pool for some time. Eight chairs, each one filled with a Jovian friend or relative. Andrew's cousin David is beside me. He's nineteen years old and attentive to my drinking needs. He also looks just like Andrew, though in skinnier, younger form. The resemblance is uncanny.

"Are you sure you're not brothers?" I ask for the third time.

Andrew laughs. "We do look alike, but his eyes are different. And we have different parents. Plus, he's adopted."

"Yes, that's what you keep telling me, but it's hard to believe."

"Aunt Constance wanted a boy like me, so she ordered him out of a catalog. That's what Uncle Jimmy always says."

"Funny man!" I say with more enthusiasm than I would had I not ingested three, four, however many mimosas.

A giant umbrella shades us; otherwise, we'd have sunburned shoulders and red noses. For the last twenty minutes, David has been going on about vodka and how "all Russians drink it." Typical man-child.

"If you don't do a shot," he says, "how can I be sure you're really Russian?"

"You don't have to do a shot," Andrew whispers in my ear on my other side.

"Not all Russians drink," I say. "That is a mere, uh, *ah!*—what do you call it?" I lose bits of my English when I drink too much.

"Stereotype?" Andrew offers.

"Yes, exactly." I pat his shoulder. "*Stereotype*. Weird American words. I mean, what does a stereo have to do with it?"

The three of us laugh. We've been laughing all afternoon, and my smile hurts.

David excuses himself to go to the bar. "Save my seat," he says over his shoulder.

David's chair is open for only a few seconds before another man fills it. This one is muscular, especially in the arms and chest, the whole of him like a wrestler—or super-hero. He has a kind face, very movie-star handsome.

Andrew reaches around me to shake his hand. "When did you sneak in?"

"Just got here." He gestures to the collection of champagne flutes in front of us. "Looks like you've been here a while."

"Svetlana, I want you to meet Fran Vasquez. He's an FBI agent, the guy I traveled to Russia with when we were in college."

"Very nice to meet you," I say, trying not to look too drunk, which takes more effort than it should.

His grin brings out a dimple in his cheek.

"Where's Lisa?" Andrew asks. "Couldn't get away?"

"Kid's sick again," Fran says. "Now she's sick, too. It's been a year since we were all healthy at the same time."

"I hope nothing serious," I say.

"Just a cold. Lisa's so sleep deprived, she can't catch a break. It's unbelievable. Kids are friggin' germ collectors."

Andrew and Fran continue a conversation about some other couple I don't know, and I sit back. The band's playing a song that matches my mood: cheerful and, I don't know, *hopeful*. So, yes, I am having a good time. Being near Andrew is enough to make me happy, and I'm glad I came to the party.

Though I do feel like a goldfish in a bowl.

And by that I mean that his relatives stare. A lot. Since the second I stepped into the yard. And not in a secret or subtle way. They do it from every angle, every distance, up close and across the wide lawn. It's like I am a magnet pulling their eyes to my body, a scientific specimen to be studied. I wonder if they do this to all of Andrew's girl-friends—not that I'm a girlfriend *yet*, but I am a date. Strange Americans. Do they all gape in such a way? Is this normal? I haven't noticed before. Helena would have something to say. Not only do pampered Americans smile too much, but their eyes bore holes into all who enter their domain. *Dramatic Helena.*

When I met Andrew's father, Edmund, he acted like Uncle Jimmy—getting close to my face, bringing on the wide eyeballs, and giving me an electrical shock that raised the roots of my hair. I swear to God, I don't think I imagined it. I have never felt such a thing. It's so strange. And then a little while later, his mother, Caroline, gave me the same weird jolt.

"Oh, shit." Fran pushes back in his chair. "Your mother."

"What? Where?" Andrew looks first one way, then the other.

Fran doubles over and pretends to tie his shoe. "Did she see me?"

"Don't worry, man. She's busy, she won't come over here.

Plenty of other guests for her to mingle—" He pauses. "Scratch that. She saw you. Here she comes."

Wrapped in an air of self-consciousness, Fran sits straight in the chair and picks at the label on his beer. What is going on, I have not a clue.

"Andrew," Caroline calls out. "You didn't tell me Fran was here." His mother rushes over, grabs Fran's arm, and bends down so she can see right into his eyes, just like she, Edmund, and Uncle Jimmy did to me. "How are you?" she says.

It seems like she might kiss him on the lips. He smiles but at the same time retracts his neck. She moves even closer, then veers off at the last second, pulling him into an embrace. "It's been too long. You need to bring the baby over."

"Well, he's sick again. So is Lisa."

"That's a shame," Caroline says. She straightens up and lingers in front of him. "Promise me you'll bring him over soon."

"Yeah. Of course I—"

"And how have you been?"

"I'm good, good. You?" He runs his hand over the top of his buzz cut.

"I have to get back inside," she says. "Dessert is about to come out, and I want to make sure Nancy doesn't get the gluten-free cupcakes mixed up with the regular ones like she did last year." She backs away, waggling a finger at him. "I want to catch up with you before you go; don't try to sneak off."

"Never," he says, back to picking his beer label and looking uncomfortable.

As soon as she reaches the sliding glass door, Fran and I exchange a look. He's rubbing the top of his head again, and I'm pretty sure he felt the same scalp-tingling strangeness I felt when Caroline and Edmund said hello to me. I wonder if he'll say something.

Or maybe I should.

He shakes his head and rolls his eyes as if holding back.

On the other side of me, Andrew says, "Go ahead, Fran. You can say it."

"What?" He gulps his beer.

"It's fine. I know my family is weird."

I turn to find a veil of guilt clouding Andrew's happy-go-lucky face.

"What do you mean?" I say. "Your mother is very sweet. Everyone here has been so ..." I miss a beat, vacillating between "nice" and "great" before landing on the former.

"Right. But they do that staring thing. I know all about it."

I tilt my head in question. "But last night, when I told you about Uncle Jimmy—"

"I acted like I didn't know what you were talking about. But I do. I know about the ..." He pulls up some of his hair in demonstration.

"Happens to me every time," Fran says. "Like little soldiers standing at attention."

I turn back to Fran, and he runs his hand over his crew cut again. "She gets right in there." He puts his hand in front of his face. "But it's fine. I'm used to it. Sort of."

"So then I didn't imagine what happened last night?" I say.

Fran gives a little sigh. "No you did not."

"How do they do it?"

He cracks his thick knuckles. His hands are huge, like bear paws. "Beats the crap out of me."

"You know what else is strange?" I say, because I'm pretty loose in the tongue at this point, and even though I have just met Fran, I feel like this phenomenon has brought us to common ground. "Everywhere I look, someone is staring back at me."

I turn my head, and every face at the table turns toward me in unison: neighbors Matthew and Eric; their stepsister, Jennifer; Uncle Colin; Aunt Sylvia; others who happen to be walking past our table.

"Yeah, but that's different," Fran says with a laugh. "That's because you're pretty. You should be used to that."

"You absolutely should," Andrew says, jumping at the chance to change the conversation.

I feel a blush creep over my cheeks as I scramble for a way to respond. Thankfully, young David returns with a tray full of colorless shots. He makes his way around the table, delivering one to each of us, and stops beside Fran with a scowl on his face. "You took my chair."

Fran cocks a brow in his direction. "If you want me to move, you'll have to make me."

David's wiry build is no match for Fran's manly muscle. Instead he steps in between our chairs and parks his skinny backside against the arm of mine.

Andrew stretches around me and gives him a shove. "Get off."

"Boys, boys," I say. "Please stop fighting before we spill this wonderful vodka." I raise the shot glass and say, "To drinks on the lawn." And then I lean into Andrew and tell him, "Drinks will literally be on the lawn after this."

"Here, here!" He raises his glass before tipping it back in one swoop.

We look at each other and grin. Our happiness somehow connects, latches together, becomes bonded. I feel as if we've been together forever. Next thing I know, we are face-to-face in a kiss.

I wake up in darkness. Not only can't I see anything, I can't remember where I am or how I got here. I'm lying on a bed; I know that much because there's a pillow under my head and a pain in my ... finger. My pointer finger, to be exact. I stretch out my arm. It collides with the lampshade, and my hand fumbles for the lamp's switch. A yellowish glow emerges. My finger is red at the tip. I must have broken a nail, bent it back, or something such as this. A dresser of white wicker with several framed photographs on top sits to my left. I get up, unsteadily, to have a closer look at a picture of young Andrew, probably about ten years old. His teeth look too big for his face. I laugh out loud.

My breath is pure rubbing alcohol.

That's when I remember how David's vodka shot pushed me over the edge. I struggled not to fall asleep at the table, in front of all those staring Jovians. Andrew brought me to this first-floor guest room so that I could pass out in peace and privacy, kind boy that he is. Adorable round-faced boy. I think I'm falling in love with him.

Oh, who am I kidding? I'm definitely in love with him.

I'm happy to discover a small bathroom attached to this guest room. Walking gives rise to a wave of nausea, but it passes in a couple of breaths. Lights over the bathroom mirror are much brighter than the lamp beside the bed. My finger throbs. I seem to have broken the nail right down to the skin. Drunken fool. I don't even remember doing it. It's not bleeding, thank goodness, so I get to the job of tidying myself up before venturing out. I find a comb in the medicine cabinet, and after I neaten my hair I use a tissue and soap to wipe away the mascara that blackens the area underneath my eyes. Then I gulp some cold water.

As I reenter the bedroom, I notice all at once the lack of party music, lack of chatter, lack of laughter. The one window in the room faces the side yard, so it's no help in determining the status of the party. Still, I'm pretty sure drinks on the lawn has ended. I must have been asleep for a long time. The sun was still out when Andrew introduced me to the guest room.

I open the door into the hallway, and who is heading in my direction but Uncle Jimmy. I consider pretending not to see him and scooting back into the room for something I have forgotten, but it's too late.

"Hey, there, Sleeping Beauty," he says, his shoulders bouncing in a giggle. A telescope with a giant zoom lens like a big metal head stuck to a tripod leans against his shoulder. "Hope I didn't wake you."

"No, no, you didn't."

He fixes his owlish stare on me. I know he doesn't mean to frighten me, but the zip of electricity that raises my hair makes me feel as though I have met with a predator.

"We're out on the patio if you care to join," he says, continuing on. "Time for a little sightseeing." He lifts the telescope in explanation.

How can he be a predator, with his button-up sweater and just-out-of-bed hair? I don't want him to think me rude, so I say, "Is this one of the family products?"

He backtracks to me, holds out the telescope. "Sure is. The T125XS. Superpower in a small package. Only forty grand retail."

My jaw drops. "Forty thousand—you're not serious?"

"I am. You can see all the way to Icarus if all the coordinates are right."

I'm floored—not that I've ever heard of Icarus outside of the mythological story.

"It's a star. Halfway across the universe."

He meets my eyes, and my scalp tingles—I focus on the wall. "Wow. That must be so neat." I never use the word *neat*; it's just what popped out.

"It certainly is. Must hurry," he says, turning on his heels. "They're waiting."

Outside, Andrew stands beside Mr. Jovian, who smokes a cigar. They're both gazing upward at the night sky. David is in a chair a couple of feet away, his back to me.

"Any aliens tonight?" I say. "Or have they all boarded their spaceships and flown back home?"

The men smile, but none of them laugh. I wonder if I have intruded, but then Andrew steps away from his father, takes my hand and kisses it. He must have felt the warmth of my injured finger because he looks closer at it and then says with his eyes, "What happened?"

I shake my head and whisper, "Nothing."

Uncle Jimmy sets up the telescope a couple of feet away. "If we're lucky we'll see old MACS in addition to Heinze."

"Maybe. They may have taken a turn," Mr. Jovian says.

Uncle Jimmy hovers over the eyepiece. "Yes, that is a possibility."

"They're sighting comets," Andrew tells me.

I guess they search for whatever is out there to see. They're the ones who build the things that enable people to view outer space, so it makes sense.

"So many people act as if the universe starts and ends with the Earth," Andrew's father says in my direction. "Why is that, do you think, when the cosmos is right there for all of us to see?"

It feels like a test question.

"Well, I don't know," I say with a teasing smile. "Maybe it's because our brains are so small. We can only handle what is right in front of us. For some, they cannot see outside of their country. For others, they cannot see outside of their state. Still others cannot see beyond the windows of their home. Many are stuck behind their border lines and inside their boxes."

I can tell from his wry grin that he didn't expect such an answer. He seems pleased, maybe even impressed.

"You see things a bit differently; I hope you don't mind my saying."

"Because I'm Russian, you mean?"

He blows out a cloud of smoke. "That. And because of your past experiences."

Did Andrew tell him I was an orphan? That my parents were Russian spies?

I smile in an uncomfortable way. I'd like an end to this conversation and hope that Andrew will save me. But I can see that Mr. Jovian would like a response.

"I have lived in two countries," I say, "which is more than many people who live in the United States can say."

"Found it," Uncle Jimmy says as he steps back from the telescope.

Mr. Jovian flicks his cigar. He turns toward the telescope. "Thank you, James."

Andrew grasps my hand. "I'm going to take Svetlana home."

"Oh, yes. It's as we thought," Mr. Jovian says in response to whatever he sees. "Isn't that interesting?"

"Indeed, it is," Uncle Jimmy says. "You think it's to do with M31?"

"Do you want to drive, or should we walk?" Andrew asks me.

"Walk. I need air."

"Cool. See you, Dad, Uncle Jimmy. Bye, David."

David turns and waves from the lawn chair he's sitting in. I'd forgotten he was there.

"Good night," I say. "Thank you for a wonderful party."

Mr. Jovian remains stooped over, his eye to the telescope. "It's been a pleasure meeting you, Svetlana."

4

On the way home, I'm quiet but only on the outside. Inside, I'm churning because I wish Andrew hadn't told his father I was an orphan. That's probably why everyone at the party was staring at me as if I were a scientific specimen of a poor immigrant person. I suppose none of these rich people has ever met a destitute Russian before.

"Is everything okay," he says with a nervousness that's unusual for him.

"Yes." I cannot look at him right now. "Can I ask you a question?" The words fly out of my mouth, rattling like leaves in the wind.

He pauses before he says, "What's the matter?"

"I have to know something."

We stop walking.

"Did you tell your father about the orphanage and the, um, my birth parents?"

He answers head-on. "I wouldn't do that unless you wanted me to."

"Then how did he know? He mentioned my 'experiences' as a Russian. What did he mean by that?"

"I wondered if you would remember," he says with regret in his voice.

My heart stops. *Oh my God, what did I do? What did I say?*

"My father sat with us this afternoon. He was next to you, so you started a conversation."

My stomach turns upside down. I cover my mouth and hold my breath. Vague images of this conversation return in blurry blips.

"Don't worry," he says, placing his hand on my shoulder. "It's nothing bad."

How could this have happened? I never talk about my past.

"Svetlana, look at me: it's okay."

His blue-green eyes reassure me, and yet my temperature continues to rise.

"I should not have had drinks on the lawn. I should *never* have drinks on the lawn."

"Please don't, um, overreact," he says.

My nose warms with the anxiety I'm trying to contain. "Don't ever say *overreact* in front of a woman. Surely, you know this."

"All you did was tell him your parents died when you were four. I think you said it was a car accident—nothing about the KGB—and you told him that you and Helena were adopted and who your adoptive parents are. He doesn't know them, but that's not surprising since they're rarely home."

I rub my forehead, raising my eyes with hesitant hopefulness. "Is that all?"

"You said that your American parents saved you from aging out of the orphanage, from being tossed onto the streets. *That's all*. It wasn't bad, I promise. My father was fascinated. He loves hearing stories about people's lives. I can tell he was impressed by yours."

I swallow. *It's not so bad. It's not so bad.*

"You're sure that's all?"

"Yes."

"Nothing about the sex trade, then?"

"No. Absolutely not. The word *sex* didn't pass over your lips—I would have noticed if it had."

I can't laugh at his joke. I'm still embarrassed, but at least I can breathe.

"Look, we all drank too much."

I start walking again, and he follows a step behind.

"I'm sorry about that. We got carried away. Except for Fran. He tossed David's shot over his shoulder and left the party because Lisa called him home."

I nod. *It could be a lot worse. ...*

We keep walking. I take his hand. He's waiting for me to say something, so I do: "Fran seems like a great guy to have for a best friend."

The anxious little wrinkles around Andrew's eyes disappear. "I'm glad you got to meet him. He's the only friend I've bothered to stay in touch with after college, but I don't get to see him much. He's busy with his job and the baby."

We near my parents' house, which seems so modest and charming compared to the one Andrew's family owns. I wonder whether he'll come in or if this will be our first parting since we met. I dig for my key and unlock the door.

He follows me inside. There's no discussion.

I have made a huge bowl of popcorn. I make it every night and eat the whole thing myself. I don't put butter on it, but I shake very much salt. Why? Because salt is the best flavor in the world.

Helena never agreed, which was good. More popcorn for me.

Andrew takes a handful, and when it reaches his tongue, his chin drops as if he would like to spit it out.

"What's the matter? Don't like my cooking?"

Nobody likes my popcorn.

He blinks and cringes. "It's good," he says, squeaking out the words.

I present him with his own bowl, which I had left on the counter behind us. It's boring, made with the proper amounts of salt and butter, the way my parents like it.

He thanks me, pops a few kernels into his mouth, and says, "Oh, much better."

We sit on the stools at the kitchen island. I'm heating the oven for an Aunt Matilda's frozen apple pie: my second-favorite snack. I don't usually have popcorn and apple pie together, but I feel like I need to do something to keep Andrew around, and pie takes thirty-five minutes in a 325-degree oven. Plus, I'm anxious due to my hangover, and only my favorite foods appeal to me.

"I hate Sunday nights. Tomorrow is Monday, and poor me, I have to go to work alone until Michael hires someone new."

Helena didn't take the cell phone we share. I have no way to contact her, no way to make sure she arrived in Moscow safely. I expect her to buy a temporary phone in Russia at some point—if she has the money for it—so she can call me and let me know she's all right, but maybe she won't bother. She doesn't want to hear me tell her how stupid she was to leave. Perhaps she will email.

"Do you like working at the ice cream shop?" Andrew says.

I pull my hair into a ponytail and drop it behind my back. "I'm grateful for the job, but I only continued to work there for Helena. We both went to college at night—our parents said there was no reason we shouldn't work and go to school at the same time—but my sister attended few classes and dropped out after a month. Not a student, Helena."

"What was your major?"

"Child development and education."

"Because you love kids?"

The oven beeps. It's preheated and ready for the pie. "I do love them." I get up, put the pie in the oven, set the timer, and return to the stool beside Andrew. "In the orphanage, I made it my job to give the children at least some of the attention they desired. From the age of ten years, I started going into the babies' and toddlers' rooms and holding them one by one, cuddling them and kissing their little noses, rubbing my face up against theirs, making them giggle." I take my hand and smush it up against my face to demonstrate. "My little shweetie," I say in a baby voice. "*Mai-ya slat kai-ya.*"

He laughs. "Didn't they have caregivers to do that?"

"In Russian orphanages, there's not much money, so there are not many caregivers. Only enough to keep the place running. And children need a lot of love. You cannot hold them for five minutes and say, 'That's it. You're good for the day.'"

"Those kids were lucky to have you."

"Yes, well, I needed them as much as they needed me."

"It must have been hard to leave when you were adopted."

"Oh, it was," I say, remembering the painful day Helena and I left. "But Miss Sonja demanded we go. She gave us no choice."

"So I have Miss Sonja to thank."

I nod shyly. "We both do." I kiss him. His lips are soft and warm, and set a tingle through my body.

The oven makes a clicking sound, and he says, "How long does it take to bake an apple pie?"

About this, I am purposely vague. "Not too long."

"You know that's very American of you, right?"

"What?"

"Your affinity for apple pie."

I can't tell if he's making fun of me. "Have you had it before?"

He chuckles in a way that lets me know I still don't understand everything about Americans. "Only about two hundred times in my life," he says.

"Oh. Well, that is lucky for you," I say with embarrassment warming my cheeks. "Anyway, to answer your question, I have a lot of experience handling children, and whatever job that I do, I would like to help children in general."

"In Russia?"

"Oh, no. I'm not ready to go back to Russia. I don't know if I ever will be. ... Helena and I differ very much in this way."

This mention of Helena brings new seriousness to our conversation. His face lacks that smiley softness he's had until now. Probably because he's thinking about my sad circumstances of living alone in the American house of my parents, who are never here.

"Don't feel bad for me," I say.

"You've been through a lot and you're so young."

"Yes, but I have KGB in my blood," I say, grinning as I make a muscle. "I can kick ass."

"I don't doubt it."

I look to the ceiling, then toward the oven, then back to him. "I do what I have to do, like everyone else. I mean, what else is there?"

This seems to cheer him a bit.

"What will you do now that Helena has left? You said you only worked at the ice cream shop for her."

Helena left and Andrew came into the picture. The festival happened. Then drinks on the lawn. Popcorn and this conversation. And soon, apple pie. It all feels so meant to be.

"I don't know," I say.

He grabs a handful of popcorn. "Do you want to be a teacher?"

"To earn a living, I would like to be a teacher. I will get my master's first, however. I have only a year left." I stop there, put my smile on, and say, "This is a very serious conversation."

"I like serious conversations."

I wonder if I should tell him what I want. What I've always wanted. Most men wouldn't want to hear so much so soon.

"But earning a living isn't everything, is it?" I say, feeling him out.

"No, it definitely is not."

"Do you want to know what I really want?"

Part of me wants to tell him.

"I do." He's sincere, fully attentive.

"Okay, I'll tell you." I pause, a bit scared of what I just got myself into. But he wants to know. *He* started this conversation.

"What I look forward to is being older and settled, with a family of my own. A husband ..." I pause there to scan his face. There's no apparent change I can detect. I'm still afraid but I'm not the kind to let my fear make a decision for me, so I keep going. "... one that I am crazy about, not some go-to-work-and-forget-about-me kind of relationship. And a child," I say quickly, "and a little house somewhere nice. I don't need the American glamour, housewives of the rich and famous, whatever that is. I want a normal family, you know? Hardworking during the week, picnics on the weekend." I can't look him in the eyes. *Have I really said all of this out loud?* "This is my dream."

He sits back, looking—what is the proper word?—*stunned.* Or not at all impressed. I'm not sure which.

I hop down from my chair. Maybe I shouldn't have gone so far, carried away by our mutual intensity, all of his serious talk, and now I may have made a fool of myself. I have the urge to hide. But where can I go? I have no reason to walk out of the room, and I can't sit here and wait for him to think of something to say. I take a step toward the oven as if this is a good time to check the pie.

"Come back here." He grabs me around my middle before I can get away and pulls me close. The only way I can avoid his eyes is to bow my head and look into his lap. I place one hand on each of his thighs. I can't face him right now.

"I'm afraid I've said too much," I say. "I'm sorry if I make you uncomfortable. Most men want to be free; I know this. But I didn't say I want this life right now. I understand patience. A good time for everything, and everything for a good time."

I'm surprised when he draws me in and hugs me tight. My whole body becomes warm and excited and at ease at the same time. When he speaks, he turns his head so that the words go right in my ear. "You don't make me uncomfortable. And I don't want to be free. Please sit down."

I sit. We're face-to-face, very close. I'm still warm from his embrace.

"What if you could have those things now? Or most of them?"

I'm not sure I understand, and I'm not bold enough to ask, so I sit there doing what I can to reveal nothing.

"What I mean is ..." His focus on me is intense, fearless.

"... I'm the kind of person who relies heavily on his gut to make decisions. I know when something is right. I've always been that way. So, when I met you that first day I came into the ice cream shop, it felt like ..." He pauses and looks to the ceiling as if he might find the right words there. "... *worlds colliding.*"

His face widens with delight, as if something big has happened.

"We spoke for a few minutes, but it wasn't about that. When I left the ice cream shop, my gut was screaming out to me."

My hopefulness multiplies. "What was it saying?"

"It was saying that I was going to fall for you. Really hard. And really fast. And that was okay, because this thing between us, it's meant to be, the same way the moon gravitated to the Earth millions of years ago and now circles endlessly. It's just *inevitable*. I don't know if you believe in 'meant to be,' but I always have. Especially when something hits me so hard like meeting you has."

"I do believe in 'meant to be,'" I say softly.

He leans forward and kisses me.

When we break apart, I touch his face. I love it—I love *him*. I want him. I feel as if I'm under some wonderful, magical spell. And yet it's so good and so pure and so new that I worry. I worry that it can't be real.

"But are you afraid it's going too fast?" I say, wishing I hadn't asked the question the second I asked it. Instead of giving him a chance to answer, I keep talking: "I didn't want to tell you before, but I dread the moment you say you're going home, the day you kiss me goodbye. I don't want to be away from you."

"I was thinking the same thing on the walk over here. If you had told me to go home, I would have, of course, but I was dreading it."

"I'll never tell you to go home," I say as a wave of sadness washes over me. It's such a happy moment, but I'm holding back the tears and feeling more vulnerable than ever.

He takes both of my hands. "If you're sure about what you want, as sure as I am about what I want, then I think you should quit your job and finish grad school—and equally important, agree to marry me and start living the life you want to live. Because I trust what my gut tells me, and if there's one thing I know above everything else, it's that I never want to be without you."

I am not shocked or appalled or in any way frightened by what he has said. It's as if he's spoken words I knew he would speak, as if this entire day, every second, every minute, was ticking toward this place, this conversation. He has proposed to me, and all I can think is *Yes. This is what I want. And I want it with you.*

The oven's timer buzzes. The pie is ready to be eaten, but I'm not hungry anymore. I have everything I need right in front of me.

I lead Andrew to my bedroom and don't bother to turn on a light. I don't tell him that he should sleep on the floor. We don't talk, but lie on the bed and hold each other, side by side, smiling like beautiful mutes, touching fingertips and faces, filling each other with so much love that I feel swollen.

There's no hurry. Our feelings have already set a wild pace, and our bodies must now catch up. What is about to happen is inevitable, written in the kind of faraway places the Jovians sight with their telescopes. I have never wanted a moment to last as long as I want this moment to last. This present. This right now.

And yet, there's no hesitancy. No "should I?" or "shouldn't

I?" These are not the thoughts that occupy my mind. In a way, I feel as if we've already done what we are about to do, like we are old souls reacquainted from another life. In another way, though, it's all new and thrilling and hot and good, like a dream that I worry will end too soon.

Our mouths come together, two parts that make a whole. Soft lips and warm, wet tongues that meet and circle and dip. A saltiness I find pleasing. I am literally breathing him in. He smells of laundry soap and maleness and brown hair and clean cotton sheets. As he removes my dress and I unbutton his shirt, an urgency builds like a motor eager to move. Our nakedness feels electric, magnetic as skin passes over skin, a certain energy like static electricity generated. I am like an ember, glowing. My mouth greedy with wanting. The sound of my own breath fills my ears.

He unfastens my bra; there's a fumbling of straps and then a tossing away. His hands wander, skimming over the terrain, eager to touch. My breasts rise like mounds in a landscape; he follows the curve of my hip with the tips of his fingers. His chest rises to solid shoulders, I graze over his back with my nails while his fingers slide to the small of my spine. He grabs with both hands at the bottom and pulls me in closer. His mouth circles a nipple, and I am tossed onto my back. His love is a force sent to ravage me. My silk underwear is tugged off, a tissue wadded into a ball. His pants, an annoyance, kicked over the side of the bed. The moment pulsates between my legs, swelling like a tide that threatens to sweep me away.

I wrap my legs around his thighs, and he enters. There is a moan—mine, his, both of ours. It is the sound of connection, the click of the key in the lock, a tack pressed into the wall, a ship moored to the quay as the ocean rolls and pitches with storm.

Afterward, happy in the dark, with nothing to entertain ourselves except for our flushed cheeks and blissful satisfaction, a poem enters my mind: old English poetry, though I don't remember the title or poet. John Donne, maybe? It's one of the few poems I remember studying, and only because I took an English literature course to satisfy core curriculum. In it, two lovers lie together and stare into each other's eyes, lying still like we do now, basking in passionate feelings. This causes their souls to release from their bodies and rise into the air above. Free from their bodies, the souls intertwine, becoming one, and form a new and more perfect soul.

This is what has happened to us.

I just know it.

Our two souls have come together as one—they are forever joined.

We sleep for a short time before I feel the jiggle of the mattress and realize he's getting up. I almost fall back to sleep, but something makes me aware that he hasn't returned, so I slide into my underwear and throw on a T-shirt. As I cross the hall, I find him staring out the back window. I come up behind him, wrap my arms around his middle, stand on tiptoe so I can gaze over his shoulder at the sky. A bright, blaring moon makes me squint. Its silvery cold surface reminds me of a field of Russian snow, and its beauty both frightens and fills me with awe.

"I'm too happy to sleep," he says, bowing his neck to kiss my arm.

His voice has a sincere rasp weaved into it. "The universe is so big, always getting bigger, and I can't believe how lucky

I am that I'm here and you're here, together at the same time and place. It's practically a miracle."

"Mmmm." I hold him tighter and press my face into his back. "I was thinking the same thing."

"Were you?" He turns around and drapes his arms over my shoulders. "You were not," he says, smiling.

"You're right. I wasn't thinking that exact thought, but I like what you said, so I wish I could say I was." I giggle. I'm giddy-tired. "Actually, I'm hungry. Are you hungry? My stomach is growling. I was afraid it interrupted your sleep."

"I *am* hungry. We never ate the pie. Or dinner, if I remember correctly."

"Should we have some now?"

"Yes. Definitely."

I take his hand and lead him to the kitchen island. The forks and plates and pie knife have awaited our return. I scoop out two enormous pieces and find some vanilla ice cream to lay on top.

It is the best pie I have ever eaten in my life.

5

ONE YEAR AND TWO MONTHS LATER

Dusk comes early these October evenings. The computer's clock says 6 p.m., and I still haven't reached my goal: at least two résumés emailed daily, no skimping. Sometimes there are no teaching jobs outside of substitutes. But I'm flexible (a word my American mother is known to use often). I am willing to take any job that's teaching related. I prefer not to substitute, but I will tutor, or even work as a daycare teacher or nanny, if I have to. I've been job searching for about three weeks. I finished the summer semester, graduated from my master's program, and took one week off. Three weeks of searching for employment is not so long, and yet long enough to know I don't like the black hole that seems to be sucking up my résumés and flushing them into the toilet of the cosmos. All of my professors told me with confidence that I'd have no trouble finding a job, and yet I haven't received even one email request for an interview.

This morning the carpenters came to work on the room above the garage, so I had to pause to unlock the garage door and discuss plans with the contractor. And then I received the daily phone call from Andrew's mother, Caroline, before having to run out for a dental appointment.

The day has sped off like a shooting star, as all days seem to.

But I'm happy. Andrew is happy. Our souls are entwined, as that lovely old English poem goes, and in August we celebrated our first anniversary.

I shut down my computer, tidy my desk, jot a note about checking yet another job website before tucking in my chair for the evening. Andrew will be home any minute, and good wife that I am, I promised to cook dinner.

Similar in size to my parents' kitchen, ours is set up in a way I find perfectly efficient. It is renovated with painted white cabinets that shine day and night (thanks to Andrew's desire for many windows and recessed lights). It's so radiant in there that I'm sometimes tempted to wear sunglasses when I cook.

The cottage (which is what wealthy people call homes under five thousand square feet in size) is solar powered (all Jovian homes are, I have been informed), and it has brand-new skylights, though the builders recommend against them, due to the possibility of leaks. My sky-loving husband must be able to check on the heavens at all times. Even the bathrooms have more than the standard one or two windows; the extras are high up so we can see out but others cannot see us when we shower.

Not that we have close neighbors. Each house in the neighborhood sits on at least one acre of land, so there's plenty of room in between. Plenty of space to breathe the cool October air while sitting on our spacious deck of ipe (an exotic wood affordable only to the children of wealthy Americans). Plenty of privacy. Or there would be if Andrew's family would stop dropping by so often and ringing the telephone even more.

After living here for about a year, all of it still feels new to me. Our marriage. The house. Andrew. I'm in love with all of the above.

My adoptive parents supported me 100 percent when I called with the news that I would be married by the end of summer. They knew of Andrew's parents because the Jovians are Kirksberg royalty. Dana and John would have stopped home for the wedding had they not just arrived in the Middle East. (I was lucky to reach Dana on her cell phone before she and John went off-grid, as they often do.) Their mission: clean drinking water for all. And that is fine. I completely understand, even though Helena had communicated with me only once at the time, and I found it more than a little depressing that none of my family attended my wedding.

If I dwell on that fact for too long, I will cry—but no, I have Andrew now. He is my family, and that makes me very happy.

I put the chicken Angelo in the oven, and my wonderful husband walks in the door, studying a piece of mail he holds in one hand, holding his keys with the other, his messenger bag slung over the shoulder. He scowls as he pushes the door closed with an elbow.

"Rough day?" I say.

I seem to have woken him from his bad dream, whatever it is. He drops the mail and the bag on the couch and comes straight for me. "I missed you," he says, grabbing me and lifting me off the ground. "So glad to be home."

"Oh, well," I say, laughing, "that's lovely to hear. Is there any reason for your distress, or—"

"The usual deadlines and ..." He looks away and mutters, "NASA."

My husband is a mysterious man. I didn't know this before I married him. He doesn't like to speak about work. I know only that his company makes the telescopes and that one of the clients is NASA, which I find impressive, but Andrew waves away like it's no big deal. Obviously, it is a big deal because he's sworn to secrecy when it comes to the NASA project and never tells me anything about it—even when it distresses him.

Whenever he doesn't want to talk, even if it's not about work, one of us simply says "NASA." It has become a code word between us.

"Well, darling husband of mine," I say as he pulls his jacket off and loosens his tie. "I still have not found a job."

He opens the fridge and pulls out a soda. "You knew it would take time," he says, popping it open. "You're not exactly living in a metropolis, and it's only been, like, a week since your last class ended."

"It's been three weeks. And it's no rush except that I'm bored. I would rather scoop ice cream than sit home all day answering the phone for your family."

A serious bit of concern pinches his face. He backs up until he's leaning against the counter. "Who was it today?"

"You mean in addition to your mother's good-morning call?"

He has the blank look of guilt. "Not Uncle Jimmy."

"No. Not Uncle Jimmy. He hasn't bothered me since the incident with the bath towel."

Andrew stifles a smile, but evidence of it remains in the crinkles around his eyes.

"It wasn't funny, Andrew," I say, but I can't help laughing as I reach for the nearest cooking mitt and throw it at him. "And I'm still angry," which is hard for me to express when my husband makes me smile so much.

Last week, Uncle Jimmy came over unannounced, and I had been in the shower, which was obvious because after hearing his hammering fist upon the door, I feared there was a fire and did not dry myself before rushing to the door in a towel, hair dripping in streams.

There he stood, staring through one of the windows that flanks the door, in his big glasses and too-long pants, all by himself.

I opened the door a crack and asked what was wrong. He said, "Nothing."

I told him that I had just taken a shower. He said he had to reset the sprinkler system unit because it had been done incorrectly. The control box for it was located in the laundry room. I refrained from shouting, "You have to do this right now, you crazy imbecile?" because that would have been rude. Instead I said, "Can you come back later when I'm dressed?" In response, he told me, "It will only take a second," and barged right in.

"He was trying to be helpful," Andrew says in his defense.

"Well, today your cousin David wanted to 'do coffee,'" I say, using the air quotes. "Do they think I sit around watching the TV? They don't take me for a serious person, Andrew. You must talk to them."

"I *have* told them. They're crazy about you and want to be around you. And how can I blame them? I'm crazier about you than all of them put together. You don't mind when *I* call, do you?"

"Not at all. That is not my point." I chew my bottom lip. I can't get angry with him. I always wanted to be part of a family—a real family—and now I have my wish.

He gets up, stops in front of the oven and opens it to see inside. "Smells good. What is it?"

"Aunt Constant's recipe for chicken Angelo."

"Oh, nice. I'm going to change." He gives me an eyebrow raise before heading into the bedroom, pulling his shirt from the waistband it's tucked into.

"I'll come with you," I say.

"So, what did Mom want?"

"Just to chat. All these chatty Americans. Man, I can't get no relief!"

He stops and eyes me. "Have you been listening to classic rock again? Jimi Hendrix, maybe?"

"Yes, I have. In between résumés. Why? Did I use it wrong?"

"Not at all," he says. "I love the way you speak."

Then he literally tackles me so that we land on the bed, his arms forming a protective cage around me. I love the clean cotton smell of him, the feel of his five o'clock shadow grazing my cheek, the look of his eyes so close to mine. Sometimes our lashes touch like the arms of spindly children playing London bridge. When this type of thing happens, the pheromones kick in and the clothing comes off, and we forget all about dinner in the oven. I've burned more than one or two trays of chicken Angelo.

He's tugging at my cotton blouse, diving into my jeans, pressing his lips to my lips. He's become an expert at unclasping bras, so good that sometimes I wonder why I bother to wear one after 5 p.m. He rolls me on top of him, and I press my hands into his shoulders, holding him down flat. "I've got you now," I say, my legs straddling him.

"Yes, you've had me for some time now." He lifts his head, trying to get his mouth on a breast. His chest muscles contract beneath my hands as he raises his head. He's not a large man, but he's strong and wiry. Solid. A lot more than I am. I never win these wrestling matches. But I never really lose, either.

I put my hand on his mouth and push him down. He sticks his tongue out and licks the palm of my hand.

"You slobbery dog," I say and wipe my hand on his cheek.

He raises his hips so that I rise and then fall. "Bring your face down here, Sveta."

I laugh. "No way, José."

"Who's this José guy? I'll kill him."

He squeezes my middle, knowing I'm the most ticklish person on the planet. I pull back, my body curving like a quarter moon before I fall over sideways. I'm laughing and squeaking out the words, "Stop. Please. Don't." His hands roam like searchlights as they pass over my chest and stomach, and pull down my jeans.

I try to squirm away, crawling across the king-size bed, but he leaps up and wrestles me onto my back. Now he's straddling me.

"Looks like *I've* got you."

I'm panting with tears in my eyes from the laughter. My nose is hot and probably swelling from the exertion.

"Calm down, calm down." He places a hand on my bare chest. "Your heart's racing. I don't want you to blow a gasket."

"That's what you do to me," I say, struggling to catch my breath. "You make me blow a gasket." And now I'm laughing because I don't think I've ever heard that strange-sounding word before.

He pulls my jeans off, one leg, then the other, and rubs my toes. "You have the cutest feet."

"How lovely of you to say." I'm still struggling for air.

He crawls back up to me and holds my head in his hands, plants a passionate kiss. The game is over. He bows his head to kiss me again. Closed eyes, heavy breathing, roving hands.

For one moment I think of the chicken in the oven and worry, but then I remember I've set the timer, so we are good.

After we eat, we put our dishes in the sink and exit the sliding door. We sit on the deck, which is what we do every night. I love after-dinner time with Andrew. It's just me and him and no telephones—we leave the phones inside. The only trouble is the beetles. They love me almost as much as his family members do. Every night I have to be careful not to get struck in the head because they come at me like little kamikazes. Of course, they don't bother Andrew at all. He says Jovian blood repels insects.

Andrew reminds me that most of the bugs will die after the first freeze. It's only October, so I don't think the first freeze will be that soon.

The sun is setting and the sky is watercolor red mixed with purple, and every minute darker hues spill into the abstract. Soon Andrew will get behind the telescope and zoom into outer space.

"You know why my mother calls every day?" he says, gazing at the skyline.

"No idea. Wait, is it because you're her baby, and she wants to know everything you do?"

He turns his head toward me, as if surprised that I've said this. "No, but you're close. Not because *I'm* her baby, but because one day you *will have* a baby."

I scoff. "One day is not today—or even six months from today." I definitely do want children, but I don't like the idea of being rushed into parenthood by anyone, least of all his mother. "Is that really why?"

"She wants grandkids, and since I have no siblings, I'm her only chance at getting them. Sometimes I think she and my father made me only so she could have grandchildren one day. She's been talking about it since I was ten years old."

I laugh. Poor Andrew. Lonely only child. And poor me. When I have a baby, Caroline and Edmund will probably move right into this house with us.

"I can't say I blame her for thinking about it, though," he says. "I can't wait to see what our kids will look like. I hope they have your eyes and legs and face and … that cute dimple in your cheek."

"Yes, yes, I'm sure our children will be stunning," I say with humor in my voice. "But I need to get a job first. No one will hire me when I'm pregnant. And I didn't get my master's for no reason."

"Of course not," he says, unfazed. "You'll find something soon."

"You know what I was thinking today? I want to go back to North Carolina, to Ashbury Falls. It was so nice, with the hills and the tulips, and the little Main Street for shopping with all the restaurants and microbrews."

"Microbreweries."

"Plus, I had you all to myself. I wouldn't mind a vacation having you all to myself for a few days. Can we please plan a trip and go back there?"

"It was a great honeymoon," he says. "Definitely too short. I liked lying in bed with you every morning."

I'm back there in my mind. The weather was perfect. Crisp mountain air even in August. Sunshine, flowers, green grass lawns, and tall trees. "Remember the castle with its tall towers and tulip gardens? Thousands of tulips in perfect rows. White and yellow and red, and that deep purple. Some of them were even striped. I want to live in that castle and look out of those windows and see those tulips."

He shrugs. "The Chateau L'Origine is cool, but I don't know about living there. Seemed kind of old and drafty."

"What's a castle if not old and drafty? You have to take the good with the bad. That's part of its beauty."

"It's a chateau, not technically a castle. And the beauty is the wine cellar, the wine tastings. Next time we need to bring a case of that Merlot back. I don't know why we didn't."

"Yes, you're right. The chateau is too big to live in. And I love our house. It's the house I've always dreamed of. But if we could lift it up out of the ground and fly it to Ashbury Falls, I would love it even more."

He brings his gaze back down to the earth, to me and the chair I'm sitting in. "Is my family bugging you that much?"

I take a breath and sigh it out. "It's not that I don't like them. You know I have love for your family. It's just that I feel like they're always right in front of me. And not only Uncle Jimmy. There's always *someone* on the phone or at the door. I never know when the doorbell will ring."

"I understand. I'll talk to them. Again."

"Thank you. Please don't hurt their feelings."

He gets up and walks across the deck to the locked stainless-steel box where we stow his favorite toy. This superexpensive magnifying glass is the third member of our family: here is my Adirondack chair and there is Andrew's, and there is the special inlay in the deck, the circle of dark wood that marks the place where he sets up the telescope each night. The circle was Andrew's idea. The "telescoping area," he calls it.

My husband is nothing if not devoted to the night sky.

The following day, Caroline calls and wants to meet for lunch. I know Andrew has not yet had a chance to speak to her, so I graciously accept her invitation, and by that I mean I use my cheerful voice. "Sure, where would you like to go?"

"Sheridan Café. It's on the corner of—"

"Oh, yes," I say. "I am familiar."

"Wonderful. See you at twelve."

I'm in front of the computer, as I always am at this time of day. I type the address for the job-seeking website and tap in a few keywords: *teacher, Kirksberg, elementary school*, etc. When I click Search, the computer screen goes black for a second, experiencing a momentary lapse of consciousness. The search comes back with zero results. So I type *Pennsylvania* over *Kirksberg*. This time, a full-time elementary school position comes up in Pittsburgh and a few tutors in Philadelphia, but nothing within fifty miles of our home. I switch off the computer and grumble. Time to meet my mother-in-law for lunch.

———

At the café, Caroline sits in a booth waiting for me. I'm five minutes early, but because she arrived even earlier, I feel as if I'm late. I kiss her cheek and sit. She smells like perfumed roses—a scent that draws my full attention because as soon as it registers in my brain, I think of my birth mother—her hair and face, smooth skin and warmth, what it felt like to sleep beside her, to have her hold me. All of this comes rushing at me in an emotional avalanche as soon as I smell that scent. I've leapt so far back in time that I'm afraid I may become stuck.

"I ordered your iced tea," Caroline says.

"Oh, thank you. May I ask, what is the perfume that you wear?"

"La Rose."

It *is* my mother's perfume. Miss Sonja at the orphanage received some as a gift once, and I asked her about it because it was so familiar. She told me many women in Russia wear it. It's an odd choice for Caroline, not at all similar to her usual powdery gardenia.

"It's lovely," I say, but I don't tell her it reminds me of my mother. I don't want her to remember that I'm a poor girl whose parents passed away when she was a toddler.

"I'll get you some," she says. "It's one of my favorites."

I would have noticed if she'd worn it before, but I'm not here to cause trouble, so I keep that to myself.

The waitress comes by with the drinks and asks if we are ready to order, but Caroline tells her to "give us a few minutes."

Caroline is a beautiful woman, but not in the usual way. Her face is both ordinary and exotic. I don't know how this is, but it's what I always think when I see her in person. She has the light hair so many American women in their fifties and early sixties do, cut to the chin in a classic bob, very little layering, no bangs. But her features are interesting. Like the men of the Jovian family, she has a high forehead that gives her an air of intelligence. Her striking eyes make me feel like she's aware of everything going on in my world, Andrew's world, and everyone else's. They're a beautiful dark brown with flecks of gold, and her brows are as immaculate as her designer outfits. Her clothes fit her to perfection. No wrinkles or bulges to be found. She is thin, though I can't imagine her exercising, and about the same height I am, maybe five foot seven or a bit taller.

"I'm so glad you could come today," she says. "I'm sorry my invite was spur of the moment. A friend of mine canceled, so I thought it the perfect opportunity."

"That's not a problem. I was job searching, and as it turns out, there are no jobs today, so I'm free."

"Oh, that's too bad." She pulls a pair of reading glasses from her purse, puts them on, and glances over the menu. "So, the house is finished then?" she says in an offhand way.

"Everything except for the room over the garage and the bedroom below it, the one that suffered the water damage when they hit a pipe."

"Yes, you told me," she says, sounding like a person who's not sure she believes it.

"Andrew's excited about having a home office that works

as a gym as well," I say, purposely remaining positive. "Some-place he can exercise, lift the weights."

"And what about a nursery?" Her strong eyes pin me to the chair. "Did you take my advice and redecorate the guest room?"

I smile and pause before I respond. I made it clear the last time we spoke that I would *not* do what she suggested at this time. I need the space for other things because I have no chil-dren, no need for a nursery. "It still has a desk and my computer in it for now. And if we have guests, that's where they will sleep. There's a foldout couch. I think I told you."

I want to save a place for Helena, though I doubt she'll ever visit. Not that any of this is Caroline's business.

"But you're not expecting out-of-town guests anytime soon, are you?" She removes her glasses and closes the menu. "The baby is going to need somewhere to sleep, Svetlana. I know you realize this. And you have a three-bedroom home, so I think it would be smart to turn one of those bedrooms into a nursery."

There's a note of anger in her voice that goes beyond frustration. She speaks to me as if I am a child she's lost patience with.

"But right now there is no baby," I say, forcing a smile. "I'm looking for a job. There will be time for a baby down the road. By then the bedroom below the garage will be ready."

I don't tell her that I'm on birth control pills, that there is only a 1 percent chance of a baby at this time because I'm religious about taking them. And even if I weren't, even if I were sloppy and occasionally skipped a pill, research says there's only a 9 percent chance of pregnancy—so, sorry Caroline, but it will not happen until Andrew and I want it to.

"When?" she says, her eyes needling me.

I take a fast sip of my iced tea, which is bitter, not at all sweet, and divert my attention to the couple at the table across the aisle. They're laughing and relaxed. The woman is leaning torward the man, hanging on his every word. I wish it were me and Andrew. I don't want to offend Caroline, but her insistence is ridiculous and I need a change of conversation. She has moved beyond suggestions into demands. I feel bullied.

"I'll let you know," I say with an air of finality.

She replaces her glasses and reopens the menu. "Yes, please do. How many will you have, do you think?"

Oh my God. Rich people assume they can tell everyone what to do.

"Andrew and I haven't spoken about that, to tell you the truth, so I don't have the answer. Only time will—"

"Haven't spoken about it?" she says, grimacing. "Well, I happen to know that my son wants a large family. He should have informed you before you married. And from what I've heard, you love children, so I honestly don't see what the problem is. Why put it off?"

"I do love children, but—"

"Good," she says, as if my decision has been made. "I think it would be smart to get started. You're twenty-five, correct?"

I'm literally hiding behind my menu at this point. "Twenty-four," I mutter.

The waitress has returned. "Are you ready?"

Caroline looks up and says, "I'll have the Cobb salad."

The waitress turns to me, but I'm too flustered to know what I want. I tell her I'll have the same, though I don't know what this salad involves and I hope it's not corn on the cob.

The waitress collects the menus and leaves, and Caroline reaches out and takes a firm hold of my hand. Her fingers are long and so are her nails, painted a combative red. "When the two of you married, I couldn't have been happier. I was thrilled, and honestly I still am. But I thought you would have started a family by now. It's been over a year, almost two."

Her disappointment beams at me like the rays of the sun, and I actually feel my face become hot. *Does she think I don't know when I was married?* Today is October 7, which means it's been only one year and two months since our wedding day. Perhaps she's confused; the lack of grandchildren has caused so much distress that her ability to count months has been derailed.

"I can promise you that we *will* have children. But I hope to get a job before I get pregnant. Then I can take maternity leave and still have a job after the baby is born."

"You mean you'll continue to work after the baby comes?" She retracts like a compressed accordion, as if this is the most bizarre thing she has ever heard. "I didn't know—"

"That I'll go back to work?"

"I guess it's fine if you want to," she says, with an offended look that defies her words.

Of course she wouldn't understand. She never needed a job. She doesn't know what it's like to make her own money, to want to do so. She was born rich and married rich—what else could she know?

"I'm surprised is all," she says in a kinder tone. Then she looks down at her blouse, fussing with it, though it hangs as impeccably as ever. "You certainly don't *need* the money."

She's right about that. Andrew and I are set for life, thanks to his portfolios and bank accounts. Still, I feel I should remind her that it's the twenty-first century and women have joined the workforce. Few stay home with the kids. Many take great satisfaction in their work. But I must be tactful. I don't want her to give Andrew grief about this later.

"I hope you don't mind my saying so," I say, "but many of

the members of your family seem to be on the old-fashioned side."

"Oh, yes," she says, startling me with the volume of her laugh. "About that you could not be more correct. And we want the family line to continue. Our family lineage is of the utmost importance to us. The *utmost* importance. It must go on. It must thrive. And you and Andrew are expected to do your part."

I'm sure my eyes have grown to the size of headlights as I am held hostage by her unwavering stare, which says, "Do you understand?" without any help from her mouth.

I nod, indicating that I get it even though I'm sure I do not. She has crossed a line into the extreme, and I won't go there with her. I cannot wait to tell my husband.

My mood is raw and prickly as I drive back to the house, so when I see Uncle Jimmy's car parked on the street, I can't help myself: I'm like a teapot about to shoot steam through my nostrils.

He's at the door, doing his usual banging. I can hear it from inside the car, with the windows closed. He turns around as I coast into my parking place in front of the garage. As I walk toward him, he says, "You've been out. Did you go to lunch?"

I wonder if his intelligence quotient is as low as it seems.

"Yes, I did. How are you, Mr. Jimmy?" I say without a smile. It is all I can do to refrain from shouting, *You were warned to stay away.*

That's when I notice he has something in his hand: a plastic card of some sort, white and shiny, with black writing on it.

"I received something in the mail," he says, lifting the card to eye level. "It has to do with your security system. I need to get in there and program it for you."

"Oh?" Why he would receive mail about our security system is beyond me, but stranger things have happened on a daily basis with this family. "It seems to be working as it should. Nothing weird happening with it."

"That's good. But the company has come up with this extra bit of security. It has to do with calling the local police and how they receive the call. It's up-to-the-minute technology. Very important." His face flattens into that of a sincere puppy dog. He knows I don't want him around—or if he doesn't, he's even dumber than I thought.

I push the key into the lock and twist the knob. "Come in," I say, digging deep in my place of niceness to find a smile for him.

He rushes past and goes straight for the white plastic box in the hallway—the brains of the security system. I head into the kitchen. The corncob salad and iced tea have left me thirsty. "Would you like a glass of water?" I ask, because I'm the perfect hostess, even to unwanted guests.

"Would love one," he shouts back.

Of course he does. He never turns down the opportunity to linger. A true hanger-outer, Uncle Jimmy is.

I get two glasses, fill them with ice, and pour the water. I put his glass on the breakfast bar. Then I gulp mine down so fast the ice falls onto my upper lip and water splashes upon my cheek. I use my sleeve to absorb it and wonder how long Uncle Jimmy plans to stay.

"And ... finished," he shouts from the foyer. "I told you it would only take a second."

He had said nothing about how long it would take.

He appears before me now, shirt untucked, hair in a whirl, plastic card still in hand. I cannot help noticing his high forehead and his light hair, which seems thinner than usual. Or maybe it's simply more windblown than usual. If I had to guess, I'd say the Jovians have some Nordic roots. I'll have to ask Andrew about that.

"Thank you," I say with mature calm. "I feel much safer now."

He tilts his head and laughs, his shoulders bobbing up and down. "I love your sense of humor."

My internal voice responds, *Well, I do not love you.* I would not say this out loud because I'm not supposed to hurt the family's feelings.

"One more thing before I go," he says. "I need to use your bathroom, if you don't mind."

"Of course." I gesture in the direction of the powder room, which is through the kitchen, but he's already heading straight for the master suite. I shake my head and grumble under my breath. I'd rather he didn't snoop around my bedroom or bath, but his manners are atrocious, and what can I do?

A few seconds later, I hear the sound of the toilet, and he returns like a walker in a walking race. He grins in my direction, gives me a split-second wave, and heads for the front door. "Well, have a nice day."

"Don't you want your water?"

"No, no. No time." He continues out, closing the door behind him.

I mutter, "Thank God," and get on with my day.

6

———

That night, after dinner, Andrew and I are back on
the deck, the two of us piled upon one Adirondack
chair. I'm in the back, and he's draped over my legs
with his upper body using my middle as a cushion. The sun
has painted the sky in glossy shades of oyster shell—pastel
pink, feathery gray, puffs of white clouds—and Andrew has
just told me about a party we'll go to in a couple of weeks, for
Fran's birthday. Lisa's throwing him a dinner party at a
Japanese steakhouse. I have never been to a Japanese restaurant, so I don't know if I'll like it, but I'm happy to see Fran
and Lisa and baby Max. It's been a while since we've visited,
and I always have fun with them.

So far I have refrained from talking about the lunch with
"Mom" and my short visit from Uncle Jimmy because I feel
like I have been complaining a lot, and Andrew told me
yesterday that he would speak to them. I don't want to nag—
then again, I want to tell him what his mother said about the
family lineage and the two of us doing our part—and whatever Uncle Jimmy did with the security system as well. I'm

putting it off for the moment. Why let them ruin our beautiful, relaxed time in front of the sunset?

"Remind me, dear husband," I say, humorously, "what is your family heritage? Is it Swedish? I can't for the life of me remember."

"Um, well, we're a big, worldly mix. My family line starts way back, probably with the cavemen."

"Did you ever notice that you don't look like your parents too much? Maybe a bit of your mother around the eyes, and your father's lean body, but definitely not the forehead. I mean, you're oval, which is nice, but your face is much rounder than theirs."

"The forehead is the European side. I never noticed it being *that* prominent, though."

"Oh, it is. Especially Edmund's and Uncle Jimmy's. Believe me."

"We actually have some Egyptian in our heritage," he says.

"That is not what I would have guessed."

"I'm not kidding. Uncle Jimmy traced our history all the way back to ancient times."

What a wonder Uncle Jimmy is.

"He's into ancestry—and DNA, which is sort of his second profession."

"Second profession? I didn't know he had a first profession. He doesn't seem to work too much. And that is strange, but then again, so is he."

Andrew doesn't reply to my harsh words, which are whisked away by the evening breeze.

"He used to work in a laboratory in Scotland."

"Scotland? Did he discover anything important? How to clone a cow, for instance."

"No, not a cow. It was his colleagues that cloned a sheep, though. He was a consultant on the project."

This rings all kinds of bells in my mind. I remember

reading about the cloned sheep in one of my school text-books. Or maybe I saw a program about it on TV. *"The* famous cloned sheep?"

"You know Dolly?"

"I think we discussed it in one of my college classes."

I suppose Mr. Jimmy is not as dumb as I thought. But I don't care. I'm not in the mood for talk of Uncle Strange Man's greatness.

"Well, that is …" And then I stop because Andrew and I have spoken at the same time. "Go ahead," I tell him.

"I was going to say that there's a reason I brought up Uncle Jimmy's interest in DNA. I have to get something off my chest."

I frown. "That is unfortunate."

"It's nothing bad. It's …" He shifts side to side upon my lap as if unable to get comfortable. "Do you remember the first drinks-on-the-lawn party, where you met everyone?"

"That is a party I will never forget."

"Oh, I know. Me, too. Um, and I'm sure you remember passing out in the guest room?"

"If you're going to tell me that we had sex, I don't want to know. Let sleeping bears lie at this point."

He laughs. "No, not that. You were in no shape for—"

"I'm only kidding, my sweetness. I would remember such a thing."

"Oh, yeah," he says, followed by a stiff laugh. "Well, that night you noticed that your—this is going to sound strange, and I apologize in advance—your fingernail was cut when you woke up?"

Alarms go off in my body and mind. "I remember," I say, not sure I want to hear more.

"Uncle Jimmy took it."

My legs spasm, causing Andrew to wobble on my lap. "You're not serious."

Andrew sits up and scoots to the end of the chair. "Yes, I am. He took your fingernail for scientific reasons, not for some bizarre collection or something like that."

"'Scientific reasons' is still bizarre." *How he can imply that it's not?*

"Right. I know," he says, "but I can explain."

Caught in a flurry of panic, I drop my head into my hands. "God, Andrew, I give him chance after chance, and it always ends the same way."

"Please don't jump to conclusions. He wanted to do a DNA test. That's all."

At that, my thoughts come to a halt because only one question matters: "Why?"

"To check your genetic makeup. He only needed a piece of hair, but he thought clipping a nail would be less intrusive, somehow, in his eccentric mind."

I press my lips tight and ride out the urge to scream. This requires a clenched jaw and a few heated breaths. "He wanted to check my DNA because I am a poor orphan?"

Andrew moves closer to me and rests his hands on my shoulders. "No, no, not at all—"

"Does he do this to everyone he meets?" I realize I sound angry. I remind myself that I'm not angry with Andrew. I'm angry with the disturbed uncle who I wish I could remove from my life.

Andrew pulls me close so that we're now side by side on the lounge chair. The familiar clean cotton scent of him calms my nerves and reminds me he is on my side. He strokes my back as if I'm a flustered cat he's trying to soothe.

"No," he says, "he doesn't do this to everyone. He did it because he suspected I was in love with you. That day at the party, it was pretty obvious to everyone who knows me. They could tell something serious was happening between us."

"That doesn't make it all right," I say, trying not to yell. "I still feel as if my rights have been violated. He came into the guest room while I was asleep, and he nearly cut my finger off. I can't even tell you how strange that is. Taking one of my fingernails!"

"I know, I know," Andrew says, deflating. "I'm not making excuses for him, but you have to understand, family lineage is a big thing for him. He only wanted a sample."

"*Family lineage*," I shout, remembering what Andrew's mother said earlier at the café.

"Yes. And DNA. He wanted to see what you were bringing to the table. It didn't occur to him that what he was doing was out of the ordinary."

The heat of my anger collects in my chest like smoldering coal.

"I'm sorry," he says again. "I would've stopped him had I known his plan."

"Would you have?"

He looks deep into my eyes. "Of course I would. I love you. I don't need to know what's in your DNA to know that."

"Ugh." I want to plug my ears. I'm tired and upset, and it's been a bad day. "Why can't he leave me alone? I know I don't come from a normal family."

"They love you," Andrew says, squeezing with the arm that's around me. "The whole family does. They don't care that your parents are dead or that you lived in an orphanage."

I'm thinking they're a wealthy American family, so of course they care that I'm some pauper who stole their son away.

"If it makes you feel any better, Uncle Jimmy said you have excellent genes."

I look up, confused, and find Andrew's roundy face flatten into a look of concern. "I mean, it's pretty obvious that you do. But as far as being disease-free and all of that, you passed the test with flying colors."

I sniffle and sit up. All of this emotion has drained me.

"If nothing else, that's nice to know, isn't it?" He doesn't wait for my answer. "Look, I know it's not normal. He loves science and he can't help himself. I'm sorry."

I shake my head. "What if he didn't like what he found? They wouldn't have let you marry me."

"I still would have married you. With or without their blessing. Nothing could have stopped—" Andrew's pocket rings. He's not supposed to bring the phone on the deck. It's our rule. Yet here it is, coming between us. Just like his family.

"Oh, shit. I'm sorry, I meant to leave it—" Something on the screen catches his attention as he pulls it out. "I won't answer, don't worry."

"Please don't," I say with an eye roll I make sure he observes.

The phone follows up with a loud "plink." A text has come in.

Andrew glances at the screen and says, "Oh—what?" He turns away from me and scans the horizon. "I have to do something. I'm sorry. I can't ignore this."

"What is it? Is someone hurt? Do you have to leave?"

"No, but it *is* an emergency." He heads toward the metal lockbox and types in the code to open it. The door pops open, and he pulls out the telescope. "They need me to locate something. Uncle Jimmy says there's an obstruction blocking his view wherever he is, and it's urgent."

Andrew carries the telescope to the designated circle and presses out the legs so that it sits in the very center.

I'm not at all convinced that this qualifies as an emergency. I mean, what is a space emergency? A beetle whizzes by my head, and I say, "I'm going inside."

Andrew is so involved, I'm not sure he's heard me.

Inside, I sit on the couch and grab a pillow to squeeze while I watch my husband through the living room windows. He hovers over the scope's eyepiece the way he always does, standing stock-still, moving the barrel of the telescope in miniscule degrees. Then he takes his phone from his pocket and makes a call. He talks for a moment while pacing the deck. Finally he opens the door and comes inside.

"It's okay," he announces.

I glare at him. "What happened? Did Uncle Jimmy think the sky was falling? Should we dig a hole and jump in until it passes?"

He gives me a look like I threw an apple pie at his head.

"I only want to know what the emergency could be," I say. "The sky's up there; we're down here. You never tell me anything."

"You don't think what happens up there affects us?" His voice has taken a turn toward the defensive. "You honestly don't think that what happens up there matters down here?"

I have touched a nerve, and that is satisfying but also worrisome. I use my strong woman voice to say, "What I think is that Uncle Jimmy is a bored old man who needs attention."

"You don't think that what I was dealing with had the potential to be an emergency?"

I feel scolded. Andrew never speaks to me in a harsh tone. "I guess I don't know," I say.

He shakes his head like he has married some dumb earthling without a clue.

"I didn't say your job is unimportant. I just don't see why Uncle Jimmy has to call as if the house is on fire. I think he does it on purpose. He's always in our business."

"This wasn't about him." Andrew ruffles his hair the same way he does when he tries to convince his stubborn mother of something. The fact that he's doing it in response to me makes me regret everything I've said, and I would like to go back to the moment before his phone rang.

"For your information, he was right to call."

"Okay. Well, I'm sorry then," I say in earnest. "I guess I don't know what I'm talking about."

A softness returns to him, a guilty kind of awareness. He tells me so little when it comes to his job. He knows I wonder about the NASA secrets, the cosmos which is his work life.

"It was about a satellite," he says. "Uncle Jimmy thought it was knocked out of orbit. Space garbage has been a real problem this year. Anyway, I don't know why I didn't just tell you."

"Is the satellite all right?"

"It could have gone spinning out of control, worst-case scenario, and it could have reentered Earth's atmosphere, but it seems to have found its way back."

"Oh, my gosh. It really could have come crashing down here—or in some part of the world."

"I'm sorry I snapped," he says.

"Please don't worry. It's just been a bad day for me. I didn't even tell you of the difficult lunch I had with your mother."

"Oh, no," he says, deflating. "You two had lunch?"

"All she talked about was babies—the grandchildren she doesn't have—and family lineage."

I can't help myself; suddenly my eyes fill. I don't know what's wrong with me. I must be more tired than I thought.

Andrew pulls the phone from his pocket and starts swiping.

"No, Andrew, please don't call her now. I can't take it. Can we go into the bedroom and talk about other things?"

He pauses, looks at me with a question in his eye.

"We can discuss your mother another time. I'm too tired right now."

He puts his phone back in his pocket. "How about I open a bottle of wine?"

"Yes, good," I say.

He comes over and hugs me, then kisses me. He's the love of my life. I could never live with myself if we were to fight all the time.

"I love you," he says. "More than anything or anyone."

I know this is true the same way I know the sun loves the moon so much, he dies every night just to let her breathe—I read that saying on a pillow in a gift shop and liked it so much, I memorized it.

Andrew gets a bottle of wine from the fridge and two stemless glasses. He says, "I am going to give you the best massage of your life."

I know what comes after his best massages, and today I need it more than ever.

7

In the bathroom the next morning, I'm fuzzy in the brain. It's the wine. I had too much, losing count after the third glass. I'm not even sure, now that I think of it, whether Andrew drank any. He left for work as usual, at least an hour ago. I was up in the middle of the night several times to use the bathroom and drink water. Now that it's fifteen minutes to nine, I reach for my birth control pill, but the pill for today is not there. I guess I took it out of habit when I drank a glass of water in the middle of the night.

I'm showered and dressed when my cell phone rings. It says, "Aunt Constant." That could be Uncle Jimmy being sneaky, so I don't answer. I like Aunt Constant the best of all the relatives, because she has never raised my hair and she's by far the most normal of them. Then again, I don't see her too often. She never does the drop-by.

And now someone's banging at the front door. I peek through the bedroom window. It's Mr. High Forehead himself. I should pretend to be asleep, but I'm so annoyed that I run down the hall with the intention of telling him what an ass he is. I fling open the door and glare at him through the glass of the storm door. He's pacing. Before I can utter a word, he raises both of his hands in surrender.

"I know, I know. I'm here to apologize. And I brought you something. He lifts a stack of Aunt Matilda's apple pies from where he put them down beside the rose bush. "I apologize for my terrible social skills. I'm basically a moron except that I'm so smart."

"I'm sorry to hear that," I say, crossing my arms over my chest. A goofy smile brightens his face, and I try hard not to laugh at him. He's a ... what-you-call? *kook*.

"I know, I know. I've worn out my welcome. And I took your fingernail. I'm an idiot!" He scrunches his face in a pained way. "I just want the two of you to be happy."

I'm frozen. *He wants us to be happy?*

"It was a very strange thing to do," I say.

"You don't understand because you don't have a scientific mind like I do. I had to make sure, for Andrew's sake. Can I please come in?" The tower of apple pies wobbles side to side, threatening to end up on the ground.

I push open the storm door, and he literally stumbles in, somehow making it across the living room without dropping the pies. He places the stack on the breakfast bar.

"Andrew says these are your favorite. I bought ten of them. Ten's a good number, so I figured ten would be good. And I apologize," he says again, "times ten, as well."

He's nuts. I realize this. Bad social skills is right. "Thank you," I say, and I hope he knows that he should leave now.

"Am I forgiven?"

I answer with a not-nice face, my upper lip curling into a snarl. I can't give him what he wants just yet.

"I'll take that as a maybe," he says.

A held-back laugh sputters across my lips. I can't help it. He's funny even if he makes me want to pull his hair.

At that, he nods and takes a seat at the kitchen table. I

guess he's staying. I pour him a glass of iced tea because he looks hot. Then I sit across from him.

"This darn summer heat," he mutters. His shirt has sweat stains under the arms, and his face is red with dribbles coming down the sides. He takes out a folded handkerchief and pats at the moisture. "I ran over here as soon as Andrew told me how awful I've been. I hope he can forgive me. I told him I would come right over with the pies, and he told me not to, but I said I had to do it. I had to let you know how bad I feel."

"I'm sure you are forgiven," I say, because it doesn't matter that I don't mean it, and he seems desperate and I can't be that mean. "Don't you ever go to work?"

I know he works for Starbright, but what he does there is a mystery. Andrew says he doesn't have a title or anything. I suppose he's a consultant.

"I'm on call. So, yes, sometimes I go to work. Not today. Not yet, anyway."

"On call, like a doctor?"

"No, no." He laughs. "I'm not a doctor."

I can see that I'm not going to get an answer, so I move on.

"You head up the Kirksberg astronomy club, too, don't you?"

"Oh, yes, but the club only meets after dark. You know, because we look at the night skies." He points upward.

"Of course."

The conversation has stalled. I have no more to say, and I hope he refrains because every time he opens his mouth, I worry what will come out.

He pretends to be interested in the dish towel that's folded on the table beside him. And then he speaks: "So, what are you doing today? Are you tired of looking for a job? Why don't you have a baby like you want to?"

Bingo. My jaw drops, and a puff of shocked air comes out. "That is not your business," I say. And while this isn't a conversation I want to have with him, I can't hold back. "Who said I want to have a baby?"

He gazes out the sliding glass door, into the backyard. "Your husband might have mentioned it."

"Or maybe you mean my mother-in-law?"

He leans forward and taps the top of my hand. "It's a good time to have a baby. Twenty-five years old. Very good time, indeed."

I back up in my chair. "I'm twenty-four and, again, that is none of your business."

"I mean, when you give birth. You'll be twenty-five."

"Will I?"

"If you were to be pregnant right now."

My eyes squint down to slits; it's my KGB look-to-kill face.

"Oh, boy, there I go again, putting my big foot in it."

He shakes his head and rubs his chin. I can see that he wants to say more but is fighting himself to stay quiet.

I, too, am wrestling because while it's none of his business when Andrew and I start a family—and I want Uncle Jimmy to know nothing about our plans—I feel a need to defend myself and what I want.

"One day I'll have a baby, but I want to have a job as well. So I must work for a year, at least—"

He sits up with bright-eyed, renewed interest, glad that I've made the next move, I suppose. "I understand. You're a working woman. It's the twentieth century."

"The twenty-*first* century," I correct him. "And these days women have choices. Your wife chose not to work. And Andrew's mother chose not to work. That was their choice. Women can do one or the other or both. You know this, right?"

"I am aware," he says, bobbing his oblong head. "I just thought because, well, you seemed so eager to create something new. Not so long ago, I mean." He pauses. Looks to the ceiling, then straightens up like a child making an oral report in front of the class:

"Love these mix'd souls doth mix again
    And makes both one, each this and that.
    A single violet transplant."

A bell rings in the recesses of my mind, and my lashes flutter with suspicion. "Are you reciting—what was that—poetry?"

He stands up, as if proud of himself. "John Donne."

"John Donne," I echo.

"You know him," he says.

It's not a question.

"I have heard of him, of course. But my major was children and education, not English."

Uncle Jimmy downs the rest of his tea. The glass makes a knocking sound when he sets it on the wood table, and I sit there, stuck in my thoughts. Something is weird about that quote. Something even stranger than the fact that he recited old English poetry in my kitchen.

"I'll be going." He stands and pulls his pants up high around his protruding middle. "Thank you for your hospitality. And again, please accept my apologies. I don't expect it to be too hard to grant me my eccentricities. I'm admittedly a strange duck. Everyone says so."

He hurries to the front door, his feet scuffling as he waddles in that chubby, older man way.

Today I'm not interested in his comedic mannerisms. I'm

stuck in my own spinning thoughts. *John Donne. Mix'd souls. Violet something or other.* The words feel familiar. I know this poem. It means something to me.

Oh my God.

The front door closes with a whoosh. I hear Jimmy's car start, and I'm left alone with my spinning thoughts.

Something about souls mixing feels familiar—and personal—and that sends a shiver up my spine. That thought, or something like it, came to me the first time Andrew and I slept together. It has lingered around me like perfume ever since. I run into my office and sit in front of the computer, pull up a search site and type in the words *violet transplant, poem, John Donne.* "The Ecstasy" comes up in various forms. I click on the first one, the text of the poem in its entirety, and read from beginning to end. The souls of the lovers leave their bodies and meet in the space above their heads. Midway through, I come across the line about the *single violet transplant.*

This is it.

The one I studied in college.

The one that came to mind when Andrew and I first slept together.

Is it coincidence that Uncle Jimmy quoted it to me?

Many people know the poem. Many have studied it. It's a love poem. But still. Why would he speak these lines? *Why today?* And if he did it deliberately, how in the hell did he get inside my head?

8

My hands are shaking as I grab my cell phone from the kitchen counter. It slips through my fingers and crashes to the floor. I reach for it under the table and then smack my head on the way up. I cannot even remember how to use the thing. I'm pressing button after button until my contacts show up and I push "Andrew."

"Hey, sexy, what's up?"

He's so unsuspecting that it breaks my heart.

"I need you." My voice wobbles like an old woman's. "Right now. I need to talk to you. Please come home."

"What happened? Is it Uncle Jimmy again? Damn him!"

"I don't want to speak on the phone. Please, can you?"

"You're not hurt, are you?"

I close my eyes. Will myself to calm down.

"No, I'm … freaking out. Can you please come home?"

"I'll be right there."

I sit in the armchair and wait for the front door to pop open. I take breaths in and out to keep my hysteria at bay. I pull my legs in close and wrap my arms around them, then bump my lips into my kneecaps. It's twelve minutes of refrigerator hum and house-settling ticks. And the question *Why is Uncle Jimmy doing this to me?*

The second Andrew walks through the door, I leap up, grab him, whisper, "Thank God." Then I gather myself so I can tell him what happened without sounding hysterical. I tell him everything about the poem and how I believe Uncle Jimmy has been reading my mind.

Meanwhile, Andrew stares at me as if he is listening to someone in the midst of a breakdown.

He hugs me and says, "He's not reading your mind. Please don't worry. He loves poetry. I've heard him recite poems a million times. All kinds, too, like sonnets and rhymes, Chaucer, Shakespeare."

I nod. I want his logic to suffice, but it doesn't. "How would he know to choose John Donne?"

"It's a love poem. He guessed, that's all. He's not telepathic, believe me."

"And you know this how?"

"Well, because he would've read my mind a million times. And second, he's not that clever."

"He's not clever at all," I shout in a sudden flash of anger. "He's rude. The last thing I want to worry about is that man poking around my brain. He's already in my face every day."

The tips of Andrew's ears turn red. "Give me one minute." He gets up, slips through the sliding glass door onto the deck, and closes it behind him.

This is my cue not to follow.

But I have to know who he calls and what he says, so I head into the living room and open one of the windows that face the backyard.

"No, Mom, listen to me." His voice is calm but stern. He has transformed into his take-charge persona. I've seen this happen only a handful of times, usually during an argument

---

with his mother. He has that "I cannot believe this shit" hardness to his cute, roundy, never-too-angry face.

"I'm not making a big deal," he says. "And neither is Svetlana. You and Uncle Jimmy have gone too far, and now you're upsetting my wife on a daily basis. … She *has been* patient. … It *is* a problem. You should see her right now. She's shaking. … Yes, he was here. That's why she's upset. … He always says something. He's a social idiot. You know that. … Yes, he brought over the pies. That's not what this is— … Yes, she forgave him. *She's* not to blame here. … No, I don't think so. It was *not* an innocent mistake. … Yes, I know he's been known to quote poetry, but this time you have to take my word for it, it was truly weird and invasive. … Will you talk to him? I *need* you to talk to him."

Another pause and then he responds in an angry, unsatisfied way. "Fine. Put Dad on."

A few silent seconds pass.

"Hey. I'm sorry to bother you. … I know what time it is and I know— … Okay. Yes. Okay. … Uh, I don't know. I'd have to ask her. … Yes, she does. She likes it very much. … Okay. Well, she's pretty upset right now. … You're right. That would be great. I'll tell her. Thank you, Dad. … Thanks, thanks. Yup, bye."

He ends the call, and the next thing I know the glass door slides open and he strides in, eager to speak with me.

"You look happy," I say, unable to hide my surprise.

"I think I have the solution."

"Really?" I blow my nose. "Are we going to kill Uncle Jimmy?"

"Better. We're moving to Ashbury Falls."

My eyes pop.

"*If* you want to, of course, but I think it's a great idea."

"Ashbury Falls?" I stifle the urge to jump up and down. "Don't tease me, Andrew."

"I'm not kidding. We can move there if you want to."

"But what about your job? And this house—and your parents?"

He crosses the room and sits beside me. "Remember when I told you that a few years ago Starbright built one of its biggest telescopes in the mountains on the border of Ashbury Falls and, uh, the next town over, I can't remember its name off the top of my head. You said there was no way you were going to tour the facility during our honeymoon."

I grab a tissue from the box on the table. "Yes, I remember."

"I can pretty much work there in whatever capacity I want since my father owns the company. And there's a house, too. A company house, used for guests and family on occasion."

I study his face for signs of joking: a twitch of a laugh or an I-wish rise of his brow. But no. Nothing like this happens.

"Dad made the suggestion we move there."

"This is an option? In Ashbury Falls?" I say, making sure I didn't hear wrong. "You realize how far that is? Over six hundred miles?"

"Plenty of buffer between us and the family if we go there."

I laugh because I cannot contain my excitement. "You're sure you're serious? I mean, are you sure?"

He tells me yes, and suddenly this day has transformed. "I love Ashbury Falls." I run at him and hug him as hard as I can. "No more Uncle Jimmy!"

"You'll still see him at holidays and family events."

"Of course, holidays. That's fine." I release him and step back. "What a relief." The adrenaline surges, and I am elated.

"I'm glad you're happy." He glances around the living room, the house we have just finished remodeling.

Perhaps he's not quite as happy as I am. "Are you okay with this?" I say.

"Yes. I am. I mean, we don't have kids yet. It's not like my mother can say we need to stay close for that reason."

"What about when we *do* have them?"

"We can always move back. If you want to. ... We're definitely keeping this house. Maybe David will live here for a while."

"This is so great." I clap my hands, already thinking of what to pack first. My computer and all of my office things. "When can we leave?"

"Whenever you want to."

"Whenever I want to," I say, letting it sink in. "Whenever I want to!"

The following night, a Friday, we get together with Fran and his wife, Lisa, and baby Max at their place. I'm sad to move away from them, to make Andrew leave his best friend, but they don't see each other much anymore. Fran's job keeps him busy at all hours, and when he's not at work, Lisa keeps him close to her and the baby. I don't blame her at all.

When we arrive at their house, Lisa opens the door in her robe and bare feet, with a towel covering her dark hair and Max, the ferocious toddler, struggling to get free from her arms. She's put on a happy face, but I see through it. She may even be close to tears.

Andrew checks his watch. "Shoot. Are we early?"

"Oh, Max, why do you cry, *moy mal'chik?*" I say. "Please let Mommy get dressed. Would you like me to take him?" I hold out both hands.

Lisa says, "Thank you," and passes him over. "I think I've

been late for every social event since he was born," she says, "not that there have been many."

"We understand, don't we, Max?" I say, smooching his fat cheek and getting salty tears on my lips.

We step into the living area while Lisa speeds off in the opposite direction.

I spend the next blissful half hour bouncing Max on my knees, playing peek-a-boo and basking in his baked-bread toddler scent. His hair is like Fran's—wavy, thick, dark brown—but his skin is coffee and milk like Lisa's. He makes a beautiful genetic mix. *Uncle Jimmy would probably want to study his DNA.* Max has a sweet personality, too, and he's boisterous, like a toddler should be. So curious. As we play together, I consider how I might smuggle him out in my purse before the night is through. Of course, I would be happy to return him the following morning. Toddlers are adorable, but also rude; they care nothing about your sleep or your showers.

Andrew and Fran talk sports—this baseball game and that. Nothing I care about, so I leave them to their male bonding. I always forget how tall and wide Fran is. He's something to look at. If I were a criminal, I wouldn't like to find him and his team of FBI officers at my door.

The TV is on, the volume low. A baseball game is about to start. Fran asks if I want a beer, but I tell him no.

A few minutes later, Lisa enters the room fully dressed and looking like a new person. She has some makeup on and shoes with a heel.

I get up from the couch to join her in the kitchen, accidentally kicking a yellow dump truck halfway across the room. Max runs after it, glad for the action. Toys and plastic parts of toys are sprawled on the floor, on the windowsill, in a pile in front of the fireplace.

"Sorry about that." Fran grabs a handful of peanuts from

the bowl on the coffee table. "Gotta be careful where you step when you come to our house."

"Max sure has a lot to play with," Andrew says.

"Tell me about it. We spoil him rotten."

I enter the kitchen and hover around the island, out of Lisa's way while she gets the appetizers together.

"You should have a baby," she says. "You're obviously ready."

I smile. I know she doesn't mean anything by it—unlike my relatives. I scoop Max up from the floor as he passes through. "All in good time, right Max-a-million?"

He's so solid compared to the children I knew at the orphanage. Gruel doesn't exactly put meat on the orphans' bones.

Max giggles and squirms, so I put him down. He points to the living room and says, "Daddy."

"I wish we put it off, to be honest," Lisa says in a low voice. "I mean, Max was not planned. Not that I'm not grateful for him, because I definitely am. Half my friends from work are on fertility drugs." She reaches into the fridge and pulls out a plate of cubed cheeses, setting it on the island before me. She removes the cellophane and pops a couple into her mouth. "It's a lot of work, you know? And it's not *fun* work. Like right now, I would be so excited to go to the office and take a twelve-hour shift like I used to. And you know I never liked my job that much." She yawns and stretches out her neck. "It's just that Max needs me so much. Literally 24/7."

"Yes. I know this about young children. And I'm in no hurry. But I do love your Max."

She pauses as she pulls a box of crackers from the cabinet. "I can't believe you're leaving so soon. It's so sudden, it blows my mind. I thought you two would be in Kirksberg forever—and you're moving when?"

"Next week."

"You won't even be here for Halloween."

"I know. Andrew has to get up there to start his new job."

I don't want to tell her the real reason we're leaving so quickly. She doesn't know Andrew's family well and wouldn't understand if I said they're driving me crazy.

"We'll take a road trip and see you guys," she says, pouring chips into a bowl. "Maybe around Thanksgiving, if *Fran can ever get a day off.*"

She said that last part loud enough to get Fran's attention.

"I'm working on it," he says.

She closes the fridge, a bottle of orange juice in hand. "So you say."

"Whoa, did you see that tag?" he shouts as cheers rise from the TV set.

Andrew says, "Nice," and I hear the clap of a high five.

"We should be back here for holidays," I tell her, because that was the deal we made with his parents.

Lisa turns back to me and frowns. "Good. 'Cause we're really going to miss you guys."

I pick up bowls of chips, and she takes the plate of cheese, and we join the guys at the coffee table.

"Speak for yourself," Fran says. "I'm not gonna miss them at all." His words are heavy with sarcasm. "This one only stays in touch because he knows I can help him get out of a jam with the law." He thumbs at Andrew.

"Why would I need help with—"

"You can admit it," Fran says. "You've always looked up to me, being FBI and all. You think I'm cool."

"Are you sure? 'Cause I knew you freshman year when you tried to sport a mohawk and—"

"Stop right there." Fran attempts to smack the back of Andrew's head but misses when Andrew ducks.

"—and were pretty goofy looking in general," Andrew

continues with a laugh. "With your bushy Einstein mustache. Lucky for Lisa, the bureau makes you shave."

Fran puffs up like a proud peacock. "See? He's jealous of my good looks."

I've seen this routine before, and I love their friendship. I'm sorry we're leaving. *Thanks so much, Uncle Jimmy.*

Lisa gives Fran a look like she thinks he's nuts or maybe she's baffled by his vanity. "Honey, you can believe whatever you want to believe, but all Andrew cares about are two things in this world: his wife and the stuff up there, in the sky. No one thinks it's that great being an FBI agent. I know I don't."

"Hey!" he shouts loud enough to make me believe she may have touched a nerve this time. "I can admit that being a Jovian is pretty hard to top, but come on, baby, it's the FBI." His eyes bulge a little, which is the most frustrated I've ever seen Fran look. "Plus," he says, "some of the Jovians are pretty strange." He makes eye contact with me, reminding me of the conversation we had about the Jovians' piercing stares and jolts of electricity in our hair.

"You're so right," I say with a laugh. "And I for one feel a lot safer knowing you're out there if I ever need you."

Fran winks at me. "Why, thank you, Svetlana. I appreciate that."

"I feel like my whole family has just been insulted," Andrew says.

"Don't worry," I tell him, "you're not one of the strange ones."

9

The road trip to Ashbury Falls feels like an adventure to yet another new life. Andrew keeps telling me he hasn't seen me so relaxed since the honeymoon, but now that we've been in the car for twelve straight hours, I'm starting to feel sick. Since reaching the base of the mountain, we've circled like vultures, around and around, surrounded by jagged rock walls and steeply sloping inclines covered with spindly evergreens that look like they've withstood years of difficult weather. Ashbury Falls is in the mountains of North Carolina, and the road we are on, the one that leads to our new home—the one we will take to get to the food store and the doctor's office and the restaurants and quaint shops of Main Street—coils up the mountain like a miles-long serpent. It's appropriately named Steep Hill Road, and I'm not looking forward to driving up and down during the icy days of winter. Already I'm wondering if we have not made a mistake in the location we have chosen for our new home.

On the other hand, Andrew seems to love mountain driving. He holds the wheel with the focus and joy of taking on an exciting challenge. His truck is getting the workout it was built for. So manly, these American trucks. What is it they say, "ram tough"? But a ram is a goat, so I don't get it.

"Are we almost there?"

"Almost," he says, glancing at the GPS. "Five hundred more feet, and it will be on the right."

"You promise that our house isn't at the top of this mountain?"

"It's only about halfway up. The Starbright International office is at the top."

"This is a very tall mountain," I say.

I roll down the window and let the autumn air rush at my face. My new town smells like the earth, soil, and moss. Fresh and crisp. Clean, like the oxygen from pine trees. A wisp of a fire in the fireplace. I breathe in and release a giant sigh of relief. We make the turn off the main road and pass a wooden sign that says "Majestic Terrace."

"There it is," Andrew says.

The house up ahead looks like the fraternal twin of the one we left behind, a sprawling ranch with beautiful landscaping, tall long-leafed pines, and a low stone wall that crosses the front lawn—I am the luckiest girl in the world.

Andrew starts his job two days after the movers drop off our things. He's heading up a new project for NASA. No surprise there. I make him promise to text me the minute he arrives at work; I don't trust that coiled-up snake of a Steep Hill Road, though I'm sure I'll get used to it and will one day laugh at how much worry it is causing. Not that I've had to drive anywhere on my own. Andrew and I have been so busy with the house, we haven't ventured out for dinner or even a stroll down Main Street yet.

If someone had told me last week that I'd get away from Uncle Jimmy and Andrew's mother *and* have a new home in a matter of days, I never would have believed it. In less than a week, we have put 90 percent of the house together, minus the wall hangings, paintings, and curtains. The neighbors are so far to either side that I don't even care about the lack of curtains. Tomorrow a woman from the warehouse store will measure for window treatments in the living room, bedroom, and all three baths. It's going to be expensive, but it's what Andrew wants and, being Jovians, there's no lack of money. I know how much Andrew loves the house in Kirksberg, so I want to make sure he's equally happy with this one. It already has solar panels, so that's a plus.

I'm showered and I've had my breakfast. Andrew has texted to let me know he's arrived safely at the office. Time for me to get to work.

I sit at my desk and boot up my computer. I'm feeling lighthearted, like I might find a job today. I love my new office. The sun beams through a picture window larger than a big-screen TV and splashes onto bare, bright walls. My view of the lake and the wooded surroundings features leaves of orange and red and yellow, and water that reflects the blue sky, endless with possibility.

I can't imagine anyone not loving this place.

Our neighborhood, Majestic Terrace, consists of about a dozen homes on an offshoot of Steep Hill Road. Many are log cabins surrounded by wildflowers, with neat woodpiles waiting to warm chilled nights. Ours is a plank-siding house with a renovated kitchen that has gleaming earth-colored granite, a proper replacement for the home we left behind. Of course, my dear husband has already hired the carpenters who will build a deck on the back for his telescope and our Adirondack chairs.

After living in the town of Kirksberg for the past eight-plus years, most noticeable to me is the blissful quiet. There are nature sounds and not much else: the chatter of a breeze through leaves, the chirp of birds, the rare buzz of a passing car. Since we arrived, I've sighted three foxes on the property, several small families of deer, and at least four or five rabbits as well as many adorable chickadees and titmice and woodpeckers.

Zero Uncle Jimmies have come to call, and that is *wonderful.*

I spent the first day in Ashbury Falls setting up my office because I wanted to look for a job right away. Even before the bed in the master wore a set of sheets, I had put my computer together, hooked up the Wi-Fi, and sent out two résumés. Yes, I'm focused. And thank goodness for technology. Otherwise, how would I do everything so quickly? If I couldn't send emails, I couldn't apply for jobs or stay in touch with Lisa and Fran, or my long-lost sister in Russia, and then I might suffer the so-called cabin fever Uncle Jimmy spoke of before "bidding us goodbye" like some old Englishman.

As long as my husband joins me each evening and weekend, I will be fine watching the foxes and the birds and not meeting David for coffee or Caroline for lunch.

Speaking of email, I must try again to reach Helena. I haven't heard from her in too long, and while I'm worried that we'll grow apart, I'm too busy to linger on my worry. I'm sure she's busy, too, planting her vegetables with her "cousin" (now boyfriend, Ivan). I've heard from her only three times since she ran away. She has no money for a phone or computer, so email's not so convenient for her. When she wants to email, she has to go to the internet café or find a friend whose email actually works. And that could explain her failure to write back in a consistent manner—though she swears she sends far more emails than I've received, and I know I do the same.

Sometimes I wonder if the problem is my computer: it has a strange habit of blinking every now and then, but it never crashes or dies, so I keep using it. Maybe there was a bad connection in Kirksberg.

Or maybe Helena's been avoiding me. Maybe she doesn't want to report that Russia's not so good. Or it could be everything she hoped it would be, and she doesn't want to boast. I have no idea.

> My dear little sister,
>
> We have been out of touch again. I miss you. How is Mother Russia? I hope she's treating you well. We've moved to Ashbury Falls, North Carolina, so please take down my new address in case you ever want to visit. You are welcome to come anytime. Here it is …

After I type in my new information, I sit back and consider what else to say. My eyes pass over the bookshelf on the right, where propped against its side is the framed aerial photograph of Chateau L'Origine that Aunt Constant and Uncle Jimmy gave Andrew and me for a wedding gift. Whenever I look at the bird's-eye view of the sprawling castle and its towers, terraces, and tulip gardens fit for royalty, it brings back blissful memories of our honeymoon.

And now we live in this town. I can't believe it.

I want to hang the picture in the living room, on the wall perpendicular to the one with the wood-burning stove, but Andrew keeps bringing it in here. I finish writing my email, then grab the picture and lug it into the living area. It's quite heavy, so I lean it against the long backyard-facing wall, then swoop into the kitchen where I last saw the picture-hanging kit and pick it up. I want to get this done before Andrew decides he doesn't want to hang the picture for some reason. I have a feeling that's why it keeps turning up in my office. He doesn't like the castle as much as I do. I'm not sure why.

A small circular table with two chairs sit in front of the far wall, so I use the tape measure to figure out how to center the picture over this table. I make a pencil mark, then take measurements and go through the necessary calculations. I'm pretty good at hanging pictures. It's not rocket science, after all.

As this thought crosses my mind, my phone makes the outer-space sound (appropriately called "Aurora") that Andrew selected to alert me of incoming emails. I check it and find a request for an interview one week from today at 11 a.m., at the Ashbury Falls Montessori School that's in search of an assistant teacher for the four-year-old class-room. I'm overqualified, but I think I can convince them that I am right for the job.

I sit back and revel in a swell of satisfaction.

It really is a beautiful day.

Four very quiet, super-private days later, during which I speak to no one other than my husband, the early November sunshine becomes lost behind a thick swath of cloud. The curtains have been ordered, the artwork hung, the email sent to Helena and not responded to, the groceries shopped for, all three bathrooms cleaned, the birdfeeder filled with seed, two novels read, three movies watched, the laundry done, dinners (and desserts) made, and the job interview still three long days away.

I am inches from admitting to boredom and, dare I say, loneliness.

My phone has not rung since we moved in. Andrew only texts on those rare occasions when he's not in a meeting.

I'm wondering who else lives on this mountain.

Does anyone live on this mountain?

Am I alone with the foxes and the fawns?

I have seen a red car speed past once or twice, so I know at least one other human lives up here.

Perhaps this is a neighborhood of vacation homes.

I asked Andrew if he wanted me to drive him to work today, just for something to do. He did a double-take to see if I was kidding, then laughed and continued on his way.

I'm doing all I can to resist playing solitaire on my telephone.

Could cabin fever have set in so soon?

Damn you, Uncle Jimmy.

———

The day has come for me to put on the interview suit: navy blue, serious, professional (yes, quite traditional and ordinary), a gift from Dana, my American mother, when I graduated college. I wish I could talk to her, but I've been trying to reach her and my father for weeks, and my messages keep going to voicemail. I'm sure that's because they're using temporary international phones. Every time they leave the country, they rent international phone lines with numbers different from the last. They put their American phones aside until they make the trip back home. Which means they will eventually hear my voice messages. They probably stayed abroad longer than planned and haven't used their American phones in months. I'll keep trying.

If Dana were here, she would help me prepare for this

interview with Mrs. Lewis. Because, yes, my palms are cold and sweaty, and anxiety fuels my every movement.

"You have nothing to worry about," Andrew said earlier this morning. "She's going to love you."

But I'm not so sure. There are many things she may not like. For instance, she may not like my accent. Or the answers I give in response to her questions.

"You're going to be an awesome teacher, and if you don't get this job, you'll get the next one," he said in a casual and unconcerned way that irritated me.

This from the man whose father gave him employment. But I don't hold that against him. Andrew wakes up happy and ready to go every day, eager to get to Starbright because he loves what he does. He's nice to everyone who works there, too, even his assistant. I hope Mrs. Lewis is equally nice when she interviews me today.

Grinning like a true-blue American girl, I drive out of the Montessori School parking lot and down the street, where I get back onto the snaky Steep Hill Road. The interview is over, and my nerves have given way to a flow of adrenaline. Mrs. Lewis has offered me the job—though it doesn't start until March, when one of the teachers goes on maternity leave. But that's okay because *I got the job!* I have the radio on, and the singer is belting out, "Those were the best days of my life," over his electric guitar.

It isn't until I pull into the driveway that I realize I forgot the Parmesan cheese to go with dinner. I consider doing a U-turn and coasting back downhill, but there's a red car in our extra parking spot and a woman standing at the front door. She holds a brown basket covered with a white cloth in one hand and knocks the door with the other.

At the sound of my car, she turns around. I take in her sun-weathered wavy hair, high-waisted jeans, and peach-colored blouse. She's short and plump in her bottom, thick waisted like many women are—what Helena would call a typical American housewife. I continue past to my parking spot in front of the garage (I have never made a habit of pulling into the garage).

"Well, hello, young lady," she says as I near. "I'm Miranda, wife of Leo, your neighbor from over there." She points to the right. "Consider me the neighborhood welcome committee."

She's tan and pretty. Her onslaught of friendliness and twangy accent make me smile. What Helena would do by way of imitation, I can only imagine.

"I am Svetlana. My husband is Andrew." I shake her hand. She has an overall youthful glow, and her eyes are as blue as tropical waters, but the skin around them radiates with fine lines.

"Svetlana, is it? What a nice name. We don't get too many Svetlanas around here."

She's so perky and sweet, like the iced tea the restaurants serve.

"My friends call me Sveta."

"All righty, then I will do the same. You have a wonderful accent."

"Oh." I look down out of habit. I don't know why I'm embarrassed when people say this. "I was thinking the same about you."

"Well, Sveta, I wanted to drop off these muffins and say welcome to Ashbury Falls. I meant to visit sooner, but Leo's father has been ill and it's been back and forth to Rock Hill for the past ten days."

I take the basket in my free hand. It's not light. There must be at least a dozen muffins in there, and the cinnamon-butter scent rising from them makes my mouth water. "They smell so good," I say, wishing I could think of a better adjective.

"I hope you like them because there's enough in there to keep you alive for days." Her dimples come out when she laughs, and I wonder how old she is. Definitely older than me. Maybe forty. Whatever age she is, she seems like she'd be fun to hang around with.

"I also want to let you know that I'm here for you, whatever you may need, whether it's help moving a sofa or the phone number for a lady doctor ..." She pauses, possibly in wait of a reply. "Or a plumber or what-have-you," she adds. "I'll be happy to help you settle in in whatever way I can."

"That's very nice," I say, remembering I'll need all of those things. I push the key into the lock and ask her to come in. I'm excited to have my first guest.

"Oh, no thank you," she says. "I didn't come here to do the drop-by. I wanted to deliver the welcome basket and be on my way. I've got to meet Leo in town." She checks her watch. "He's probably wondering where I am."

Shoot. She's so friendly and *normal*. I could have shared the news about my job with her. We could have talked about the restaurants in town, the stores.

"Okay, well, thank you for stopping by. And thanks for these." I raise the basket.

"Believe me, I'll happily take a rain check." She's backing away. "Anytime you feel like you want some company, swing by my house for a visit. If the red sedan is there, then so am I. And I mean that. Sometimes I feel like I'm the only one up here with the foxes and the deer, so I welcome the company."

"It *is* quiet up here."

She pulls open the car door. "Don't worry, you'll get used to it." Then she gets in and starts the engine. "And happy Thanksgiving a little early," she says with a wave.

It probably will not be happy considering we are going home to see Uncle Jimmy, but she doesn't know that.

I go inside and celebrate my new job with a homemade muffin.

———

Andrew bursts through the door just like he used to in the Kirksberg house: the day's mail in one hand, briefcase in the other, a stern look on his face as he shuffles through the junk.

I run from kitchen to foyer and stand before him. I've been keeping my secret inside all day, purposely not calling or texting. "I have been offered a job." I bend into a balletic bow, followed by a celebration jump that's more cheerleader than ballerina. "My interview was so good Mrs. Lewis offered me the position right away. She told me to think about it overnight, but I don't need to because I already gave my answer."

I run at him and leap like a flying squirrel onto the trunk of his body, causing him to scatter the mail and drop the briefcase as I plant kisses on various parts of his face.

"Oh. Wow," he says as he regains balance. "That's great, honey. Of course Mrs. Lewis loves you. Why wouldn't she? You're amazing, and I'm not saying that because you're so cute."

"Yes, but the job doesn't start until March. One of the teachers is pregnant and will go on maternity leave."

We kiss again, but only for a moment because he's stopped to whiff the air.

"What's that cooking? Smells great."

I squeeze him in a hug once more before dropping to my feet. "Lasagna."

His eyes grow large. "Dinner. Now, please."

I love this about him. He never fails to compliment my mediocre cooking—like I never fail to compliment his.

We sit at the kitchen table. The sun spreads a pink glow over the walls. I cut the lasagna and transfer it to our plates. He brings the salad out, the sparkling wine. He sets the bottle down, and I say, "Oh, I see," knowing wine means we'll be in the bedroom after dessert. Or possibly before.

"I realized today that it can get really quiet up here, on this mountain," I say. "I had no one to share my good news with."

He blows on the lasagna, steam bending in the breeze. I've seen him burn his mouth a million times. He always comes home so hungry. He says that he's so into his work during the day that he forgets to eat. I tell him he needs to take care of himself.

"But that's what you wanted, right? Privacy. I'm sure you'll have a bunch of friends once you start working."

"As a matter of fact, I made a friend today. Her name is Miranda, wife of Leo."

"Wife of—" He squints at me. "Is that something you made up?"

I shake my head. "She said it like that. 'I am Miranda, wife of Leo.'"

He's about to shovel a forkful of lasagna into his mouth when he drops his head and laughs. "How old is she?"

I shrug. "Forty-something ... maybe. She made cinnamon apple muffins as a welcome gift."

"I love her. Bring on the muffins."

"With lasagna? Sounds unappetizing."

"You're right. Save them for dessert."

"And I didn't tell you the best thing about my new friend: when I invited her to come in, she said no *because she doesn't do the drop-by*," I say with emphasis. "Can you believe it? Except I wouldn't have minded her company today—"

"That's perfect," he says, but the words lie flat, without enthusiasm.

I'm just noticing there's something going on, something more than his usual hunger. It's preoccupation, or maybe worry. Something is churning inside his brain.

"Andrew?"

He looks up with an air of sheepishness, as if he's been caught doing something bad.

"How was the galaxy today?"

That's what I sometimes call his work. The galaxy, the cosmos, hyperspace.

By now the sun has all but gone down, so I lean back and switch on the chandelier above our heads: a pretty stained-glass light with a bowl of purple grapes, red apples, cheerful oranges. Fruit salad.

He gives up on the piece of lettuce he was trying to level onto his fork and meets my gaze. "It's fine."

His lips move as if he's about to speak, but he doesn't. I am thinking he wants to say more, but because it's something about work, he's not supposed to. I've seen this face of his before. The "confidential" face. The NASA face.

We continue to eat. I wait for him to say something.

He finishes his lasagna and asks if there's more.

"I always make an entire casserole dish for my hungry husband," I say, trying to make him laugh.

He gets up, serves himself, comes back.

I wonder how long he'll be silent.

After a moment he says, "So, you know how I head up several projects for NASA? I mean, I know you know, but ..."

"Like you did back home."

"Right. And you know about Kirksberg and the spaceship that landed in the 1960s?"

What a question. "Ohhhh," I say as if I am in revelation. "Is that why Kirksberg hosts the UFO Festival every year?"

He's not amused. "But you know the spaceship is real, right? That it wasn't a hoax or something Russia sent over to mess with the United States."

I wipe my mouth with my napkin and clear my throat. "I have always believed it was real. And Russia would never do that." I open my eyes very wide in a humorous manner so he can see the sarcasm.

"Right," he says with a weak sort of laugh. "But not everyone believes it was real."

"Yes, yes, the nonbelievers. It seems pretty obvious to me. So many people saw it in the sky and then in the woods. They even saw the men in white suits who rushed into the town and took it away. I mean, come on, America. Just because they told you there was nothing to see doesn't mean there was nothing to see."

"Right."

"Talk about brainwashed," I mutter. "People are strange."

I look up from my plate, and I can see that he's waiting for me to stop talking.

"My work with NASA has to do with that spaceship."

Andrew has turned a shade of pink.

I sit up. It's the least I can do to look more serious. The conversation was heading in this direction the whole time, but I am still surprised to arrive at this place. "And you are allowed to tell me?"

"No. I'm not. I shouldn't. But something exciting is happening, and I—" He pops a tomato into his mouth. "I feel like I *should* tell you. And I want to tell you." He wipes his mouth. "In a way, it involves you as much as it does me."

He's never this serious, and for some reason it makes me act nonchalant, all happy American smiley-faced wife. "Well, I can keep a secret as long as Uncle Jimmy's not here to see inside my head."

I expect him to find me hilarious, but he doesn't even

grin. I push my plate away. Suddenly this conversation has sharp edges. I feel as if I must proceed carefully.

"What is it?"

He rubs his hand over the five o'clock shadow that darkens his jawline. "There was a being aboard that ship. At least one. Maybe more."

"Oh, my goodness. Have you seen it?"

"I've seen photos. The body itself is in a vacuum-sealed container, stored at the Pentagon, or … they may have moved it. But that's not what's new. What's new is what they've discovered about its DNA—" He scratches his head and plants his elbow on the table, then props his chin on his fist. "And this is the really crazy thing: the DNA matches closely with a number of my family members'. Like …" He gazes at me with droopy eyes, heavy with what might be guilt—or maybe shame? "… very closely."

My mouth opens and the word *uh* drops out.

"I know," he says.

"Why would that be?" I'm experiencing a mental jolt comparable to what it would feel like if the Earth collided with the moon.

"I don't know. I told you our lineage goes way back. Uncle Jimmy claims it can be traced to ancient times. But I always thought that was wishful thinking on his part."

I'm nervous because I can't read Andrew's body language. He smiles like this is wonderful news, but then his eyes fill with deep concern, resting on me then the window then the table then his own hands.

"Why would the UFO be related to your ancestors, even if the family did begin that far back in history?"

He shakes his head, looking like he wants to provide an answer but can't come up with anything. "Some scientists believe that alien creatures are responsible for the origin of mankind. And this tie to human DNA would help prove that

theory. If nothing else, it's evidence that humans and whatever beings may live in outer space are a lot more similar
than they are different."

I stare at him. "Does the DNA match other families, too,
or just yours—I mean, *ours?*"

"I'm sure it's not only ours, but I don't know." He pushes
away his plate of salad and leans back in the chair, then
bounces forward again. "I know it sounds crazy."

"Which relatives?" Before he can get a word out, I gasp
and say, "*Uncle Jimmy.* This could explain every—"

"No, actually." Andrew says, remaining perfectly still. "Or
I shouldn't say no, because I don't know. His name didn't
show up anywhere in the report."

"Whose did?"

"My cousin David."

"David? He's so young. Who else?"

"I don't know. Several are listed, but many of them aren't
referred to by name."

"How are they—"

"Letters and numbers. X99, L14, Q09. Code names, I
guess."

"That's strange."

"Yes, it is. Very."

"So how do you know those code names refer to people
in your family?"

He looks away for a second, rubbing his forehead as if all
of this has caused a stabbing pain. Then he returns my stare
with one of his own. "The file I read was called 'Jovian Line.'"

The moment slams into my stunned face. "The entire
report is about the Jovian family?"

He rakes his hand through his hair. "I wasn't supposed to
get it. It was meant for the guy who got a promotion so that I
could have his job. Trey Clemens. He moved to Kirksberg,
and I moved into his job, and this file reached its destination

—meaning Trey's desk—a day late. It was in a regular manila envelope, the kind that all reports arrive in, with nothing but the company seal printed on it. No name or address. So I opened it, and I saw the letter addressed to him … but it was my job now, so I glanced over the file, trying to figure out what it was, and then I saw the file's name and, well, I couldn't *not* read it."

"Of course, you couldn't help but see. You did nothing wrong," I say, though something tells me this is reason for worry. "What will they do?"

"Who?"

"The people at work. If you weren't supposed to see it."

"Oh, I'm sure it's fine," he says, shrugging and waving it off now that I have the pallor of nervousness on my face. "Don't worry. I'm just pissed because I feel like they've purposely kept this from me. All of them. The company. My father. … And I don't understand why. I mean, this is big. It might be *enormous*. They should have told me about it."

"Maybe they just found out, too. Maybe you actually were supposed to get the file, but yours went to Trey in Kirksberg. Where's the file now?"

"I sent it on to Clemens in the Kirksberg office."

"Good." Our eyes meet again, and I try to appear unconcerned, though I can't help that I am. This is not a family secret of the ordinary kind. "He won't know you're the one who sent it?"

"I put it in a new envelope and told Jake, my assistant, to send it out like I would any other file or information. Clemens'll have it in the morning."

"So, then it should be okay, right?"

His face has the pale-gray sheen of illness. "I'm sure it will be. But I'm wondering what to say next weekend when I see my father—and everyone else."

Thanksgiving weekend. Four days of mingling with the Jovians.

"Ask him when the two of you are alone. I'm sure it will be all right."

"Yeah," he says as if trying to convince himself. "I'll just ask him."

Two weeks later, while sitting at my desk in my very serious home office, I open my calendar and it occurs to me that I never got my little red friend. We are in the first week in December, which means it has been about six weeks since my last period. Can that be right? It was due right before we moved. I didn't think much of it when it didn't come. I thought maybe it would be super-light this month. Or maybe it would be a couple of days late. Either way I fully expected it to make an appearance—and then we became so busy with the move that I forgot about it.

So I went from one package of birth control pills to the next with no trace of a period. I have googled this dilemma and found that if I prove to be pregnant, the extra hormones will not harm the fetus. Which is a relief because as I said before, I'm religious about taking every single dose.

Except I might have missed one back in October, a little chickadee in my brain reminds me. The night Andrew and I went to bed with the bottle of wine, and the pill was missing in the morning. Maybe I dropped it down the sink? I wasn't so drunk that I wouldn't have remembered doing such a thing.

Or maybe I was. I drank most of the bottle myself. So it's either that I lost the pill or someone stole it. Like Caroline. Ha ha. ... *Would she stoop that low?* Probably. But I can't remember her using my bathroom, so she wouldn't have had access to my pills. Only Uncle Jimmy was dumb enough to use our bathroom instead of the powder room—and he did it last month. He wants me to be pregnant, too ... but using my bathroom so he could dispose of one of my pills would take his weirdness to absurd heights.

And yet, I can't convince myself that it's out of the question.

There's only a 9 percent chance when a pill is missed, I remind myself. My cautious side tells me I could be pregnant. And wouldn't that be typical? The second I get away from Uncle Jimmy and Caroline and move into a new, beautiful home— and line up a job—we have to move back to Kirksberg because I'm pregnant? Seems unlikely. Later today, I'll go to the pharmacy and buy a home pregnancy test to rule it out. I'm sure I'm worried for no reason.

Stress can make a period late.

Helena's was late all the time for no apparent reason.

After lunch, I head outside. I'm raking the fall leaves the way my parents' landscapers used to, when I see Miranda's red sedan coming up the road. I wave her down. Her radio plays some kind of country music through the open window. Sounds very much like a teenager driving up.

It's nice to see a friendly face. "Hey, Sveta. How's it going, chicklet? Don't you love this crisp autumn air? Hard to believe it's already December."

"I know. It's beautiful. And I'm well, thank you. I'm wondering if I can ask you for those phone numbers for the plumber and the, uh, doctors you mentioned. I'm due for a checkup and don't want to put it off for too long."

"Of course I can. I'm so glad I caught you out here. I wanted to see if you and Andrew can come over tonight for a little barbecue. I'm coming from Food King and already have all the stuff, and it's about time I meet young Mr. Jovian, don't you think?"

I'm searching for an excuse not to have dinner, but it's Friday and we have nothing planned. "Oh, you don't have to—"

"I know I don't *have* to, but I really want to. Please don't make me eat alone with Leo again. All he talks about is planets this and comets that. Stars this and black holes that. Half the time I have no idea what language he's speaking."

"Sounds like my husband," I say with a laugh. "Does he happen to work at Starbright International?"

"More than half the village of Ashbury Falls works there, so yes," she says, as if this were one of those mundane facts of life.

"That's where Andrew works as well."

"Well, that settles it. You're coming over."

Maybe it would be good for us to go out. I smile and say, "What time would you like us?"

"How about six-thirty, seven o'clock?"

"That sounds good. Thank you, Miranda."

"And don't bring anything," she shouts as she pulls back onto the road. "Not one thing."

———

Miranda's food could not be more comfortable. Is that what they call it? Comfortable food? Full of fat and grease and salty flavors—but in a good way. A delicious way. Barbecued chicken and skinny riblets. Homemade macaroni salad.

Dumplings she calls hush puppies, no idea why because they don't look at all like dogs. Also some kind of creamy crab dip and crispy cheese things. Fritters? Is that even a word? Anyway, it's nothing I've eaten before, so it's a relief that it all tastes so good. I'm afraid Andrew has made a pig of himself.

We'll have something called mud pie after we have time to digest. The name is unappetizing, but Miranda's description of this chocolate delicacy makes my mouth water. As soon as I walked into their house, Miranda handed me the doctors' numbers and plumber and landscapers, and many others that I didn't ask for, as promised. I'm happy to have this list because the pregnancy test I bought at the pharmacy appeared to be positive. Maybe. It also may have been negative. And by that, I mean there was no black line to indicate pregnancy after four minutes, but there was a black line after five and a half minutes. And then two minutes later I checked again, and the line was gone. So, does it count? I have no idea. I'll go to the doctor and have a real test done.

In the meantime, I'm determined not to drink too much, but Miranda keeps trying to fill my glass. She's too good a hostess.

Like my husband, Leo is preoccupied with the night sky, so we have taken seats on the stone patio out back. Miranda and I recline on lounge chairs while Leo and Andrew set up a telescope. It's the same one we have at home, which isn't surprising considering they both work for the company that makes them.

I'm trying to listen to their conversation, but Miranda keeps asking things like what Russia is like, and did we leave family in Kirksberg, and what kind of job am I looking for?

"I found a job in town," I say. "I start spring semester at the Montessori school. Assistant teacher of the four-year-old class. I'm super excited."

"Well, that is wonderful. Congratulations. Do you need more wine? Should we make a toast?"

"No, no, please. I'm a very light drinker. What about you? Do you work?"

"I volunteer at the public library once a week. And my sister owns a boutique on Main Street, so you can find me helping the ladies in town pick out sexy outfits for their special occasions."

"That sounds fun," I say.

"If you ever need anything, I can get you a real good discount."

She must not know Andrew's family owns Starbright International and that he is the sole heir to more dollars than there are stars in our galaxy.

"That is very kind," I say.

My attention reaches across the patio to my husband's conversation when he says, "Yeah, I heard there was a DNA test. Do you know the details?"

Over Thanksgiving Day weekend, Andrew had asked Edmund about the file he'd come across, and Edmund denied knowing anything about it. When Andrew told him what he had seen, Edmund shook his head and said he'd look into it. Then his phone rang and he took the call.

Leo puts his hands under his thighs and sits up straighter as he looks thoughtfully upward. His gray hair and pale skin make him seem a lot older than Miranda—and maybe he is.

"I did hear a rumor a couple of weeks ago, but I don't know how accurate it was."

"My assistant told me about that rumor," Andrew says, "which just goes to show that the assistants are always the first to know." He laughs, as if this is the most casual conversation in the world.

Leo steps up to the telescope, leans in toward the eyepiece and makes adjustments with one hand.

Andrew continues, "Something about a new technique to extract the blood and infuse it with the chemicals in the panel."

"Well, I for one am so glad to have you two in the neighborhood," Miranda cuts in. She's not one for silence from what I've seen, and she's already told me that she's tired of Leo's sky talk. "We need some new, young bodies up here. Not that the other neighbors aren't great, but most of them spend the entire winter indoors. I can't do that."

"Do they?" I say as Andrew says something about a file. I wish I could get his attention because I don't think he should talk about this with a new acquaintance.

"Well, yeah, I mean, some of these folks are in their seventies and older, so I get it," Miranda continues, "but it's nice to get out once in a while. Leo and I like to ice skate and cross-country ski. Or, if nothing else, sit out here and have a barbecue. I mean, have you ever seen so many stars? On a clear night like this one, the Milky Way spills right over our heads and through those mountains in the distance."

"That's why we moved here," Leo says, joining our conversation. "And, of course, because Starbright built their new facility. The minute we came up here, I fell in love with Ashbury's night sky. I knew we'd made the right choice."

"Andrew is always looking through his telescope as well," I say.

"I'd be surprised if he wasn't," Leo says. "Hey, are you two into hiking? There's a great trail up the road that leads to one of the larger waterfalls. We'll have to show you."

"You know what else they'd like, hon?" Miranda says. "The chateau. Have y'all been to L'Origine?"

"We took a tour during our honeymoon," I say, perking up with enthusiasm. "The tulips were in bloom. It was beautiful."

"So romantic," she says.

I can tell Miranda is a flowery, romance-novel type of woman.

"All that color in those neat rows," she says. "We'll have to head over there together. They have wine tastings all the time. That would be fun for the four of us. But we might have to get a driver. Can't be going up Steep Hill after a wine tasting. Especially me. I'm not good behind the wheel even when I'm sober."

"That's right," Leo says. "Don't want to endanger the lives of our neighbors more than you already do."

She presses her lips into a smirk. "Leo's always making fun of how I drive. It's not that I go too fast. If anything, I drive too slow."

I pass her an empathetic smile and take the tiniest sip of wine. "I'd go back to L'Origine anytime."

"You know it's right over there." She points to a place beyond the lake. "Right there, lined up beneath the moon. If there weren't so many pine trees, we'd probably be able to see one of the towers from here."

"Wouldn't that be amazing?"

"It would."

I gaze over the lake, wondering what the castle gardens look like this time of year.

"Hon?" Leo says, shaking me out of my thoughts.

"Yes, Leo?" Miranda turns toward him.

"Serious question now," he says, once again hovering over the telescope.

Miranda winks in my direction. "Yeah, go ahead. Lay it on me."

"When are you gonna bring out that mud pie?"

"I know his stomach like a book, I swear," she whispers. And then she uses both arms to push herself up and out of the chair. "I'm on it."

Leo takes a step back from the telescope. "Check this out, Andrew."

My husband steps up and looks through the eyepiece. "Wow, isn't that—holy crap, it's moving so fast. How did you ever—you're a real talent."

"Been doing this a long time," Leo says, puffing up with pride. "It's a dark red color, though that's hard to see with this scope. I homed in on it yesterday with the Mission X1,000 at work."

"How long have you been with the company?"

Leo stares into space. "'Bout thirty years. Started in Denver, Colorado, my hometown. Sometimes I tell people I was born in a Starbright office."

"What are you looking at?" I say.

Leo brings a pair of binoculars up to his eyes. "It's called 'Oumuamua.'"

At first I think he's joking, but he doesn't so much as grin. "And what is that?"

"Basically, a cigar-shaped space rock from another galaxy," Andrew says.

"A space rock," I say under my breath. "Of course."

———

On the walk home, I ask Andrew if he ever sees Leo at work.

"He's in a different department, on a different floor, so no, I usually don't. But he says he heard about the DNA test."

"Yes, I know. I was spying on your conversation. Have you forgotten that I come from a long line of Russian spies?"

I love to make him laugh.

"He also heard that the results were inconclusive," he says.

"But they weren't, were they?"

"Far from it."

"You didn't tell him—"

"I acted as if I knew no more than he did."

"Good. I think it's best to tell no one."

"I'll wait and see if Uncle Jimmy knows anything. I had asked him about it when we were home, but my mother called me away and he never gave me an answer. If he won't tell me anything, I guess I'll hope for the right moment to bring it up to Dad again. I can't imagine why he wouldn't know about it."

"Maybe it's not real. Maybe it was a joke."

"Yeah, I don't know. It looked real."

We have reached the sidewalk in front of our home. I haven't yet told him about the pregnancy test because as soon as he came home we had to run right out so we wouldn't be late for Miranda and Leo. I want it to be a special moment for us, and it has been a hard thing to keep inside. But now that we're alone, I take a deep breath, surprised that nervous jitters have twisted my tongue considering how many hours I forced the words back. "Andrew."

He looks at me.

"I might be pregnant."

He stops short, and the hand that holds my hand pulls my arm taut as I naturally step forward. My body reels back like a yo-yo spinning on a string, and he gathers me in, all smiley and excited. I love how he looks at me like I'm the greatest thing that ever happened to him. He wraps his arms around me, then bumps his forehead into my own. "Are you kidding?"

"I would never kid about this."

We stand there, grinning at each other, our noses rubbing. We shift foot to foot, two hearts as one.

"But you're on the pill."

I feel as if someone is watching us from above; the moon's big, bright face is everywhere.

"It's a small chance, but—"

"You don't think you're just late?"

"I really don't."

My intuition has been telling me that I may actually be pregnant.

"Well, that figures, doesn't it? The second we move away, *boom*, there it is."

"I was probably pregnant before we left." I step back but continue to hold his hands in front of me. "I hope you're not angry. I'm not ready to move back to Kirksberg, even if I am pregnant, which I may not be. I don't have morning sickness or anything."

"*Angry?* I could never be angry about this. And believe me, I'm not ready to move back, either." The darkness under his eyes looks strange in the violet rays of moonlight. Like he's sick, but I know he's just tired. Tired from the move, tired from his job.

"There's no way we're packing everything up and moving back," he says. "We've already moved twice in two years. I can't even think about doing it again right now."

In spite of what he said, the serious rumple of his brow makes me wonder if he actually *is* considering it, and it worries me. But then he says, "We don't have to tell my parents right away. It takes nine months to make a baby, right?"

"*If* I'm pregnant, you mean. I said I *might* be. I'm not for sure. Plus, I just got a job, one that I want, and it won't start until the teacher goes on maternity leave in the spring."

He's grinning like he's happy and proud no matter what the circumstances. His roundy face and big eyes are so cute; no wonder his mother still hovers over him even though he's twenty-nine years old.

I giggle. I don't know why. I feel girlish and excited. Nervous in a head-over-heels way, and closer to Andrew than ever, imagining our entwined souls floating around the ether. And yet it is not without worry.

"But your mother and Uncle Jimmy, I dread—"

"We'll figure it out. We won't tell them until we have to. And if they demand that we move back, we'll just ..." He pauses, thinking. "Oh, I don't know. Hide away in the L'Origine Chateau until they promise to leave us alone."

"I like the sound of that. Just the two of us in a castle sounds fun."

"Yeah, I know you wouldn't mind."

"Don't say it like that. *You're* not the one they were stalking."

"Believe me, I'm not denying they can be stifling."

I hug him again, pulling our bodies together, breathing his clean scent. We kiss in the moonlight. I hope the neighbors aren't watching.

I know the moon is.

———

Before going to bed I boot up the computer and find an email from Helena. What a wonderful day this is.

> Where have you been? I have written several times, and you do not reply. I will keep trying because I know you. My Sveta would not purposely torture me like this. Every week I try again. I have much to tell you. Write back to me please!

How is that possible? Russia's email must be more unreliable than I thought. I write to her several times a week. I look for her emails every day. I open my spam folder and check that, too. Nothing. No notes from Helena.

I wish she would just get a phone, but since she does not, I will continue to email. I know her money is tight.

I open a new message box.

My dearest sister, how are you? I hope you and your farmer are well. Kidding aside, I have not received your emails, though I wish they would come through because I want to hear all of your news. I have written to you many times as well. We have moved to Ashbury Falls, North Carolina, and I will start a new job soon. I hope you get this message. Please keep trying. I miss you.

Much love, Sveta

It's as good a time as ever to try calling my parents again.

I dial the number for Dana. Once again, I leave a message. Then John. I tell them all is well, that Andrew and I are fine. Then I say that I might have news. "Please call me. I love you both." I hope I reach them before I have my first child. And that's a bizarre thought that makes me want to laugh and cry at the same time. *Of course I'll hear from them before then.*

I take the list of phone numbers Miranda wrote for me from my purse and place it next to the computer. Tomorrow I will call the doctor.

The flimsy white paper gown has never been a favorite. Obviously. Who wants to get undressed and sit on a paper mat? I want even less to lie back and lift my feet into the angled metal stirrups and scoot my behind down toward the table's end. The pee-in-a-cup pregnancy test I took at the nurse's request proved as inconclusive as the one I took at home. Frustrating. So I have undressed and will have the full examination. Dr. Falugia seemed nice enough based on the three seconds I saw him speaking with a patient as I made my way to the nurse's station. My doctor in Kirksberg was a woman. Not that I care. Woman, man; the trip to the GYN is not at all a sexual experience. Most of the time I only want to have the annual Pap smear and get on with my day. But this is different. There may be a baby inside of me, and if there is I will be both joyous and afraid. Joyous for me and Andrew, and afraid of having to move back to Uncle Jimmy and Caroline.

A tap on the door precedes the doctor and his thick black hair, graying at the temples. He enters with his nurse assistant just one step behind, a tired-looking, middle-aged woman, short like a child. She reminds me of an elf.

"Hello," the doctor says as he snaps on the gloves. "Very nice to meet you, Svetlana. I hear you're from Russia."

"Yes. But I've been an American citizen for nine years now."

"Lovely," he says. "And what brought your parents to the U.S., if you don't mind my asking?"

"I was adopted. I was sixteen when I came here."

"Oh, okay. Lie back for me?"

I do.

"My adoptive parents are world citizens whose home base is in Pennsylvania," I add.

"Okay, scoot on down now."

I make the awkward journey, flat on my back and treading to the end of the table.

He then does the internal exam, rummaging around for a moment. "Hmm," he says. "Oh, yes, there it is. Oh sure. That's pretty positive to me."

What that means, I have no idea.

He steps back and switches on a light. "I'm going to get a quick Pap." He inserts the whatever-it-is and pokes with what feels like a stick. And like that, the whatever-it-is tool is removed and Dr. Falugia pulls off his gloves.

I prop the upper half of my body by the elbows. "You said 'That's positive'?"

"The walls of the womb appear to be thickening. In other words, preparing a soft bed for its new arrival. Will this be your first?"

My heart thunders in my ears. I gasp, then squeeze my eyes closed while a surge of emotion rises like a tree sprouted and climbing the rungs of my chest. I've got happy, chatty batches of leaves tickling the inside of my head. I can't form a spoken word, but I'm thinking, *Dobrota, dobrata,* which means *goodness* in Russian. I am pregnant! I open my eyes wide and say, "Wow."

A smile appears on the doctor's face. "I'll take that as a yes."

There's a tap at the door, and a second nurse appears behind it.

Dr. Falugia's commanding voice rolls over whatever she may have come to say: "She's about eight to ten weeks. Better do an ultrasound to nail it down."

"I think it's more like six," I say.

"We'll find out for sure." He winks at me, then addresses the nurse who has yet to fully enter the room. "Ultrasound, please, Jessica."

"Oh, okay," she says, "I wasn't sure you were speaking to—"

He tilts his head in a disappointed manner. "I am. Thank you."

She rushes back out.

"Okay, Mrs. Jovian, remember that you're doing everything for two now. Amy will give you a prescription for prenatal vitamins and a schedule of forthcoming visits. It was a pleasure meeting you. Call if you have any concerns or questions."

"Thank you," I say, overwhelmed by my own happy thoughts.

He excuses himself and leaves.

My eyes meet the little nurse's eyes, and I feel electricity pull at my hair. This strange occurrence has not happened since I left Kirksberg. But as soon as I feel it, she turns away and the buzz fades. I don't think much of it because I'm pregnant, and the cause may only be my excitement.

I'm going to have an ultrasound!

Amy the nurse says, "I'll be right back," and slips out the door.

The reality of my pregnancy falls upon me like a big, bouncing baby. I'm going to be a mother. Andrew will be so happy! We'll be parents. I can't wait to tell him it's definite. Why am I grabbing my forehead? Why is my breath coming in and out in rapid, shallow gasps? What's so different at this moment from the hour before, when I only knew a child was possible? I guess I never believed it would happen.

Wait till I tell Helena. My heart aches to call her. But all I can do is attempt another email. Something must be wrong with my computer. Or hers. And I need to tell my parents, too.

The nurse named Jessica returns with the ultrasound machine on wheels. "First off," she says, "do you want to know the sex? I always have to ask."

"We're going to wait," I say, because Andrew needs to be here for that.

She makes the wire connections and switches on the screen before doing all of the things I've seen the technicians on television do: spreading the cold gel across my abdomen, gliding the handheld scanner over the gel, and turning up the volume when she detects the squeaky-sounding heartbeat that makes me laugh and also cry. Soon enough the scan emerges from the machine, and she passes it to me. It resembles the night sky, with a Milky Way background and a glowing orb at its center.

"The baby is the size of a strawberry, probably ten weeks old," Jessica says, as she wipes down the handheld scanner, "but the doctor will confirm."

I can't take my eyes away from the picture. "It's beautiful."

Jessica stops what she's doing to have a closer look. "Wow, that's a lot more detail than we usually see, though I don't know why that would be."

"Is it?" I say.

She must be worried that she shouldn't have said what

she said, because she shrugs and casually adds, "It's different for everyone. Maybe we ordered some higher-quality thermal paper. I'll ask Dr. Falugia."

While she dismantles the machine, I say, "Do you think I can use your computer to send a quick email?" I know this probably sounds strange, so I add, "My computer at home isn't working, and I want to tell my sister in Russia the good news. She doesn't have a phone at the moment. She dropped it and broke the screen last week."

"Oh, that's the worst," she says with a frown. "Sure you can. Get dressed and meet me in the hall."

———

I hurry into the house as if Andrew might be there, though I know it's too early in the day and he's still at work. I cannot help rushing around. Should I call him? I pull the sonogram from my purse and say, "Hello, my little strawberry baby."

On the way back from the doctor, I pulled into Greenie's garden shop, near the Montessori School I will soon work at, and I purchased the wrought-iron bench I had wanted to buy the last time we were there, when we picked up a rake and some other yard tools. It's the perfect gift for Andrew, considering our first night together, when we ate our steaks of cheese under the stars during the Kirksberg UFO Festival. The armrests are decorated with moons and other heavenly bodies carved into wood pieces, and the planks of the seating and backrest shine in a deep midnight-blue stain. I love it, and I know Andrew will, too.

Mr. Greene will deliver it in a few minutes. One of his workers was loading it into the van when I drove away. I told him I want it to go on the grassy part of the yard, beside the weeping willow tree, overlooking the lake. I also said I would leave it to him to find the just-right angle to the moon, and I laughed at how Jovian that must have sounded. He smiled and said he knew what I meant. I was tempted to tell him that I'm so happy right now I could die, but this was my first time meeting him, and I knew he would think me odd.

———

Andrew pulls into the drive at 4:30 p.m. The bench is in place, the sonogram in my pocket. The muffins have been made (apple, of course; I had to do something to kill three hours). I have left "I'm pregnant" voice messages on both my mother's and my father's phones, but who knows when they'll get them.

Andrew walks in, his new briefcase in hand, looking handsome and healthy … except for the dark circles under-scoring his eyes. He has been stressed since he read that stupid Jovian file. But not tonight. Tonight, he'll be on the moon with happiness.

I run over to him and give him my usual you-are-home greeting and kiss. "I couldn't wait for you to get here," I say, grabbing one of his hands. "Come with me."

"What's that I smell?" he says. "Muffins?"

"Yes, I made them for you. But they will come later, and what I have to show you will only take a second." I pull him through the kitchen, and he grabs a muffin from the top of the stack and shoves it into his mouth. We're still moving because I cannot wait another second. I slide open the door to the backyard and place my hand over his eyes—sort of— he's moving, and his legs are longer than mine so it's diffi-cult. He continues to chew, dropping crumbs as he strides out the door, already finishing the muffin, probably wishing he grabbed two. Now he's laughing with his mouth full and saying things like, "Are you feeling all right? Did you hit your head? Have you been drinking? Are we going swimming in the lake?"

"Very humorous," I say. "Please follow quickly and try not to choke."

I guide him down the wood steps that lead to the grassy beach. The weeping arms of the willow hover over us like a thatched roof. The autumn sun is already starting to give way to dusky blue-gray with a few hints of pink, like the cheeks of babies. I won't yet remove my hand from his face.

"Remember that bench that you knew in Kirksberg? The first night we spent in the park eating chiz steaks? I have bought you your very own."

Finally, I remove my hand so he can see.

"Cheesesteaks?" His eyes widen as if expecting to find a pile of sandwiches on a platter for dinner alfresco, but then he catches sight of the bench. "Oh, wow, our own bench. That's so cool."

I continue toward it, pulling him along with me. "Look at its arms. There's a moon and stars."

His easy laughter tells me he's as excited about it as I am.

"It's beautiful. Thank you, honey."

He sits, and I sit beside him.

I take his hand. "Like our first night, when I fell in love with you."

"And I with you," he says, gazing over the lake and then up to the sky, that infinite expanse that forever pulls him away from me. I'm lucky when I have his attention.

"It's not my birthday, so ..." He raises his brows in anticipation. "What's up?"

"You're right. It's not a birthday gift. It's a something-else gift," I say in an excited tone.

"Well, I know you went to the doctor today, so do you have something to tell—"

"Yes, Andrew! It's a *baby* gift, you are right." I pull out the sonogram and hand it to him, so happy I might pop like a balloon.

"You are? *We* are? Oh my God, we are." He takes a second to study the picture before grabbing me in a hug. "I thought about you all day. I didn't want to get my hopes up. But, wow. Is that him ... or her?" He sits back and holds the picture in two cupped hands as if it were the baby itself.

"I don't know what it is, but it's about ten weeks—or that's what they tell me. I think it's more like a month or six weeks, but they are the supposed experts."

"Wow. Oh, wow." His face is so bright with happiness that I swear light is beaming from his pores. He kisses me and gives me a devout I-love-you embrace, pulling me in. The hug I give him does not reflect how strongly I feel, how desperate I am to hold him.

We pull apart. He looks at the picture again, then looks at me. No words come out of his mouth. He reaches for me and draws me in, and we stay like that, on the bench, holding each other as the sun becomes absorbed by the horizon and the night sky rises up from the ground with spectacular swirls of windblown purple and red, an abstract of the sort I've never seen before.

After that, we go back into the house, all lovey-dovey and ready for the bedroom. As soon as we enter, however, we stop short and suck in our breath because someone is knocking at the front door.

We huddle together and lean into the cabinetry wall, poking our heads around just enough to get a glimpse. "Miranda?" we whisper simultaneously. I only think so because I saw a bit of red and figured it was her car in the drive.

"Did you park in the garage?"

Neither one of us ever does.

"No," he says.

"She'll see that we're both here. What should we do?"

He peers around again. "She has a basket of something. Probably muffins. If you hadn't made a batch today, I'd let her in."

I jab his arm and struggle to keep my laughter in check. "If you'd rather talk to Miranda than go into the bedroom with me ..."

"She's leaving," he says.

"I hope she's not angry."

"She didn't look angry. Maybe she'll leave the basket by the door."

The thump of a car door precedes the motor trailing away.

"Come on." He leads me out of the kitchen, tiptoeing through the living room and past the foyer, though Miranda is no longer there for us to evade. Energized by our sneakiness, we run together like two fugitives into the bedroom. He releases my hand and jumps full-body onto the bed. I dive on top of him because we are still young enough to act like children.

He rolls me onto my back and lifts my shirt a little so he can view my abdomen. "So, this is where it all happens, huh?"

"Yes, my darling genius, I believe so. You have planted the seed, as they say."

He grins. "Looks like a good home for a baby. A little small, but ... I wouldn't mind living in there for nine months."

"Don't remind me."

"I'm sure the time will fly by."

"Yes, like a rocket. But it's more like ten."

"Ten?"

"Ten months, not nine."

As he rubs my middle, his expression softens, his smile fades. "You know, I think I might be jealous of the little guy."

Later, while we're eating a dinner of microwaved macaroni and cheese (I was so busy baking the muffins, I prepared nothing for dinner), Leo's at the door in his Dockers and green polo shirt. Southern-man casual attire.

Andrew answers, and I turn to face the backyard because I cannot help but scowl. *What is it with these two today? They're acting like Jovians.*

"I'm so sorry to bother you," he tells Andrew, "but my Wi-Fi's out, and I need to reach my brother in the Amazon. It's a true emergency, or I wouldn't bother you at dinnertime."

"Come in, come in," Andrew says, backing up and closing the door behind him. "You have a brother in the Amazon?"

"He's a scientist studying the healing properties of a rare flower, among other things."

"Wow. Interesting line of work."

Leo turns and waves at me. "Hey, Svetlana. Sorry to interrupt."

I wave back. "Hello, Leo," all nice and American neighborlike.

"Problem is," Leo continues, "my dad's not well and there's no way to reach Bobby except via Skype—I've tried calling, and 90 percent of the time calls to the jungle don't make it through, so I was wondering if you would mind if I—"

"Of course, of course," Andrew says. "Follow me."

"I would have sent it from work today or tomorrow morning, but I just got the call from my stepmother and unfortunately it's bad news that can't wait."

"I'm sorry to hear that." Their conversation fades as they head down the hall toward my office.

I spear a few macaronis and take my time chewing. I

don't want to finish my dinner before the father of my unborn child returns to his meal.

Something tells me this is not about Leo's brother or his dad. I'm not the kind who relies on her intuition the way people like my husband do, as if it were an email straight from the powers of the universe, but seeing Leo at the door after Miranda came over a couple of hours earlier with another basket of goodies, I cannot help thinking something is up the same way Uncle Jimmy used to pop over with his strange requests. But Miranda and Leo are not Uncle Jimmy, and they have not bothered us at all until now. So this is only a small reservation that I have.

Besides, I'm having a very nice day and don't want to waste time worrying over dumb things. If Leo wants to snoop in my computer—or toy with it—he can. It's never worked properly anyway.

Still, why would he do that?

I'm afraid my in-laws have made me paranoid.

Andrew returns. "He's using the computer for a minute."

"Okay," I say, and I put on a crooked smile and crossed eyes, hoping Andrew will laugh—which he does.

A minute later Leo comes rushing down the hall. "All done. Thanks so much. Sorry to intrude."

"I'm sorry about your father," I say.

"Thank you. You two have a wonderful night." He reaches the front door and he's gone.

We finish our dinner. Andrew takes the plates to the sink, then comes back and sits down while I finish a glass of water.

"So," he says, "speaking of fathers, I spoke with mine today."

"Oh? And what did Edmund have to say?"

"It's what he didn't say that's interesting. He asked how you were and if everything was okay with the house and work—you know, all the normal stuff—but he failed to mention the file. So I waited until he was ready to hang up, and at the last second I said, 'Hey, did you get a chance to ask around about that file I told you about?'"

Andrew frowns, then lifts the jar of honey in the center of the table and picks at its label.

"And?"

"He didn't waste any time telling me it was inconclusive."

"But it wasn't."

"No, it wasn't," he says, adding a shoulder shrug to his drooping posture.

"What about the name on the file? Did you ask him why it was named after your family?"

"I did."

"And?"

"He said it doesn't matter what it was called because the lab work was inconclusive." Andrew pauses to rub his eye. "And insignificant, and apparently that's all he wants to say about it."

"Oh."

"Yeah. So that's the end of that."

"I wonder why—"

"Who knows?" Andrew says with an angry edge. "I guess he doesn't trust me."

"How can he not trust you? You're his family. *You're* the most trustworthy man on the planet."

"I know," he says with a fleeting grin.

"Well, maybe we've made more of this file than we should."

He breathes like a depressed person: low in his chair and loud through the nose. "I guess so."

"Please don't be unhappy tonight. We have a baby to think about. And names to discuss. Who cares about all of this lineage stuff? It's the past. The baby is the future. *Our* future."

At that, his face lights up. "I do have a few favorite names."

"So do I," I say, happy that he's letting the other stuff go. "Shall we discuss them?"

"If you don't think it's too soon."

"Not at all," I say. "You go first."

This pregnancy thing is unpredictable. For weeks I remained my usual shape, going about my business, eating everything I wanted and still waking up slender. It was wonderful, to say the least. Ice cream. Christmas cookies. Popcorn. Pizza. Apple pie. (So much apple pie.) Andrew and I both gorged ourselves during our five-day holiday with the family in Kirksberg (a surprisingly low-key Christmas with few decorations and even fewer gifts). Then January came and went, and my body remained the same. Through most of February I began to doubt Dr. Falugia's expertise, but then this morning, finally, with February at its end, I woke in the shape of a pregnant guppy. My stomach itself has become an apple pie—and by that I mean if I took a full-size pie and belted it to my middle, this is what I would look like.

Oh, and my boobs have ballooned. Yes, I've become the symbol of motherhood. Extra-soft and womanly. All of my jeans are too tight to zip, and my butt looks huge when I check it out in the mirror—believe me, I will not be doing that again soon. It frightened me, to tell you the truth. I have never looked more adult, more like a mommy. If I wasn't so stubborn, I would have switched to sweatpants, but I can't do it. I'm not a sweat suit type of person. Maybe I'll change my mind soon, though. According to Dr. Falugia, I am about twenty-one weeks pregnant. Nineteen more to go.

I will give birth to a summer baby, late June or early July. (I'm still not convinced Dr. Falugia has correctly pinpointed the day of conception, but who am I to argue?) If the baby arrives in August, I will know I was right.

During our Christmas visit to Andrew's parents' house, we were careful not to tell Andrew's mother and the rest of them that a baby is on the way. But like I said, I hadn't yet blossomed at that time, so all we had to do was keep our mouths shut, and with a little bit of pretend drinking on my part, no one suspected a thing. Which reminds me: Uncle Jimmy said I would have a baby by the time I was twenty-five, and it looks like he will be right. My birthday is June 8.

It's been hard to sleep. Not to *fall* asleep. I can do that anytime—because I am building a human being inside of my body, and that in itself is exhausting. So, I fall asleep easily, but then I wake up four hours later. No matter what time I lie down, I wake up four hours later. It's a pain in my big pregnant butt.

Tonight, I fell asleep at 8 p.m., and now it is midnight and I'm wide awake, hungry, and suffering dry mouth. I turn in the bed and notice that my husband is missing. Perhaps he's in the kitchen eating another meal. I get up. Put the robe on. Slippers scuff through the dark hall into the living room where moonlight spills like water over the furnishings. He's not on the couch. Where is he? I pass the eating area and stand at the sliding glass door. He's not at the telescope. I open the door. Could he be on the bench?

As I cross the deck, the night air finds its way through my clothes, and I unwrap my robe and cinch it tighter. He has to be here. He's not the kind who goes out and has a beer with the boys when he can't sleep. Does anyone do that? Outside of movies and television shows, I mean. I reach the end of the deck and breathe relief. He's on the bench. Legs outstretched, arms crossed over his chest, head tipped back. Asleep or stargazing? With him, it could be either.

I come around the side of the bench and stand in front of him.

The moon has made him vibrant. His skin appears white violet, almost silver. He's smooth, like a sculpture of himself. I've never seen a more attractive man. I adore him. And I know how lucky I am to be a wife who adores her husband.

I tap his foot with the tip of my slipper. "Andrew, hello? Earth to Andrew."

He twitches, then opens his eyes and blinks a couple of times as if he has no idea where he is. When he sees me, he says, "Oh, hey." He raises his arms and straightens into a stretch, squinting in my direction. "I dozed off?"

"Looks like you have fallen asleep on a wooden bench like an old homeless man." I look up to the sky. The moon is too bright. It's not letting the stars show off. "Were you searching for planets?"

He shakes his head. Due for a haircut, his longer length of hair makes him look younger than his twenty-nine years. "I was thinking about things."

"It's cold out here." I sit on the bench beside him. "Is something wrong?"

He looks away, scratches his forehead.

I take his hand and twist his wedding band around his finger. "Are you nervous about becoming a father? The pregnancy book I'm reading says it is perfectly normal for men to feel strange and worried before—"

He smiles and shakes his head. "I couldn't be more excited."

"I thought so." I scoot closer, take his arm and drape it across my shoulders. "So what is it? Is it NASA that's bothering you?"

"No, not NASA this time." He breathes in and scrunches his shoulders. Some kind of angst is making him tight. "I don't know what it is."

"Hm," I say, not wanting to push. I will sit here in silence if that's what he wants.

A second later, he says, "Like, are you happy?"

"Am I happy?" I say, with a laugh. "Why wouldn't I be? My body's becoming huge, and soon I'll have stretch marks like an elephant—who wouldn't be happy about that?"

He grins at the moon. "But you like where we live and the people we've met, and the fact that you'll be working soon?"

"Yes, I do. I like all of it."

"And you like that you'll be a mother soon?"

"Of course. Why are you—"

"And you're happy with me?" His words have rushed out of his mouth, and now he's holding his breath in wait of an answer, which is strange considering I've never given him a reason to ask such a question. "Are you happy you married me?"

The air catches in my throat. "Really? Are you really asking?" I take his face in my hands. "You, my darling husband, are the best part. You are *everything*. Everything starts with you."

I press my lips up to his, feeling his warm breath across my face.

I've brought a genuine smile to the surface, not only on his mouth but in his gorgeous blue-green eyes.

After that, whatever rock had been weighing him down has toppled from his shoulders, and he looks like I have given him a wonderful gift. He needed to hear it for reasons unknown. For reasons I can only assume I will never know.

He gathers me into a smothering-close hug. I return the enthusiasm.

He says, "I just love you so much. I guess it's scary."

I pull back and look into his eyes. "I know. Sometimes it's overwhelming."

He's so serious tonight, his face is like stone. To tell you the truth, he has frightened me. There's something ominous about this conversation, but of course I don't want to think bad thoughts. I tell myself it's because things are so good. I worry when things are too good.

"It comes over me sometimes," he says. "I'm so happy I can't breathe. I feel as though I'll split at the seams."

"We're very lucky. Me, you, the baby." I look down at my wide apple pie of a stomach, and he touches it. Then we hug each other so close it's like we're one. Me, him, and the little being in the belly between us. It's the first time I truly feel like there are three of us in this family.

In the morning, it's very cold. Frost on the edges of the windows flanking the front door twinkle like sugar glaze in the bitter morning light. Andrew emerges from the bedroom showered, hair brushed, dressed in his "important office man" clothing. I don't know if it's hormones or love or what, but from where I stand in the kitchen he strikes me as seriously handsome. I want to take this moment and frame it. Keep it in a shadow box hung upon the wall.

"Do you have to go to work? We were up so late. It would be nice if you could call in sick."

He levels a look in my direction that says, *Don't tempt me.*

"But I got up and showered," he says. "If I'm going to have a day off, I want to sleep in."

"You're right." I look away and then look back again, shooting him a seductive bed-headed pout. "But still."

"I guess I could." He stands in front of me, considering my offer for a flash before saying, "Nope, I've got a lunch meeting at noon. The Texas guys are flying in—I have to remind Jake to send the car."

"Even when you reject me for Texas gentlemen," I say, "I still love you."

"You know I would never reject you."

"Yes, I know. You're crazy for me."

I put my arms around him and breathe in his soapy clean scent. I, on the other hand, have not showered and plan to go back to bed for at least an hour. The baby is tired!

My breasts are like two sofa pillows butting up against his chest. I shift to get a better hold. I don't have a bra on, and I'm sure he notices. He gazes at me with second-thought eyes and kisses me for real this time. Last time was just playing.

Then there's more embracing and kissing, spinning around the kitchen in a pushy kind of waltz or other dance—I'm not too familiar with the names of old dances—and he's to the point where he would like to devour me. Only he pulls away in a sudden burst of stoicism. "Nope. Can't do this. Have to go to work. Very important." He finger combs his hair into shape and fixes the places his shirt has tried to escape the waist of his pants.

I pull at his belt buckle. "I almost caught you in my trap, didn't I?"

"I really don't want to go." He rolls his head in a quick neck stretch and fills himself with a deep breath. "I'll take a day off next week. We can go to lunch and the movies maybe."

"After a morning of late sleeping?"

"Yes," he says and gives me another kiss. "So … do I have everything?"

"Briefcase," I call out.

He finds it on the floor by the kitchen island. "Check."

"Suit jacket?"

He lifts it from the couch, drapes it over his forearm.

"Beautiful face and body," I say.

He smirks and says, "That would be you."

"Thank you so much, kind gentleman."

"I feel like I'm forgetting something," he says with rumpled eyebrows.

"Yes, you are forgetting to sleep with me. Other than that, maybe your wallet?"

He pats the back pocket of his pants. "Got it."

"Keys?"

He finds those in his front pants pocket.

"I'm afraid you are ready to go, my love."

He grins. "Off to the cosmos ..."

"I shall be here, counting the hours until your return." I pretend to swoon like a bad actress, back of hand to forehead and all.

He heads to the foyer, opens the door, turns for one last look at me, thinking what a wonder I am (he must be thinking this because I am just that ... wonderful, ha ha), and he's out the door.

I turn to the refrigerator and open it up. I decide that I'll have strawberry yogurt and maybe ...

The front door clicks open.

Andrew is back.

"I feel like I'm missing something," he says.

Like an excited child, I run after him as he strides into the bedroom. He stops just inside the doorway. Head tilted. I can almost hear the wheels in his brain spinning like a car stuck in mud.

"Wallet, briefcase, suit jacket, keys. What else could it be?" I say.

He laughs a little and drops his head. "I guess it's the meeting. Jake needs to confirm the driver."

"That must be it. You almost forgot, but now you have remembered. Don't worry. All is well."

I meant for him to laugh, but he doesn't.

"Yeah …" he says, shrugging in an unconvinced way.

"Maybe you wanted to touch the baby again." I step up to him and bump my front into his side. "Go ahead."

He does. Then he plants another kiss on my lips and says, "I'll see you later."

"Okay," I say and watch him move down the hall.

The front door clicks open and then closed.

———————

Sirens rise up from the mountainside, a spinning sound that circles my head like a raptor. It occurs to me that I have not heard a siren since leaving Kirksberg. I'm sure people in town hear them all the time, but up here on the hill, there are not many people to have emergencies. And I'm glad. I don't care for this sound.

Probably someone has crashed their car on the snaky road I hate so much. Hopefully Miranda's home fast asleep and not "endangering the lives of others," as Leo said when joking about her bad driving skills. The road may be slick from this morning's cold. Jack Frost's handiwork. Though, I don't think there was enough frost to ice the roads. I wonder what I will do when it snows and I have to get to work. I suppose school will be closed. Or delayed. I loved snow days when I was in high school, and I'll love them even more when Andrew is snowed in with me.

I lay there for a few minutes before deciding I don't want to go back to sleep. I get up. Make the bed. Andrew's side always requires more tucking in. He has the size eleven feet that rip hospital corners to shreds. I lift the mattress and shove the sheet underneath. After this I will check email. It's been a few days, and maybe Helena has—

An urgent knock on the door gives me a minor stroke. I grab my baby belly in a protective manner and freeze. It can't be Andrew again. He has a key and would never knock like that, scaring me as if the house is burning.

My breath speeds as I rush down the hall. *It better not be Uncle Jimmy.* It was an Uncle Jimmy kind of knock—and now the landline is ringing. I can see Miranda at the door, face up to the glass, looking through, unsmiling. Her nose and cheeks are red with cold. I give her the "one second" finger gesture and rush to the telephone in the kitchen, grabbing the receiver. "Hello?"

"Svetlana, are you alone?"

It's Caroline. Andrew's been fielding family calls for weeks, so I have not spoken to her in a while—I've been hiding out because I didn't want to lie about being pregnant.

"Um, not really," I say, heading back toward the front door so I can let Miranda in. "Why?"

Miranda is more than just cold. She's blinking rapidly, and her eyes are watery. I unlock the door and pull it open.

On the phone, Caroline says, "I'm sorry." Her voice sounds strange.

My hair stands up like sticks from my head.

Miranda presses her lips together and comes closer as if expecting me to fall. Her chin is jumpy, curling up—she's losing the battle to stave off a full-blown cry—and her nose is running.

I question her with my eyes.

"Caroline?" I say. "What's—"

"It's Andrew. I'm afraid he's no longer with us."

I lose my legs. All at once the floor has risen up to meet me. The phone has escaped my grip and clatters against the foyer's tile, broken into pieces. My head doesn't know which way to turn. "Andrew?"

But he was just here. He kissed me and touched the baby. … He held us and said, "I'll see you later."

Then he got into his car … and drove onto that stupid snake of a road.

The sirens rise up in my memory.

My body is a knot. A convulsing knot, too tight for normal breathing.

What happened to him?

I cannot speak. Cannot form words. Don't want to hear my own voice ask the question.

Miranda comes closer. Slowly, as if approaching an injured animal. "It's okay. You're okay. It's going to be okay." She has me in a half hug and pats my back.

Why is she here?

I'm stuck in a crouch on the floor, staring into the beige tile. The convulsions have stopped. I'm breathing again. I wish I were alone. I wish this wasn't real. I can't think.

"It's okay," she says again. "Let's get you up."

But it's not okay. The news has already reached me. It's too late for okay. *Andrew is no longer with us.* He was here, and now he's gone. It's not okay. It will never be okay.

I sit on my rear end. I can't stand. Not yet.

"What happened?" The words press through my choked throat. They don't sound like me.

Miranda blinks a few times. Drawing the courage, I suppose. This can't be easy for her.

"Uh, well, a little while ago Mr. Limehouse found Andrew's truck wedged into the guardrail on the shoulder down about a quarter mile from Starbright. It was still running—the truck—sitting there, idling."

"On our road. Right here? Right up the hill?"

"Yes, right here on Steep Hill Road. You know that part

where they've had problems with falling rock? There's a guardrail there."

I picture it in my mind.

"Mr. Limehouse passed Andrew's truck going the opposite way, so when he saw it sitting there, he pulled over to check if everything was all right. The bumper was hanging from the front of the truck, but otherwise nothing seemed wrong. The windshield was intact, there weren't any dents or scratches, no other cars involved—"

"I don't understand. Are you saying Andrew didn't crash?"

"No one knows for sure. But it doesn't look like it. Chief Mahony says he may have passed out or maybe he pulled over because he didn't feel well. He didn't appear hurt. There was no … blood." She blinks as the word hangs in the air. "I'm so sorry. As soon as Leo called, I ran over here to tell you."

"But Andrew is young. He's healthy. No reason to pass out or feel ill. He was fine this morning. He just left for work." I say all of this as if that should make a difference, as if it will render this horrible news null and void.

"Did he have any health problems, or maybe he was on medication or some—"

"No. Nothing." I grab my stomach and the baby. *The baby.* I squeeze my eyes closed and raise my hand. "I should stand."

Miranda helps me to the couch. Then she returns to the foyer behind me. I hear her putting the parts of the phone back together.

Meanwhile, I'm thinking this isn't right. There must be some mistake. Andrew can't be dead. He wouldn't do this to me. He wouldn't do this to the baby.

I'm staring into the carpet.

My hands are shaking.

I am not in the present.

I want nothing to do with the present.

My heart would kill itself right now if it knew how.

I'm floating backward, inside my head to where Andrew still lives.

We're in the kitchen dancing a clumsy waltz, thinking of the sex we should have, wishing he could stay home from work.

I'm breathing his breath, feeling his warmth, loving his laugh.

Touching his face. Feeling his body against mine.

Now we're in the bedroom.

I'm adoring his smell and his hair. His roundy face and blue-green eyes. Watching him worry over his day. Watching the wheels in his brain spin.

He says he has to go.

I ask him to stay.

Please stay.

His hand crosses over my stomach.

The baby reaches for him from the inside.

We are three pressed together.

On the bench in the backyard …

Andrew is filled with love for us and splitting at the seams with happiness.

I am overwhelmed.

The moon watches in the sky above the backyard.

I'm saying I love you in the kitchen, in the bedroom, on the bench outside.

I'm saying stay, stay, *please* stay.

He says, "I'll see you later."

There must be a way to get back, to claw my way back. Backstroke my arms in big windmill circles and kick my feet as hard as they will go, swim through space and through time to get back to him.

He's so close. He was here only moments ago. If I can get

back, just a little bit, I'll find him at the front door, in the bedroom, on the bench. Smiling at me, saying he loves me, holding me. Smelling good, looking beautiful, loving the baby.

I'll tear through atoms if that's what I have to do.

I'll tear through seconds, minutes, time itself.

I cannot stay here, in the present.

I want nothing to do with the present.

It should not be that hard to get back to a few minutes ago.

"Okay, goodbye."

It's Miranda. She has ended a phone call and now joins me on the couch and asks, "Do you want me to call anyone?"

My eyes are dead. I'm seeing the world through dead, wet eyes.

Just Andrew. I need to call Andrew.

Miranda pats my knee. "Don't worry. You don't have to call anyone right now. Sit here. You don't have to do anything."

I'm alone. No one to call. My parents are … I don't know where. I've left them so many messages! Helena, in Russia, has no telephone. Helena doesn't even answer email.

I'm alone. But in my head, I'm not. My husband still lives inside of me. Our souls came together years ago. His soul mingled with mine, and in this way we are forever.

When I think of us that way, I almost feel all right.

Except for the wall between us. The wall of time separating us. He's on one side and I am on the other, and we're both thinking of each other and trying to figure out how to tear the wall down so we can get back together.

"Do you want anything? Maybe some tea?"

I leave my thoughts for a moment and stare at Miranda. What else can she say at a time like this? She's not built for catastrophe. She's built for picnics and wine tastings.

Barbecues. Apple muffins. Sexy outfits for special occasions.

"No," I tell her. And then "Yes," giving her something to do so I can be alone to figure out how to get back to a few minutes ago.

She crosses the room to the kitchen. Opens and closes cabinets in search of a cup. I don't tell her where to look. I'm in no hurry for her to come back.

I want to stay inside my head. That's where I can see Andrew on the bench in the moonlight, in the bedroom wondering what he's forgotten, in the foyer ready to leave. Dancing with me in the kitchen. Reaching out to touch our baby.

Stay with me, Andrew. Please stay. Why didn't I make him stay?

Miranda returns with the tea. I don't take it when she holds it out, so she places it on the coffee table in front of me.

"Thanks," I manage.

The front door opens and closes.

Leo walks in. Head bowed, somber expression. I've never seen him in a suit. His formal work clothing. It's strange what you notice in the midst of catastrophe. "I'm sorry, Svetlana." He embraces me with the smell of coffee. I cannot speak. I am inside my head, clawing my way backward through time.

This can't be real.

Maybe it isn't. I would love to wake up and find myself in bed, fresh from a horrible dream.

Leo squats in front of me. His voice is gentle: "Listen, the ambulance took him. They're going to keep him until ..." He pauses and clears his throat. " ... funeral plans are made."

I nod. "How do you know this?"

"I was there. After the police arrived. I recognized his truck and pulled over on my way to—"

I gasp at the picture inside my mind: the blue pickup with Andrew in the front seat, unmoving. I feel as if I have driven up to the truck myself.

"I want to see him," I say.

Leo looks at Miranda for a second, then back at me. "Of course. You can do that."

I want to be in Andrew's presence.

I want to hold his hand and tell him I'm sorry.

I won't believe it's true until I see him.

"When can I see him?" I say.

"I know the police chief," Leo says. "I'll call and ask."

"Thank you."

"There will be an autopsy to rule out anything unusual," he says, his eyes on the screen of his cell. "Not that any foul play is expected. It's just, with such a young man and no witnesses to the accident, that's what they do."

He meets my gaze.

Foul play.

He asks, "Are you okay with that?"

I just want to see Andrew. I don't care what they have to do. He's still here on Earth for me to see, and I want to spend every second I can with him.

I nod, and Leo stands and pulls something from his pocket. "Chief Mahony gave me this, for you."

Miranda's head tilts in question. I cannot see her face.

I reach for whatever he holds. He presses it into the center of my palm.

It's Andrew's wedding band, smooth and cool, shining, still new. Just like my own. Having his ring makes it more real. I unclasp the plain gold chain I wear around my neck and thread the ring through. Miranda helps me close it.

I can't stay here, in the present.

I want nothing to do with the present.

It shouldn't be that hard to get back to a few minutes ago.

If they would leave me alone, I could claw my way through the past, find Andrew standing in the bedroom or at the front door. I could stop him from leaving.

The baby kicks the side of my uterine wall, and I jolt.

When I look up, Miranda and Leo are staring down at me. Pale, unsmiling.

"Are you all right?" they say in unison.

I rub my side. "I need to see Andrew."

———

I sit in the backseat of Leo's car, feeling like a child.

The headrest cradles my skull like a sleeping baby that lulls back and forth at the mercy of each winding turn of this snake of a road. I don't want to see the place where it happened, the guardrail that caught him. I might fall apart if I do. And that's not why I'm here.

I'm going to see Andrew.

I have nothing to say.

I don't care how heavy the silence becomes.

———

We arrive at an office complex. Leo drives toward a four-story rectangular building with Starbright International in black letters across the top and windows that reflect like mirrors. It's a solitary structure on a mound of higher ground, a regular office building except for the large circular protrusion rising from the roof like the head of a giant—the telescope, of course.

In the surrounding parking lot, I count only a few cars. I haven't been to Andrew's work since we arrived in Ashbury Falls. When we lived in Kirksberg, I sometimes dropped off food or met him for lunch in the cafeteria. I imagined this building would be more like that one, where at least five hundred people work. This seems like a place for fifty. I never asked Andrew how many people he worked with, but I remember Miranda saying half the town worked there. There's no way half the town of Ashbury Falls works inside this building.

"What are we doing?" I say.

Miranda turns around, wearing a twitchy sort of smile that I have no doubt she means to be reassuring. "Everything is fine," she says.

Leo pulls to the back of the building and parks in one of the many empty spaces. He switches off the car and twists around to face me. "He's here."

He can't mean Andrew. Why would Andrew be here? Andrew didn't make it to work today.

"I don't understand."

"His father, well, you know he owns the company, and—"

"Yes?"

"He wanted Andrew brought here."

"That is strange," I say, noting the nervous red flags flapping in my brain.

"Well, it's not that strange considering what's done here. Scientifically, I mean. There's a refrigerated room, and that's where they've brought him. For the autopsy. Mr. Jovian wants his own people to do it."

At that, Miranda places her hand upon my shoulder. She nods, encouraging me to accept this factual oddity as if it were normal.

"Edmund wants his employees to do it?" I say. "The scientists at Starbright?"

"Yes," Leo says. "I suppose he doesn't trust anyone else to do it right."

"And the police have agreed because the Jovians are wealthy?" I look to Miranda. "Is that right?"

"We don't know," Leo says before she can answer. "But if you want to, we can call Chief Mahony, and you can speak to him yourself."

I want to see Andrew. I don't care about anything else. If an autopsy has to be done, and Edmund wants his scientists to do it, that's fine with me. I shake my head. "So, I can see him?"

Leo eases back. My answer seems to have let some of the stiffness out of his posture. "Yes, of course."

We get out of the car. I'm holding my middle as if it were the baby who needs the support. But I need the baby more than it needs me right now.

Everyone I love goes away.

───────────

As we walk through the corridors, Leo and Miranda flank me, poised for my impending collapse. Or maybe hoping to make me feel less alone, which is an impossibility right now.

I feel an unusual brand of excitement. My brain has not entirely accepted that living Andrew will not be present for this meeting.

Part of me assumes all of this death will go away as soon as I see him again. That he'll sit up and say, "Thank goodness you're here. That was a close one."

And I'll say, "They told me you were gone."

And he'll laugh that adorable laugh of his and say, "That's ridiculous. I would never leave you."

───────────

I insist on going in alone.

Miranda and Leo hover outside the door.

It's not their business. This is my husband.

The room is cold and metal. Tiles of white and silver. Shiny. Hard. Sharp edges. Even the air is void of softness. It is winter here.

He is there. Lying flat on his back on a metal table. Covered up to his waist with a white sheet. Shirtless. Cold, but not shivering. Still. Too still.

Andrew.

It's not like sleeping. This stiffness. This ... *unmoving.*

This is not how Andrew looks when he sleeps.

His eyes are closed. His face offers no expression. It's not like him. Where is the mischievous grin? The happy color in his cheeks?

Where are you?

You're not in there, in that body.

You have flown away, and this shell is merely where you lived on Earth.

His soul is in the air, mingling with mine, invisible and content.

There are no bruises that I can see. No cuts. No scrapes. Only smooth, pale skin. A placid expression. No broken bones. No sign of foul play.

I take his hand. But it doesn't feel like Andrew's hand. Cold. Hard. Already something else.

I thought I would get to see him one more time, but now I know for sure: he's already gone.

Back at my house, I can't wait to get inside. There's more Andrew here than in that refrigerator at Starbright. I fling open the door, and Miranda follows close behind like an annoying dog. Leo has dropped us off. I wish she went with him, but she insists that I need her. "I don't think you should be alone," she says.

I spin around. "To be alone is exactly what I want."

At this, she doesn't sigh or scowl. Her expression is one of imperviousness. "I promised your in-laws I'd stay with you. They're worried."

"My in-laws? You don't even know my in-laws."

"Chief Mahoney spoke with them on the phone, and they, uh—" She fumbles for words. "They relayed a message—requested that someone, a neighbor or friend—"

"Fine," I say, hating every second she makes me stand there and listen to her. All I want is to get back into my bedroom where Andrew's things are. His clothes and the bed and ... all of our stuff. "I'm going to lie down," I say. "I'm exhausted."

"But you're all right? I'm here for you, Sveta. Whatever you need. I know you feel horrible."

"I'm good," I say, stifling the urge to shout, *Leave me alone.*

Released from this conversation, I rush down the hall and enter the bathroom, stopping short at the entrance. I take in the sight of Andrew's things, objects he touched and handled only hours ago. On his side of the double vanity, I find his toothbrush in the cup he used and the soap in a dish with a puddle of water, and the towels he dried himself with, the hand towel still holding the cinched shape of his hands squeezing it. On the vanity, I find a piece of hair on the marble. I lift it. It's Andrew's. A tiny piece of him. His cells.

My already burning eyes well with tears. I open the drawer and find a plastic vial, an old prescription with only two pills inside, which I drop into the drawer. The vial will make a safe place for this piece of hair, which I plan to keep forever. Something to show the baby when he or she is old enough to understand.

I close the vial with its child-proof lid and head into the bedroom. I place the vial on the top of my dresser, next to the picture of us from our wedding day. The two of us in the photo are completely unaware of what the future holds.

Now that I have his hair, I can look at a piece of Andrew whenever I like. This strand of hair has just become my most prized possession.

I reach into the laundry basket and rummage past socks and underwear, another damp towel, and a pair of leggings I wore yesterday. Finally, I reach the shirt Andrew wore last night. I bury my face in it and inhale him. My body tingles all over. Some of the pain siphons away, though the wound underneath still throbs, fresh and swollen. If I'd known Andrew was going to leave today, I would have paid better attention. I would have held him longer, kissed him more. Stared into his eyes and told him I loved him over and over again. But I did tell him, didn't I? I tell him every day.

If I had known, I would have held on and never let go.

Smelling him like this brings him back to me. It's like I have clawed my way back to a place we both dwell.

I drop onto his side of the bed with his shirt covering my face. With eyes closed, I reach for his pillow, pull it close to me as if it were his body, his chest. I remember what it feels like to hold him, to be held. I imagine his hand on the back of my head, his fingers weaved through my hair. I want to open my eyes and see if he's there, but I know the spell will break if I do. I keep my eyes closed and let the feeling go on as long as it will.

I wake with a start.

"Don't panic."

It's Andrew's voice.

I'm frightened, but I don't know why.

Where is he? What time is it? What day? The light coming through the window is dull afternoon light. I try to sit up, but my neck hurts from sleeping with his thick pillow balled up under my chin. Andrew likes firm pillows. I like soft. I force my stiff neck to turn, groaning as I stretch the kinks from the muscles—and then I remember that he's gone, and a great swell of devastation pulls me into a ball like one of those dried and crusty millipedes on the carpet in summer. My eyes squeeze shut so tight that I'm afraid they may sink into the center of my skull and become stuck. I'm breathing as if pulling air through a thick cloth mask.

A voice hovers like a cloud nearby, its familiar inflections muffled through the wall. Caroline's know-it-all entitlement causes a shiver up my back. She's not speaking to me, but she's here. In my house.

The family has arrived.

Maybe this is what Andrew meant by "Don't panic"?

His voice sounded so alive, so real. Was it only my mind playing tricks?

There's a tap at the door, and I picture Caroline's shiny red fingernails.

Shouldn't they have called first?

"Svetlana, it's Caroline."

How did they get here so fast?

"I'm here," I say, hoping she won't hear my dejected voice through the door.

"I'm coming in."

Of course she is.

I open my swollen eyes, and what I see is surprising: designer pants, beige; silk blouse, ivory; blonde bob, freshly washed and shining.

Caroline looks as stellar as ever.

"Oh, my dear," she says in a *tsk-tsk* way, observing the rumpled, bedraggled mess that is me. "You're so changed from last I saw you."

I sink into self-consciousness. But then Caroline clasps her hands together and raises them to her lips, her mouth curving with delight. "It's wonderful."

Wonderful?

She continues on her walk to the end of the bed, adjusting her expression so that it's no longer delighted, but solemn. She turns to me and holds up one hand. "First, let me say that I know you are pregnant. I was told a few hours ago, before flying down here to see you. Please don't feel like you need to hide it anymore."

I look down at myself. I suppose she might think I was trying to hide under the sheet wrapped around my middle, but the thought hadn't crossed my mind. As a matter of fact, I forgot it was a secret.

"That would be impossible to do at this point," I say.

"No need to apologize," she says in a loud, assuming voice. "I'm not angry with you."

I wasn't going to apologize.

Her brows rise. "How far along are you?"

"Um." I clear my throat. Shouldn't she say something about her son? The skin across my forehead tightens; my mind underneath is straining. "Eighteen weeks," I say, but I'm not sure that's right. My brains became scrambled this morning. It might be twenty.

She smiles and nods as if this pleases her. "And the sex of the child?"

We don't know, don't want to know, and even if I knew, I wouldn't tell her.

I shake my head. I have no words for Caroline. Especially now that I can see Andrew was right: she cares more for her grandchild than she cared for him. I wish Andrew were here. I need him now. I find her so offensive, this woman in beautiful clothing. Why does she look so normal? Why doesn't she care?

"If you don't know yet, it's fine. I'm sure you'll find out soon."

When I frown, she blinks and remains still before speaking again. "Perhaps we can discuss the baby in more detail after you're showered and dressed. I'm sure doing so would help you feel better."

Is that your excuse? You showered this morning and now you feel better, or is it something else? Please tell me your secret.

"How do *you* feel, Caroline?"

She gazes blankly at me before shifting her eyes toward the windows. Perhaps she has read between the lines. I don't know because I truly don't know her well.

"Of course I've seen better days," she says, doing her best to appear humble, something I've never seen her do. I've never seen her show vulnerability of any kind. "But we Jovians carry on through thick and thin."

I'm tempted to smother myself in the folds of Andrew's pillow.

My voice shakes when I say, "Andrew died only this morning."

She looks away. Possibly she's in denial. Or maybe shock. Though she doesn't strike me as one who's in shock. She seems like a person with something going on below the surface, someone preoccupied with trying to appear a certain way ... casual? Maybe she wants something from me and she's afraid to ask for it. Or she's angry with me about hiding the pregnancy from her—angry with her son for hiding it as well—and it's hard for her to act normally because of that.

"It's a pretty room," she says, I assume, to move on from this awkwardness. "I love the blue-and-white color scheme. French country is a favorite of mine."

"I assumed you decorated," I say with a frown. *This is no time for niceties, Caroline.*

As soon as she leaves, I'm calling both of my parents' phones and leaving another message. I need someone here. I need my own family.

"Mmmm," she mutters. Her gaze passes over the dimly lit windows and stops at the dresser. Something there interests her. She steps toward it, hovers for a moment as she views our framed wedding photo. Then she lifts the vial that holds the piece of Andrew's hair.

My whole body goes cold. That vial is *mine*. All I have left of him.

With manicured fingers, she holds it up to the light.

"He had beautiful hair, didn't he?" she says, smiling like a proud parent.

The urge to yell, *Put it down!* balloons up my throat.

Instead I simply answer yes and hope she doesn't notice that my response is stiff with restraint.

She could take the vial not because she wants it for herself but because she knows how much I want it. And what could I do? I am powerless. At her mercy. My KGB side would want to wrestle her for it, but a pregnant lady fighting a rich middle-aged woman in designer clothes is a bizarre thought.

And so is my life at this point.

Maybe she's angry because I'm the reason Andrew decided to move six hundred miles from her, to this place with its steep hills and falling rock.

She replaces the vial and turns her attention to me.

I want to tell her that she may go now. That she's dismissed. But she's Andrew's mother, and I can't do that.

"There's something important I must ask," she says, wearing her seriousness like a badge or a uniform. "As you know, we need to make plans for a funeral."

I bow my head and close my eyes. How will I survive this?

"What are your wishes?"

I wait for more, but there's only silence.

My wishes?

I had assumed she and Edmund would make all of the decisions. I had assumed they would tell me what *they* wanted.

"All I mean is, what type of funeral would you like to have for Andrew?"

I have begun to shake. She's glaring at me. I don't know how to answer this question. I shrug up to my ears. "He never said anything about what he would like. He was so young. We didn't discuss—"

She tilts her head. "For instance, would you prefer burial or cremation?"

"Uh." I sniff and rub my eyes. She may as well have asked

what type of salad I would like for lunch because that is how not-upset she seems to be right now. My nose is about to run. I whisk a tissue from the night table.

"I haven't yet thought of this," I say with difficulty. It's hard to speak when all you want to do is bawl like a baby. "I can't believe he's gone."

Why can you? Why are your eyes clear? Why are you not crumbling?

I'm afraid that I hate her right now.

I think she gets the hint because her shoulders droop, and she goes blank in the face. "I'm extremely saddened. He was my son, after all."

Was he? At this point, I have to wonder.

"But we must carry on," she says, standing a bit straighter. "Don't you agree?"

I refuse to answer the question. I have no intention to stand tall and carry on with the Jovians at this time. Cowering under the covers and clinging to Andrew's pillow is where they'll find me.

Caroline passes me a smile, and when I don't respond she clears her throat. "Why don't you take a shower and then join us in the kitchen? I'm sure you could use something to eat."

I would much rather stay right here, in our bedroom. I'm not hungry. I don't want to eat. I may never eat again. And I don't want to plan a funeral for my husband. I'm not ready to do that. *Come back tomorrow and try again!*

"For the baby," she says, reminding me.

I nod and say, "All right," in the hope that she will go.

She takes a few steps in the direction of the door and then stops to look at me once more. "Edmund is here, and Aunt Constance and Uncle James as well."

My eyes bulge with the effort to conceal my feelings concerning this news. Uncle Jimmy is the last one I want to spend time with.

"I'm happy to see you, Svetlana. I've missed you and Andrew both."

She swings the door open and strides out, her head held high, *carrying on through thick and thin* like some kind of automated mannequin.

It doesn't seem real. Nothing about this day seems real.

When I step out of the bedroom with wet hair dripping on the shoulders of my sweatshirt, I find my mother- and father-in-law seated on the living room couch across from Aunt Constant in an armchair. All three of them are fixed upon the photo of Chateau L'Origine that Aunt Constant and Uncle Jimmy gave us as a wedding gift.

There are nuts in a bowl on the coffee table as well as glasses filled with brown liquid and ice cubes in front of each one of them. Scotch, maybe. Something the wealthy drink during a tragedy.

"Hi," I say, thinking, *So glad to join your party.*

The refrigerator closes with a slap; Uncle Jimmy spins around, and his big glasses point in my direction. He must have been foraging in my refrigerator. Probably set his sights on apple pie. Or beer.

No scotch for Uncle Jimmy.

Edmund rises from the couch and reaches me as I enter the living room. "So good to see you," he says in a subdued tone I've never heard him use.

Before I respond, he's hugging me. He is taller than Andrew, but something about him feels the same. It's strange because I never noticed before. Edmund has never shown much affection. He's more of a lean-forward-and-half-hug type of person. I've never seen him full-body anyone. Not even Caroline.

But this is not normal circumstances.

When he releases me, Aunt Constant appears beside him. A foot shorter than I am, her head tipped upward, sad-faced and pink in her wobbly cheeks. "You poor girl," she says as she reaches to embrace me.

She's not crying.

Then again, neither am I. For the moment, my tears have gone dry. My eyes are as swollen as overripe plums. I feel sick, beaten. Weak.

I sense Uncle Jimmy's approach. He takes deliberate steps the way you might approach a frightened doe in the backyard.

But I have nowhere to go.

It's the same old Jimmy: hair mussed as if it's 7 a.m. and he just rose from bed. A button on his cardigan misaligned so the two halves of the sweater don't match. His pant legs bunched up on the tops of his shoes. Eccentric, annoying Uncle Jimmy, and yet something about seeing him comforts me. I don't understand it. My own feelings feel odd to me. Maybe it's the fact that he's so familiar. Or maybe it's that, in spite of all his eccentricities, Andrew loved him.

"Hello," I say.

He's still five or six steps away, and I hope he doesn't expect me to run into his arms. This is not going to happen.

"So, it's true," he says, grinning. "You're going to have a baby. I knew you could do it." He claps his hands together and folds his arms up to his chest as though he can hardly contain his satisfaction.

He is bursting at the seams.

And not a word about Andrew. Not one of them has said a word about Andrew. What is wrong with these people?

He moves closer, an outstretched hand leading the way. "May I touch it?"

"No," Aunt Constant says.

But Uncle Jimmy continues to walk toward me, begging with owl eyes.

"Oh, I, um …" I laugh a little to stop from groaning. "Okay. Yes."

Jimmy is a child granted a toy. He's in awe of me and my baby belly—and I don't hate him for it. On the contrary, I can feel his happiness. Actually *feel* it. And I can't help but smile back at him. Happiness must be contagious.

He rests his hand on the shelf of my newly expanded stomach and stands stock-still as if his hand and arm make up some kind of listening device, his gaze pointed in the direction of the sliding glass door, the backyard, and beyond.

I stand there, a bit awkward with this man's hand on my midsection, until he returns to Earth, to the living room, to me. He raises his brows and says, "Fantastic."

He's literally glowing. A lot more than I am today.

All I can think is, poor Andrew will never see his child, and strange Uncle Jimmy will.

But I suppose it's good that the baby and I have people who care.

It could be much worse, considering I have no idea where my parents are and the chance of Helena coming back is zero.

"We Jovians are so lucky to have you," Uncle Jimmy says as he bows his head, possibly in a gesture of respect.

The chill of my angry feelings for him warms, and some of that heat rolls up my throat and threatens tears.

"Not to worry, sweetheart, not to worry." He pulls me in for a hug. "We'll take care of you. You and the baby. You're part of our family, and we love you."

He pulls back and stares me in the face with watery blue eyes. "You're our pride and joy."

Pride and joy? I think, as the buzz of electricity spreads across my scalp. I know he wished for a baby in the family, but I didn't know pregnancy would raise me to such high esteem. Should I be flattered? I can't help that I am.

When he releases me, all four Jovians gather around like a fence, their perfumes and aftershave mingling into a strange and dizzying scent. Aunt Constant and Caroline wear the empty gazes of the overwhelmed. Edmund says, "He's right. We don't want you to worry about a thing. We're all here for you."

It's too much for me to bear considering the opposition I've leveled in their direction. The guilt of knowing they only want to care for me pulls at the walls of my throat. My eyes well up this time because I am loved, and I've been mean and angry and my husband is dead and I'm scared, and it's true that they are strange, but I need them now. Even if I don't love them or trust them 100 percent.

Aunt Constant passes me a tissue. The others continue to hover close. I feel I should say something. "I loved Andrew more than anything in this world." I am cracking like an eggshell on the inside. "And I'm lucky to be part of his family."

Edmund exchanges a glance with Caroline. Uncle Jimmy grins as if he knew I loved him all this time and was merely hiding my admiration. Aunt Constant says, "Let's get you a sandwich."

Three of them find seats in the living room while Aunt Constant leads me to the kitchen table.

The first thing I feel when I reach the table is that it's strange to sit here without Andrew. Aunt Constant fusses around, opening and closing drawers and cabinets as she gathers what's needed to make me a turkey sandwich and a glass of milk, both of which she places in front of me now.

When did I last eat something? What time is it? What day?

Outside, through the glass of the sliding door, the sun is dropping into the lake. Evening's dark purple and jagged streaks of crimson appear to be engaged in some violent struggle as my first night without Andrew approaches.

It seems like a lifetime ago I saw him, and I miss him so much already. It feels unfair for me to eat when he can't. I know that makes no sense.

And yet, when I lift the sandwich to take a bite, something happens. A switch is flipped. My stomach awakens, becomes a monster that wants its prey, and I eat so fast that I have to wash it down with the milk or it will become stuck in my throat. Aunt Constant doesn't ask if I would like another; she simply makes it and places it on the plate where the last one used to be.

The baby is growing. And I haven't eaten all day. *Oh my gosh. I haven't eaten all day.*

A phone rings, and my first thought is, *Andrew.*

Caroline has the cordless house telephone beside her on the couch, which she answers before the second ring. "Hello, David," she says, inspecting her fingernails. "Yes, we're all here."

Edmund and Jimmy murmur something as they walk through the kitchen. Jimmy winks at me as he passes, and they exit the house onto the deck. I've slept through the day, and it's already time for the telescope. Day in, day out, *through thick and thin,* the Jovians remain true to their night sky.

"Oh, yes, the flight was perfect," Caroline continues. "Clear skies. ... Lovely. Forty-five degrees. ... Yes, you should. ... The hotel is beautiful. ... Okay. I'll tell them. ... See you soon."

How cheerful Caroline is. And thank God she doesn't want to stay with me. I may need the Jovians, but I don't want to live with them. So glad hotel accommodations are to her liking.

I can't help but scowl at her as she walks into the kitchen, approaching Aunt Constant, who's rearranging the refrigerator. "David will come in the morning," she says with a smile that shows her teeth.

"Wonderful," Aunt Constant says. "Please tell Edmund and James."

Caroline turns on her heels, passes me at the kitchen table, and opens the sliding glass door. Once outside, she proceeds to the men.

I want to yell: *Have fun. Enjoy the sights!*

They're acting as if they're not surprised Andrew died, like they knew it was going to happen. Could they have known? And if they did, what does that mean? The Jovian file Andrew told me about barges into my mind, and my thoughts cascade: he wasn't supposed to see it. His father denied it was real. Uncle Jimmy didn't acknowledge it. Edmund insisted his people perform the autopsy. Caroline's only son has died, and she's talking about the beautiful hotel.

My face blooms with heat that rises into my ears. Could they have killed him? But no, the police chief reported no signs of foul play, no evidence of wrongdoing. I saw Andrew's body myself: it was smooth and unblemished. No cuts, bruises, broken bones. He didn't crash his car. He simply pulled over and passed out.

Aunt Constant slides into the seat in front of me and ushers me out of my thoughts. Her manner of sitting is odd, with arms straight down at her sides. "I wanted to talk to you about something." Her words appear in a motherly way because everything about her is motherly: her petite body and soft, wrinkled face; the curls of cropped gray hair. She's what my American mother would call "down to earth." Nothing like Caroline and her stringent beauty.

"We wanted to give you the opportunity to have full control of the funeral arrangements," she says, "but on second thought, we realized that would be difficult for you right now, wouldn't it?"

Mention of the funeral takes my breath away. "Uh, yes, I—"

"Would you like us to take care of it? You can tell us if there's anything you don't like along the way, and we'll grant whatever wishes you have."

Thank God one of them gets it. I want to hug her. "That will be a very big relief, thank you."

"I thought so," she says. "You know you can always come to me, right? If something is bothering you, or if you need someone to listen. Goodness knows, Edmund and Caroline can be intimidating, and Jimmy's—" She pauses as if she can't think of the right word. "Well, you know he tries, right?"

"Yes," I say, with a smile. "I know."

"And you and I understand each other, don't we?"

Out of all of them, she's the most normal, so I guess I could say that's true. Regardless, it feels good to have an ally. Without Andrew to protect me, I'll need one.

"I have a question," I say in a hushed volume, "and I don't want to ask Caroline."

She leans in and nods.

"Did Andrew have any medical problems that he maybe didn't tell me about? I don't think he did, b—"

"He didn't. And he would have told you. He loved you so much."

I press my lips together and draw in a shaky breath.

"Eat up, my dear," she says, as she stands. "You must stay healthy, not only for yourself but for the baby."

She pushes in the chair and heads toward the stove.

I can relax after that, knowing the group of them will go back to their luxury hotel and that soon I can return to my bedroom and concentrate on bringing my husband back to life in my mind. Because that's all I want to do.

On the deck, Edmund looks through the lens of the telescope and Uncle Jimmy gestures big circles with his hands while Caroline listens to whatever he's saying. I guess they know the combination to the lockbox. Why wouldn't they? It's the same one Uncle Jimmy purchased for us in Kirksberg.

I say, "What's going on out there tonight?"

Aunt Constant turns so she can see. "Looks like the usual to me."

If Andrew were home, he'd be out there with them. He was out there last night and the night before and all the nights before that—and if only I could backstroke my way to an earlier time, I would be out there with him.

With each second that passes, we grow farther apart.

He's stuck in the past, and the universe is dragging me into the future.

1 4

"Cremation," Caroline says with confidence. "That's the Jovian tradition."

"Yes, it truly is," Edmund replies. "All the Jovians make that choice, and I have no doubt Andrew would want the same." He doesn't look at me when he says this, though I feel he is speaking to me specifically.

Two days have passed since the family arrived, and this morning we are packed together in a booth at the Sheridan Café. Five of us sit on puffy pleather benches meant for four: me, Caroline, and Jimmy on one side; Constant and Edmund on the other. The remnants of omelets and French toast crowd the table in between. They tell me funeral plans have been made, and now we must discuss the matter of what happens afterward.

"No headstone then?" I ask, disappointed because I wanted someplace to go to be with him. Not that it matters so much, but … I don't know. Maybe it does matter. Or maybe it will someday.

"You can still get a headstone," Aunt Constant says. "Do you want him to have a headstone?"

"But what will be buried there, if his body is cremated?"

"You can put the ashes in an urn, and the urn goes underground." She shows me with her hands how tall an urn might be. "Is that what you want? To put the ashes—"

"Or you can keep some ashes for yourself," Caroline interrupts. "In a small bottle next to your photograph and Andrew's hair."

I can't tell if she is making fun of me. As much as I would like to carry Andrew around with me in a vial, I'm not sure that's a healthy thing to do. "And would you like to keep some of the ashes, too, Caroline?" I say.

She says, "Sure," but looks like she couldn't care less and is already thinking of other things.

"What about spreading some ashes in a place that he loved?" I say. "Isn't that what people do? Maybe by the bench in our backyard?"

Aunt Constant sits in her usual way, with her arms straight down at her sides. "That is a lovely idea."

Edmund yawns.

The waitress comes by. "Everything all right?"

"Please bring Svetlana more milk," Caroline says, pointing to my empty glass.

I want to tell her no, but Jimmy, seated in the innermost corner of the booth, throws his arm out in front of Caroline and me, and says, "Can I get another beer?" He's another one who appears bored with funeral arrangements.

"So, cremation, headstone, small vial of ashes for Svetlana and for spreading in the backyard," Constant recites. "Are you getting all of this, James?"

"Oh, yes ma'am. I got it," he says, draining his first beer with one hand and pointing to his skull with the other.

It's 10 a.m.

I don't understand this family.

Later, when Aunt Constant and the others finally leave me alone in the evening, I slip into the bedroom and inhale Andrew's pillow. When I'm satisfied with that, I sit up and lift my cell phone from the night table. I'm not sure I want to do what I'm about to do, and yet I know for sure that I want to do it. I go into my contacts list and press "Andrew: work." After a pause, the ringing begins. Once, twice, three times. My heartbeat flutters, and I tense all over, every breath stiff with anticipation. Click. "Hello. You've reached Andrew Jovian of Starbright International."

Hearing him speak sends a bolt of life through my brain. It's as if he exists on some other plane, as if he isn't dead but only misplaced. I implode with a mix of longing and excitement.

"At the moment I'm away from my desk, but if you leave your name, number, and the planet you are calling from, I'll get back to you as soon as I can."

My ears prick like antennae.

Was that his message? I don't remember him saying that. When did he change his outgoing—the signal to let me know it's time to record my message vibrates in my ear. I hang up.

What a joker he is!

I laugh so hard the mattress shakes. I lift the wedding band I wear around my neck and kiss it.

I've heard his voicemail message so many times, and, wow, that was strange.

I call again and wait impatiently for the three rings to pass.

"Hello. You've reached Andrew Jovian." It's definitely Andrew's voice, his usual hello. My heart flutters and blood pounds in my ears as I continue to listen. ... But this time the expected message plays with the ordinary wording. It's businesslike and professional. No mention of *planets* whatsoever. And that's not only disappointing but baffling.

I suppose my mind is playing tricks on me.

Tomorrow I will attend my husband's funeral. I'm tired and emotionally drained. Am I hearing things, too?

Or maybe Andrew is trying to reach me from beyond. I survey my bedroom as if he might step out from in between molecules of air. If he wanted to haunt me, I would welcome it.

The next day, dark and dreary, the skies leak tears, as they should. The misty drizzle reflects my mood. If it were a few degrees colder, the outside would become a beautiful snow-white wonderland—and that would not be appropriate for this horrible day. I'd rather see gray and dreary than something bright and beautiful right now.

Of course, I'm wearing a black dress, black stockings, black heels. I can't wear makeup because my sadness will spread a mess across my face. I'm pale and swollen eyed, and have been shaking with nerves since I woke up an hour ago.

I'm holding our wedding photograph in my hands. I feel sorry for the young couple pictured there. They strike me as so innocent, their smiles so clueless. There was no way they could have known the tragic end to their story.

My mother-in-law is outside my bedroom door, speaking on the phone. "Well, of course you're coming over after the funeral. ... Good. ... No. ... I know how busy you are. ... Okay, David. ... Yes, it will be fine. I'll see you shortly."

A second later, her voice strikes my bedroom door and shocks my ailing heart. "Are you almost ready, Svetlana? The car will be here in a moment."

I open the door to a brilliant surprise: Caroline dressed in a shimmering gold top and rich tobacco-colored pants. Her hair is done, lashes thick and glistening, heels high. The colors by themselves are an assault on my wallowing misery. I feel puckered, peeled, riddled with holes, and the sight of her is an astringent that stings.

The exasperation must show on my face because she says, "Oh, yes. I should explain the way I've dressed. This, too, is a Jovian tradition. Many years ago, Edmund's mother decided that those who did not want to wear black to a family funeral should not feel obligated. She was no fan of dark colors. For Edmund Sr.'s funeral she wore crimson, I believe it was, and she asked others to wear bold colors as well. 'He was a bold man and would have preferred it,' she said."

It sounds like a crock, and I want to say, *That is peculiar, Caroline.* But I'm much more accustomed to Jovian eccentricities than I was a few days ago. I am convinced their ancient lineage, wherever it comes from, probably explains why they're so weird. And what do I care? My husband will be put to rest today. Besides, I asked his parents to plan the funeral. If everyone shows up in a rainbow of colors, who am I to complain?

Caroline and the others will go back to Kirksberg tomorrow morning. I am ready for the family-in-law to leave.

———

A sleek Jovian limousine takes us ever upward. As far as I can tell, we are near the top of the mountain, not far from Starbright International. The service will take place at a lookout point. I'm told that during the spring, tourists come here to admire a picturesque chasm created by a tiny stream, which after centuries of flowing through solid rock created the deep divide that is this gorge, a natural wonder dotted with mountain flowers and greenery. But it's not spring, and it's not green or flowery. It's March 3, forty-four degrees, and a dismal drizzle continues to fall from a thick, colorless sky. Gray piles of snow turning to slush decorate the sides of the parking area. As I get out of the car, all I know is that I will not near the chasm's edge today for fear I may be tempted to fling myself over.

Away from the edge, in the flat area where we will have the ceremony, folding chairs create perfect rows in which Andrew's family, friends, and acquaintances—all of them in traditional dark suits and dresses covered by formal dress coats—sit under wide black umbrellas that resemble protective pods. I wonder why they didn't cover the entire area with a tent. I've never seen an outdoor memorial in the winter, but like I said, I asked my eccentric in-laws to handle the details.

We Jovians are the last to arrive. The front row of empty seats awaits us. Only the chair at the far end is occupied—I see what I think is the back of David's head. The chair rows pause in the middle to make an aisle for walking similar to a floor plan found in a church. As we pass through the center, I notice Miranda and Leo occupy two chairs in the last row, and Fran, whose broad shoulders slouch to such a desperate degree that I can't even be certain it's him, sits alone. Lisa and baby Max are not here. Maybe they are sick again. The rest of the chairs are filled with people I may have met once or twice, and those who aren't familiar at all. Co-workers, probably. Friends of Caroline and Edmund.

As I follow Aunt Constant (wearing black like me—I knew Caroline's story about a bold-color tradition was a crock), David stands and greets Edmund with a handshake. I'm tempted to run ahead, to push the others out of the way so that I can get up close and study his adorable face. *Andrew's* face. I'd forgotten how much they look alike. I wonder if that's why David hasn't been to see me; maybe the others told him to stay away, to spare me the pain.

Aunt Constant has taken a seat and now motions for me to do the same. The bubble of an umbrella connected to my chair via a metal pole thrums with the pop of light rain, the sound of fingers tapping above my head.

Ahead of us, there is no casket, no body. That's fine with me. I feel no need to view the empty shell that is Andrew. A large framed photograph propped upon a metal stand sits protected under an arbor-shaped tent. Where they found this picture, I don't know. It's like a high school photo, only it's recent and he wears a suit. Most likely it's the one they use when he writes something for Starbright's corporate newsletter. Next to the framed picture stands a podium, also sheltered underneath the small tent. A microphone reaches up from it like the stem of a flower.

The music of a violin quartet comes to the end of a song (I hadn't noticed the music until now, and I see that the musicians sit under yet another tent that's a few yards back and to the left). I am eager for the ceremony to begin and end.

A young guy with the skinny build of a teen walks down the center aisle and stands behind the podium. He's quivering like a feather, and I can't help but feel bad for him. It's not an easy thing to speak at a funeral.

"Good afternoon," he says, his voice difficult to hear even with the help of the microphone. Suddenly he lurches forward in a spastic move and bumps the microphone with his chin, causing it to collapse. One of his knees must have given out.

"Sorry, sorry," he says, straightening both his body and the microphone. "And, uh, thank you for coming."

He's too upset. He shouldn't have volunteered to speak.

"I'm Jake Clapper, and for a short time Andrew was my

boss at Starbright." He tries to smile but only makes it half-way. "Andrew was a super-nice boss, super-nice guy. Didn't make me get his coffee, or anything."

A few flutters of laughter rise up behind me.

"He had this calm way about him. Never got upset or angry. One time I sent an important memo to the wrong people—at the wrong company—and he didn't even get mad. He said he did the same thing his first week of work, though I don't think that was true. I think he made it up so I wouldn't feel stupid. He was really smart and never would have done something like that."

His voice trails off, and he makes a sniffling sound before knocking the microphone with the back of his hand and watching with a pained look of shock as it falls over and then dangles from its wire. He whispers, "Shit," which the microphone picks up and broadcasts through the speakers, as he grabs for and replaces the mic to its stand. "I'm sorry, Andrew," he says, shaking his head. "As you can see, I'm still doing dumb things." He tilts a grim face to the sky, mouth wavering with humiliation, and rushes away.

I wonder whose idea it was to ask him to speak, considering he was Andrew's assistant for only a few months.

A moment of silence occurs before Edmund passes in front of me.

He reaches the podium looking distinguished in his expensive suit and black raincoat. "Thank you, Jake." Edmund adjusts the microphone for his taller frame. "We know how hard this is for you, and for everyone who loved Andrew."

He pauses. The rain comes down a bit harder, and he looks up and smiles. "I suppose the heavens are showing their understanding of our pain, perhaps their compassion for the situation. My son was a wonderful kid. A great person. I miss him already, as I know all of you do."

Unlike young Jake, there's no quiver in Edmund's voice.

"Andrew would have made an excellent CEO, but he didn't want that. Not now, maybe not ever. He wanted to be on the ground floor, handling the telescopes, improving them, because that's how much he loved the night sky. From the time he was a small child, he set his sights on the stars." He pauses, smiles a proud smile. "I'd always hoped he would become an astronaut. But I should have known better because Andrew had his two feet planted firmly on the ground. He was human through and through ..."

The words detonate in my ears, and once again the file Andrew found comes to mind. Could this be what Edmund is referring to? Why wouldn't he discuss the file with Andrew?

"... And a wonderful husband. He loved his wife, Svetlana, very much."

I snap back to the present moment and try to look pleased ... or grateful for Edmund's kind words.

"He loved her the second he met her. That's what he told me. He said, 'Dad, she's the one. I'm sure of it.'"

With that, I think I just died. Again.

Aunt Constant pats my shoulder. It's merely a pat, but it feels somehow awkward. Hesitant, on her part. Don't ask me how. It feels ... wrong.

And I don't like what I'm seeing: Edmund and Caroline's strange brand of strength in dealing with Andrew's death, their odd way of planning the memorial, their lack of misery or any emotion at all. None of this is, dare I say, normal.

When I look down the row of immediate family members, no one is crying. Not Constant or Jimmy or even Caroline. Yet, I hear the sniffles behind us. Andrew's friends and co-workers have no problem displaying their sadness.

Again, I wonder, did the family know Andrew was going

to die? Or are they so unusual that they don't think death is sad?

The rain grows in strength, making a loud patter against the umbrellas that hover over each chair. It's an orchestra of drums. A rhythm of raindrops. An asteroid shower colliding with satellite disks.

Edmund continues to speak, unfazed by the weather.

Water beads up on my jacket, my hair, my skin. I've got a chill in my bones that keeps my body in shivers.

I'm so sorry that you died, Andrew. I'm sorry you didn't get to see our baby. I'll tell him or her all about you. I promise. I miss you and I love you, and the baby does, too.

And then, even louder than the drumming rain, someone has coughed into the microphone and set off a screech like the brakes of a rusted steam engine.

I look up to the podium and find Uncle Jimmy.

He swipes the knitted hat from his head; spindly hairs dance like wispy flames in a fireplace. His taupe-colored trench coat buckles around the shoulders and the chest. It's too big. Maybe it's not his. Maybe he grabbed it from the rack at the café the other day and made it his own. I wouldn't put it past him.

"I'm not the greatest public speaker," he says, holding the hat with both hands like a humble pauper. "I thought it might be nice to recite a poem. I believe it's appropriate for the occasion."

He glances at me. "I hope you like it."

A frightened smile bounces over my lips. *If he recites John Donne's "Ecstasy," I will kill him.*

He clears his throat.

The rain continues, determined to drench us.

I cannot wait for this whole thing to be over.

"It's called 'A Clear Midnight' by Walt Whitman."

Thank goodness for small favors.

Uncle Jimmy bows his head. He appears to be centering himself. Drawing the courage, maybe. Apparently he knows the poem by heart because he has no note cards. No soggy scrap of paper to read from.

"This is thy hour, O Soul," he begins, his voice resonating through the speakers. He pauses to scan the crowd of onlookers.

The forceful pattering of rain slows. I look up at the sky, which is gray and dismal. A colorless wet blanket.

> ... thy free flight into the wordless,
>   Away from books, away from art,
>   the day erased, the lesson done.

Like a crowd of talking people who gradually quiet, the rain has dwindled to nothing. The thrumming upon umbrellas has halted, and a hushed silence has become the backdrop to Jimmy's words. It's almost as if the mountain itself—the sky, the ground, the nearby chasm—is listening.

Jimmy continues in a louder volume:

> Thee fully forth emerging, silent, gazing,
>   pondering the themes thou lovest best—

He raises his face to the heavens, and the gray sky blanket cracks down the middle, then splits apart. A brilliant burst of sunshine spills through the tear. It rolls toward the crowd like a wave cresting upon the land, the light flooding my vision as it passes through me, taking with it my sadness like a layer of grit washed from the surface of my skin.

I'm light as air, relieved of the weight of misery.

Uncle Jimmy moves closer to the microphone, and the next words ring like bells in my ears:

Night, sleep, death and the stars.

I gasp and close my eyes. I don't know what it means, but my hair pulls up from my scalp and my body buzzes with bright energy. For a moment—for one astounding moment—I feel pure, sparkling goodness. That's all. *Dobrata.*

Maybe it's Andrew.

Maybe it's his goodbye.

His spirit soaring to the heavens.

I have to assume it is.

I open my eyes and scan my surroundings to see if the others experienced what I have experienced. If anyone looks as astounded as I feel. But it is business as usual: the sad assemblage awash in cold, damp air gazing numbly at the ground or at Uncle Jimmy. The sky above has returned to its previous form and color. Wet-blanket gray. Steady drizzle.

No one, as far as I can tell, is astounded at all.

15

The moon is enormous, and I can see Andrew's cute, roundy face in it.

It lights the deck, the weeping willow, the lake —everything I can see. Everything Andrew used to see. The day may have been dreary with drizzle, but tonight the sharp bite of winter has moved in and skies are clear. I have a sweatshirt over my black dress and Andrew's down jacket over that, a wool scarf around my neck, and a matching wool hat, and I'm wearing sheepskin boots instead of heels. The need for formality is over. Most of the Jovians and whatever guests remain at this gathering are drunk and enjoying the warmth of the family room's wood-burning stove.

"This is nice," Fran says as we pass through the back door. "I hate being around drinkers when I'm not one of them. Even if it is thirty-five degrees out here. You warm enough?"

"I'm used to it. Andrew and I came out here every night after dinner. You know how he is with the telescope."

Fran points to the right. "I see the sacred circle."

"Every house has to have one," I say, and then, "Does yours have one?"

"No, but then again, I'm not a Jovian and I've never owned a Starbright telescope."

The sliding glass door pulls open, and I turn to see who's there: Miranda and Leo hover just inside the door. She pokes her head out, her blonde hair highlighted by the glow of indoor lights. "Will you look at that moon? Oh, Leo, it's gorgeous."

"It's for Andrew," I say.

"Yes." She puts on a sad face. "Wow. It's cold out here. Wouldn't you rather be by the fire?"

"I need air," I say.

We smile at one another. I'm lucky to have such a nice neighbor and friend.

"Well, we're heading home. I wanted to say good night."

As I go in for a hug, I notice her tired-looking complexion, the overall puffiness of her face. She liked Andrew, and I can only assume she's been crying a lot. Leo reaches from behind Miranda to place a supportive hand on my shoulder. "Take it easy, kiddo. Call us anytime."

"Please do," Miranda urges me with raised brows. "We're only fifty steps away. I can be here in a flash for any reason, any reason at all."

"I will. I promise."

"I'll stop by in a day or two to see how you're doing."

"Okay." As my gaze lingers on her face, I fill with admiration for her. She's become like family.

"Nice meeting you, Fran." She waves at him and then turns to go but stops midstep. "Oh, Fran, I almost forgot: Caroline needs you inside for a minute. She wants you to put your number into her telephone."

"Yes, ma'am," he says, following them inside.

The sliding glass door closes. I start to walk away, and then I hear it slide open again.

David is there. A hopeful little zing rushes through my

chest before I realize he's not Andrew. David has been watching me from afar since the funeral. I'm sure it's hard for him to approach me, considering I'm the poor widow and he's a kid. Well, a young man. He must be twenty-one by now.

"Oh, David, you just missed Miranda and Leo. I wanted you to meet them."

"We met earlier." He closes the door and steps out. "Mind if I sit with you? Getting kind of stale in there."

"Of course. Fran went inside to talk to Caroline for a second. She wants his phone number, probably so she can stalk his baby."

I notice he doesn't laugh, and then Fran passes through the door rubbing his head. He must have experienced the Jovian jolt.

"David's going to sit with us," I tell him. I turn to David and say, "We're going down to the bench. It was Andrew's favorite place to look at the stars, and sometimes he would fall asleep there like an old homeless man."

I chuckle at my own joke and realize that being with Fran and David has made me lighter hearted. As much as that's possible.

The two of them follow me down the steps into the yard, and all three of us squeeze onto the bench together, which is no easy feat, considering I'm sitting for two and Fran is as wide as a hockey player. But it's good to be close because the winter chill becomes chillier for those who sit.

I keep waiting for Andrew to appear. My random thoughts tell me he must be talking to someone inside or he must be doing something for Caroline or using the bathroom or getting another drink. The new thoughts know he's not, and I'm glad for all of the people around me today to keep me from wallowing.

Now that I have David up close, I can study his face.

He's most like Andrew in his roundy cheeks and sandy hair. And though his eyes are a similar color, David's are sharper than Andrew's were. His overall countenance is sharper. He's also less readable. I can't tell what he's thinking. Probably because I simply don't know him as well as I know Andrew.

"So, David," I say. "There's something I want to ask you. You were adopted, and so was I. I'm wondering why we haven't spoken on this subject. Or do you not like to—"

"I don't mind." His head is tipped back, and he wears a pleasant expression, one of ease, contentment. "Everyone knows I'm adopted. I think they forget because I look so much like Andrew. Plus, I went from birth parents to Jimmy and Constance the day I was born."

Slowly, he turns toward me, evading direct eye contact like he always does. "Do you mind that I mentioned how I look like him?"

"Can't exactly hide it, man," Fran says.

I shake my head. "I like it. Andrew did, too."

I expect David to give me a smile or make some wordless connection with his eyes or reach out and touch my hand or shoulder, but it doesn't happen. He simply tips his head back again and gazes upward with that astronomer's look of satisfaction.

He's not the usual David tonight, not the eager-to-please fellow I've come to know. Come to think of it, we've always been drinking when I've seen him in the past, at family parties and holiday celebrations. It's understandable that I'm seeing a different side of him. The death of a favorite cousin would do that to anyone.

"Your father gave a nice eulogy today," Fran says.

"He did," I say. "Before he spoke, I was nervous about what he had planned, but it touched my heart."

Once again, David returns my emotional gaze with a stoic

one. His blue-green eyes avoid mine, and more than that, they express nothing. They're not the eyes of Andrew at all.

"It was nice," he says.

He's definitely more Jovian than Andrew ever was. I had thought about sharing the experience I had during the funeral ceremony, how I saw the sky open up, but I'm afraid he'd look at me as if I were crazy.

"I wanted to ask you," David says, "now that you're alone, where will you live?"

Now that you are alone is not a phrase a new widow wants to hear, but I don't think he means to be rude. Besides, I feel like Andrew is still close by. Maybe even watching over me. And what is the rush with all of these people? Caroline asked the same question this morning.

"This was my home with Andrew. I'm not leaving it, not for a while, at least."

Fran places his hand on my arm.

"I thought because you're pregnant you might want to be closer to family and friends," David says, as if it's a no-brainer and I have no brain of my own.

"You mean leave Ashbury Falls? And, what, go back to Kirksberg?"

He sits up straighter. "I thought you'd want to be with us."

I *don't* want to be with them. If I move back, they'll swarm me like bees.

Fran gives my arm a little squeeze. "You know, Svetlana, maybe you should think about moving back to Kirksberg. You're going to need help with the baby."

Andrew and I never told him why we left Kirksberg. He and Lisa knew Uncle Jimmy showed up at the door far too often, but we never told them the extent to which he and Caroline pressured and bullied me. As good friends as they are, we didn't share the family business.

"You still have a house in Kirksberg, all set up and waiting for you," David says. "You lived there with Andrew, like you lived here with Andrew."

"Yes, I know." I blow on my cold hands, stalling for time. If I move back, I'll lose my independence from the family, my *space*. Uncle Jimmy and Caroline will be at the door every day. I can't. I just can't. And if David thinks I'll agree to this right now, he doesn't know me at all.

"Or if you wanted me or my mom or Caroline to, one of us could stay in your spare room, here, for a while."

"I don't have a spare room," I say in a blunt tone. "Do you mean my office?"

The family probably put him up to this. They want to control me.

Oh, Andrew, please don't leave me alone.

David hesitates before responding. He has to know he's touched a nerve. "I'm trying to think what Andrew would want. And I don't think he'd want you to be alone. Pregnant. On top of a mountain."

He wouldn't want me to live with his family, either.

Before I can think of a way to respond, David stands, raises his long arms, and stretches out his back. "I've had a headache all day. We can talk about this later."

"That's a good idea," I say in a more positive tone. "It's been an emotional day, and I can't think about the future right now."

Fran holds out his hand to David for a shake. "I'll see you later, man."

I stand and try to connect with David eye to eye, but he eludes me, as usual. "Are you okay? I didn't mean to snap at you."

"I'm fine," he says.

I give him a hug, but he's not too good at hugs, so I don't think it helps.

A few minutes after David leaves, the baby starts kicking. When I pat my belly, it presses into the place where my hand lies. Feels like a little foot. *Did I forget to eat again?* I've been eating more than ever, it seems, since the relatives arrived. Lucky for me and baby Sonja or baby Evander (my pick for a girl, Andrew's pick for a boy), Aunt Constant and Uncle Jimmy went food shopping and to Costco, and we're stocked for at least the next two to three weeks. If there's a snowstorm, I won't have to dig out of the house. I can stay here, in my bed, dreaming of Andrew.

I lean back on the bench and straighten my legs now that David has left us more room. Fran has been talking about little Max and the funny things he says, and it makes me want to hurry up and have this baby.

Maybe it will look like Andrew. I would love that.

"I'm surprised Caroline hasn't stolen your Max; she wants grandchildren so badly," I say, hinting at the negative feelings I have for my mother-in-law.

"Whenever I went to one of the Jovian parties, Andrew told me to guard Max with my life, so I did," he says, laughing. "Seriously. Lisa used to become really protective when we visited. Some kind of mommy paranoia always came over her."

"I don't blame her. Remember the day I first met you and you told me about your hair raising whenever Caroline greets you? Does it still happen?"

He rubs his hand over his short hair as if the mere mention causes the sensation. "Literally every time."

"I thought so."

"It happened earlier today when I met Miranda and her husband, Leo," he says.

My face drops into a baffled frown. "But they're not Jovians."

"Well, it happened."

This spoils my theory. I was thinking the Jovians' ancient DNA must cause a strange electrical storm in some normal humans' brain circuitry.

"What is the cause of it, do you think?" I ask, to see what he says. I can't tell him what I think. I doubt he'd believe it has anything to do with ancient DNA or aliens, and then he'd probably make me promise to go see a psychiatrist.

He puffs out his cheeks and shakes his head. "Beats me."

"What did Andrew say when you told him it happened?"

"He thought it was hilarious. Didn't want to believe it. One time he said I must be 'really sensitive,' which pissed me off."

"Well, I believe you. But it doesn't happen to me as much anymore."

"That's because you're one of *them* now."

Our eyes meet, and we hang onto the silence that follows his words until we both break into smiles.

"I'm *not* one of them," I say with a laugh. "Maybe I'm just used to it. Don't tell anyone, but I don't think I'm strange enough to be a real Jovian. Though Andrew was not strange at all. Maybe he was adopted and never knew it."

Fran's wide shoulders jiggle as he soundlessly laughs.

"But they *are* strange, Fran. I can't be more serious about that. Except for Aunt Constant. She's mostly normal."

"And all this time I thought Uncle Jimmy was your favorite."

"Uncle Jimmy," I say with a sigh. "He's starting to grow on me. I think maybe we can get along now that we live six hundred miles apart." I'd like to tell Fran what happened today, during the ceremony, but I'm not sure how to begin. I turn toward him. "I loved the poem he read today. It made me feel better in a way I'll never understand. Like, I know this sounds 'out there' but when Uncle Jimmy read that poem, I felt like Andrew was there, looking down or ..." I realize this is not a good description of what happened, but I can't find the right words, "present in that clearing. With us."

Fran's nodding, probably because I've said what everyone says at funerals. I'm tempted to tell him how I feel like Andrew has been communicating with me in his own ways, but he might think I am a silly widow, desperate for a sign from my dead husband. Seems better to keep it between me and Andrew.

"I think Uncle Jimmy's a good guy," he says. "He's definitely different, but he has a good heart. All the Jovians do."

I'm not so sure Caroline and Edmund do, but I won't say this out loud.

The baby has settled, and the sky has darkened. The moon moved farther away so the stars can shine. When I locate Orion's Belt, a wave of hopefulness washes over me. Andrew always searched for Orion first to get his bearings before looking for other constellations, planets, satellites, meteors. *I can't believe he's gone.*

I guess I've been silent for a while, and Fran says, "What are you thinking about?"

"Andrew," I say. And then I whisper, "Did you notice that Caroline doesn't even act like he is dead? She's been cheerful, 'everything as usual' since she arrived in Ashbury Falls."

"I'm sure it's denial."

"Right. But a funeral is where you're supposed to show your feelings. Did you see her cry?"

"I did not."

"She wore too much makeup to shed a tear."

"Yeah, but everybody grieves in their own way. She's a strong lady. She probably saves it for when she's alone, or with her husband."

"Maybe. But it doesn't feel right to me. And not only that, a lot of things don't feel right. Sitting here with you, talking, is the most normal I've felt since Andrew—" I put on the brakes, but it's too late "—left me."

If I wanted to make myself cry, I've done a good job of it.

And now Fran's riled as well. "He *didn't* leave you. If there had been a choice, he would be right here next to you." He reaches out and takes my hand. "Of course it doesn't feel right. It's *not* right. He should be here. He was one of the good ones." He shakes his head and groans. "I loved him, and I'm so pissed that he died."

I place my hand on his back. I've never seen Fran this upset. "I know, I know."

I give him a second for the swell of emotion to pass.

"Did you know Edmund had his scientists examine Andrew's body?"

Fran's face twitches with surprise. "Edmund's Starbright people performed the autopsy? Why did they do that, do you know?"

"Edmund doesn't trust the doctors in the hospital, I think. When they found Andrew, he hadn't been in a car crash. They say he pulled over and died of natural causes. They didn't even tell me how he actually died, you know that?" I say. "I'm afraid to ask."

Fran rests his hand on my shoulder. "It was his heart."

I suck in my breath, and my own heart flutters.

"A defect he probably had since birth. It just gave out. I'm sure no one wanted to break it to you."

"Oh … my … poor Andrew." I grab onto Fran to keep from falling into a well of despair. I'm crying again. I can't help it. "Thank you for telling me. You're a good friend. I don't know what I'd do if you weren't here today."

"Of course I'm here."

So his parents *didn't* know. Or they knew, but they never did anything about it. Maybe they couldn't do anything about it? I sniffle and wipe my tears. We sit back. I rub my baby belly and look up at the moon again, and think about my husband and his roundy face and how much I'm going to miss him.

"Are you okay?" Fran says.

"As okay as I can be, I guess."

"Yeah. I get that, but you *will* be okay. I know you will."

I turn to face him and give him a sad smile. "How long will you stay?"

He puffs out his cheeks, and I know I won't like his answer. "I'm in the middle of an investigation, like always. I wish I could stay longer, I really do, but ..." He looks down, presses his lips together. "I have to leave in the morning."

With that, I am whisked out of the modicum of comfort I'd found the moment before.

"And there's more," he says, avoiding my eyes. "I know this isn't the best time to tell you, but like I said, I'm heading out in the morning so—"

"Go ahead. What is it?"

"I've been transferred to DC. Lisa and I are moving."

Andrew has just died and already things are changing, moving forward, leaving him behind. Nothing stays the same. I drop my head, suddenly afraid for no reason I can put into words.

Fran grabs both of my hands and pulls me toward him so we're face to face. "DC is actually closer to Ashbury Falls. But it doesn't matter where I am. If you need me for anything, call me. Anytime, okay?"

"Okay," I manage, though I'm jittery and weak.

"Don't just say you will," he says in a tone that borders on harsh. "Make sure you do it."

I want to take him up on this. I want to latch onto him, to

feel his support, but I know I have to be strong on my own. I can't be a third wheel on someone else's marriage.

"Same goes for Lisa. Whenever you want to talk, whenever you have a question about the baby, or whatever, she wants to be there for you."

"Thank you. Tell her thank you for me. I'll stay in touch."

I won't tell him how bad my record for staying in touch with people is.

He sits back. "And don't be polite about it. I don't care what time it is. Between work and Max, I'm up pretty much around the clock these days."

"I'm sorry to hear that, but I promise not to be polite."

"If anyone so much as looks at you the wrong way, I'll take care of it."

That makes me laugh for a second. But I'm not the type to bother someone else's husband.

"Andrew would have done the same for Lisa." He grabs my hand again, this time to look at my wedding ring. "The moonlight glinted off this thing and nearly blinded me. That's some rock he gave you."

I smile. "I think it came from outer space."

"No doubt. An asteroid maybe?"

"I wouldn't put it past him," I say.

In the morning, while I'm toasting an English muffin, not yet out of pajamas, my hair wishing for a brush, Aunt Constant shows up at the front door. Uncle Jimmy's rent-a-car idles in the drive; I can make out his high forehead behind the wheel.

I open the door to a cold wind that blows back my hair and draws tears from my eyes. Why does every gust of moving air make me feel like Andrew's trying to tell me something?

Aunt Constant remains outside. She's wearing rust-colored corduroys and a white knit sweater. "I wanted to try one last time to convince you to come home with us."

"Oh, thank you, Aunt Constant, but I can't leave yet. I'm not ready."

I'm staying here with Andrew, thank you very much.

"If you change your mind, please call us. I'll be more than happy to make all the arrangements for the transportation of your things."

"You'll be the first one I call. I promise."

She smiles her wobbly cheeked smile. "We're going to check up on you quite a bit. And David will be working up here from time to time, so he'll drop by. Don't hide from us, Svetlana. We want to help."

The David thing bothers me. I feel bad about not wanting him to stay with me in this house. This is one of the many Jovian family homes, after all. I don't own it, and neither did Andrew. Aunt Constant has been so nice, the least I can do is give her an explanation: "I'm sorry I can't let David live here."

"It's fine. We just wanted to offer."

"You've all been so nice," I say, for lack of a better word.

"We only want what is best for the baby. And you, of course."

"I know."

"Make sure you drink lots of milk."

It's sweet of her to worry. "You're my favorite, you know this?" I say with a laugh.

"And you know that my name is Constance, not Constant?"

She has never corrected me before, so I'm taken aback. "Sometimes I forget. But, yes, I know." I wonder if she is angry. Her face is sort of blank. "It's only that Andrew thought it was funny when I mispronounced …" I try to explain but can't find the words fast enough.

She reaches the car and waves one last time before getting in.

As soon as I lock the door, I abandon the English muffin and run back to my bedroom, to my wedding photograph and my strand of hair and Andrew's laundry, which I'll never wash. I leap into bed, kiss the wedding band that hangs around my neck, and grab his pillow. It smells only a fraction as strong as it used to.

But it is enough.

16

I was supposed to prepare the nursery. Caroline kept calling to remind me. I kept telling her I would get around to it soon. But I didn't. Months passed, and I still couldn't. I was too busy living inside my head. Enjoying Andrew's company, even if it was only a ghost of the real thing and our time together felt more like watching reruns of a favorite television show than it did real life.

One morning in May, when the sun shined brightly and the temperature climbed, I was surprised to see that the snow had melted and robins were running this way and that across the lawn. The petals of flowers giggling in the breeze unknowingly hurt my feelings. *Not yet*, I thought. *Too soon*. I'd assumed the harshness of winter would outlast my feelings of utter devastation and was in no hurry to move on, for the days to grow longer, for the Earth to tilt nearer the sun. I'd been content living under ice and snow and blankets, and could have done so for several more years. Or at least months. Unfortunately spring arrived in spite of my wanting to tell it to go back where it came from. By the time I accepted it, it was June.

Refusing to move forward is difficult to do when one is pregnant. There are doctor appointments and hunger to deal with—and shopping for new clothing becomes a necessity. But I've managed to remain sheltered and alone, for the most part: just me and the baby and my thoughts of Andrew.

At this point, my stomach ascends from my body like a mountain pressed up from the Earth's core. I cannot see my toes on the other side. It is June 8—happy twenty-fifth birthday to me. Not one person, Jovian or otherwise, has called to wish me a happy day, and that's fine. I am in no mood to celebrate, no mood to become older than I was when Andrew still lived on this planet.

Besides, I have an OB-GYN appointment, and Dr. Falugia is doing an internal exam because I have complained of backache. He wants to check my cervix for changes.

"It hasn't softened," he says when he's done. "You can sit up now."

As I do, he says, "So, how's it been going otherwise? Feeling good?"

I have little to report, which I'm glad about. "It's hard to sleep, but that's not new. And I can't sit too long or I start to lose my breath. But I've read this is normal?"

"Yes," he says as he attaches the stethoscope to his ears and listens through my stomach wall. "Any contractions?"

"A few. Not many. Once in a while. He moves a lot."

Soon after Andrew died, I asked to know the sex of the child. I wasn't surprised when I was told it's a boy. I was glad because I can name him Evander, the name Andrew wanted for him.

"Moving ten or more times in two hours is a good thing."

"Then it's a good thing," I say.

"What else?"

"Honestly, I can't wait for my due date."

He smiles. "You're in the final stretch, so I'm not surprised to hear it."

"Not quite," I say, hoisting myself to an upright position. "I'm due next month."

The doctor's face forms a question. "Are you certain? Looks further along to me. Let's check your chart—Amy?"

The elf-size nurse hands him the paperwork with no expression at all. Probably thinking about what she'll cook for dinner tonight. The doctor browses midway down the page. "Your son is over nine pounds, Svetlana. You're growing a rather large child. And he gained two and a half pounds in the last four weeks."

It's more a question than a statement, and I don't know the answer. That seems like too much. Can this be? I sometimes wonder if Dr. Falugia and his nurses know what they're doing. Then again, the baby's sudden weight gain could explain the mountainous stomach—it's noticeably bigger than the one I carried last month. "Is this bad news?"

So far, Dr. Falugia has downplayed every concern I've ever had, and I expect he will do the same now.

"Not at all, not at all," he says, regaining an air of professionalism. "You must be hungry these days. Have you been eating a lot?"

"Like a pig."

I am too tired for politeness.

He pages through the chart, then returns to the most current information. "The baby is twenty inches. That's more in the range of overdue than ninth month."

My ears prick like a rabbit's. "Does this mean he'll come early?"

Please say yes.

Dr. Falugia hands the folder back to Nurse Amy, who's nodding with confidence. Apparently she thinks so.

"Not necessarily," he says. "Be sure to take note of the

number of contractions you have, and head over to the hospital if you get more than four per hour."

I say okay, but the idea of having more than four contractions an hour makes me sweat under the arms. Could this be happening so soon? Or maybe this is a precaution on the doctor's part.

"You and the baby are both healthy. You'll be fine," he says.

The door to the room cracks open with the *tap-tap* of someone who's trying to be polite, but I still startle. It's Jessica, the nurse who makes the sonograms, and her down-turned mouth gives away her distress. "Dr. Falugia? We have a situation."

"Okay, well, we're about done here."

"Are we?" I want to say, but I don't.

He steps back. "Take care, Mrs. Jovian. Call me with any concerns."

He rushes out, and I turn to Amy, still standing before me. "I suppose someone is in labor."

She lifts my folder from the counter. "I wouldn't doubt it. The moon is full."

"The moon," I say, wondering why that should make a difference.

"More babies are born on the full moon than any other time of the month. I'm surprised you don't know that."

"Why would I know that?"

She drops her gaze to the floor suddenly, like a self-conscious teenager. "Being a Jovian and all."

"Oh." I get down from the table. "Right."

I don't hum a melody in the car on the drive home. Nor do I tune in to a radio station. Not today. Today the wheels of my mommy brain are spinning. Dr. Falugia has all but said Evander is ready. Does that mean he could show up any day now? Sometimes I wish Dr. Falugia were a little less laid-back and a lot more specific. I thought I had at least another month before I had to worry about four contractions per hour.

Why can't you be here? I ask the Andrew in my mind. *I'm so nervous. Not that I can't handle it, because I know I can, but because … I don't know why. I'm nervous for no reason. And I wish you were here. I always wish you were here.*

I no longer feel that I can backstroke through time and touch my husband. He has slipped away like a kite cut from its string, blown into the heavens, far away from me.

But that doesn't mean I can't talk to him whenever I want to. I speak to him often. Maybe he can hear me. I thought I heard him this morning, like the last time when he told me not to panic. This time he said, "You're going to be a wonderful mother."

It was definitely his voice. His words. And it gave me confidence, at least for a little while. If he is watching me from above, I want to make him proud. I am grateful whenever I hear his voice, whether I am making it happen or he is.

I'm not always alone. Miranda and Leo drop by almost every day. I'm lucky to have them nearby, and I'm grateful for their friendship. I wish my job at the Montessori School had come through, but the woman who gave birth changed her mind about staying home with her baby. She took only two weeks of maternity leave, so I wasn't needed. Since I was pregnant and in mourning, I didn't care. Mrs. Lewis says she'll let me know when she has another opening, and hopefully I'll be ready.

I'm thinking I should try my parents again on the phone. Even if I don't get a response, I continue to try. Eventually I'll get lucky and reconnect. We have to.

As I pull into the driveway, once again, someone is standing at my door. Today it is the Andrew look-alike, young David. I park and grab my purse. Getting out of the car has become a big to-do for me. I hoist my legs over the side and use both arms to push my behind out of the seat. My arm muscles are more toned than ever.

"Well, hello, Mr. Jovian," I say. "What brings you to Ashbury Falls?"

The sun is shining in his eyes, which have narrowed down to slits, and he gives me one of his small smiles, though most of his smiles are small. "I'm checking on you, as per Caroline's instructions."

That's what I love about David. He comes right out with the truth even if it sounds rude. Like the other Jovians, he has forgotten my birthday, and that's perfect. I'm twenty-five with no intention of celebrating.

Caroline sends David to see me at least once a month. I still feel bad when he stays at a hotel, but I don't want him to stay with me. He looks too much like Andrew, and the idea of sleeping under the same roof with him when no one else is around feels wrong.

I unlock the door and say, "Well, here I am. All five hundred pounds of me and my oversize baby."

"You look good," he says in his usual reserved manner. It has taken me some time to get used to non-party David, but I do like him. He's sweet in his own way. And caring, in his own way. He always asks how the baby and I are doing. Are we eating enough, sleeping enough? Do we need anything? He brings organic vegetables and free-range chickens and milk, always the milk.

Today he follows me inside with a couple of bulging canvas grocery bags. I see carrots, heirloom tomatoes in colors like deep purple and orange, green beans and Brussels sprouts. Brilliant red peppers.

"Did you have a doctor's appointment?" he asks.

I put my purse down on the breakfast bar. "Yes, I did. And guess what? I have a very large baby growing inside of me. A ten-month baby to be exact. Not a nine-month like he should be. And to tell you the truth, it's giving me a backache. Would you like a drink? Water, iced tea?"

"No," he says, lifting the bags onto the counter. "Will he be here soon?"

A few weeks ago, I slipped and referred to the baby as "he" in front of David, who picked up on it like a dog with perked ears. But revealing the secret isn't a big deal at this point, considering the little guy with his tiny wee-wee will soon be out and about for all to see. I swore David to secrecy, and even if he didn't keep it to himself, no one has acknowledged knowing.

"He may, David. He very well may."

"But that's good, right? Because you look like you wouldn't mind losing a few pounds."

I have removed the peppers and green beans from the bag and am midway to the refrigerator when it dawns on me that he's trying to be funny. When I turn, he grins off into the distance and emits an air chuckle.

"You told a joke," I say. "I knew you had a sense of humor in there."

He's nothing like Uncle Jimmy, who's always laughing, and Aunt Constant, who's always sweet. But then again, they're not blood related.

"Normally the funny stuff only comes out when I drink," he says.

I put the vegetables in the bin and grab a bottle of water, then stand across from him at the breakfast bar. I pat his head. "That is cute. Have you been drinking today?"

"Oh, no. That's not what I meant."

He's so serious. I want to tell him, "It's okay. You can relax around me." Instead I say, "I'm only kidding with you."

I gulp the cold water, suddenly thirsty. It gives me a painful cramp in my forehead that makes me double over and moan.

David eyes me like a curious animal. "Are you okay? Do you need an ambulance—"

The pain recedes, and I'm able to stand straight again. "What? Oh, no. I only drank too fast. This is freezing-cold water. I'm fine."

"You said he might be here soon," he says, sitting back in the chair.

"I don't mean *today*. God, I hope not, even though Amy the nurse says it's a full moon. Is it a full moon tonight, David?"

"Yes."

Of course he knows.

"Well, he may come in a couple of weeks," I say, rubbing my lower back. "If he comes sooner than that, I will be surprised. Full moon or no full moon."

David has the look of someone who's holding back something he'd like to say.

"What is it?" I ask.

"Maybe I should stay over."

I can see that I've worried him. "Oh, no, no, no, David. I'm sure tonight is not the night—"

"I could sleep on the couch."

"I shouldn't have said anything. Honestly, I'm fine. He's not coming. A woman knows these things. Please don't worry."

The contractions began some time ago. Maybe three hours. At first I convinced myself they were the false kind, but now I've had three tsunami-strength labor pains in the last hour and the medicine I took for my back has yet to make any difference.

I need to pack a bag for the hospital in case this is really happening, so I head into the bedroom. From the closet, I pull out Andrew's backpack on wheels, unzip it, and toss it onto the bed, then go to the dresser to gather the clothing I'll need: the robe Miranda bought me from her sister's shop, pajamas, underwear. When I bend for my slippers, my midsection balls into a fist.

Not again!

This can't be happening.

Where's my cell phone? I think I left it in the bathroom.

I shuffle a few pained steps to my night table and swipe the cordless house phone from its surface. It's only by chance that it's sitting there considering I rarely use it. David called someone when he came over earlier, so he must have left it in here. But why was he in my room? As I'm thinking this frivolous nonsense, the fist in my midsection reaches full strength, weakening my knees so that I lower to the carpet. I'm lying on my side on the floor, and I can't stop myself from howling like an injured animal.

It has only been ten minutes since my last contraction. Amy was right: the moon is doing its best to raise the tides of my amniotic fluid and pull the baby out of my womb.

Andrew said I will be a wonderful mother, so I know it will be all right.

Miranda's number is keyed into speed dial for emergency purposes. Number 2. I remember when she did that for me, and I told her it wasn't necessary. And now here I am, calling her because Evander is on his way. Number 1 is still Andrew's work number, though they have long ago taken his voice mailbox away. His number is not the number I need right now. I suck in a breath and press the 2 with my thumb.

Miranda picks up right away. "Please tell me you're dying for company," she says in her usual twang.

"I need you," I say in between gulps of air.

"Sveta? Oh my gosh, what's wrong?"

"The moon is—" The pain whisks my voice from my throat.

"Hold on, honey! I'm running out the door. Won't take but a minute to get there." Then she yells, "Leo, it's Sveta. I've got to go."

I hear shifting sounds of movement and Miranda's heavy breathing as she runs. I'm still on the floor, and I don't know if the front door is unlocked.

"Okay, okay," I say as the fist starts to let up. "You can slow down. It's passing. It's, wow, that was ..."

"I'm almost there," Miranda says, huffing and puffing.

"Please don't hurt yoursel—"

Something thumps against the front door. And now I believe I hear Miranda's slapping palms. I use the bed for leverage, pulling myself to a stand, and carry my weighted middle down the hall, one hand holding the phone to my ear, the other wrapped around the bottom of my baby belly.

I turn the latch and lean against the adjacent wall, still breathing like I'm coming off several flights of stairs.

"I need to go to the hospital," I say.

Now that she's in front of me, Miranda has regained her composure. Her movements are slow and thoughtful, not at all harried. Probably because she wants me to remain calm. "Are you sure it's not Braxton-Hicks? They can be convincing."

"That was the fifth contraction in an hour. Doctor said more than four and I should—" I'm hit with the start of another wave of pain. This one moves even more swiftly, curling my toes and making me grit my teeth. I lower to the living room floor.

"This will be …" *Oh God, oh God,* "number six." I barely squeak out the words.

Miranda takes the phone from my hand. "I'll make the call," she says.

17

The cry of a bird rouses me. At first the image of a seagull comes to mind, but then the bird calls out again, and I realize it's a crow. I can imagine its glossy black feathers as dark as the buzzing space inside my head. *Am I asleep?* Whatever dark demon hovers inside me makes it hard to think. *Was I in an accident last night?* I'm sore all over. My brain feels stuffed. Heavy. *Where is Andrew? Where am I?* Something has happened, but I don't know what. I'm on my side with my face in the pillow. I can't lift my head. When I try to turn over, my body doesn't cooperate. It weighs too much. My eyelids won't budge. I'm stuck in the buzzing dark. The wind whips around the corner of—*where am I?*

The crow caws again, sharp and ominous, a cry that cuts through the black buzz in my head.

I cough, and my body spasms. Shooting pains cross my abdomen. I reach for my baby belly, but it's changed. I'm lying on top of a heating pad. *What's happened? Where is little Andrew—or, no, we decided on Evander.* I am no longer pregnant. My hair stands up straight from my head. I remember that Andrew is dead and open my eyes.

The light hurts my brain. *Where the hell am I?* I twist around, withstanding the crush of pain that turning from stomach to back causes, like a blade ripping from ribcage to loins. I'm a human wound, panting the way I might had I been stabbed. A moment of stillness, and it becomes more bearable. I open my eyes again. *I must be dreaming.* I'm in a bed with white sheets and blankets, in a room of gray stone laid like oversize brick. Opposite the bed, there's a window and a door. To the left, a four-drawer dresser with a framed photograph on top. *My wedding photo?* A small metal urn and plastic vial sit beside the picture: Andrew's ashes and strand of hair? I reach for his wedding band hung from the chain around my neck, but it's gone.

What the hell is going on? This isn't a hospital room. Where are Dr. Falugia and Nurse what's-her-name? Where are Miranda and Leo? Where's David?

I call out, "Hello?" but my voice is small. I'm alone in this stone room. Alone with my staggering heart and shooting pains that feed the awful headache in my brain. *Why can't I remember anything? Where's my baby? Could he be—?* No, I can't think it. He's alive. He has to be alive.

I remember nothing about the birth. Only the contractions and the full moon, and how Miranda came to help. I writhed in pain while she called an ambulance.

I sit up as best I can while my stomach muscles complain and my breasts bump together. The space between my legs burns, and I still myself, waiting for the flames to tamp down.

Where's my baby, my Evander? What happened to him? Is he alive? Please don't tell me he died. Where have they brought him? Where am I?

"Help me," I say as loud as I can.

To the left of the dresser of drawers stands a wheeled tray, a wicker hamper, a pair of white slippers. This is not a hospital. *Who brought me here?* Miranda was the last one I saw, the one I called, the one I trusted. "Miranda?" I try to shout, but it's a whisper.

My pulse swells in my ears. Maybe if I shut my eyes, I'll fall back to sleep and wake up in the hospital. But what if I don't? What if I'm not dreaming?

Where's my baby? Where's Evander? Why have they taken him from me?

I'm so tired. It's like I've been drugged. I sink into the mattress as if it were a bed of sand, and pass out.

Again, the bird caws. This time I open my eyes right away. I have been sleeping on my back. The ferocious headache has receded and now merely hums. I push up on my elbows, but even this causes the muscles in my middle to scream, the space between my legs to smolder. Droplets of sweat rise from my brow. *Where's my baby?* In front of me loom the same walls of stone. The dresser with photograph, urn, vial. The cart and slippers and hamper.

"Where am I?" I say.

No one answers.

"Hello?" I call. "Somebody help me, please."

I hear the murmur of voices. The cry of an infant. *My baby?* The sound propels my nerves to urgent heights, and I fumble out of the bed, only to be brought to my knees by the pain in my lower half. I crawl the rest of the way to the door and press my hands against the wall to brace myself as I struggle to stand. The white nightgown drops full-length past my knees. I punish the door with my fists. "Let me out of here!"

Tears leak from my eyes.

I hear nothing on the other side of the door. No one. Perhaps I imagined the sound of a baby, the murmur of talking.

The floor is cold against my feet. My tears have wet the neckline of my nightgown. My body doesn't feel like my own. *Where's my baby?* I'm shivering. Feverish. I wrap my arms around my middle as I succumb to a wave of nausea.

Why can't I remember what happened?

I stagger to the window. Not clear glass, but a dark tint. Only a dim shade of light filters through, not enough to brighten the room. Through it, I can see that I'm high above the ground. I would guess four stories. Below looms a landscaped yard with mounds of bushes, tall trees, exotic plants that seem out of place. It's too pretty for the surroundings of a hideout or prison. Everything appears in shades of gray, but I can tell the sun is shining. The sky is probably blue. A thick lawn rolls downward, meeting with patio stones.

Where is Evander?

Why am I being held hostage in a beautiful place?

Something about the perimeter of flowers brings a shiver up my spine; the blooms have a single head and long, gracefully curved leaves. All of them crowded together in perfect rows.

I scratch at the plastic covering and am able to peel back the size of a penny. Through it, I see that the flowers are yellow and red and pink.

Tulips.

The only tulips I know grow at Chateau L'Origine.

I passed out again soon after my excursion to the window. While I slept, someone was here. I heard them close the door when they left, and I struggled out of bed, my foot stuck in the twisted sheet. Once free, I rushed to the door and put my ear against it, then banged on it with my fist as I begged them to come back.

They had left me a tray of food next to the dresser, on the metal cart. A peanut butter sandwich, glass of milk, slice of apple pie.

Apple pie?

Have I really been kidnapped?

Andrew's parents are rich, so maybe the kidnappers think the Jovians will pay a large sum for me and my baby. I have no doubt Caroline will pay any amount for the return of the grandchild she always wanted. If he is alive. *He has to be alive!* Could Miranda be the kidnapper? Or maybe somebody barged into the house, pushed Miranda aside, and whisked me away? I can't remember anything after Miranda called the ambulance.

I'm suddenly starving. I'll be able to think more clearly when I have food in my stomach.

The sandwich goes down easy. I rise from the bed and stand beside the window. The sun lowers in the sky like a watery, glowing orb through my tinted window. What time does the sun set? It must be around seven or seven-thirty. A mother deer appears on the grass, cautious, with ears pointed and alert. Her baby follows close behind. They nibble the bushes at the edge of the drive. I tap on the glass and both of them straighten up, check all around. "It's not you who are in danger," I want to say. But they don't see me. I'm high above the ground, locked in a stone tower without my baby.

It is enough to make a person crazy.

I'll soon have to use the bathroom, and this creates a worry. Do they expect me just to go wherever? What kind of people are my captors? I'm thirsty. I found some bottles of water on the bottom shelf of the cart and I want to drink—but then I will need the bathroom, so I don't know what to do. And I don't want to sit around in this nightgown. I have a vulnerable, naked feeling. The burning in between my legs is much better now than when I first woke. A thick pad covers my underwear, and it is in need of a change. Again, who is caring for me? Or maybe *caring* is the wrong word. Yes, definitely the wrong word. *How are they feeding my baby?* I suppose there's formula for that. I had wanted to breastfeed—my milk will be here soon, and then I'll be even more uncomfortable. I told Andrew I would breastfeed for two months for the purpose of good immunities. If only Andrew were still alive. At least I would know someone was searching for me.

A knock at the door startles me, and I consider falling back onto the mattress and feigning sleep, but I'm too late. I'm fully upright as the door opens, and Caroline, beautiful clothes and all, steps in.

"Svetlana, how are you feeling?"

Baffled, I stare her down. I don't know where to start or how to respond. What the hell is happening? Who are the kidnappers? What is *she* doing here?

"I'm sorry if you were frightened, but all of this is for the best."

She's so calm.

My heart thumps with rage in my ears.

I can feel my eyes bulging.

"For the best? Being held prisoner is for the best?"

I'm glowing like a flash of heat lightning. Like a fired gun. Like a brand.

She says nothing.

"Where's my baby, Caroline? What are you doing to me?"

She raises one graceful hand as if to say, "One question at a time." Her posture remains strong. As unemotional as ever. "Now, Svetlana, you know I would never hurt you or the baby. I couldn't let you take him to that awful hospital."

As usual her explanation strikes me as phony. An excuse. A cover for some truth she doesn't want to reveal.

My heart's speeding, and right now I'm doing all I can not to lash out. "The hospital was perfect," I say with a shaking voice. "Andrew said it received five out of five stars. I wanted to go there. I would like to go there now, actually. Please take us there."

Her expression remains the same. "What I'm trying to say is that your baby is special and deserves the very best, which is why—"

"You drugged me so that you could bring me here and make me miss my child's delivery." I smack my own forehead.

When I look up, she's standing there like a full-body portrait. No response whatsoever.

What kind of bullshit is this?

"Where's my baby? Is he here? Bring him to me. Please, Caroline. I need to see him." My voice fills the entire room. I'm shaking so hard it's difficult to breathe.

She frowns as if I am a rude little girl.

"Caroline, please," I say, my voice quivering. "I would like to feed him. And I'm going to need a bathroom for myself."

About this, Caroline smiles. "Yes, of course. From now on the door will be unlocked to the hallway, which leads to a bath at the end. You'll find everything you—"

"I *need* my child." Tears speed down my cheeks. "What are you feeding him? *Are* you feeding him?"

"He's thriving on the formula we've made for him."

I didn't want to feed him formula! What could be better than the milk of his mother? Who else is in on this scheme? I'm sure if Aunt Constant knew, she would do something about it. I need to call her. I need a phone, but I can't freak out and have Caroline walk away and lock the door behind her. No matter how desperate I feel, I must stay in control.

I clench my jaw in an effort not to become a raving lunatic. If anyone is a lunatic, it's Caroline. There is an ache in my heart that grows every second she keeps Evander from me. I'm afraid it may spin out of control, and I'll have a heart attack.

I sit back and swallow the bile that rises up my throat. "I need to see my child," I say. "I'm *dying* to see him, Caroline."

"Yes, well." She strides across the room to the one window available to me and touches the small hole I've picked out of the tinted plastic. "I had to see you first. I needed to make sure you were fit before I brought him in, and now that I see that you are …" She passes me a stiff smile of approval, like I've been a good girl and if I continue to behave, I will be rewarded. "You're such a young soul, but then again, so was Andrew."

Inside I'm groaning in agony. *What does that have to do with anything?*

She walks back to the room's entrance and opens the door wide. She points to someone down the hall that I can't see and says, "Bring him in."

Seconds later, a door opens and closes in the near distance. The *tap-tap* of footsteps precede a tiny woman in a nurse's uniform carrying a bundle pressed to her chest. It's Dr. Falugia's nurse. The elf. *Amy.*

She's in on it, too? And Dr. Falugia, possibly.

The bundle gurgles as she hands him to me. Evander's big, watery eyes find mine and latch on—we are finally together, and my jagged nerves flatten and fall away, the pain of longing melts and runs off. Everything inside of me becomes soft and warm. He is so plump and delightful, with sky-pink cheeks and baby sounds, and I can breathe again.

He has Andrew's beautiful, soft blue-green eyes.

I'm in love.

My heart can beat again.

"He's marvelous," Caroline says.

I will her words to disappear.

If she tries to take him from me, I will kill her.

I don't know when Caroline left us, but she let Evander stay. His body against mine is pure bliss. It's the happiest I've been since Andrew passed. I could gaze into his eyes forever. He has Andrew's roundy face, too. My brown hair color and silky texture sit on top of his head, but I know that may change. He's big. A big handsome boy. Sturdy. Not like the wrinkled newborns I've seen. More like a one-year-old child than an infant. Dr. Falugia was right when he said I was growing a large baby. And that's strange considering Andrew and I are both average size—and Evander arrived a month early. I wonder if being Jovian has something to do with it. Jovians and their ancient DNA.

"You are by far the best birthday present I ever got," I tell him.

He smiles at me. He gurgles and kicks his fat legs. I can tell that he knows who I am. He spent months inside of me before I gave birth and Caroline took him away. I have no trouble nursing him; he seems to know just what to do.

He can already hold and squeeze my finger.

He's smart like his father.

When I observe him and the knowing look on his face, the way he focuses so intently on my every move, I have a feeling that somehow he already understands the world.

I gaze at him all night until I can't stay awake any longer.

———

In the morning, Evander and I are cuddling in bed when I hear a key in the lock down the hall. A door opens in the near distance and a few seconds pass before the wicked witch barges into our room in her business-as-usual manner. A silent girl follows behind with a tray and places it on the cart beside the dresser, then disappears.

"I've brought your breakfast," Caroline says.

I see that, but I don't wish to exchange niceties. There will be no thank-you for Caroline.

"I would like to see Aunt Constant," I say without taking my eyes off my sweet son. "Or to speak with her on the phone."

Caroline hovers over us, too close for my taste. "That's not possible at the moment. Perhaps tomorrow. I need to take Evander now."

I whip my head around and gape at her with fierce accusation. "How do you know his name?"

She takes a step backward. "Andrew told us before he died."

I sit up, hold Evander more closely to my chest. I'm ready to fight her, if I have to. "Told who?"

"Us. His parents. His family."

"But how could he have? We didn't even tell anyone I was pregnant."

"Oh, it was before he met you," she says. "We asked him to select a name."

Is she joking? Who does this kind of thing? And if it's true, why didn't Andrew tell me?

"That is strange, Caroline. And so are you."

I've never been so blunt, and I'm not sure how to

continue the conversation. The truth is, I don't care anymore for politeness. Politeness vanished when she took me from my home. There have been things I wanted to say to her in the past, but I held back for the sake of getting along. None of that matters anymore, so I take it a step further.

"You knew Andrew was going to die, didn't you?" I hope my words hurt. "You knew he had a heart problem."

She backs up a step and crosses her arms over her chest. I can't tell if she's upset with what I've said or baffled by it. She may be waiting for clarification.

"You hardly cried at the funeral. You and Edmund both. It's not normal, how you two reacted."

She bows her head. Shows the usual self-restraint. "I'm sure our behavior seems strange to you, but it's simply a matter of perspective. We have a different set of beliefs than you do."

"You don't believe that death is sad?"

"Nothing dies, Svetlana. Energy is neither created nor destroyed; it is only transformed."

I knew they had some out-there philosophy. And they probably have a strange religion to go with it.

"I don't understand what you're saying. I'm not a physics major. I don't work at Starbright."

"But you know enough to realize—"

"That you tell me nothing," I say, finishing her sentence. I should ask if she killed Andrew, or had him killed because of the file he read, but I'm afraid.

"What do you want to know?"

I guess this is my chance: "Did you ..." my voice quivers, "... kill him? Or have someone do it? Fran told me about Andrew's heart condition, but I don't know if I believe—"

"Kill him?" she says, loudly. "We desperately wanted him to live." Her eyes open wider than before, and I experience a rush of relief. It's the most genuine thing I've ever heard her say, and the resulting happiness darts from place to place in my body, too excited to settle.

Then she says, "You and Andrew could have had many wonderful children."

And like that, it dissipates.

It has always been about the children.

It was never about Andrew.

She never loved him.

How can this be?

She's waiting for a response.

I say, "Okay, well, you brought me here instead of the hospital. You took my child as soon as he was born. Where do you take him, by the way?"

She shakes her head and tries but fails to appear casual. "For a walk, for some fresh air."

"Without me? Without his mother?"

Her expression goes blank. Uncaring. "You've been recovering. I've done nothing that would not have been done had Andrew lived."

Her words singe my brain. "If Andrew had lived," I say through clenched teeth, "*none* of this would be happening."

She steps toward us and pulls back the blanket that has gathered in front of Evander's face. She's smiling on him, and I want nothing more than to carry him away from her, to go somewhere where she is not.

"Years ago, I gave birth to Andrew here," she says.

"Against your will?" I say. "Were you drugged, too?"

"What difference does that make?"

"A huge one, Caroline. How can you not know this? Did you have your baby here because you wanted to or because you had to?" My voice quivers with anger. Evander reaches up and touches my chin and neck. His baby cheeks flatten with concern.

Caroline grimaces in that "why can't you be easy?" way.

Of course she won't tell me. She's a kidnapper. Kidnappers never tell.

"You don't like that question? Well, I have many more. Like who else knows I'm here? I suppose all of the Jovians do, or have you and Edmund taken us on your own? Are you even married to Edmund? Are any of you Jovians really married?"

I'm not sure why I've asked these last two questions; I suppose they've been simmering below the surface for some time.

Caroline steps away, approaches the window. She looks through it, up to the sky. "What is marriage, except an agreement of one form or another? You are who you are. That's all. There is no ownership amongst beings. You know this better than most after what you've been through."

Yes, I know this all too well, and many other things. I know that I've been kidnapped by a crazy person and/or a family of them. I know that Caroline outranks Uncle Jimmy on the strangeness scale. And that Edmund most likely is not far behind them. For all I know, Aunt Constant may be, too. But I need her to be different. I need to call her so she can help me get out of here.

Caroline moves toward the entrance of the room and hovers there. "Your clothing is in the dresser. We brought comfortable pants and tops, pajamas, socks, underwear. If we have missed anything, let me know."

"How nice of you," I say in my deepest deadpan.

"James will be in to see you tonight, somewhat late, around midnight. Evander will stay with me and Nurse Amy after dinner."

"Midnight? I have a meeting with Uncle Jimmy at midnight? Should I bring my poetry book, or is it a meeting of the Cosmos Club?"

"It's important" is all she says, but even that makes me angry.

"Being with my son is important. I'll need to feed him."

"You can feed him beforehand, and if he gets hungry later, we have the formula."

The formula that renders me expendable.

"And how do I know you won't run away with him?" I say.

Her eyes bore into my own. "We're family. You can trust me more than anyone on this planet to keep him safe."

"But I don't trust you not to steal him. Don't you get that, Caroline?"

She always wanted a grandchild. She doesn't care that Andrew died. She no longer needs me now that I have given birth. She has the formula.

"When one owns nothing," she says, "there is nothing to steal."

That evening, Nurse Amy takes Evander. I let her only because I want to see Uncle Jimmy. I think I can probably convince him to let me call Aunt Constant. I head into the bathroom down the hall. It's small. Enough for a tiny sink, a toilet, a tub. White tiles all around. There are clean towels on the rack and soap in the dish. I draw the water. It's warm. The bathtub is not long enough for me to stretch my legs, but the sensation of floating feels wonderful to my postpartum body. When the tub is full, the water drips from the faucet and echoes to the ceiling. It's so quiet that I'll fall asleep if I'm not careful.

I'm easing down low, my earlobes dipping in, when I first hear someone talking. "Come on, Evander. Come on, baby boy. What a good boy you are." It sounds like Amy, and I suffer a spasm of jealousy because she's with him and I am not.

Somehow the sounds from below are reaching me, way up here at the top of the tower. But how? Is there anything below this floor? Is the sound of Amy's voice traveling through the plumbing all the way from the ground? Is the tower empty in the middle? A cylinder of stone? I'll have to ask Uncle Jimmy when he gets here. Not that he'll tell me. In the meantime, Amy gets to play with Evander, and I'm up here waiting for my strange uncle to arrive.

After I dress, I pass the time moping in front of my tinted window, staring at the grounds, which is like staring at a black-and-white negative. There's little outdoor lighting as far as I can see. Maybe a spotlight or two shining from the castle wall. Caroline left her watch on the dresser so I will know what time it is, and now both hour and minute hands near twelve. Maybe Jimmy, the absentminded professor, forgot this appointment. I open the door and prop it with the metal cart so I'll hear him coming.

Part of me wants to lie down and go to sleep. Another part is jittery with cold sweat and nerves. My mommy brain keeps reminding me that I don't know exactly where my child is. I wish they had left him here with me. I wish I'd refused to let him go, but Caroline is his grandmother. And I am kidnapped. I have no idea what they'll do to me—or him —if I don't do as they tell me.

It seems an eternity before I hear scuffling outside the door. A man's voice mutters *12:27, 12:27, must hurry, can't be late.* His head is bowed over his wristwatch as he stumbles over the transom and stops short inside the room. He wears the usual baggie pants, thin whirl of hair, and glasses that give him the look of a wise old bird.

His cheeks bulge as he smiles wide. "Well, hello, fine young lady. Congratulations on the dashing baby boy you've brought into the world. And you picked a good birthday for him, too. Very appropriate—very apropos as they say."

I don't care what he means by that. "The moon picked his birthday," I say. "I had nothing to do with it."

"But you know about giving birth on your own birth date, right?"

"Of course I do," I say, though I don't, and right now I don't care. I'm sure it has something to do with the tilt of the Earth and the constellations and dark matter floating above our heads.

"You and Evander will get along swimmingly." He grins like a crazy person.

"That is good to know, I suppose," I say in monotone.

He freezes, then juts his chin in question. "You're not happy."

"That is correct."

He takes one small step toward me. Doesn't want to frighten the doe before him. "What's wrong, if you don't mind my asking?"

"For one, Caroline has stolen my child."

"Oh, no, no, no." My words seem to have agitated his brain. "Your child is here. He's just in a different part of the chateau."

So, I'm right. I'm hidden away in the Chateau L'Origine like a cartoon princess. My memory flashes back to my honeymoon, the moment Andrew and I came upon one of the castle towers up close and said how "cool" it was.

"Do the Jovians own this place or something?"

How crazy this is!

"Um." He looks up to the ceiling. "That's not something I'm prepared to talk about. What I can tell you is that you and Evander will be together again as soon as we get back."

I whip my head in his direction. "Back from where? Are we going out?"

"Yes, yes, we are."

"Why?"

"We have to. There's no other way."

I didn't imagine we'd be going out. *Why would we need to go out?* "No one tells me anything. I'm glad I changed out of my pajamas."

THEY WILL BE COMING FOR US

"Me, too," he says so seriously I almost laugh.

"Where are we going?" I don't trust him, and I don't want to venture too far from Evander.

"Oh, don't worry, don't worry, it's good."

I frown as a grumbling sound rises up my throat. I can't help it. The politeness is simply gone. *Good for who?* I wonder.

"Please don't be mad," he says. "This is important, and you're going to like it, probably even love it. I set it up for you and for Andrew. I know how heartbroken you've been —" He checks his watch again. "Too much talking. We have to go."

It sounds like I may be heading to the afterlife to see my husband, which would be lovely except that I can't leave Evander with these warped people. They can do with me whatever they will do, but I'll fight to the death to stay alive for my child.

He offers me a hand up from the bed; his fingers are fat and warm. He loved Andrew, I know he did, in spite of his eccentricities and his bad social skills. Would he hurt me?

"We have to leave now if we're going to make it," he says.

I stand, but not quickly. I'm still fueled with low energy and discomfort in many different parts of my body. And I'm a little bit afraid because who knows? Caroline may have given him the order to take me into the woods and shoot me, so do I want to rush ahead with this plan? They don't need me anymore. They have the formula.

"Follow me." Uncle Jimmy takes the lead down the hallway to the door that is usually locked.

I don't want to follow him, but at the same time, I feel like I should. I need to know more about why this is happening to me, and right now he's my best chance.

My body doesn't move the way it did a few days ago. I no longer have the off-center balance of a heavy belly. But now my skeleton feels rusted and stretched. My middle and groin have improved but still have much healing to do. It's good to move, though not too fast. Around and around the dark staircase we go, like water spiraling down a drain. I was right about the tower's stone cylinder. There are no stories in between, only a medieval staircase that leads to the ground.

We reach the bottom, where Uncle Jimmy pushes open another door and takes my hand, guiding me through a dark, cramped passage and down another shorter staircase to the outdoors. A heavy wooden door opens to an influx of air.

I hadn't realized how damp and dusky the tower was until I breathed this wonderful air that smells of grass and dew and earth all mixed altogether. "I feel so much better out here," I say.

"Of course you do. Human beings are meant to get lots of oxygen. You know that."

The earthy scents make me miss my home on Steep Hill Road. The deck out back. Nights spent stargazing with Andrew.

"Come on, hop in."

He gestures to a bug of a car. A shimmering light-green color. I have no idea what kind of car this is. I have to hunch to get into the passenger seat without hitting my head. Will Uncle Jimmy harm me? Where are we going? After Andrew died, I felt he and I had made a connection, that we had come to terms with our disagreements on some unspoken level. I accepted him and his social strangeness and eccentricities. I believed he cared about me. And I love Aunt Constant. Would she let him hurt me, even if Caroline asked him to? I want to trust Uncle Jimmy, but why are we running out in the middle of the night, camouflaged in darkness, with no one around to see? Why not take me out in daylight with the rest of the world?

The car purrs to life, and Uncle Jimmy turns left, navigating the drive that passes the side of the castle and then around to the front entrance, which oddly is not well lit. "Why is the entrance so dark?" I say.

"This isn't the entrance," he says. "I mean, it *is* an entrance, one of them, but it's not the public entrance. There are many entrances."

He heads up the dark drive and takes a right onto the equally dark road. We begin to ascend, passing no other cars. I am jostled side to side in the seat, as the road curves and the engine labors. I reach for the hand grip above the window and hold on. My ears grow cloudy with pressure. The grasshopper of a car strains as it makes its way up and up.

"Where are we going?"

He points in the distance: "The highest peak."

"In Ashbury Falls?"

"Correct. Not the highest peak in the world because that would take too long to get to, and we only have seventeen minutes—and a ten- to twelve-minute hike yet to go."

"A hike? I don't know how well I'll do hiking in my condition."

"An amateur hike. You can manage. I'll help."

He's more insistent than I would like. What if I say I can't, or don't want to? Will he make me? How badly does he want to get me into the woods?

"I'm still weak from the delivery."

"It's fine. I'll carry you. Don't worry. It has to be tonight. The calculations are clear. We came up with the answer together."

The hairs on my arms rise with alarm.

"Who is 'we'?"

"Caroline, Edmund, myself." He sits up straight. Proud, maybe. Unfortunately I cannot share in his enthusiasm.

After about ten minutes of careening through the darkness, the car slows and Uncle Jimmy leans toward me to better see out the passenger-side window.

"What are you looking for?" I ask, nervous that he may drive into a tree.

"We have to get off right about …"

His words hang in the air.

A small break in the trees appears, and the car jolts to the shoulder and skids to an abrupt stop. Without a moment to settle, Jimmy pops open his door and steps out.

"This is where the hike begins?" I say, checking around as I undo my seatbelt. "Is there no trail head, or something to mark it? If we're hurt, people will find the car but won't have any idea which way we went."

Or where to find my dead body, should it come to that.

He has opened my door at this point and offers a hand up. "It's only ten minutes," he says, checking his watch. "Then we'll be where we need to be."

I'm out of the car and pushing my arms into the cardigan I'd tied around my waist. It's a cool mountain night like those Andrew and I used to spend searching for planets, our bodies close and warm, enjoying our time together. I suppose this wouldn't be such a terrible place to die, if that is why Uncle Jimmy has brought me here.

I can't decide whether to trust him or fear him, and whether I'm being paranoid or sensible. He could be a hit man for Caroline and Edmund. They're not even married. And she gave birth to Andrew in the chateau. And didn't cry at Andrew's funeral. I know she won't cry at mine, either. Still Uncle Jimmy may be eccentric, but a killer? I can't picture it.

"It's through here," he says, leading the way in his boots

and baggie pants. "It has to be dark, away from all of the lights. Hurry now. I know you're not feeling your best. Tell me if you want me to carry—"

"No," I say.

Last thing I want is to be that close to him.

We follow a vague path littered with sticks, needles, pinecones, one I would have veered off several times were I making this hike on my own. It winds around the trunks of trees of all different sizes. The piney scent wakens my senses and somehow makes me feel stronger. If I weren't so unsure about Uncle Jimmy and what he was getting me into, I might enjoy this midnight outing.

As it is, I hope not to find some strange ceremony going on at the journey's end—and I definitely hope not to become a human sacrifice.

"Almost there." He checks over his shoulder to see where I am.

After a few more minutes of walking with him waving me on, he pushes through a break in the forest.

I jog the last few steps to catch up, passing through the same opening in the trees. We have reached a clearing the size of a bedroom. Compared to the darkness of the forest, the moonlight that enters freely here fills the space with cool blue light that resembles water. At the center of this clearing is a circle of rocks with a telescope set up in the middle, similar to our wooden deck at home. Uncle Jimmy is gazing upward, and when I do the same, the stars spread before me like a thousand winking eyes.

A weight lifts from my shoulders, and some of the tension in my head siphons away.

"See?" Jimmy says. "I knew you could make it. You're a strong lady."

I've seen Uncle Jimmy's look of delighted eagerness before. When he used to come over to our house to show

Andrew something he'd located in the sky—a comet or nebula or one of the planets shining in a vibrant, unexpected color—he always took great pleasure in sharing.

So he wants to show me something.

I'm pretty sure he won't kill me.

"What are we going to see?" I say.

He does nothing to stifle a full-belly laugh. "I can't bring you all the way here for a surprise and then tell you what it is."

Like a bird that sticks out its feathered tail as it pecks the ground, he bends over the telescope and hovers in a "searching" stance. This telescope is bigger than those I have used in the past. Bigger than the ones we have at home and in Kirksberg. Getting it up here must have been difficult.

Uncle Jimmy searches in silence. It's the only time you can be assured of silence when Uncle Jimmy is around because the telescopes are so sensitive that the mere action of speaking words guarantees jiggles of air molecules that can shake the view off course.

I can't imagine what he wants me to see.

What could be so important ... unless this is merely a trick to get me away from Evander.

Still in bird position, he thrusts one hand in my direction and waves me over. "Okay," he whispers. "You have to look through and keep your sights to the left of Jupiter."

He backs up, and I take his place, bending over. The view through the lens is beautiful. Bright spots of stars, bursts of red-orange, fluffy light clouds of crimson and maroon. Space is far from black and white alone. "Jupiter is the reddish one?" I ask.

"Correct. Tonight it is. Now look to the left of Jupiter; you'll find Callisto. You know Callisto?"

"I think so. It's the bigger one?"

"Yes, that's it. Keep your sight on that empty space near Callisto. You see it?"

"You want me to keep looking at the place where there is nothing?"

"Exactly."

"Okay." I blink so that I can continue to stare. "Can I ask why?"

"You'll see," he says, all happy mischief.

Seconds tick by. My neck starts to strain. "I'm very tired, Uncle Jimmy. I'm not sure I can keep—"

"You have to. This is the best part, and you're almost there."

I take a noisy breath and stifle the urge to yell, "This better be worth it."

"Okay, okay," he says, "hooooold," drawing out the one-syllable word. "Keep looking at that empty space. Keep looking. Five, four, three, two—"

A tiny bit of light twinkles in the space where I have been looking, unfolding like the wings of a dusty moth in the place that a moment ago was black and empty. The little moth grows in size and intensity as it spins like an atom, its wings wrapping around itself. It is bright white and becoming a solid sphere before my eyes, twinkling with explosion and doubling in size. I believe I'm watching a star form. It's spinning in place, glimmering like simmering light, sparking and growing brighter every second, every breath, until it's so bright, I can no longer tell whether it is deepening in intensity, spinning or burning or ...

It has arrived. I feel as if I know this light. This light is strangely familiar. And happy. I know how bizarre that sounds. But I can feel its happiness. I think I know this star. My heart pounds with anticipation. A poignant sort of bliss washes over me. I'm eager. Hopeful. I love this star and want to look at it forever. Reach out and touch it. Pluck it from the sky and cup it in my hands.

"Is it—" I'm afraid to ask.

"Yes," he says. "It's him. It's your Andrew."

Euphoric.

That's the only way to describe my feelings right now. We are in Uncle Jimmy's grasshopper of a car, heading back to the chateau at normal speed, but my mind is up there in the little clearing near the top of the mountain. I'm still watching the part of the sky near Jupiter and Callisto, basking in that white light, that beautiful star illuminating the heavens.

When Andrew's star arrived out of nowhere, I knew for sure my spirit lies with his, that our souls are intermingled. They have truly become John Donne's *single violet transplant.*

I know this without a doubt.

I just do.

I really do.

My eyes know it. My head knows it. My spirit knows it. I would know him anywhere, in any shape, in any form, in any body. It is Andrew. Andrew has become a star.

I'm crying happy tears.

"Does it happen for everyone?" I say.

Uncle Jimmy takes his focus off the road; his glasses glint in my direction. "What's that, my dear?"

"Do all humans become stars when they die?"

A sad smile crosses his face, and I realize that I'm an ordinary person who married someone from an extraordinary family.

"No," he says, and he checks his watch. "We have to hurry and get you back. Caroline says you need your rest, and it's time for you and Evander to sleep."

I nod and grin and hug my knees to my chest because I need something to hold.

I'm too happy to sleep.

I may never sleep again.

————————

When I arrive back at the tower, Nurse Amy and Evander are there, along with a bassinet next to my bed. "He didn't want the formula," she says. "I think he was waiting for you to get home."

She may have smiled when she said it, but I'm not certain. She passes the baby, and he reaches for me with a clinginess that lets me know he has missed me. His baby laugh swells my heart as he hugs me and rubs his face into mine. I pull up my shirt so he can nurse.

He's heavy. Nurse Amy tells me he weighs almost twelve pounds.

I know this is not the usual for a newborn. When Evander was ready to be born, Dr. Falugia said he was over nine pounds. It's only days later and he's already three pounds heavier? I wonder what kind of giant he will turn out to be.

I don't remember my own parents being especially tall, but then again, I was a toddler when they died. Edmund is taller than average, so I suppose Evander takes after his Jovian side. And who knows what that might mean?

"Do you know why—" I turn to ask Nurse Amy, but she's gone.

"It's just me and you tonight," I whisper into Evander's ear.

He gurgles and makes a happy spitting sound.

"You love Mommy, don't you, Evander?"

When he's finished nursing, I lay him on his tummy in his bassinet, and he turns over and sits up like an older baby would. "Look at you! You're such a big boy." I wish I had my child development book from college. Before he was born, I had reread only half of it, and there are particulars I know I've forgotten. Could this type of behavior and growth still be within the range of normal? Is he advanced because of his large size—or is it something else?

He watches me as I remove my shoes and prepare for bed.

He calls out to me with burbles and coos, and raises his arms in my direction.

I lift him and carry him to the window. I point to the sky and say, "You see up there? That's where Daddy lives. Whenever we want, we can look up and find him." I pick off a bit more of the tinted plastic that clings to the glass of the window and locate the general cluster of stars that Uncle Jimmy pointed the telescope at. "Look through here," I say. He tries to see through the little hole, but I know he can't see what I want him to.

That's okay. I will continue to pick at the window.

Eventually Evander and I will have an unhindered view of the sky.

19

Caroline comes up each morning with the silent girl behind her carrying the breakfast tray that she places on the cart before leaving as quietly as she came. The girl's job includes tending to my laundry, taking away dirty dishes and garbage, and general cleaning. Never does she turn her mousy head in my direction; never does she acknowledge my presence. She wears a long dress with an apron, a maid's sort of uniform.

Four weeks have passed since Uncle Jimmy took me to see Andrew's star. I have lived in this tower for more than thirty days. A few nights ago, I heard fireworks booming for the Fourth of July, but I didn't bother to see if I could watch them brighten the sky. Fireworks don't seem so special when you've seen your husband's star take shape. It did remind me, though, of how much time has passed since I first arrived.

This morning, as I rock Evander in my arms, Caroline asks what type of books I like to read. Someone must have told her I've been bored up here. Probably Nurse Amy. It's easier to complain to her in more insistent ways than it is to complain to Caroline.

"I haven't read a book in ages, but something classic would be nice. *Wuthering Heights* or *Pride and Prejudice*. Or maybe something with an old, dusty tower. Maybe Rapunzel. Do you know Rapunzel, Caroline?"

She shakes her head.

"That is ironic," I say. I'm often sarcastic, but she doesn't seem to notice.

"And we need children's books. I must read to Evander. He requires mental stimulation."

"Of course. I'll get them."

"How much longer will we be here?"

"A week or so," she says.

Her answer is always the same.

But why are we here? What are we waiting for? I get no real answers. Probably they are waiting for something to pass through the cosmos. An asteroid or a pile of space garbage. Who knows? These relatives of mine, I realize, have their own space-related existence. They worship the cosmos the way Christians and Muslims worship their gods. The night I saw Andrew's star made me realize I don't care about them. He's watching over me and Evander. We're his family. Caroline and the others haven't tried to steal Evander from me, so I think we're okay—for now.

Still, it would be nice to have at least some of my life back. Some privacy and independence. To cook my own meals—not that their food isn't good. A car to drive my son to the playground or to my home, where I can come and go as I please without a team of black-uniformed security tracking my every move. (I've seen them in the garden trying to blend in with the shadows.) I feel sick thinking of all the ways Evander and I are prisoners. I'm not happy that I've given into this situation, but what am I to do? I don't know what they'll do to us if I try to run—and even if we did, where would we run to?

I suppose I can continue to complain. They can't keep us forever. Caroline says we'll leave soon. Where we are going is another mystery.

"I still don't see why we can't go home," I say for the thousandth time. "A child shouldn't grow up like this. Evander needs to go outside and see other children. Preferably in *daylight.*"

Momma's boy that he is, Evander bit the last three "playmates" who tried to take him outside and push him in the stroller (they use a bicycle lock to secure it to a tree outside so I can't use it without supervision): the silent girl was one of them, and her finger remains wrapped in bandages for several days now. (Yes, Evander already has several teeth.) It seems that he wants most of all to be with me. So they have allowed us special privileges. We may walk the grounds any night of the week after 8 p.m. under cover of darkness and the watchful eye of the black-uniformed security squad. And by "grounds" I mean the area surrounding the tower, which is mostly hidden behind the castle itself. As Uncle Jimmy said, we're nowhere near the public areas of L'Origine. I have yet to look through the window and find a wayward tourist lost in the confines of our secret garden with tulip-lined pathways.

Caroline knows I won't get far on my own with my fast-growing child on my hip and the diaper bag that needs to go with him, so I'm sure she doesn't worry too much about an attempted escape. The door to the staircase that leads to the ground floor is left unlocked during the evenings, when we do our walking around. And Uncle Jimmy installed solar ground lights to mark the paths.

It's a strange existence. There's no doubt about it.

Caroline stands at the window, taking note of the hole I have picked through the tinted vellum, now the size of a grapefruit. "We can't have anyone see you; you know that, Svetlana?"

Obviously. No one can know I'm being held here against my will.

"Who will see us?" I say. "Tourists aren't allowed back here, and even if they wandered over accidentally and saw us, do you think they would assume a kidnapped woman and her child were being held captive in one of the towers in the Chateau L'Origine? I can hardly believe it myself."

In the meantime, I need to see my husband through this window, even if all I can see of him is a vaguely familiar portion of the sky, in which he is one of many tiny specks of light.

"Maybe," she says, staring into the distance.

"More important, what if I need help? What if, heaven forbid, Evander has fallen and hurt himself? It would be good to have a way to contact you when the door to the staircase is locked, wouldn't it? I would like a phone."

"If you have an emergency, you can stomp on the floor. Someone will hear you."

"Stomp the floor?"

Her response is silence. Stillness. She gapes at me the way one might gape at an idiot who doesn't understand the simplest of concepts.

"I'm not sure someone will hear me," I say. "Last I checked it was a long way to the first floor."

I hope my tone bothers her and that my questions get under her skin. But somehow I don't think they do.

―――――――――

Last night, as Evander and I drifted to sleep, he said what sounded a lot like "I love you." Garbled, for certain, but the sounds were there. I didn't imagine it.

He's on the verge of five weeks old.

Everything about him—his body, his mental capacity—is accelerated to an obvious degree. He's not what they write about in the books. And he's surprisingly expressive. His eyes tell me everything I need to know. This morning, he suspects something's wrong. He's been watching me since I woke, calling for me to hold him, to lift him out of the bassinet.

I'm pretty sure he was watching me while I slept, too, and while I slept, I heard Andrew's voice again. This time, I was sure I would turn over and find him lying beside me, whispering in my ear.

He told me to get out.

He said they wanted to use Evander to do something terrible.

He said, "You must get away, Svetlana. You need to listen to me."

His words spin through my mind as I go about the morning routine with cold, scared hands and chills running up and down my arms. First, I change Evander, and then I feed and cuddle him. I put him in the bassinet so I can dress. Together we gaze out the window to see what the weather is like. The azaleas have bloomed out; their crusted flowerheads tire of these dull rainless days and wait for one of those angry showers to pound them into the soil below.

All the while I swear Evander knows something has happened, that Mommy is not her usual self this morning. He has a suspicious glint in his eye, a focus that's even more prevalent than his usual. "What is she up to?" he seems to be thinking.

Does he know that Andrew has told me to leave this place?

If he does, he doesn't have the words to say so. Yet.

The hours pass slowly.

My breakfast is delivered in silence.

Caroline doesn't come, which is a relief because I don't

feel like small-talking with her. It's also suspicious. She must have some business to tend to, and so do I. I'm considering how Evander and I can escape. Andrew says we must leave, and even if I only imagined or dreamed I heard his voice, it's probably true. We're prisoners here. Prisoners of our own family, and this is no way to raise a child.

Nurse Amy checks on us midmorning.

I tell her we're fine, and she leaves.

Normally she would find an excuse to hang around and play with Evander, but she must have something pressing to do because she stays for only five minutes. I wonder what's going on. Or maybe it's nothing. But Caroline didn't show this morning, and now Amy is in a hurry, so I do think it's something. Plus, I may be more sensitive because of Andrew's message, but I sense some strange activity in the air. Whatever it is, my feelings are not the usual.

Evander and I read books. We gaze out the hole I've picked into the plastic. We nap. He decides that today he will crawl. He's too young, but it's happening before my eyes, so I know it's true.

The silent one brings lunch. I say, "Hello."

She leaves without a response.

When she returns, I say, "You don't say hello?"

She stops what she's doing and turns around. Her wrists are as thin as broom handles. Her cheeks, soft with youth, suggest that she is maybe twelve.

"What's your name?" I ask in a friendly tone.

She bows her head.

"Don't be afraid. I won't tell them you spoke to me."

Still, the bowed head. This one is stubborn. Or afraid.

"I'm Svetlana, and this is Evander. I'm sure you already know who we are."

Her eyes flick toward the door.

"You can talk to me. No one is coming," I say with confidence. "Caroline would have come this morning, and Amy was already here this afternoon. Are you afraid of them?"

She says nothing, turns back to her cart, to the laundry in the basket, to the empty glass on the dresser's top.

I hold Evander up so he can balance on two wobbly legs. He's determined to stand. "What a strong boy you are." I kiss the soft patch of hair on top of his head.

The skirt of the girl's dress skims the floor as she picks up a toy here and there and places them in the crate against the wall. The room is in order, and I know she will leave.

"Wait." I lift Evander from the ground and ease him into the bassinet. Then I walk toward her, stopping a yard away.

I'm more than a foot taller than she is.

I squint one of my eyes to nearly shut. "I have something in my eye and no mirror to see it. Can you please tell me if something is there?"

The girl's bony shoulders rise a notch. For her, this is a dangerous request. She doesn't want to, but if she doesn't do what I ask, I may complain to Caroline or Amy later, and then she will be in trouble. It's a lose-lose for her. She points in the direction of the bathroom. "There's a mirror in the—"

"Please, I can hardly open it. Just look," I say, stepping up to her.

She nods, her small face so tense that it's pinched.

I use my fingers to wedge open my eye.

When she looks up, I feel no zap of electricity. No strange, hair-raising sensation. Her eyes are earth brown. Her face, heart shaped.

She's not one of them.

She's a little girl with small hands and skinny arms. My KGB mind has sized her up.

"I can't see anything," she says, "maybe splash some water in it."

"I will. Thank you."

She turns back to her cart, pushes it out the door.

"One more thing," I say.

She stops, her shoulders creeping up to her ears.

"You never told me your name."

"No," she says and continues on her way.

―――――――

Caroline shows up after our dinner. She pops through the door with a wide, more-plastic-than-usual smile. "How are we today?" she says, sounding like a schoolteacher.

I close the book I'm reading. Evander has been drowsing upon my lap, but with the flurry of activity that is my mother-in-law, he rouses. I say, "To what do we owe the pleasure of this change in schedule?"

"I visit my grandson every day. You know that."

"Not this late in the day."

"Oh, well, yes," she says. "I was busy overseeing the gardening this afternoon and unable to come at the usual time. And now I need to take Evander downstairs to the doctor's office for an exam."

"Doctor's office? The Chateau L'Origine has a doctor's office?"

"The wing we live in does."

"He was sound asleep. Can't it wait until tomorrow?"

Her gaze is steely. Even though I've given her her life's dream in Evander, she has yet to warm to me. "No, I'm afraid it can't."

"Well, I want to meet this doctor. Evander is my child, and I insist."

Caroline remains calm and seemingly carefree. "You've already met him. You may not remember. He came to see you when you first had the baby. You were understandably exhausted."

She has an answer for everything, and so do I: "No, actually, I was drugged. Drugged is not the same as exhausted."

I frown. I'm tired of this game, and I don't want her to take Evander.

"Why did you bring me here? Why are we locked in a tower?"

"Please, Svetlana, do we have to do this right now?"

"If you want me to stop asking questions, you should answer some of them. Have you ever been imprisoned, Caroline?"

"It's the best for Evander. I know you don't understand, but you have a very special child who has special needs. And you're not imprisoned. You come and go as you please."

"We go for walks in a garden that is guarded. That is not the same as being free." A fire smolders under my words. "Do you think I'm unable to care for my own child?"

"That is not what this is about. You're a wonderful mother."

Evander grumbles and makes a squawking sound. He's trying to stand, so I support his upper body. He can almost do it himself. When I grab around his waist, I notice his onesie is wet. "My special child needs a change."

Caroline backs up to the entrance of the room where she belongs. Evander flails his arms and legs as I manipulate the diaper around his bottom. It's a game to him. I'm kicked in the face or upper body every day. Not too hard, of course.

Soon as I'm done, Caroline is next to me and Evander reaches his arms out to her. I was hoping he would cry when she came for him.

She gets him situated on her hip and rushes toward the exit, heels tapping like rock hammers against the floor. The shoes are fancier than usual. "We'll see you in an hour or so. Why don't you take a nap or read the book I brought you? Evander will be back before you know it."

I want to run after them, to pull Evander out of her arms, to tell her that she can take him over my dead body—but it's important that I remain alive.

We have to get out of this tower.

20

I have been standing beside the window for at least fifteen minutes. The view is the usual. The path of solar lights stretches down the dark expanse of lawn into the gardens. I don't expect Caroline to return Evander in an hour. The vague "hour or so" she gave as an estimate most likely means she doesn't want to reveal how long it will really be.

Who schedules a baby's doctor appointment at night? And what wealthy homemaker oversees the gardening at a chateau? I can't see her caring about flowers or plants.

Caroline's excuses are lame. They have always been lame.

My nerves are up. Something must be happening tonight, and Andrew told me to get out. Why does Caroline need Evander? Have I made a terrible mistake letting her take him? What else could I do? I'm sick with regret and shaking with nerves.

I open the door to my room and pad down the hall, wondering if anyone below ever listens for me. The second door is closed and locked. This is not the usual. For a few weeks now, Evander and I have been allowed access to the garden after the sun has set.

I head back to my room, put on my sneakers, and gaze out the window once more, angry thoughts heating the inside of my head. The moon is up; the stars are like pinholes in the black fabric of the sky. I wish Andrew were here with me. *What should I do? You say we must leave, but when? How?* I wish he would speak to me.

A flash of light skips across the yard like a stone skimming the surface of water. Not one car has driven back here in all the days I have lived in this tower. I've seen mother and baby deer, a few blackbirds, the same fat squirrels, and that is all. The light disappears for a moment, but then returns, growing brighter. Maybe it's Uncle Jimmy come to see me.

A limousine slinks up, pauses, then makes a sharp U-turn before going back the way it came.

We have visitors. But why? Maybe it's the doctor for Evander. Would he arrive in a limousine? And if he's been to the chateau before, would he get lost and end up back here, where no one ever ends up?

I go around the room, grabbing supplies—diapers, a blanket, the cereal Evander snacks on—and throw them into the plastic bag that lines my empty garbage pail by the door. I place two bottles of water in there, too. If we do get the chance to get out of here, we'll need these things. Then I go to the bathroom and lie in the empty tub to see what I can hear. The distant chime of music rising through the pipes is a surprise. It's classical. The music mingles with the murmur of conversation, the clink of pots and pans and shuffle of footsteps. I can't tell exactly what's going on, but it's more moving around than usual. More talking.

A party?

Why would Caroline want Evander for that?

I return to my room and stomp the floor as well as I can in my sneakers. I have to get out of here and see what's going on. If Evander's in danger, I'll never forgive myself. I get on my hands and knees and pound the floor with my fists.

Nothing happens. Just as I thought. I could be dying up here and no one would come. I grab the hardcover book from my bed and drop it from high above my head. Several times. Still nothing. I walk over to the dresser. Maybe I could lift one side; I'm feeling pretty strong. I bend my knees, grip its edge, and lift it maybe an inch and a half. When I let it drop, it makes a good, solid thud. Wood against wood. If that doesn't get them—

The door down the hall opens.

I leap into my bed. "It's about time," I say with a weak edge to my voice.

The silent one enters, the spindly girl who doesn't want to be my friend. I've pulled my knees to my chest and put on a scowling face that I hope makes me appear ill.

"I need to see the doctor. I'm bleeding." It's the first thing that comes to mind. "Don't bother to get Caroline. I know she's busy tonight." I lurch sideways as I groan—the pretend pain is unbearable.

"Okay, okay, I'll, um—" She stutters over the sounds I'm making. "I'll be right back, hang on."

Before she has a chance to get away, I spring from the mattress, shove her into the wall, grab the plastic bag of supplies and water out of the garbage pail, and run. She has fallen to the floor, a small cry escaping her usually mute mouth. I close the second door with a thud behind me and turn the lock in spite of feeling bad for what I've done. I hope I haven't hurt her. I drop down the stairs, sort of running, sort of stumbling, close to falling. I drop and drop and drop. When I near the bottom, the cool night air reaches up to me.

I can see that the door is ajar, as it often is. I'm excited by this escape, this daring act, but also sickened by it. *What will they do if they catch me?*

Doesn't matter. Andrew said we have to go, so we have to go. I run out and reach the side of the chateau, where I drop to a crouch in the bushes, which have hard, pointy leaves. I'll leave my bag of supplies here until I've found Evander. The tower wall rises beside me like a cliff. I'm a mouse sitting at the foot of an elephant, catching my breath while I gaze up the side of the monstrosity I've been living in.

Behind me, the scuffling of feet draws my attention. Two men and a woman in security-squad black race out the door and down the solar-lighted path. Unlike me, the silent one has a key and has already escaped my room and alerted the others. A dog flies out the door next and my heart jolts. It's a German shepherd.

On hands and knees, I scuttle through the bushes in the opposite direction, suffering little injuries inflicted by a bed of mulch. The chateau is as wide as a hospital building. There are windows above my head. No light comes from them. When I'm halfway across, I stand and peek into the closest one. The room is dark. And empty. No heavy medieval furnishings outfitting the space like in the rooms I remember from our honeymoon tour—no goblets or vases or metal tableware. No tapestries with pictures of horses and knights.

I wish Andrew would speak to me again.

As I resume my crawl through scratching leaves and painful mulch, hoping the wind doesn't deliver a whiff of my presence to the German shepherd in pursuit, I would like my husband to provide more-detailed instructions.

What am I supposed to do?

I continue crawling along the castle wall, rising only to look into a window every now and then until I have reached the end of the building. I glance around the corner. In front of me, the long driveway that leads to the street glistens with bright lighting that bounces off shiny parked cars. Expensive sedans, SUVs, and stretch limousines. Whatever gathering Caroline hosts tonight is not a small affair, not one of her drinks-on-the-lawn get-togethers. From the looks of the vehicles, it might be an assembly of world leaders.

The arched wooden entrance surrounded by heavy stone is maybe fifty feet away. I'm still on all fours, still hugging the wall. Classical music reaches out to me in a scattered jumble of notes. It's light and serene, not like a celebration exactly, but soothing. The double doors are propped wide open. Who do they welcome? I hear no chatter, no laughter, no individual voices telling polite stories. Only the music.

What could Caroline want with Evander tonight?

I crawl past an ornamental bush in the shape of a spiral, and a moth flies out and flutters over my head. I am crouched beside the stairway that leads into the castle. Through the two enormous front doors, I see no one. No guests, no security squad. Only a vacuous hall decorated with deep-red carpeting accented with gold, and white walls with massive red and gold wall hangings. I pull myself up to the top step and throw one leg over the brass handrail. As soon as I've cleared it, I rush into the corridor and am staggered by the extra-tall ceilings and wide-open space. I don't remember this from the tour Andrew and I took.

Where can I hide?

I am a fish out of water in frantic search of a pool or puddle I can leap into. I keep my head down and walk, my legs powered by overzealous adrenaline. Across the way, the corridor opens to a dining hall where a couple of servers dressed in black and white set a table decorated with gold chalices and candelabras with gems that sparkle. If they look into the hall for any reason, surely they'll find the lady in the black leggings and gray T-shirt and sneakers a suspicious sight. I keep moving, rounding the corner where I see a set of entry doors leading into what must be an auditorium of some sort. A place for assembly.

Beside each door stands an enormous, human-height vase —glossy red pottery with decorative white tree branches reaching out like a bouquet of smooth and leafless sticks from the top. I squat behind the first vase I come to and consider what to do next.

My breath is coming fast, and my heart flaps like a nervous gerbil trapped in the spinning wheel of my chest.

Through the doors of whatever I am sitting beside (an auditorium? theater? ballroom?) I hear the sound of hushed conversation. Then someone speaks above the rest, but I can't make out words.

Could this be it? Caroline's gathering?

No wonder she was so busy today.

With a startling *whoosh*, one of the doors farther down the hall opens. I freeze, still crouched beside the glossy vase. Fast footsteps near, and I bow my head, praying I won't be discovered. The footsteps continue past, and when I ease out to take a look, I see the back of a disorderly man staggering away. Someone like Uncle Jimmy in what looks like an ill-fitting suit, rumpled with wrinkles. Maybe it *was* Uncle Jimmy. He wouldn't dress properly for a formal occasion— which this must be, considering the venue—and he would probably become drunk and need the bathroom in the middle of a meeting. Except that this man seemed to have more hair than Uncle Jimmy.

It might have been him.

At this point, the assembly room is so quiet that I wonder if I'm wrong about the whole thing. Maybe there is no gathering and the man who left was tidying up the place, or cutting through it to get someplace else. Now I don't know what to do. I can stay here and open the door a crack to glimpse what's inside, or I can move on and search for Evander in another part of the chateau. I want to open the door, but I'm afraid. I press my back against the wall and wait.

Through the door come the sounds of shifting, perhaps standing or sitting, then a collective released breath: "Ohhh" in unison.

So there are people in there.

But is Evander? Caroline said he had an appointment with the doctor. Maybe she wasn't lying. Maybe what's going on behind this door doesn't have anything to do with the Jovians at all. Maybe the chateau has been rented to a Fortune 500 corporation, and I have made a mistake.

Oh, Andrew, please help me!

I stand by. If someone were to open this door, I'm not sure I could pull back and slip into the corridor fast enough to get away undetected, though it might be possible to remain behind the door and go unnoticed as the group passed right by me.

"Bar-starban," a magnified voice says.

I heard it clearly.

I don't know what it means.

The speaker continues. Some words jump out at me: something about "night sky." Something about "Jovian."

Electricity dances up and down my back like leggy water bugs zipping across a pond. I can't tell whether I've given myself the shivers or the source of this strange feeling is beyond the door.

The voice says something about a "child." And then, "Like our ancestors who came before."

The gathering responds with a unified "ohhh."

The doors in front of me swoop open, and I duck behind the vase before it's possible for me to see what's inside. I am prepared to be grabbed, roughed up, dragged out, returned to the tower. Tortured and locked up for real this time.

But no one follows. No one appears. I remain crouched and shaking.

Nothing happens.

The doors remain open.

My insides prickle with frantic nerves.

Whoever had been speaking must have finished, because the talking has stopped. Once again, I wonder if I haven't imagined the gathering I assume lies beyond the entrance. I don't hear any people sounds. No coughing or whispers or scuffing of shoes upon the floor. Maybe there's no one beyond these doors. Surely someone would have come out if they suspected I was here. Surely they would have investigated.

I stand. With breath held, I inch my way forward until I can see inside.

The room before me is much like a planetarium, stretching as tall and wide as a small mountain. Pews line up under an expansive glass ceiling that provides a clear view of the sky. Row after row of them. Filled with ... people. Regular people. An ordinary crowd, not an empty seat available.

I expect to hear shouts, for someone to stand and point, for others to run toward me.

No one, as far as I can tell, has noticed me.

I stand there, a couple of steps inside the room, feeling like I do in dreams when I'm exposed and vulnerable and waiting to be discovered. But no one so much as looks my way. I can't imagine why.

As I consider turning around and running out the way I

came in, the man nearest me, a man similar in looks to Edmund, turns his head. He sees me but makes no response. And then the people from his row all turn their heads in unison, each one of them, all the way across to the other side of this strange cathedral, where the row ends. Forty or fifty people, maybe more, gaze upon me with wide eyes.

Now I can see they're not regular people, though they each wear different clothing, suits and dresses, fancy attire. They have hair styles and various skin tones, black and white and tan, but they are all of the same slender build and vacant expression.

They are as still as owls, and as unblinking.

Not one of them levels so much as a word in my direction.

I can hear the sound of my own shaking breath. And all I can think is, *Why does no one come at me?*

In the next moment, their discovery of me spreads like fire up the rows, each row turns to look and look and look —*flick, flick, flick*—clicking like a camera on time-lapse until the entire building stares upon me at once.

A baby lets loose a cry that shoots upward like a flare gun.

Evander. *Where is he?*

I'm drawn toward the stage, moving in that direction in spite of the multitudes who see me. I must find Evander. I can't worry about whether or not anyone will try to stop me. The lighting onstage is strange—bright bursts sparkling in my eyes keep me from seeing clearly.

I'm just short of the steps that lead to the stage when I hear, "Svetlana."

It's Caroline. Clear and unmistakable. I skid to a stop and spin around.

She's in the front row. Seated in the center beside her pretend husband, Edmund, her "there is no ownership amongst beings" partner.

Evander cries out again. It sounds like "Mommy."

I whip my head around. There he is. On the stage. Held by … someone. Some *thing*. A man or … my vision blurs, and I'm not sure. One second it looks like a man, the next it's long and drawn out, not entirely solid. I can see my son on the stage in front of all of these strange, synchronized people. But the thing that holds him—what is it? It has no face. *Why is that creature holding my baby?*

"Svetlana, it's all right," Caroline says, her voice the usual combination of stern and calm.

I glance back at her and Edmund. Miranda is there, too, and Leo. Dr. Falugia and Nurse Amy. Aunt Constant!

What the hell? They know each other? They're all in on this? How long have they been here? Why didn't Aunt Constant come to see me? Why hasn't she helped get me out? Why haven't Miranda and Leo?

The lights continue to spin and sparkle, but Evander is there. "Come," the thing holding my baby says with a deliberate gesture of his too-long arm and too-long hand.

I'm the mother deer on the grass. Ears pricked, limbs shaking. Frozen in fear and worry. But I need my child. I'm not leaving without him.

"I'm here," my voice quivers, "for Evander."

"Ah." The crowd releases an airy cloud of acknowledgment. I'd almost forgotten they were there; they're inhumanly quiet.

Caroline stands and says, "This is the mother of the child. Svetlana Jovian. Wife of Andrew."

I remember meeting Miranda: *I am Miranda, wife of Leo.* Andrew and I had laughed about it.

Then the creature holding my baby says something in a language I don't understand. *Kah nagga neigh wood allami sun kah nagga.*

In a unified motion, the crowd nods its hundreds of heads.

I'm certain that I might at any second wake from this awful nightmare. But I have to get my baby, so I start up the steps to the stage on shaking legs that may not get me where I need to go.

What will this thing do when I take my baby?

No one tries to stop me from nearing the stage.

No security squad or Jovians.

The wavering thing waits for me to approach. Out and then back, this way and that. Solid, liquid? A blur. At once it is average height, and then it grows taller and leaner. Its head, longer. Stretched. At once it is both solid and transparent. It wavers up and then back down. Evander is perched upon its arm, as he would a human arm. But this arm is long and smooth and trembling like a shadow or the flame of a candle.

It is clearly not human.

Maybe it plays tricks on my mind.

But Evander is there. Of that I'm sure.

It holds out a long, lean arm and gestures again, with the same arm motion it used before. "Come."

I'm frozen. Afraid. A doe who wants her fawn.

When I can't get myself to move any closer, Evander stretches his little arm and makes the same gesture the creature used to urge me forward.

Evander is not afraid.

I step forward with my hair raised, my scalp scalped. I'm having trouble taking breaths.

The thing holds Evander out to me.

"I can take him?" I bow my head in fear. Every cell in my body vibrates. I can hardly walk, hardly breathe, hardly keep my fear contained.

Evander is probably wondering what's wrong with Mommy.

I reach out and grab him.

The thing lets me.

I take a few steps back and gulp the air. Tears run hot down my cheeks. Evander touches my face, concerned.

The creature continues to waver: up and then down. Long. Stretched. Smooth. A blur.

I waste no time sprinting down the aisle in the direction of the door through which I came. It's a long aisle, but I'm determined to get through without being detained. I'm panting as if I have already run miles. One look over my shoulder, and I realize no one is chasing after us. No one has left their seat. Caroline does not even call my name.

Where will we go? Andrew didn't tell me this much. Only that we must leave. I now have my baby. For whatever reason the crowd let us go. The thing on stage let us go. Caroline, Edmund, Aunt Constant all let us walk out of that place as fast as my legs would go.

As I reach the outdoors, I remember that we will need many things.

I have no money. No car. All I have sits in a bag at the foot of the tower.

But I've made it outside with my child. Down the front steps, onto the asphalt where all of the cars are parked. My footsteps *slap, slap, slap* as I run.

I continue along the side of the castle, back the way I came. Past the windows that reveal empty rooms, over the mulch that crunches loudly with every step I take. When I reach the doorway to the stairs that climb the tower, I search for the plastic bag filled with diapers and water. It's gone.

One of the security squad must have found it. I hesitate. We're going to need those things. We won't get far without them—doesn't matter. Andrew said we have to leave, and now we are free. We have to keep going.

As we cross the drive, Evander grips me with anxious hands, and I gaze into the distance, at the darkness dotted with pools of the solar light. I pause at the garden's entry. Is this the way we should go? We've never made it to the edge of the property, to the end of the garden. I have no doubt the grounds spread for miles or at least acres. But we'll come to a road or a neighborhood eventually, I suppose? Or maybe not. Maybe all that's out there is the woods.

Headlights bounce toward us, and I hurry down the garden path, down the steps to the first tier.

The car has turned onto the drive and creeps along. Whoever it is must be looking for us. I duck into the rosebushes as Uncle Jimmy's light-green grasshopper of a car inches closer. Evander cries out. The motor purrs. Jimmy has the passenger-side window down and is squinting into the darkness. Would he be driving if he were going to make us go back to the tower?

I stand, adjust Evander's weight on my hip, and step back up to the edge of the drive.

The lenses of Jimmy's glasses are like satellite dishes over his plump cheeks. "There you are! Get in, no time to waste."

I don't move. My heart's pounding and I'm a million degrees hot.

"Hurry or we'll miss our chance," he says in a loud whisper.

"They let us go," I say.

"They know you don't have transportation. How far will you get with a baby that size and no car?"

He's right. I need a car. I look left and right. Then back at him. "Fine, I'll get in. But you need to get out."

"I can't do that. Nobody wants you driving in a panic. I'll take you wherever you want to go."

I say nothing. I should run the other way. He's one of them—whatever they are. But it's weird because I'm not afraid of him. He's different. I've always thought so. He took me to see Andrew's star.

"You promise you will drive us where I want to go?"

His head bobs with eager enthusiasm. "If you hurry up and get in."

Evander's weight strains my arms. I'm already struggling.

"I want to help you," Uncle Jimmy says, his eyes round with innocence.

"That's funny coming from someone who let Caroline lock me in a tower."

"I did not let—" He huffs. The red hue of his complexion penetrates the darkness. "If I had my way, that never would have happened. *Never.*" His hushed voice cracks with strain.

I want to believe him. Too bad every one of his relatives have lied to me. I scan the garden grounds. Maybe I should run for it. Jimmy's not that fast, and no one else has come for us. We might make it.

I turn down the garden path and start a slow jog, which is the best I can do. Evander touches my face, and I look into his eyes. Andrew's eyes. I want to cry, and I would if I had time, because I'd love to go with Uncle Jimmy, but no matter what he says, he's still one of them. A Jovian. People with ancient alien DNA. Followers of a blurry thing with gangly arms and legs. Who knows what that thing is, what it can do? The thought of that alone makes me want to run.

Jimmy's voice cuts through the garden, loud and clear: "Andrew trusted me."

That's true, and for some reason it produces a lump in my throat. I stop. I'm panting.

"And there are bears in the woods. Saw one on the side of

the road the other day. Not to frighten you, but you should know they're out there."

I have to worry about bears now, too?

"I'm not like them, Svetlana. You know I'm not. I wasn't at the assembly. Did you see me at the assembly?"

I didn't see him there. Unless he was the man in the corridor. And that would mean he left early. To go where? Back to his car because he knew he'd have to pick us up? But that man was wearing a suit, and Uncle Jimmy has on a plaid shirt and khakis.

"I'm different," he says.

Evander makes a little coo that goes up in pitch, a question sound. Thank goodness he's not a squirmy child. My arms throb with his weight. My chest shines with sweat. I wish Andrew would tell me what to do. I feel about ready to collapse, and I haven't even gotten anywhere yet.

When Uncle Jimmy sees us coming his way, his smile is as genuine as one of Evander's. I know a real smile when I see one, and I haven't seen one since I woke up in this place. "I guess it's either you or the bears," I tell him.

Maybe if we had the stroller we could have escaped on our own. But the stroller wouldn't wheel through the woods.

Uncle Jimmy sits up straight and adjusts the rearview mirror. "I'll help you any way I can."

"I want to believe you," I say, checking out the back seat. It looks like a good place to catch my breath. If Uncle Jimmy tries anything funny, like bringing me back here, I suppose I can strangle him while he drives.

I open the door and climb in. There's a baby seat on the far side, and Evander allows me to set him in it and snap the safety straps. I seatbelt myself in beside him. He seems excited, and I remember that it's his first time in a car.

"I took the liberty of grabbing a few things from your room," Uncle Jimmy says.

How did you know I would need them? How did you know I would need you?

"Can we go, please? Before I change my mind?"

He punches the gas, and my head jerks backward. I look around for something to hit Uncle Jimmy with should Plan B become necessary. There's a diaper bag stuffed full of things at my feet. Maybe I can find an umbrella or a—

"I filled the diaper bag and threw in a couple of bottles of water and formula, crackers and such. Blankets," he says. "Oh, and your wedding picture and other Andrew treasures."

His fat-cheeked smile greets me through the rearview, wide with thoughtfulness.

And here I was dreaming of ways to kill him. *What would Andrew think?* I wish I could trust Uncle Jimmy. Of all the Jovians, he's the only one with real feelings, as far as I can tell. As eccentric as he is, and as alien as they are.

I say, "Thank you," as I rummage through the bag and find the plastic vial. I pick it up and make sure the hair is still there. *I demand that you tell me what to do, Andrew!*

At this point, we're flying down the driveway out front, the tires squealing as if we're participants in a race in which we're the only contestants. Out the back window, I see that the front doors to the castle are now closed. The many parked cars remain in their neat rows. No one watches us leave. No one chases us.

They have let us go.

"You'll take us to my parents' house in Kirksberg?" I say. I know they probably won't be home, but if they happened to be I would be so happy. And if they're not, I know how to get into the house without a key, and I will buy an alarm system and turn their home into a fortress and call the police—or Fran, yes, I can call Fran—the second even one Jovian sets foot on the property.

"I'll be happy to."

"Can I use your phone?"

He presses his lips together. "Best if we stay off the phone for now," he says.

I didn't expect him to grant me all of my wishes. I sink low in the seat.

Evander giggles and gurgles and squawks. To him, it's all a game.

21

W e have traveled a couple of miles now, and still I see no headlights in front or behind, no one following after. Evander has had some of his formula, and I have guzzled a bottle of water. The adrenaline that helped me escape has waned, and I'm able to breathe again, to think again. I focus on Uncle Jimmy's eyes in the rearview. "Sometimes it seems like you can read my mind."

"Me? Oh, no. I can't do that. There's only one who has access to all, and that's the supreme being."

"Do you mean the thing I saw on stage?"

"Yes."

"What is it?"

His face drops. There's no laugh in his cheeks, and his expression is as stern as I've ever seen it. "I'm afraid I can't say. But even if I could, you wouldn't understand—not that you're not intelligent."

"Evander wasn't frightened of it. It was holding him, and he wasn't afraid."

"He has no reason to be."

"Well, I've never been so scared in my life. I've never seen anything like it."

"That is understandable."

I want to tell him what I'm thinking about this supreme being. And I want him to tell me if I'm right. He says he wants to help. Does he? How far does our special bond go?

"I was thinking that the supreme being looked like a, uh, like it might be like the, uh, *thing* that landed in Kirksberg in the 1960s. Andrew told me NASA found the body of an—" I'm afraid to say it. I sit there, biting my lip, trying to come up with the right word.

"*Extraterrestrial*," Jimmy offers.

"Yes," I say, relieved he spoke for me. "They found the dead extraterrestrial in the spaceship, and it's kept in a vacuum-sealed tank somewhere, but maybe that's not true. Maybe what they have is only a decoy, or maybe there was more than one of them on that spaceship and the one that survived has been living on Earth for some time. For decades. It's possible, right?"

Uncle Jimmy rubs the scruff of his chin. "I'll tell you, Svetlana, that's not a bad hypothesis, but please, let's not speak of the supreme one. It's just best not to."

Though I have many more questions, I refrain. I don't want Uncle Jimmy to stop telling me things.

A moment of silence lapses, and then I say, "Do you know that before Andrew died, he saw a file at work? A report about the Jovian family. He told me it compared the Kirksberg alien's cells to our family's cells. I'm sure you know this."

He continues to drive, failing to meet my eyes in the mirror, his head dipping into a nod.

"Andrew said David's name was mentioned in particular. But we didn't understand—"

He clears his throat. "David is special."

"He's not your son."

"No."

"You have no biological children."

"None of us on Earth do. We had only Andrew."

This is a strange thing to say. I'm both confused and don't want to offend. "But *Caroline and Edmund* had Andrew. And Andrew had cousins, so *some* other Jovians do have children."

"Yes, but ..." His forehead furrows, and a sharp crevice marks the center of his steep brow. He seems to want to speak and at the same time to hold back. Unfortunately for him, holding back is not something he's good at.

"Andrew was all of ours," he says. "He was what we all wanted. He's why we're here."

I don't ask where else they would be. I'm trying not to get stuck on the disturbing possibility that underneath his clothing and glasses and whirl of hair, Uncle Jimmy may be a creature like the one I saw onstage. But he seems so human. So imperfect and eccentric. Far too human to come from outer space.

"Okay. So Andrew was all of yours, and all of the other Jovian children were not?"

"They weren't born here," he says. "That's the thing. The difference, I mean."

I get the feeling that he's parsing his words, as if he fears our conversation might be overheard. Or maybe he's afraid I'll betray him, that I'll tell Caroline everything about this conversation. I'm sure he's not supposed to tell me anything.

"I swear I won't repeat anything you tell me," I say.

"Oh, I know you won't," he says, as if unconcerned.

"I'm still confused. It seems to me the Jovians want children most of all."

"That's exactly right. We want children most of all."

"But you can't have them. Or most of you can't?"

"Well, there have been problems."

"Like, fertility problems?"

He gazes into the mirror and nods.

"If you want children, I know where you can adopt many. Petranko, for one, Moscow, St. Petersburg ..."

He chuckles. "You're a sharp cookie. And I understand adoption. I think it's a wonderful thing for people to do. Humankind has a heart of gold," he says in a tone of bitter-sweet. "On the one hand, at least."

"And on the other?"

"It also has a heart of destruction."

"Yes, well, some people have bad intentions, but in general, I think—"

"That humans are good. I agree. There's a lot that's good about them."

I sense that he's holding back. "But?"

"They've become lazy over time. They're taking the easy way out. Not doing what needs to be done. The leadership has been weak, corrupted. And the masses are simply not using their heads. They need strong stewards to focus on the real issues, *life* issues. They're too busy fighting each other, too busy trying to quote-unquote win."

"Right," I say, knowing this is leading somewhere, and I don't want him to stop before he reaches wherever that is.

"Among other things, they haven't treated the planet well. That's not something we can ignore. We have a responsibility."

"And by *we* you mean the Jovians?"

He doesn't reply. He's chewing his bottom lip and staring at the road as if there's something distressing out there.

Meanwhile, we've reached the bottom of the mountain, and Evander has settled into his car seat, his eyelids closed. The quiet persists and minutes pass, and I wonder if that's all Uncle Jimmy will tell me tonight. I don't want to push, so I sit back and wait.

Just when I think the conversation is over, Jimmy fidgets

in the seat as if he can't get comfortable. He opens the window and then closes it a second later. I sense tension building. All at once, he shakes his head and rubs his hair—now I know why it's always in a whirl. "The problem is ... the thing is ..." He sniffs loudly. "In a nutshell it's a situation with the DNA."

It seems as if he's halfway talking to me, halfway thinking out loud.

"We're pretty sure that if there were more Jovian DNA in the human species, things would be different, better. And when you think about it, it makes a lot of sense."

"You mean, people would be smarter if they had Jovian DNA?"

"They already *have* Jovian DNA. Some of it. Always have. But if they had more—like Andrew did—they would likely be smarter intellectually, but also ..." He flicks on the car's blinker and takes a quick right turn. The wheels screech, and I wrap my arms around Evander's car seat. "... more connected and attuned to the planet and to their fellow humans. Basically, to all natural things. Do you see what I'm getting at? With a greater amount of Jovian DNA, respect for the universe as a whole would become ingrained, a natural aspect of the human existence. A sense of the universe in its greater form would come from within. And with it, a sense of responsibility. Humans would in general become a more benevolent species."

I think of how Andrew's love of the night sky and for all things in the cosmos came as naturally as his need to breathe.

All of the jostling back and forth has woken Evander, who reaches out and grabs a lock of my hair. I hold back a squeal, and he lets go, then raises his arms and scowls: his fat legs bounce up and down as he kicks the bottom of the car seat, and his brow rumples. I'm pretty sure he wants me to let him out of the seat so I can hold him. I search around the diaper bag and find a stuffed toy. It's a spaceship. He swipes it out of my hand and bites it.

"You found it." Uncle Jimmy's eyes brighten like a child's. "I bought that spaceship for him last time I was at the toy store in Kirksberg."

"He likes it."

"I would do more for him, if they let me."

"If who let you?"

"Oh," he says and shakes his head. "Doesn't matter."

Who else could he mean but Caroline and Edmund? But he's right. It's not important right now. I need to get back to the conversation about DNA. "I'm not sure I understand what you're saying," I say as blithely as possible, feigning ordinary conversation, which this definitely is not. "The Jovians want to repopulate the planet with their own children? But you've had difficulties and only Caroline and Edmund—"

"No, no, that's not it. We don't want to repopulate. None of us wants that. We simply want to assert the power of our DNA. If we slowly but surely inject a greater amount into the population, then over the course of generations, human minds will change. Humans will evolve as a species. They'll become more conscious of their surroundings, of nature and the world around them."

The thought frightens me. If humans become more Jovian, will they also become unfeeling and cold? Andrew wasn't that way, but he could have been, considering the genes he inherited from Caroline and Edmund. And if Andrew's parents are Caroline and Edmund, isn't he more Jovian than human? I'm confused, but I also don't want to overwhelm Uncle Jimmy with questions.

"You think that if humans become more Jovian, they'll take more interest in the Earth and the planets, outer space, the cosmos in general? Like Andrew did," I say.

"Evolution is quite natural, as I'm sure you already know. We want to influence the worldview. We want humans to care for each other and the planet. For *all* planets. Our lineage will work its way into humanity and eventually will be reflected in their belief systems and ways of living. The first humans who have this mutation will have certain advantages over ordinary humans. Greater intelligence, more advanced physical attributes. They'll move into leadership positions in the social structure, leadership roles, probably become presidents and prime ministers and businesspeople who head up large companies and build other platforms upon which to assert their influence. Granted, it will take decades before we see substantial change. But time is relative. A few decades to a human makes the difference between young and old. A few decades to the cosmos is the width of a piece of hair on the time line. We're confident that the DNA will make for a better, healthier Earth. And a healthier human race that's far less violent and far more capable. Believe me when I say it will have an enormous effect on the universe as a whole."

The universe? This is a lot more than I ever imagined Uncle Jimmy to tell. I don't know what to say. He's talking about a mutation of the human race. The genetic engineering of a new human, one that will eventually lead the people on this planet.

As we continue along Route 206, I wonder how much of this Andrew knew. From what I can tell, very little. But he was secretive when it came to work, so maybe he was secretive about this as well. Then again, he was surprised to find the Jovian file—and he told me about that right away.

"Do you see now why Evander is so important to us?" Uncle Jimmy has been watching me from the rearview mirror.

I freeze. The answer is there, like a hair in my mouth, but I'm too scared to pull it out.

"He's the first of the new generation."

The words are like a punch in the stomach.

How did this not occur to me?

Evander has the new DNA. Andrew's Jovian lineage mixed with mine. He's the new human. I have stopped breathing. My hands are shaking. I'm blinking in fear and wonder.

"That's why the assembly was called and all the fuss was made about him at the chateau," Uncle Jimmy says. "They did the same when Andrew was born."

What will they want from my child?

"Who were all of those people? Where do they come from?"

"They're Jovians. They come from many places." He points to the sky.

My mouth is dry, and I'm breathing too fast and becoming lightheaded. "That is hard to process," I say. Suddenly I don't know what to do. Jump out of the car? Scream? Cry? Then I remember that my husband is a star, and somehow this helps regain my sense of calm. Still, I can't stop my voice from shaking. "You say you're different. You're not one of them. What does this mean?"

"I'm from a different place."

He exits the road and stops at a stop sign. Then he takes a right onto Route 14. Is he really taking me to Kirksberg? I don't know these roads well enough to have any idea.

"There's nothing to worry about. We only want Evander to grow up and meet a young lady like yourself, and have many children. The immediate family will encourage him—"

"The same way you all encouraged Andrew."

"Yes."

"Only he died."

He sighs. "We haven't had a lot of luck so far. But combining species on a nonnative planet takes time. It's a mostly unnatural act. The gestation period for us is years, not months, for one. And we're honestly not at our best in human form."

He gives me a quick glance, and I attempt to hide my shock behind a blank expression. Human form. Jovian form. Alien form. Andrew was human. As human as I am, as far as I know. He may have had their DNA, but ... what about the others? What does a true Jovian in Jovian form look like?

"You know," Uncle Jimmy says, breaking me out of my spiral of panic. "It was a miracle when Andrew was born—the fact that all the recessives came together the way they did. He was 65 percent human. More than any of us. The two of you could have had many children."

Andrew had wanted many children.

Evander's legs are splayed as he pulls on his big toes.

"You are saying that my child is the first mutant. But he's human, right?"

Uncle Jimmy says, "Of course," without hesitation.

Evander grins like he's played some mischievous joke on me. I swear he knows everything. Probably even more than Uncle Jimmy.

"He's human and he's Jovian, just like Andrew was," Uncle Jimmy says. "Only he's even more human than Andrew was. And stronger physically because you have excellent genes; I've already told you that. You and Andrew have created a truly marvelous child."

My stomach turns with the realization that my good genes have contributed to making the Jovians' new world mission a reality. I have no doubt his Jovian side is the one fueling his rapid mental and physical growth. It occurs to me that he could turn out to be seven feet tall. Or a genius. Or both.

"Andrew died, but he played his part before he left us," Uncle Jimmy says with the low energy of a person truly saddened. "His heart gave him a disadvantage. We knew he wouldn't be long for this world. It was written in his DNA."

I bow my head. *They knew!*

"I'm sorry if that hurts you."

"Yes, well," I say softly because I'm beyond hurt. "Was there no medicine or cure for this heart problem?"

"No, there was not. I assure you."

I suppose that may be true. They wanted him to live. They wanted him to reproduce. They would have cured him if it were possible.

"And what about Evander? He may have inherited the same—"

"He didn't. I've already checked. He's as strong as can be. Evander the mighty," he declares with pride.

So my child is safe, in that vein, at least. But that's not all I'm worried about. There's so much more. "The thing is, Andrew cared ... and he loved people. And I'm sorry if this hurts you, but Jovians don't care so much. And that makes more sense to me now, because Andrew used to say that the cosmos in general is not a benevolent place—so where they come from, perhaps this is normal."

"I would agree with that, but Earth and nature in general are not benevolent, either. Think of the sea, and storms, earthquakes. Nature doesn't give fair warning. Nature does what nature does—it does what it was made to do—regardless of who gets hurt. Volcanoes stream into villages, hurricanes spin into coastlines, earthquakes shake the land to pieces."

"Yes, but humans are different. They empathize. They help each other get through the hard times."

"Sometimes they care, and sometimes they don't. And Jovians are a nonviolent people, a tolerant people."

I think back to my encounters with Caroline. Every disagreement I've had with her, every time I was rude and sarcastic. She never even raised her voice. I've never seen a Jovian commit an act of violence. A little while ago, a whole cathedral full of them let me leave the assembly with their hope for the future.

"They may be nonviolent, but they thought nothing of kidnapping me," I say, thinking the Jovians probably don't see the enormous difference between their emotion and human emotion. Maybe Uncle Jimmy doesn't see it, either.

"Do you believe I have feelings?" he asks.

"I think you do."

"You have my promise that we won't harm Evander in any way. We will simply encourage him to live a full life, to go forth and procreate."

There's a happy-go-lucky twinkle in his eye.

"Where's the harm in that?" he says.

I don't feel quite as pleased about it as he does. Perhaps because he makes this plan sound so simple and right, and I'm not sure it is. If it were, why didn't they tell Andrew about it? Why didn't they tell me?

"It's for the best," he assures me. "For everyone."

Every one of the Jovians? Or everyone on Earth?

Evander grabs my hand and squeals as he pulls it toward his chest. I take the spaceship from his lap and zoom it over his head. No matter what kind of special he is, he's just a baby. And he's mine.

We've been on the road for an hour and a half and have many hours left to go when my eyelids fall closed. I'm thinking about my parents and how surprised they will be to see us— if they're home. I have to believe there's a chance. Maybe they've been trying to reach me for weeks. I am desperate to see them, and for them to see Evander. I don't know how I'll tell them all that's happened, or even if I should. They'll want to call the police, or worse. To think that my parents, advocates of amnesty, have a daughter who has been held against her will. ... Dana and John will be livid. It's been just me and the Jovians for so long. It would be nice to have some of my own family to help me.

They could be home. And even if they aren't, Evander and I could be okay there.

As I drift toward sleep, I find myself in a memory of my parents' kitchen. Dana roasts a chicken, organic and free range, and the aroma makes my mouth water. She puts together some dark greens and colored vegetables, an African dish, I think it is. John's in front of his laptop, researching their next trip, determining the area of most need. Helena's not here. She's in her room, being her aloof self. Now that I think of it, she often hid from them, coming out only to feed and water herself. My asocial sister.

John says something about an eco-village in Tanzania. He shows me photographs on his computer. A bright place with dusty, sunburned ground. Might they still be there? He and Dana had been working on this project on and off for years. Global warming has taken a bad situation and made it worse, wreaking havoc on the water supply.

Dana tells me they are helping the townspeople build a rainwater harvesting tank. "It doesn't seem like much," she says, "but it will change many people's lives."

"During the rainy season, the water fills the tank," John says. "It's a godsend for the rural areas."

Dana smiles at me. "Such a simple solution, but what an effect it's had."

My parents always find a way to help others.

"Humans have an enormous capacity to adapt," Dana says.

"We have everything we need to exist happily on this planet. We only have to discover ways to use what we have at our disposal."

I look at her with admiration.

She smiles and says, "Adapting is the key."

The trill of a cell phone raises my lowered lids. I twist and stretch my arms. There's a pinched muscle in my neck. My head was cocked sideways. We're still in the car. Evander sleeps beside me. The light snore of his in-and-out breath is comforting. Outside the window, it's dark.

Uncle Jimmy sits behind the wheel, as straight-backed and owl-eyed as ever.

I raise my arms and stretch. "Where are we? What time is it?"

He doesn't answer. He alternates between taking glimpses of his phone and watching the road. With a noisy breath out, he furrows his brow. Then he places the phone into the drink holder and continues to drive.

"What is it?" I ask.

"Nothing. Nothing for you to worry about."

"They know you have us."

"They do. But it's not for you to worry."

That doesn't make me feel any better. I lean back and let the seat hold my weary head. The car speeds forward: the gray hum of the road helps dissipate my alarm. "Listen, there's something you need to hear," he says, a flat note of danger weighing on his voice.

My ears stretch.

"The Jovians know human beings aren't perfect and never will be, that they're thriving in many ways and failing in others. But life is complicated. Humans are complicated, and the species has to change if it's to survive."

"Okay—"

"Unfortunately it's come to the point where the life of this planet depends on that change. It's change or die."

Our eyes meet in the rearview. His are unflinching and stern.

"Evander will set off a new phase of evolution," he says.

"Yes, you've already told me."

"I know that frightens you. But you must remember that the only constant in this world is change, and you'll need to let it happen."

"What do you mean 'let it happen'?"

"I mean it's going to happen. And it's going to be out of your hands the same way it was out of Andrew's hands."

His words have ignited my insides. The surface of my skin feels burned. "You're scaring me."

"I don't mean to. It's important for you to know that whether you try to stop it or not, it *will* happen."

I don't know what to say. Do the Jovians think I will try to stop my own son from growing up and having a family? Why would I do that? If they only want Evander to grow up and have children of his own, why would I try to stop him? Uncle Jimmy knows more, and he's not telling me. He didn't tell Andrew, and now he's not telling me.

"Andrew didn't even know who he was, did he?" I have raised my voice, I can't help it. "He didn't know why they wanted him to have children so badly. They never told him. *You* never told him."

"No," he says.

"That's horrible. You know that, don't you?"

I would continue to express my anger, but Evander is staring at me with a sad expression flattening his cheeks. I grab his hands and say, "Who's awake?"

We drive for about fifteen minutes before Jimmy speaks again: "Will you take a look at that?"

I look all around and see nothing out of the ordinary.

"Through the sun roof. The supermoon."

A burst of light fills my eyes. It's like a giant iced-over snowball hurling through the sky. Much bigger than I've seen before.

"Luna truly is a beautiful thing," he says, "but she's only the closest thing. The closest thing in a cosmos of ever-expanding size. People can't understand how much is out there. They can't see the big picture and Earth's potential part in it. Earth is far more important than they know."

"Important to other planets? Is that why the Jovians care? Because they need Earth for something?"

The Jovians may be a nonviolent people, but they have power. Power that reaches far beyond Earth. More than enough to manipulate me and my son, and maybe even the entire human race.

Uncle Jimmy says nothing, but now I can't stop talking.

"When I met Andrew, I just wanted a normal life. We fell in love. We both wanted a child. A home. Work that we care about. I wanted to make a difference to the children in the world. Maybe that doesn't matter. Maybe nothing matters."

"It does matter," he says, "and you will. You've *already* made an enormous difference by giving birth to Evander. And you had a wonderful husband. You *still* have him. Andrew will always be there. In the sky. Your souls forever entwined."

"John Donne," I say with a laugh.

I doubt any of the Jovians believe in comingled souls. Not even Uncle Jimmy in spite of how it seems at the moment.

I kiss Evander's nose. He's groggy. "Where are you really taking us?"

"To your parents in Kirksberg."

"I'm sorry that I don't trust you."

"Whether you do or you don't, I'm still taking you there."

Something tells me it doesn't matter whether he is lying or not.

———————

We drive all night and straight through the morning, making few stops for food and restrooms. I have been dozing and startle at the jarring of a pothole in the road. The sun breaks through a layer of summer haze as we pass through my old neighborhood in Kirksberg, and my heartbeat radiates to the top of my head. *Home.* Finally!

Please, please, please, please, *please be there!*

Jimmy pulls up to the white Colonial house, which looks exactly the way I remember except that I see nothing through the windows. No curtains, no blinds, no electric candles.

A For Sale sign stands in the middle of the front lawn like a sentry on duty. New Moon Realty.

"No, it can't be." I throw the car door open and leap into a dripping-hot summer day. Sticks and oak leaves litter the front lawn as if a thunder storm passed through last night. I remember when Dana and John decided to paint the door Colonial red. They must have given it a fresh coat because up close the smell of paint is potent. "Dana, John, it's me!" I ring the bell. When no one answers, I climb over the railing and into the bushes so I can stand on tiptoe and see through the window. Inside, the foyer appears cold and uncaring without the sideboard where Dana used to put the mail and the keys and a vase of dried flowers. The living room strikes me as indifferent without the soft furnishings and artwork. Without lights. Without parents or a sister.

They could be anywhere.

I run back to the car. "Did you know?" I shout.

"That they moved?" He shakes his head. "No, I did not. "

"Do you know where they went?"

"If I didn't know they moved, how would I know where they went?" He scratches his chin. "I'm sorry. I wish I did."

I stand on the front lawn, suspended in space, an astronaut without a mothership to land on. I want to run. Uncle Jimmy won't catch me. But Evander. I can't leave him. I'll never leave him.

"I'm going to stay here. I know how to get in."

His face drops. "I don't think that's wise."

I glare at him. "Oh, no?"

"It's better to cooperate when it comes to dealing with the family."

"I'm not going along willingly, if that's what you mean."

"It's your decision, but it will be easy for them to ..." he pauses, "retrieve you. Both of you. Or even just one of you." He raises his brow and tilts his head. "That's not what you want."

The idea of being separated from Evander melts my insides. I knew we wouldn't get away. I'm powerless against them.

There's nothing for me to do except get back into the car, and that's why I'm already slinking around to the other side, shoulders drooped, feet dragging. I grab the handle and open the door.

"I know a nice place where you can live," Jimmy says in a regretful tone. "As a matter of fact, not long ago you lived there with your husband. It's your house. You remodeled it yourself."

I clench my jaw. He stares at me, unmoving. At least he's not trying to make a joke of it.

"They're never going to let us go, are they?"

"Listen, you have more freedom than you think. You really do."

"How is that?"

"You're smart. You'll figure it out. I have faith in you."

"So you're bringing me back to them? This was your plan all along."

"I'd hoped your parents were home. But even if they were, it would likely make little difference."

I want to pull my own hair.

"It's temporary," he says as his hands take the wheel at ten and two. "Everything is temporary. Remember that."

That's a lovely thought, but I don't see how it can help me right now.

T he door to my house is locked. I'm knocking at my own front door. Through the sidelight, I watch Aunt Constant approach. She lets us in. The clock on the wall says it's almost noon. How she arrived at the house before we did is only one of a thousand questions spinning through my head. Probably she hopped into her starship and has been waiting for hours.

She reaches for a hug from me but gets only a cold stare. I will never forgive Aunt Constant for her fake friendship. Evander, on the other hand, claps his chubby hands when he sees her. "Hi, big boy," she says, all sweet and grandma-like. "Hi, James," she tells Uncle Jimmy. Then she closes the door behind us and reactivates the alarm.

Miranda and Leo enter the house through the sliding door in the kitchen and take a seat at the table in the living room, beside the photo of the Chateau L'Origine. My head burns at the sight of that photograph, and I'm sure I've turned bright red. "Why is that here?"

Caroline and Edmund, like tall, slim royals, rise from

their seats at the kitchen table. "David moved in months ago," Caroline says. "He must have—"

"No way in hell." I hand Evander to Uncle Jimmy, walk over to the bird's-eye photo of the chateau, and rip it from the wall. The hook that secured it flies over Leo's shoulder, just missing his face. I wonder what color he would have bled if the nail had hit him. I march back to the foyer with the framed photograph in my hands. It's big and awkward to carry. I have to do a balancing act, leaning the bottom part of the frame into my thighs, freeing up one of my hands to open the front door. When I do, the alarm sounds. With an angry groan, I heave the picture into the air as if I am shot-putting a boulder. The sound of cracking glass as it skids across the asphalt fuels the rage inside of me and makes me feel strong.

"How dare you hang that photograph. ... Are you all crazy?" My voice cuts across the room as my nervous, fluttering hands push the hair from my face.

The wailing of the alarm makes Evander cover his ears with his hands. I take him from Uncle Jimmy, kiss his cheek, and tell him I'm sorry.

Uncle Jimmy closes the door and goes to the security box to key in the code. The alarm stops. Caroline's phone rings. She tells whoever is on the other end that there's no emergency.

Lies come easy to her.

No one says a word or makes a move in response.

They are a nonviolent people.

They don't understand me.

They're letting me have this tantrum.

With a whoosh of the sliding glass door, David comes in from the deck. He's bigger than the last time I saw him. Grown, filled out. More manly. He looks like Andrew more than ever. If I didn't know better, I would have thought he was a clone.

Maybe he is.

Or maybe Andrew was.

Anything is possible at this point.

"Hey, Svetlana," he says.

"Hello, David."

If we were alone, I would ask him why he didn't come to the chateau to help me fight for my freedom. Of all the Jovians, I would have thought he'd at least try.

I wait for someone to say something. So far, all they do is stare.

Caroline steps forward. "We want you to stay here, in this house. Will that be a problem?"

I produce a deranged kind of laugh. I can't help it. I feel out of my mind at this point. "You're *asking*? That's unusual, considering last time you kidnapped us."

"We're sorry you see it that way—"

"How else would I see it?"

Caroline bows her head. A gesture of apology? Regret? Sympathy?

"All of us would like you to stay," she says.

How kind of them.

"You sound so sincere, but I'm afraid some of you are better actors than others. For instance, you, Miranda. You have a real talent. I thought we were friends. I didn't realize we were also relatives."

She never raised my hair, but Fran said it happened when he met her and Leo. That's when I should have put it together. "I believed you wanted to help me get to the hospital. What a wonderful liar you are."

I expect a response of some kind. Anger, outrage, accusation. She remains unaffected.

"Each one of us has a part to play," she says.

Spoken like a robot.

"The Jovians would like me to stay here," I say, musing. "The problem is that I don't feel I have a choice. And I know that what I want doesn't matter to you. It doesn't matter to any of you."

Caroline and I stare each other down. It's a long three seconds.

"What is it you want?" she asks.

"Freedom. For me and Evander."

"You shall have that. Here. In this house."

I don't wish to talk circles with Caroline. She's not going to give me what I want, and I would like her to leave. *Get out of my sight, Caroline.*

Instead I say, "Fine. I'll stay here. But not with you, Caroline, and not with *them*." I tilt my head in the direction of the others. "Evander and I will stay alone."

"I will stay with you," she says. "I'll help you with the housework and—"

"Please," I say. "You don't know how to do housework, and—"

"Constance, then."

"Ha." I glare at Aunt Constant. "I'm afraid that is even less desirable."

Caroline takes a few steps toward me. Her face gives nothing away. I'm afraid she might try to whisk Evander from my arms, so I step backward, toward the bedroom.

She puts her hands on her hips, her red-polished nails shining like glass. "If not me or Constance, then it will have to be David. Or we could all go back to L'Origine if you'd like."

I drop my head and groan, but they probably don't understand such body language. I take a breath before speaking again. "Uncle Jimmy, please."

"I'm afraid James has somewhere else he has to be."

Uncle Jimmy remains beside the front door, which makes

me think he'll be gone in a matter of minutes. "It's true, Svet-lana. I would stay with you if I could."

"Fine. Then David. But I want you to know that I *hate* you." My teeth clench and my heart accelerates in my chest. "I hate *all* of you for what you're doing to me and Evander. None of you knows what it means to hate someone, what it feels like to hate, because you have no goddamn feelings!" My voice reaches a higher octave, screeching a bit, but I'm determined not to cry in front of this crowd.

"I'm going to my room. Evander and I are tired. No one follow us."

As we pass Uncle Jimmy, I give him a look. He has broken my heart. But I don't hate him, even if he did bring us back here. Something sincerely regretful lingers in his drooped shoulders, and I wonder if the two of us are in similar boats. If he had a choice, I'm pretty sure he would let us go, let us live our lives the way we want to live them.

He would have granted me all of my wishes.

Evander and I make the walk to my bedroom with the others' attention boring into the back of our heads. Once inside, I lock the door. There's no lock on this planet strong enough to keep them out, but I still have to try.

We are hungry, but we find some breakfast bars in a box on the bedside table and we eat them. Anything to avoid confronting the family again. Soon after, Evander, tired from the long drive, falls asleep and so do I. But now it is evening, and I am awake.

I go to the window and look up through the branches of the tall maple. Andrew may not be in this house, but he is overhead, a bright light burning through the darkness. Knowing he's out there makes me feel better, stronger. I can do anything knowing he's there, and maybe he can see me, too.

As quietly as I can, I open dresser drawers, the ones that once stored Andrew's clothing. Instead I find women's underthings, cotton tops, clothes I didn't buy myself, all of it in my size. I open the door to the walk-in closet. It, too, is filled: blouses, skirts, and pants hang from the bar. Jeans and more casual things are folded on the shelving above. A shoe rack holds a pair of sneakers, a pair of heels, a pair of black boots. Everything looks brand-new.

Andrew's side of the closet holds baby things. Little boy onesies, sneakers, shoes, a supply of diapers, lotions, wipes.

A few cardboard moving boxes sit on the floor under the hang bar. Some are open, and I recognize items from my bedroom in Ashbury Falls: the contents of my nightstand, for instance—hand lotion, lip balm, one of my child development textbooks. I guess the aliens packed my stuff and brought it here. *How thoughtful of them.* Another box contains my jewelry and hairbrush, pens, sticky note pads: things from my office. In the corner of the closet, I find a box of children's books. Andrew and I bought them together the week before he died. I sift through, excited to see them. With a few of the books in my lap, I sit cross-legged on the floor, and the hopefulness I felt when I found out I was pregnant returns to me—the happiness and feeling of oneness as a family—but this feeling arrives within a swell of sadness, and I long for Andrew again.

I'll always long for him, I realize.

I pass over the Dr. Seuss books and come to a larger one. *The Life of a Star*, with watercolor illustrations. Deep purple skies of outer space mingle with rosy bursts of newborn star gases. I remember this one and how excited Andrew was to find it. As I page through, something slips out of the book and falls into my lap. A thin notepad. Maybe three inches in height. I open it and find scribbles of Andrew's handwriting. Mathematical equations and scientific phrases and facts. Strange, incomplete thoughts. Notes from a lecture, maybe?

When did he do this? And why would it end up in Evander's book?

The notepad has maybe thirty pages, only half of which have writing on them. Small, cryptic, scribbly thoughts. Nothing I can follow or understand. But the word CLONE jumps from the fifth or sixth page in capital letters. The sentence that follows appears to be a definition: the aggregate of genetically identical cells or organisms asexually produced by or from a single progenitor cell or organism.

Did he purposely hide this note so I would find it? He couldn't have—he didn't know he was going to die. But it was hidden. I have no doubt he was hiding it from someone.

The family, maybe.

The thoughts scribbled from one page to the next have no obvious beginning or end.

I continue turning pages and come across another word in all capitals. This time the word is SON. The sentence is not a definition but a random thought: "It is best for both the father and the SON."

My hair stands straight up the way it does when one of the Jovians stares me in the face. He means Evander. But what about him? Evander is not a clone.

Heat rises from my neck into my ears because I don't know what it means, but I feel like I should. It must be important if Andrew hid this notebook. These are the only two words capitalized. *CLONE* and *SON*. It can't be a coincidence.

I put the notepad back inside the pages of the star book and bury the book in the middle of the stack that fills up the moving box.

I throw myself on the bed. I feel like I am being watched. I wouldn't be surprised to find a hole in the wall and an eyeball behind it.

The sheets smell newly cleaned, their cotton scent prominent. The pillows, stiff and unused. It's a new bed, not the one I shared with Andrew. When I turn over onto my back, a blinking dot of a red light draws my attention like a beacon, on and off, in the far corner of the room. I sit up so I can see better. It's a video camera hung from the ceiling.

We are no longer stuck in a tower, but now they will watch us.

Emotionless idiots from another planet.

Tomorrow I'll find a broom and knock the camera to the floor. I look forward to hearing it crack beneath the soles of my new boots.

They're a nonviolent people, so what are they going to do about it?

It's still dark when I wake with a start. My brain is spinning. I was in the midst of a dream. Something about a thousand Evanders and me searching for the original.

But there he is, sound asleep. Safe in his crib. I'm in my bed. I'm safe as well.

My heart slows.

And then I remember. The notebook in the box of children's books. The video camera across the room. I open the drawer of my night table and search for the pen-size flashlight I kept ages ago. It's still there.

I drop to the floor. Crawl into the closet. The video camera can no longer see me. I dig through the box and find the notebook. Switch on my tiny light and page through. There is the CLONE and there is the SON.

"The Jovians want children most of all," Uncle Jimmy had said.

Children who will plant their DNA in the mainstream and change the worldview. But that would take a long time, wouldn't it? One Jovian child at a time, considering the majority of them are infertile and Evander is years away from reproductive maturity.

It will take generations. That's what Uncle Jimmy said.

If they clone Evander, it will happen a lot faster.

And Uncle Jimmy knows how to do it. Uncle Jimmy helped clone Dolly, the sheep in Scotland.

Would he clone Evander? And if so, when?

But Uncle Jimmy's the one Jovian who understands. The one who actually cared about Andrew, who supposedly cares about me and Evander. He's different.

He said himself that he doesn't always agree with them. He didn't agree with the kidnapping or how they kept us in the tower.

Maybe Uncle Jimmy doesn't know of this plan to clone. It's possible Andrew learned about it at work when he looked for more information about the Jovian file. They kept Andrew in the dark about certain things, so maybe Uncle Jimmy's in the dark, too. Who knows why they wouldn't tell Uncle Jimmy their plan—or maybe he knows and he didn't tell me because they're going to do it no matter what. He basically said that nothing I do will make a difference.

A swell of sickness constricts my throat, and sweat sprouts from my underarms. I don't want this for my child. I can't let them do it. I need to talk to Uncle Jimmy. I need to find out if it's true. I put the notebook back in its hiding place, then crawl into bed. Evander pops his head up. He's been watching me through the bars of the crib.

23

J ust a touch of light colors the sky when Evander and I venture out of our room. To my relief, we find no one sleeping on the couch or sipping scotch on the rocks at the table. I give Evander some graham crackers and a bottle of formula from the fridge, and I stuff myself full of milk and cereal. Then we return to our room.

I put Evander on the bed and sit beside him, but he slides off the side and takes a couple of steps. He should not be walking, obviously. He isn't but a month and a few days old, and yet he laughs as he waddles along, using the momentum of almost falling to speed him across the carpeted floor. He crashes at the end but doesn't cry. Instead he rolls onto his back and kicks his legs in celebration.

I can't help but laugh with him. He's like a miniature superhero. An eighteen-pound toddler at the age of one month (I just weighed him in the master bath). And maybe this ability to walk makes sense because he's already so big, thanks no doubt to his special Jovian DNA.

He *is* marvelous, as his relatives like to say.

Later, when the sun is up, we enter the living room and

once again I'm ready for pretty much anything: alien convention, apple pie–eating contest. But only David is present, sitting at the table with a cup of coffee and a newspaper splayed before him. I hesitate mid-step because for a second I thought Andrew was home—then David looked up and his stern eyes, so different from my husband's, gave him away.

"Good morning," he says.

I say good morning. Evander, in my arms, makes spit bubbles in reply. I find a blanket draped over the arm of the couch. David watches as I spread it onto the floor for Evander to lay on. My baby is a happy clam with his feet in the air.

David sips his coffee, turns the page.

Even if he only pretends to be human, I'm glad to see him this morning instead of Aunt Constant or Caroline.

I put an English muffin into the toaster. "I need to speak to your father. Do you know when he'll come by?" I check the clock. It's 7:43 a.m. "I'm surprised he's not here already."

I walk over to the cordless phone and lift it from its perch on the wall. There's no dial tone, and I'm not surprised.

"He has an assignment, somewhere else he has to be."

My ears perk at the news. "Yes, I know, but he already left?"

"What do you need to talk to him about?"

The toaster pops, and I check the muffin. Not dark enough. I push it back down. I'm not sure I should tell David about the note pad I found. Or anyone else. "Oh, uh ... I left some of Evander's things in his car." It's all I can think to say.

David responds with one of those blank Jovian expressions.

"It doesn't matter." I turn away.

My muffin pops the second time and I butter it, then drop into the seat across from David. I'm eager to pick his brain.

"Your father seemed upset last night."

"Did he?"

"He's so different than the rest of the Jovians." As soon as I say it, I'm afraid he'll be offended. But it's David. Not stern Edmund, who's probably the supreme being's next in line, or Caroline, who has not even once engaged in a truthful conversation with me.

David takes his time folding the newspaper and putting it aside. He's not smiling. He's not the David that Andrew and I used to hang out with at parties. Maybe it's because Andrew's death made him grow up. Or maybe he was always like this, and I never noticed because I didn't try too hard to get to know him.

"If you're talking about his overactive imagination," he says, "then I agree. He also has eccentricities the rest of us don't have. That's pretty clear."

"That's not what I mean," I say, feeling like I should defend Uncle Jimmy. "What I mean is that he cares— genuinely cares—about other people."

Again, the stare. David's eyes are vacant.

"Be careful, Svetlana."

"Be careful?" I say, laughing as my neck retracts. Young David is telling me to be careful. "Of what?"

"The others."

Is he trying to warn me? It sounded more like a threat than a warning. But why would that be when the Jovians are a nonviolent people, and I am living under their roof, as *they* want me to? I must act like I'm unafraid, that I have nothing to hide. I take a bite of my muffin and speak with my mouth full. "I know they're watching me while I sleep, but Uncle Jimmy says they only want to take care of me and Evander. Is that not true?"

David responds without moving in any way. He's as still as a glass of water. "You should be careful because the Jovian family is strong, and they won't tolerate uncooperative behavior. They can make things difficult for you."

"Oh," I say, averting my eyes. "I didn't realize—"

"That what you said and did yesterday drew attention?"

"I was going to say I hadn't realized I'd ruffled some feathers, but I'm beginning to think I've offended them—and you—so I will take your advice and be more careful about how I behave from now on."

He says nothing.

I hunch down and soften my voice. I don't want to make David mad. I'm running out of allies. "I was upset yesterday and—"

Evander toddles by.

"Oh, my goodness!" I leap from my chair. "You've walked all the way across the room, you amazing boy. Do you see this, David? This is not the usual for an infant of five or six weeks."

Evander speeds past the table and doubles back into the living area, crash-landing on the blanket spread on the floor. I follow after him, joining him on the blanket. "Do you want to fly like an airplane?" Grabbing the trunk of his solid little body with both of my hands, I roll onto my back, press my feet into his middle, and lift him into flying pose. A look of joy spreads across his face, his chin shining under a wide, drooly smile.

"He's a marvelous child," David says, in a somber tone more common to Edmund's than his own. "Perhaps you'll produce more."

My ears rise to attention; I'm not sure I just heard what I heard. Evander wobbles off-balance. I lower him to the floor and sit upright, careful to adjust my angry attitude so I don't come across as harsh. "Have more children? But my husband is dead."

"Not right away," he continues with eerie calm. "We all have a part to play."

Miranda said the same thing last night.

Why do I feel like a child in David's presence? A child who's being told what to do? I get up and return to the refrigerator. I wonder if the others have brainwashed him or told him to feed me their Jovian bullshit. The David I knew never spoke this way, never in this tone. I pull out a container of yogurt and grab a spoon from the dish-drying rack.

I walk back to the table and once again sit. "In life, you mean? We all have a part to play in life?"

"I mean that the family would love it if you would bear them more children."

His blunt manner rattles my nerves, and I drop my spoon, which clatters when it reaches the floor. I pick it up, walk back to the sink to rinse it off. As I reach for a towel to dry it with, I say, "I need to talk to your dad."

It's the only change of subject I can think of.

David makes a steeple with his fingers. "He probably told you too much and now he's gone."

I hang the towel over the oven door. I'm in no hurry to rejoin David at the table. "*Gone*. As in forever?"

"I don't know."

"Who would make him leave?"

"No one would make him."

"Then he'll be back at some point? Or are you saying something bad has happened to him?"

His ceaseless stare makes me want to shake his shoulders. This is more than stare-worthy news. This is his father we're talking about. His father on Earth, that is. I wonder if Andrew ever saw this side of David. I know I never have.

"No one will discuss it. Not even my mother. I've already tried."

His cup of coffee is mostly full. Probably because he doesn't actually drink coffee.

In the quiet that follows, I stir my yogurt and wrestle with the thought of *bearing the family more children*. How do they suppose they can convince me to do that? And with who? Which Jovian do they think I will sleep with?

That night, in my dream, Helena and I are girls in the orphanage playing twenty-one questions, in Russian, of course. Helena hates this game because I always win, and I never need all twenty-one questions to do it. She can pick anything—person, place, or thing—and I can guess the correct answer after about ten questions, leaving plenty to spare.

We sit on the top bunk, whispering so as not to wake the other children. In the corner of the room, a red light blinks like a video camera.

We have gone back and forth with the questions, and I have guessed, "Russia," winning the game again.

But Helena doesn't grow angry as she used to in real life. Instead she laughs. She rolls back like a beetle and laughs and laughs as if it's the funniest thing she's ever known.

Finally I say, "Why do you laugh?"

She grins as her convulsions subside. "Because I know a secret."

"You tell me all of your secrets."

"I don't tell you all of my secrets. And I'm not telling you this one." The laughter resumes. She grows pink in the cheeks.

"Then I will guess it out of you," I say, thinking myself clever.

"You can try."

"You are the lost princess Anastasia?" I say.

"No."

"*I* am the lost princess?"

"No."

"You are married."

"That is not a secret, dear sister."

"My husband is dead?"

"Yes, this is true. I'm sorry to say."

"You didn't come back to me."

She hesitates, and I sense regret on her part. "That is not a question."

I start to cry. I reach for her, but she rolls back, once again laughing. This starts a fire within me. "Stop. Please, Helena."

She doesn't, and I am starting to hate the sound of her laughter.

Finally, she says, "Your American family is a joke."

"What do you mean? Mom and Dad? Caroline, Edmund?"

"*I'm* your family."

"Is that the secret?"

She stares at me. Blank-faced.

Like a Jovian.

"Be careful," she says.

———

About a week later, after breakfast, David follows me into my room and does a double-take at the empty corner in which the video camera formerly hung. It met *not* with a broomstick—as I couldn't find one of those—but with a children's picture book. A large one. Before he can ask me about it, I say, "It's so beautiful outside. Want to go for a walk? Let's go for a walk. Evander needs air."

By the time I've changed Evander and gathered everything I need for this outing—sippy cup and cereal spread over the tray he sometimes uses as a drum—and have strapped him into the stroller, thirty minutes have passed. David waits for us on the couch in the living room. He appears to be meditating.

"Ready," I say.

He makes no reply but jumps to a stand and strides to the front door, holding it open so I can push the stroller through.

It's already eighty degrees at 10 a.m., a sunny late-July day. "Did you put suntan lotion on?" I ask him.

"No."

"I wonder if I should put some on Evander."

"A moderate amount of sunlight is good for humans. Don't worry."

Spoken like a true Jovian. We head down the sidewalk, which is not smooth but up-and-down angular, thanks to the roots of the trees that line both sides of the road.

"What did you want to talk about?" David says.

I don't remember saying I wanted to talk. David is not much of a talker. I said we should go for a walk this morning because I wanted to distract him from the video camera, and also because it looked like a nice day. Still, I never got my answers about Uncle Jimmy, so I may as well take advantage. "I guess I want to ask you about your dad. Since you're his son, you know him better than most—"

"He's my father."

Strange reply.

"Yes. Right. To me, he seems different from other Jovians."

David lifts a stone from the ground and studies it, rubbing the film of soil from its surface. "We're all different. But you are perceptive, and that's a good quality to have."

He speaks as if he has a chip on his shoulder, like he's smarter than everyone else. He didn't do that when Andrew was alive.

"I think he's more human," I say, testing the water.

"Yes. He's more human, but he's also less human. And it would take ages to explain, so I won't." He drops the stone upon the ground, then kicks it so that it lands at the base of one of the oaks that lines the sidewalk.

"But he's Jovian?"

"He comes from a different place—a place of origination —so he has different strengths and knowledge. But he's Jovian, yes. You know of his work with DNA and fertility?"

"He mentioned Dolly, the sheep—" The stroller gets stuck on a bump in the sidewalk; I press on the handlebars to get the necessary leverage to raise the front wheels.

Evander giggles as the stroller bounces up and down.

"It's thanks to James that Andrew was born," David says.

The *James* in that statement gets my attention.

David's eyes meet mine, and my hair follicles snap, buzzing with the zap of electricity I've come to know so well.

"Andrew was our miracle," he says. "It's not a simple thing to make a human out of two Jovian cells, but James made it happen. What he did wasn't unlike what the ancients did thousands of years ago, when they created the first humans."

Uncle Jimmy had said *Andrew was all of ours*, is that what he meant? A test tube baby?

David pauses and stares at me until I utter a quick "uh-huh." My lips are probably quivering, and I'm afraid to reveal any knowledge of this topic of conversation.

"Andrew's birth was my father's big moment," David says. "He's very proud of his work."

Prouder than the other emotionless Jovians ever could be.

We continue to the end of the block and take a right-hand turn.

"And what you said the other day was correct; our emotions are not the same as human emotions, but believe me when I tell you that we know pride and satisfaction."

I nod sheepishly.

"And dignity," he adds.

I should have been more guarded with my comments since returning from the chateau. David is not turning out to be the ally I'd hoped for.

"I know I've insulted the family," I say, "but I do have great respect for all of you."

"That's good," he says, stiff as cardboard. "My father's greater capacity to feel gets him into trouble. When it comes to you and Evander, for instance."

"Is he in trouble now?"

"*Trouble* is not the right word," he says.

"If it's because he gave us a ride to Kirksberg, I was asleep for most of the trip. I was upset, and I was angry with him. We didn't talk much."

"The fact that he took you away from L'Origine is a problem. He shouldn't have done that."

I stop the stroller. I can't help but accuse him with my eyes. "So, you wouldn't have helped me if I'd run into you that night? I always thought you and Andrew were close. I thought you cared about us and understood us in ways the others don't."

"I would have done what's best," he says, without a trace of regret. "I care about you and Evander more than you know."

While he's spoken the right words, the emotions behind them are lacking. I sense no love in the sentiment. He sounds like Caroline and Edmund, and I can't help but wonder if he's trustworthy.

"I'm glad I can count on you," I say. "Thanks."

He's staring at me again. Reading my face, or trying to. I've fooled him before. It's not that hard to do.

The sunlight streams through leaves that chatter overhead, making mottled light of the rays that color the side-walk below our feet.

Evander shouts, "Go, Mommy!"

I start walking again, and David follows.

"Is it so bad living with the Jovians in a nice house with all of your needs taken care of? I would think that after being an orphan, your greatest wish would be to surround yourself with family."

"Is that *your* greatest wish?"

"I was adopted at birth," he says. "I have never considered myself an orphan."

He's right; we've had very different experiences when it comes to being adopted. But if he's asking this question, he mustn't understand humans. Maybe he's too young to under-stand, or maybe it's not possible for Jovians to understand. What they've given me isn't a loving family. They've forced themselves upon me. Kidnapped me. He knows this. But he doesn't get it.

"There's something called personal freedom," I say, "and after they locked me in the tower, I will never forgive them."

"Freedom is that important to you?"

I'd smack my own forehead, but I don't want to offend. "Freedom is practically everything."

He does nothing in response, and I have no idea what he's thinking.

"They aren't trying to punish you," he says.

"Being locked in a house or a tower *is* punishment. And people need more than the basic necessities to be happy. I'm surprised you don't realize this. Would you want to be locked up and told what to do?"

A bird flies past Evander, who squawks with glee. "Bide-y," he says, pronouncing it pretty well.

David seems not to notice. Or care. "I have observed that humans talk about *happy* a lot."

The idea that he's been impersonating a human for twentysomething years and still doesn't understand the concept of happy is baffling. "David," I say as seriously as I can, "it's what we live for. To be happy, to set up a life that we like. To be with the people we want to be with. To *choose* how we spend our time. I want to be able to cook and shop and hang out with my friends. I want to take Evander to the park for a walk. And I don't want the family telling me when I can do these things."

For a second, I feel hopeful. Maybe if I get through to David, he'll convince the others to let us go—or at least to give us more freedom.

"But *we* are your friends," he says. "*We* want to do these things with you."

I seize the sarcastic laughter building inside of me. "Friends don't … they're not …" I don't want to insult him. "Family is not the same as friends."

Some kind of thinking seems to be going on behind his stern eyes.

"We should go out. Do something fun."

For a flash, I wonder if he's asking me on a date. I tilt my head and say, "We are out."

"I'll take you to the mall. You like to shop."

"Will they let us go to the mall?"

"Why wouldn't they? You'll be with me."

After the conversation we had this morning about my "producing more children," I can't help but wonder if he wants to sleep with me. Is this why the others have allowed him to stay here? Because he looks like Andrew, and they're hoping I'll bear the Jovians more children?

Then again, if he takes me to the mall or out to lunch or dinner, maybe the opportunity to sneak away will present itself. I need a plan for just in case.

"Shopping would be nice," I say with a nervous quiver in

my voice. "Because someone has purchased clothing for me, but most of it is not my style at all."

He feigns a laugh, but I see right through. It's forced. He's playing the game of being human. "I can watch Evander while you try on clothes," he says.

I'm smiling as if I like this idea, like I'm so grateful for his suggestion.

"Do you think they'll let me have a phone? The mall can get really busy, and I'm worried Evander and I might get separated from you."

He picks up a stick from the ground and tosses it into a pile of debris on the side of the road. "Maybe we can borrow Caroline's. I'll ask."

I try not to look too excited. "Thank you, David."

He says nothing in return. The silence settles in between us as we walk back to the house.

24

A few days later, I tell David I'm baking an apple pie for us from scratch.

He doesn't respond. Something out the back window has preoccupied his interest. Evander is out there, chasing a butterfly as best he can—someone fenced the yard while we were in Ashbury Falls (probably Uncle Jimmy)—and David appears to be looking at the sun? A cloud? Who knows?

"I have to go on my computer and get the recipe," I say. "Be right back."

I'm halfway to the office, and he hasn't acknowledged me.

When we first returned to the house and I realized that my computer was here, I asked David if I was allowed to use it and he simply said, "It's your computer."

Which makes me suspicious. My computer has not worked properly since I married Andrew, and I'm sure whatever messages I write or websites I look up, the Jovians are monitoring my activity. It would explain why so few of Helena's emails have reached me the past two years, and the same goes for the ones I've sent to her. Still, I have to try.

Maybe I should use Andrew's account. Yes! I'll use Andrew's account.

I boot up the computer. My home page is my email provider, so I find Helena's address in my address book and jot it down. Then I go into Andrew's email account, happy to find the account is still there, and type in his password, which of course I know. A wave of nervous chills climbs my shoulders as I type my message in Russian:

> Trying to reach you. Please write back with a phone number where I can call you. Very important.

I click send.

Then I search for the apple pie recipe and print it out.

My computer pings, and I jump at the sound, expecting to see David in the doorway of the room, catching me in the act of receiving an email.

But he's not there, and a new message is. It's from Helena. I must have caught her at the computer:

> Svetlana, is it you? I cannot believe this. Are you in Russia? There is a phone where I work: 117-323-555-9911. Is anything wrong?

My fingers stumble with too much speed as I type:

> All is well. I miss you. Will call soon.

Then I close the email account, clear my history, and shut down my computer.

When I return to the living room, David has moved outside, just beyond the sliding glass door. As far as I can tell, he's staring straight at the sun. Meanwhile, Evander runs circles between him and the flowering plants that have attracted the butterflies. He's pretty good at toddling at this point and rarely falls.

I have been in touch with my sister, and a surge of happiness threatens joyful tears. Instead I mix the filling for the pie and pour it into the piecrust. I think of Uncle Jimmy and how he once brought me ten pies as an apology. I wish I could talk to him. I hope he's okay. The Jovians are a nonviolent people, so I'm sure he's fine. What can they do to him, except maybe make him stay away from me and Evander?

Pie making takes an hour or so. When it's done David says, "Feel more free now that you've cooked something?" No smile. No ha, ha. Just blank eyes and unsmiling lips.

"I do," I say, though the baking has little to do with it.

"Good. Let's go to the mall."

"What about the phone? It's always so crowded there."

"Don't worry," he says, "if you disappear, I'll find you."

———

David follows me into a women's clothing shop, but the stroller proves difficult to maneuver past mannequins and displays, and he decides to take Evander for me and wait by the entrance. I collect a few pairs of pants and tops, and make my way to a fitting room.

While back there, I consider asking the salesgirl or one of the many shoppers if I can borrow their phone, but I know how odd that will sound to a stranger. Besides, it's long past work hours in Russia so calling Helena won't help, and I don't know Fran's number at home or at the FBI. There may be a general number for the FBI, where I could simply ask for Officer Vasquez. He must be wondering where I've been, why I've been out of touch. Then again, if he called Caroline to ask for me, she would have provided convincing reasons for my failure to answer the telephone.

She probably tells anyone who asks that I'm in Russia visiting my sister.

The prospect of escaping the Jovians surges like boiling water through my brain. I'm hot and sweaty in this top I don't yet own. I wasn't prepared for this outing. This will not be the day Evander and I get away. I have no phone, no car, no destination to go to or hide in. At the moment, I don't even have Evander.

I try on the clothing and take two pieces to the checkout. There, behind the cashier's desk, hangs a poster of a silver spaceship hovering over what appears to be Main Street America, an advertisement for the Kirksberg UFO Festival. This year, it takes place July 30—this weekend. A person could get lost in a crowd like that one.

With a spring to my step that David no doubt assumes is inspired by my purchases, I meet my two chaperones at the entrance of the store. Evander raises his arms. "Up, up, uppie."

He learns a new set of words every day. This one arises out of necessity. He toddles so well at this point, I know that he wants to practice his new skill. But the crowd in this mall is far too large for him to roam free.

I point across the corridor, at a store that's bustling. "I'm going over there."

David turns to see. "Fine. We'll come with you."

"You don't have to. I would never leave without Evander. You know this."

He stares at me with his sharp eyes and roundy face that reveals nothing.

"Take him to the kiddie rides," I say with a smile. "He'll love the mechanical spaceship that makes buzzing sounds and jiggles around. I'll meet you over there in a few minutes, after I find some jeans to wear."

I can't tell what David is thinking.

I start to walk, then turn to see if they've headed in the opposite direction. I'm surprised that they have. "You'll need quarters," I call out.

I would think David is too far away to hear me, but he raises his hand, signaling that he's got it covered.

I enter the store, bombarded by its too-loud rock music. Groups of shoppers linger around, talking loudly. Some are there to hang out, it appears; others are looking for clothes in earnest. I find a pair of jeans that may make a good fit over my post-pregnancy body, and head to the fitting room. I'm halfway there when I hear someone behind me shout, "Oh my God, Svetlana, is that you?"

I turn and find my old boss from the ice cream shop, Michael, looking as he used to in his ripped jeans and flannel shirt.

He's laughing. The sight of me has made his eyes tear. He comes right up and gives me a sturdy hug. He says, "Holy crap, I'm so glad to see you."

He never acted like he cared for me or Helena too much, so I'm surprised. "Great to see you, too," I say.

"Where have you been? We've all been so worried." He steps back and rakes his hand through shoulder-length hair.

What can he mean by this?

"Andrew and I moved to North Carolina. Did you not know?"

"I heard, I heard," he says, "and I'm so sorry for your loss."

His eyes stop short of meeting mine. "Thank you," I say.

"Your parents must be so relieved that you're back, just to know where you are."

My parents! My hand flies up to my chest. "We haven't been in touch. I went to the house, but—do you know where they are?"

"They moved a few months ago. You didn't know?"

"Oh, well, I ..."

His face grows serious, like he's remembering a sad memory. "They assumed you went back to Russia like Helena did."

"I would *never*," I say, squeezing my eyes closed.

"They said they hadn't heard from you much after your husband passed away, and when they tried to reach you, nothing got through: no phone calls, texts, not even email. It was really strange. They were pretty freaked out."

"Oh my gosh …" I rack my brain for some kind of an answer. "I went away with my husband's family for a while. And I lost my phone so—"

He reaches out and squeezes my shoulder. "I'm so glad you're okay. You should call them, like, as soon as possible."

"I don't know their new phone numbers; they're always getting temporary lines for their trips. I don't even know where they live. Do you?"

"Uh, I think Connecticut or, wait, that's not right. My parents told me …" He strokes his stubbly chin and stares up at the ceiling as he tries to come up with the answer. "Was it upstate New York? I'm pretty sure. Near Albany somewhere. You can call my parents and ask them. They'll know."

"Thank you, I will."

"Give me your phone, and I'll put my mom's number in your contacts."

I'm thinking up an excuse for not having a phone when Evander rolls up in the stroller and makes a happy screeching sound. David's right behind him; his eyes are sharper than usual, like he's focused on something unpleasantly interesting. And that something, I realize, is Michael.

Michael sees him and takes a step backward. His face has gone pale. Maybe he has experienced the hair-raising phenomenon.

"This is David," I tell him. "A cousin of Andrew's."

"Very nice to meet you." Michael holds out his hand to shake.

David hesitates before reciprocating, and I can tell Michael finds it odd. Probably he thinks David is my boyfriend.

"And this is my son, Evander," I say.

"Wow ... he looks exactly like you." Michael bends over and jiggles Evander's foot. "Hey, little man. You're a cutie, aren't you?"

"Uppie!" Evander demands.

"Yeah, I bet you want out. Run around, cause all kinds of trouble—"

"We have to go," says David in an eerie-calm tone. "Good-bye, Michael." He takes my hand in his own, something he's never done before, and pulls me while pushing the stroller toward the exit of the store. I stumble as I tell Michael, "I'm sorry I worried you."

"Call my parents," he says.

Once outside the shop, Evander lets out a frustrated howl. His tears flow over his cheeks and down his chin. He rarely cries, so I'm surprised.

"He didn't like the rides," David says.

I wonder how David managed to get him back in the stroller.

Evander continues to make a scene, fussing and kicking and crying. The crowd walking past slows as they observe us.

I squat in front of him and wipe his face. "I'll carry you," I say. As I undo his restraints, he gives me the pouty lips and eyes that express, *Why would you tie me down like that?* His lashes have bunched up like the plastic lashes of a baby doll. I pull him up to my hip and adjust his weight.

"See, David? Even little children don't like to be held against their will."

He responds with a blank expression. "Why would you call that man's parents?"

"Michael is my boss from years ago. His parents want to offer their condolences."

All of a sudden Evander wriggles like a fish in a net, forcing me to bend forward so he doesn't drop on his head. I waver as I place him on the ground and he slips from my grasp. Next thing he's waddling into a stream of people that usher him away from me.

"Shit." I trip over the stroller as I go after him, pressing through the lumbering crowd with my heart in my throat as Evander finds empty spaces to slip through. I'm exasperated as I push forward, telling people "I'm sorry" as I rush past. And then, finally, an open space in the crowd appears, and I'm able to close the gap between us.

David all the while remains only one step behind me.

25

The gang is all here.

Always a party at my house.

Caroline and Constant putter around the kitchen, though the only thing that seems to be cooking is boiling water. Miranda, Leo, and Edmund talk on the deck out back. When it becomes dark, they'll set up the telescope. I hope they don't stay too late.

Everyone is here except Uncle Jimmy, the one I want to see.

I tend to Evander, who is tireless today. He skipped his nap and has no intention of rescheduling. All he wants to do is walk. Or, more precisely, run. I'm following him around the house the way I would a hyper puppy.

"Mommy, run," he says. "Chase!"

"I'll get you!" I say, taking the bait.

His vocabulary continues to grow at warp speed: in addition to *Mommy, uppie, run, birdy,* and *chase,* he can now say *home, car, store, nana* (for *banana*), *cookie,* and *i-cree* (for *ice cream*). He is nothing less than exceptional in so many ways. I plan to teach him Russian, but those lessons will have to take place behind closed doors.

He speeds into the kitchen, and the two ladies hop out of his way as he rounds the table and circles back, toddling right into Caroline's arms. I stop short at the breakfast counter, keeping a buffer between us. I hate that he loves her. But he does. I can tell that he does.

"The Kirksberg Festival is this weekend," I say.

The two ladies raise their heads in sync.

"Yes, it's early this year," Caroline says.

"I would like to go."

Blank stares. Slow-blinking raptor eyes.

"Evander would love it," I say, as if I don't know what those stares mean, "and I haven't been to the festival in many years."

Caroline straightens Evander's T-shirt and pulls up his elastic-waist pants. "We planned to take the child."

"And leave me home?" I cross my arms. "He's my child, Caroline. I gave birth to him, remember? I mean, *I* don't actually remember, but I'm sure you do."

"Yes, I remember." She holds her head high as if convinced she's done nothing wrong. Then she says, "You've given us a marvelous—"

"A marvelous child. Yes, I have. And David says I can go to the festival. He says he will take me and that you won't object."

This is not a lie. I asked him only yesterday, during our trip to the mall.

Again, the stares.

And then a surprise: "Well, then I guess you can go," Caroline says.

"Yes, you can," Constant adds.

May their oddities never cease.

"David also says I can have your phone in case Evander and I become separated from the group."

This paints a frown upon Caroline's face. "I doubt very much he said that."

I put my hands out to Evander, who yells "Mommy" in Caroline's ear as he squirms out of her hold, roughing up her silk blouse. It's fun to watch him treat her rudely, and yet I have never seen her reprimand him.

He runs the few steps to me, and when he gets here, I jiggle him and smooch his ear. "Ask him," I say.

After Evander ran off at the mall, it was easy to convince David that we need a phone in crowded places.

Caroline leaves us in the kitchen and pulls back the sliding glass door to the deck. Evander sees the door is open and wriggles to the floor. "Gramma!"

Another word he's learned, to my dismay.

She turns and waits for him to pass through.

Caroline will probably tell David that he needs to stop making promises and spoiling me. I'm sure she's jealous of our friendship on some level. I've noticed that David is a favorite of hers. Plus, she won't want to give up her precious cell phone.

"I made meatloaf," Aunt Constant says.

I want to tell her she can cut the homemaker act.

"Would you like a piece?" She goes ahead and retrieves it from the refrigerator before I can answer. I've fed Evander several bottles of formula today, but I can't remember the last time I ate.

"Where's your husband? Do you know?" I ask her.

"On assignment."

"Yes, I've been told. Do you know for how long? I want to call him."

She slices the meatloaf, puts it on a plate, and presses the buttons of the microwave for heating. Then she turns to me.

"Maybe I can help you with whatever it is you want to talk to him about."

Her face is so natural when she smiles. Those soft, sagging cheeks are deceiving. I can see why I fell for her faux friendship.

"No, you can't. You made that clear when I was kidnapped."

"I'm sorry you're unhappy with me," she says, but her apology is flimsy, without empathy. It's just words.

The microwave beeps, and she places the plate in front of me along with a fork.

I look up at her. "Uncle Jimmy was sent away, but he'll be back, right? Can you tell me that much?"

"I can't tell you because I don't know."

Her bright-blue eyes seem not to care. I detect no wifely concern. Her face shouts sincerity and older-lady sweetness, and yet I don't see anything beyond that.

The savory scent of her meatloaf makes my mouth water. I take a bite and wonder if she's been to cooking school. How far do these Jovians go in their efforts to appear human?

"Are you and Jimmy married? Caroline says you're not."

Her Jovian stare is even more vacant than the others'.

"It's funny how none of you know what to say when I speak the truth."

She slides into the seat across from me, arms hanging oddly at her sides as usual. "You should remember that we have our own truth."

I think of the creature at the assembly. The supreme being. Does it dictate their truth? Uncle Jimmy said it was best not to speak of it.

"If you see or hear from Uncle Jimmy, please tell him I made an apple pie and I'd like him to come over and have some with me. I'm worried about him, and you should be, too."

Caroline returns from the backyard and stops in front of us. "I'll give you my phone during the festival."

If she were human, I might say, "I told you so," but she's not, so I won't.

I scan the backyard for my child. He's perched upon David's arm, poised as a little gentleman, as if he's listening to the conversation that's taking place in front of him. With David on my side, the two of us might get out of here.

After I eat, I'll give Evander a bath. He loves water. And now that I know I'll have Caroline's phone at the festival, I need to put my KGB brain to work.

"Svetlana?" Caroline says, startling me from my thoughts. "Be careful."

I give her my best Jovian stare. "Don't worry. I won't lose your phone."

That night, I'm too wired to sleep, staring at the ceiling and listening to my stomach growl. I'm thinking about heating another piece of Aunt Constant's meatloaf, but I'm too lazy to get up, and if I do, David might hear me and then he'll get up as well, and I don't feel like talking to him.

The fact that the festival is this weekend and I'll have Caroline's phone is almost too good to be true. If she changes her mind, I don't know what I'll do. I think she has Fran's number in her contacts. I remember he put it there the night of the funeral. But did she keep it? Will she delete it before handing over the phone? I have no idea.

If I can slip away for a moment without getting caught, I may be able to call him. He may be able to help me and Evander get out.

I raise my head from the pillow. Evander continues to

sleep. I get up, stand over him. His peachy cheeks and plump lips have relaxed into serenity, not a worry in the world. I squelch my desire to smooch his chubby face and wake him up.

Something pings off one of the windowpanes. It's either a wayward beetle or the tap of a fingernail. I turn and see Uncle Jimmy's high forehead and saucer lenses through the glass. If I wasn't so glad to see him, I'd scream in horror.

Thank goodness I killed the video camera.

As I near the window, Jimmy mouths the words, "Open it."

I do. The alarm doesn't go off.

"I disabled the system," he whispers. Beyond the window screen, his head hovers at sill height. His body is wedged in between evergreen shrubs.

I've never been so excited to see Uncle Jimmy.

"I've been so worried about you. Are you okay? Are you in trouble?"

"No, no, not for the moment." He's out of breath and pale in the moonlight. The notches under his eyes are like carvings in wood, like he hasn't slept for days.

"You've been on the run?"

"Yes, I have. But never mind that. I'm good."

Clearly he's not. He's fidgeting like a frightened person. The mulch and debris below crunch under his nervous feet.

"What have they done to you?"

"Nothing," he says, avoiding my eyes. "It's fine." Then he looks up at me. "I had to see you and Evander one last time. I have to tell you something because ..." He swallows, as if sidelined by a feeling of overwhelm. "Because they're sending me away—for good—and I want you to know. You *need* to know."

I have that oh-no feeling like time is moving too fast and it's so slippery I can't get a grip on it. "What is it?"

He tilts his head back and draws courage from the sky. "Andrew was mine ... my son."

"Yours?" Now I'm the one with the owl eyes. "How is that ..." I stop myself when it dawns on me that Caroline must have slept with Uncle Jimmy, of all people, even if she and Edmund aren't really married. But, wait, Andrew was a test tube baby.

"Back then, I worked extensively in the lab," he says. "I was in charge of getting Caroline and Edmund's cells to unite, but it wasn't working. It hadn't worked twelve times. No matter what I did, the cells just wouldn't form the zygote." He pauses, stares into the distance. "So I did an experiment: I replaced Edmund's cells with my own. I didn't expect to be successful. Those two have a more direct line to original man than the rest of us, but you never know when it comes to the Earthly world, and, well, I did it. One of my cells did it, and it's the best thing that ever happened to me."

"Oh, Uncle Jimmy." I drop to my knees so that we're close together. "Did Andrew know?"

"No. He never did."

"Does anyone else?"

"Possibly, um, David—"

"That means Evander is yours, too," I say in a whisper shout as I come to this realization.

"My beautiful grand-boy." Tears glisten in the corners of his eyes. His smile is a jumble of happy and sad; his emotion, so real that I want to reach out and hug him.

"You've done me proud, Sveta. I'm so glad Andrew met and fell in love with you. I wanted to tell you. All this time I wanted to tell you." His nose is red.

I lift the screen and cup his chin in my hands. His warm, imperfect, stubbly face. "You can't let them do this. We can run. The three of us will go someplace together."

He shakes his head. "I wish we could, my dear, but there's

no place for me to run to. Go and wake Evander for me. I have to see him one last time."

I rush to the crib and lift him out. His head wobbles as he wakes with a hiccup. He sees me and gurgles, his mouth full of drool. "Look who's here," I whisper, propping him up right next to Uncle Jimmy's face. "Your favorite."

"There he is, the little sleepyhead." Uncle Jimmy sniffles. "Evander the mighty. You be a good boy, you hear? You do what your momma tells you."

Evander reaches out to touch him and makes a sound like he's trying to speak.

"Listen," Uncle Jimmy says, scratching his chin. "I have to tell you something else, and I don't have much time so. ... They want to clone him."

"What?" It's a dose of adrenaline straight to my heart. My brain spins, and I grab the windowsill for support.

"Don't let them do it," he says.

Andrew was right. The CLONE and the SON! And Uncle Jimmy knew. My heart races. I feel as if Evander and I are under attack. I'm tempted for the both of us to jump out the window. "Can't we come with you?"

"I wish you could," he says, shaking his head.

"Where you are going isn't a place for us?"

"No. It's not."

We're alone. We are all alone.

"How will I stop them?"

"They'll have a much harder time once I'm out of the picture, but you still have to protect him. I know you can figure a way."

"I'll leave Kirksberg as soon as—"

His pale eyes grow sad as he bows his head and takes my hand. "I'm sorry I can't be more help. I'm afraid it's written in the stars."

"What do you mean?"

"You and the Jovians. Your life with us. But don't worry, you'll find the freedom within your confinement. I know you will."

"You can't mean that." My thoughts flash like an electrical storm.

He checks his watch and then pushes the window screen back down. "I have to go. I'm sorry. They're coming for me."

A horrible lump blocks my throat. "Where are they sending you?"

He turns, points to the sky. "You see Orion's Belt? The star cluster on the left, it's called 'Mintaka.' That's my home, my place of origin."

I look up through the window and find the three stars in a row. The same constellation Andrew always searched for first. When I look at Uncle Jimmy again, his eyes are soft and he shrugs a little.

"Nothing is lost. Nothing created. Everything is transformed," he says softly.

"I'll miss you." My voice cracks.

Evander places his hand on my cheek.

"Close this and lock it." Jimmy gestures to the window.

As I push the glass down, the bushes shake and he's gone. He just disappears. I look up and see a flare speeding toward the sky. A tiny white fire flung headlong into the night, rising higher and higher, until it becomes one with the darkness.

Evander and I gaze at the heavens together.

A knock on my bedroom door startles us. The light goes on. David walks in, fully dressed in jeans, T-shirt, sneakers. He's wide awake. I wonder if he ever sleeps.

I squint from the brightness and swipe at my tears.

He joins us at the window. Stands a foot away from me. I smell something musky ... aftershave? The one Andrew used to wear.

"I thought I heard you," he says. "It's a nice night."

I feel his eyes on my face. He's studying me. "Yes," I say. "It is."

"Evander woke you?"

"I think he had a bad dream." I meet his eyes and then flick mine away. I don't want him to recognize my fear.

"Want to go out back and sit on the bench until he gets tired?"

I shake my head. "I'm not feeling well."

"You look pale."

I wish he wouldn't study me so closely when all I want to do is burst into tears.

"How about I take Evander and you can sleep?"

I hesitate. Would he hand him off to the others so they can clone him right now?

He holds out his hands.

"Are you sure? Aren't you going back to sleep?"

"You know me. I hardly ever sleep."

I can't think of a way to say no without offending him, so I kiss Evander's cheek and pass him over. Without the extra weight to steady my hands, they're shaking like frightened children. I clasp them together.

"You want to go watch the stars?" David asks him as if he were asking an adult.

"Daddy," Evander answers with a big smile.

"Yes, we'll get the telescope out and look at Daddy."

Then he turns to me. "Good night."

With Evander in the crook of his arm, he crosses the room.

I remain by the window, unsure of what to do.

David has paused by the bedroom door. "Get back into bed."

With slow reluctance, I climb onto the bed and slide under the sheet and blanket. Perhaps I should go with them. I could say I've changed my mind. But I'm barely holding it together. Uncle Jimmy has left us. And our life with the Jovians is written in the stars.

David waits. "You know how you asked me if James was different from the rest of us?"

"Uh-huh, yes," I say, adjusting my pillow, as if the subject no longer interests me.

"You were right. He's the most different of all."

I think of the supreme being. *Wouldn't it be the most different of all?*

"You are very astute, Svetlana," David says, and he closes the door.

26

I n spite of the heat wave, this year's festival is the most crowded I have ever seen. Even in my cotton shorts and halter top, I'm glistening with a layer of sweat. My companions are not. I never noticed before, but none of the Jovians perspire.

I push Evander's stroller over the bumps of downtown Kirksberg's old root-mangled sidewalks. The wheels are nearly flat, weighted down with my supersized child, bottles of water, containers of applesauce and yogurt in a lunch cooler, and the diaper bag bulging with supplies.

Caroline's cell phone sits in the front zipper pocket of that bag.

Caroline herself walks on the left side of me, with Constant on the right. In front of me are Leo and David, and behind is Miranda. I have my own secret service today.

We stopped for lunch at the café and have begun wandering from exhibit to exhibit, making our way up Main Street at a turtle pace. An enormous Styrofoam solar system spins across the road in front of the toy store. Leo, in particular, likes this display. He says they come close to replicating the true orbits of each planet. The next display features papier-mâché spaceships that hover around the different entrances to the library. David tells me these are not lifelike at all. I would like to remind him that we're at a UFO festival, and it's for fun. Not everyone here is an alien. But I don't think he'd like that, so I don't say it out loud.

"You know the spaceship that crash-landed here in the sixties?" he says.

"Of course." I turn to face him as if I'd hate to miss even one word.

"It was a Russian scam. The scientists at Starbright proved it decades ago."

"Did they?" I ask, wide-eyed with false glee. "Are they sure?"

"The goal of the Russians is to spread chaos and mistrust of the government," he says. "They achieved both with one minor prank."

I don't believe a word of it.

Many of the children at the festival hold the controls to a drone or other remote-control flying object. Evander points and shouts, "Look it!" But I don't find any of this as delightful as he does. Uncle Jimmy has been sent away. He was the only one who cared, and now I plan to run even though he says there's no use in trying.

"I-cree," Evander shouts.

We have just finished lunch and none of the adults want ice cream. "Soon, baby, soon. We're going to see the rocket launch. Whoosh! Up in the sky."

"Whoo," he shouts and kicks his legs.

It's only a matter of time before he demands to be let out of the stroller.

Every year, the rocket launch takes place in the green space beside the gazebo. As we approach, I can see that a crowd has already formed in anticipation. David ushers us through the fenced entrance, and somehow the tide of people drifts apart as we near. A pathway opens for us to pass through. It's a strange phenomenon I notice right away, but none of the Jovians acknowledge it. The people here don't even look our way, and yet they move just enough so we can pass with ease.

We reach the front row. Before us, a wobbly temporary fence stops the crowd from going farther. Several yards beyond that, a sizeable launchpad made of two-by-four planks and many thick metal bolts awaits the countdown.

The people in this area wear the chagrins of those who have been waiting too long in direct sun, but as soon as my family members arrive, the festivities begin. A man wearing a silver astronaut costume, helmet and all, steps up to a microphone. "Welcome to the annual launching of the Kirksberg rocket," he shouts above the noisy cheers of the crowd.

He goes on to provide some interesting facts about rockets, the NASA space program, and why they're both so important. Then he talks about the small missile we're about to see launched and gives a brief description of rocket science, though not many people seem to be listening as they chat with friends and sip drinks out of paper cups and straws. Still, the crowd claps when he's finished his speech.

Finally, he climbs the ladder below the contraption and lights the fuse. As it spews bits of light like a sparkler, he leaps down to the ground and runs to safety. The wire continues to flare, and when the little blaze reaches the end of the line, the rocket boosters ignite with a loud fizzing sound and the projectile takes off, leaving behind a blast of heat in its wake.

Evander claps. The rocket thrusts; its flame of a tail scintillates like a diamond in sunlight.

A round of applause rises from the crowd as they wave

miniature American flags. It is not as spectacular as the parting of Uncle Jimmy.

"They finally got smart and had David build the ship," Aunt Constant says.

David, her pride and joy. How human of her.

"It always needed more thrust," he says.

The man in the space suit comes back to tell the crowd that the rocket will land in the Atlantic Ocean, somewhere in between Mexico and Egypt. Too bad Evander and I couldn't have hopped aboard. Then he says, "Only kidding, it should land about a half mile away, in the high school football field."

"I-cree!" Evander shouts, and when I look at him, he raises his arms and says, "Uppie."

"Not yet, baby. You want your rocket?"

He reaches with his hands.

I dig through the bag and come up with Uncle Jimmy's rocket doll, along with his words in my mind: *Don't let them do it, Svetlana.*

I must be brave.

"How about ice cream?" I ask the others, fanning myself with a brochure from Cerino's pizza parlor that I picked up on the way in.

The Jovians stare. They couldn't care less.

"You look hot," Caroline says. "Someone can drive you home, if you'd like."

"Thank you for your concern," I say, "but I'm fine."

A line of customers dribbles like a slow-moving stream from the ice cream shop onto the sidewalk and up the road. People stand around in their neon green makeup and flowing robes, their pointy Spock ears. I tell the Jovians that Evander and I can go in and that since we are the only ones who want ice cream, they can head over to the bookstore to kill some time.

None of them respond to this suggestion.

"I'll go with you," Aunt Constant says. "The others will be fine right here."

This time it is I who fails to respond.

We join the long line and inch our way toward the shop's entrance. After twenty minutes or so, I'm expecting Aunt Constant to suggest we come back another time. But then a crowd of people leaves all at once, and suddenly we have made it to the steps in front of the entrance. I can see the two girls who work the counter in their paper hats and hair pulled back into sloppy ponytails, like me and Helena used to. Then I remember how Andrew came to my rescue when Helena stranded me on festival day, and the memory cuts a chasm through my chest.

"Mommy all right?"

Evander has been watching me from his stroller.

"Uppie," he says.

I squat in front of him, so we're at the same level. "Not yet. Soon, sweetie."

"Uppie, now," he demands.

"Soon."

He wriggles violently in the seat, and his T-shirt rises up to reveal his bare chest. A nude bandage under his arm comes into view, the sight of which draws my full attention. "Did you get a boo-boo, Evander?"

"Uppie," he says again, and then he screams. The sound is ear piercing, like a train screeching to a sudden halt. He's never done this before. I think he may have damaged my eardrums.

Aunt Constant looks at me with a squinty question in her eyes.

I shrug at her. "He wants to get out."

He screeches again, this time, a long, trailing sound that raises my shoulders to my ears. Someone in line behind us yells, "Jeez!" Another grumbles, "Nice set of lungs, kiddo."

"You better pick him up," Constant says.

I undo the straps and grab around his waist, pulling him upward. He squirms, and I lose my hold as I lift him. The little imp jumps to the ground and sprints. I shove the stroller in Aunt Constant's direction and run off with the diaper bag slung over my shoulder. It bounces around my back as I shout, "Evander, get back here."

This is not part of my plan for escape.

I run, desperate to keep the red of his shirt within sight as he dodges the legs of children and adults. People try to stop him as he passes, but he evades them all. Two weeks ago, he couldn't even stand, and now he's like a miniature sports player. I don't know whether to be frightened, angry, or proud.

He finally stops when we are three, four blocks from the ice cream shop and I am out of my mind with worry that I'll never catch him.

"Mommy," he says, panting. His chest heaves. He's so solid, a muscle baby.

He raises his arms so I can lift him and take a quick second look at the bandage under his arm. *Could they have taken a skin sample?* With one arm, I support his twenty pounds and with the other, I unzip the diaper bag and pull out the cell phone. I have to make the call now. We may not get another chance. But I'm sweating terribly. My arms are slippery, and Evander is heavy, even though he's clinging onto me.

The phone shoots out of my hand and clatters across the sidewalk. A piece of plastic has broken off the top. A woman who looks a lot like Miranda picks it up and hands it to me.

My voice shakes as I thank her and continue to walk, trying to keep pace with the flow of people in front of me. If the phone is broken, then so is our plan. ... I press the home button and the screen comes up. The glass is cracked. I touch the phone symbol and scroll through contacts. Fran's number is there. I press it.

Nothing happens. No ringing. No beeps.

I'm out of breath and desperate. I don't have time for this. Evander is sliding downward, out of my grasp. I get a better grip on him, and press the contact number again. This time it rings. I check behind us. No Jovians as far as I can see. I stop under a tree. The shade helps a little. A stream of people pass while I catch my breath.

I tell Evander, "It's okay, baby."

"Mommy," he says, and he pats my neck.

The phone continues to ring. It switches over to voice mail. Fran's voice. I'm nervous. I don't know what to say. The beep sounds, and I start talking. "Fran. It's Svetlana Jovian. I'm at the UFO Festival in Kirksberg. I'm calling from Caroline's phone. Please call me back." I fumble the phone again, but this time it lands on the grass. I pick it up. "I need help, Fran. I need your help."

I end the call and start to walk again. I don't know what to do next. What if he doesn't return my call? He may be on assignment, or ... who knows where he might be. He doesn't even live in Kirksberg anymore. I call him again. "Fran, I don't have much time. They're looking for me. I'm going to the park in the center of town. I'll hide there for as long as I can. Evander is with me. There's a bench by a grove of trees." I stop. What else should I say? "I need to get out of here. Please send someone."

I look around us. *Where are we?* I get my bearings and cross the street. The park is a few blocks up and to the right. I think.

"He'll be there," I tell Evander. "Let's call Aunt Constant."

I press the buttons. She answers right away.

"I'm on my way back," I say, panting loud enough for her to hear. "He played a game of hide-and-seek, but I found him."

"Thank goodness. We were so worried. Where are you?"

"In front of the Holy Shots bar," I lie.

"All the way over there?"

"I got turned around, but I'm heading back toward the ice cream shop now."

Silence.

"Hello?"

"Be careful, Svetlana."

I swallow. "What do you mean? You don't believe me?"

She hangs up.

I drop the phone in my bag, get a better grip on Evander, and start running as fast as I can. I'm not in great shape, so I'm struggling. I can feel my face getting red with exertion. I see the entrance to the park, marked by its bright-yellow police tape. My phone is ringing, but I can't pick it up. It could be Fran, but it also could be a Jovian, and I can't risk dropping the phone or Evander.

At the entrance, a sign says, "Park Closed for the Duration of the Festival." I duck my head and step in between rows of yellow tape. I remember the park and its paths as if it were only yesterday that Andrew and I came here to eat alfresco. The sun reaches down with its scorching rays as if drawing us in. We're the only ones here. The crowd from the festival dutifully remains outside its perimeter.

Evander looks all around, a question on his face. He's puffing his chubby cheeks. "Mommy?"

"We're going for a little walk. Nothing to worry about," I say. After the run and with all the fear in my body, it's hard to breathe and speak at the same time. "Daddy loved this park. I always wanted you to see it."

This is our only chance. If Fran hasn't received my message, my attempt is for nothing, and I don't know what the Jovians will do to me. They might take Evander or send me to some distant planet. I scan the area—the flowers I would find beautiful on any other day, the grassy carpet of green, the tall shade trees—as we move deeper into the park. I expect Caroline or Edmund to pop out at every step.

In the distance, I see the grove of pines that marks our destination. Andrew's bench. If only Evander and I were going to meet him, I would be so happy. I wouldn't be afraid.

We pass through the cluster of pines and arrive at the bench. "This is it," I say, trying to sound more cheerful than I feel. I place Evander on the wood boards that make up the seat, and I sit beside him, one hand on him at all times to make sure he doesn't topple. My hair, my halter top, my neck and face are sticky wet. I'm breathing hard. It's taking longer to catch my breath than I would like.

If the supreme being reads minds, it knows where I am. What I've done. What I plan to do.

"Svetlana."

I turn.

David has entered the park behind us.

We're caught.

But it's only David, so maybe he'll help. He said he would have given us a ride away from L'Origine. But he didn't actually do it. Uncle Jimmy did. Come to think of it, I didn't see David at the assembly.

As he walks toward us, he says, "What are you doing?"

I get up. The diaper bag slung over my shoulder swings around and hits me in the back. Evander's weight strains my spine as I lift him. Sweat drips into my eyes. "We're resting," I say, taking quick steps backward. "Andrew and I used to come here. I was showing Evander this bench, where we had our first date."

Evander tilts his head and makes a little coo that goes up in pitch, a question sound. He's wondering why I'm frightened, why my voice shakes, why I'm backing away from David.

And then Evander does something that frightens me even more than meeting David here: he extends his arm and gestures the way he and the supreme being gestured onstage that night in front of the assembly. "Come," he says, waving David closer.

Evander is not the supreme being. I know this for sure.

But maybe David is.

"Very astute, Svetlana."

His voice is void of anger, void of compassion, void of humanness.

I'm pretty sure he has read my mind.

He resembles Andrew in body and face, but now that I see him this way, with the hunt in his eyes, I can't believe I ever thought they looked alike.

He has stopped a few steps from us, every second transforming into something else, growing taller, his arms elongating, the fingers stretching. His face becoming a blur of smoothed features and empty black eyes.

He reaches with his long arms for Evander, and I lunge backward, tripping over my own feet. "David, please!" Somehow I remain upright. No one is going to take my son. I scramble back as best I can, then turn and run up the path, jostling poor Evander, who begins to cry.

"Svetlana!"

It's Fran's voice and David's voice, both at the same time.

I whip around. I see three people by the bench. Fran and a man and woman I've never met. They all have guns raised and pointed at the wavering thing that is David.

David turns toward them. He is motion and light and movement. Ever-changing organic matter. Inhuman and human at the same time, glimmering like the flame of a candle growing ever taller.

He is the leader of a nonviolent people.

But Fran and his agents don't know that.

David's voice drops from the sky. It seems to come from everywhere all at once. "Where will you go, Svetlana?"

"I won't let you do it," I shout. "I won't let you take him!"

"We'll never hurt you. We are your family."

I'm still moving up the path, struggling to put space between us. "I do not feel the same way," I say under my breath.

Fran and the woman make a run past David—one passes in front of him, the other behind him—but he doesn't attack them. When they reach me and Evander, they push us behind them, forming a protective wall between David and us. The third agent, his face collapsing into a horrified scowl, trips and falls as he backs away. "I'm sorry," he shouts as he scrambles to a stand and runs in the opposite direction, out of the park.

Fran and the woman take the FBI stance. Arms leveled, guns ready to fire. He says, "Stay back, man. Svetlana's coming with us."

"Did it hurt you?" she asks.

"Not yet," I say.

"She can go wherever she likes," David says. "Earth is not that large."

"Don't threaten her," Fran shouts.

A massive crack like thunder strikes my eardrums. Some invisible force descends from the sky and slams into the earth like a high-rise toppling over sideways. The earth below our feet shakes as if it's been hit with a gigantic hammer. The vibration causes tree limbs to fall and the land to ripple. A glowing light surrounds David, a nimbus that turns his elongated body into a silhouette.

He's a lighted cloud. A spirit hovering. A swirling oblong of energy.

The air becomes cool and buzzy. Darkness descends. Suddenly it's night. Suddenly all is silent. Fran and his agent remain in front of us, ready to fire.

I look up, expecting clouds above us, but there are none. The black sky and its cloth of speckled stars becomes clear above our heads. A strange green vapor glows where David's oblong silhouette previously hovered. I feel a force of energy emanating from that general area—or, actually the force is a pull, not a push. It's a tug on my hair, a kind of gravity. I hold tighter to Evander as it strengthens. The diaper bag pulls painfully. Fran and the woman's FBI jackets flap as they would from a gusting wind—but the air is still. Their guns fly out of their hands as if attracted by an enormous magnet. I twist my arm in such a way that allows the diaper bag to slide from my shoulder and break free of me.

The neon vapor that once was David has stretched and thinned, grown as tall as a giant redwood. Rocks fly at it. Tree limbs swirl around it. Leaves spin like windblown snow. Evander holds tighter, and I do the same.

I keep my head down and squint my eyes to see. It's trying to pull Evander from my arms, but I'll never let go. I'd rather die than let go.

All at once, the stretched form snaps into the shape of a sphere floating maybe six feet above the ground. The size of a child's red playground ball, it brightens as it shrinks, still tugging at me with fierce force, challenging me to hang on longer than I believe I can. I watch that orb grow smaller and smaller, dwindling to the size of a coin. When it gets so small I can no longer see it, it explodes with a bang greater than any thunder I've ever heard. My forehead touches Evander's like one last kiss.

The Earth staggers, and a blast of white light jets upward into the sky, then speeds back toward the ground, toward me. I hear a sound like a grenade go off inside my skull, and every hair follicle on my body stands at attention. A lime green plasma envelops me, tugging at my legs and arms and making them shake. And then my vision is lost in a lighted blur, and I can no longer see.

In my mind, thoughts and images of Andrew come to me, my sweet husband smiling in my direction. I reach for him and he fades. Uncle Jimmy appears next and then Aunt Constant follows, as well as Caroline, Edmund, Miranda, Leo. Then people I've never met. *Jovians* I've never met and yet somehow I know them to be Jovians. Hundreds of them. Maybe thousands. Finally, I see David and baby Evander.

After that, I'm careening through a galaxy of seemingly endless stars and black space. Something rises in the distance. A small, smooth sphere growing larger. A planet. Its gravity pulls me, draws me into its orbit, makes a tiny moon of me. As I near, its vast red spot stares at me like a single unmoving eye. I feel them inside my head—my Jovian family —and they feel me. It's like souls mixing. We are, all of us, part of this blinding white light passing into the great beyond in the form of an electrical wave.

It doesn't hurt.

It is not violent.

It simply rushes through like a cold breeze traveling from one place to another.

And then it lets me go.

After that, I can't hear anything, not even my own beating heart. And I wonder if I'm dead. But I can't die. I can't allow Evander to lose his mother. I think of my own mother and how much I love her, and I continue to hold him tight.

When I open my eyes, I'm lying in the grass. The sun's rays come from above like golden ladders that lead to heaven. The summer breeze rolls over my skin. I feel Evander's weight motionless upon my chest.

It's done. Over.

We're still together.

"He's gone," Fran shouts, and his footsteps rush toward us.

For a moment I think he means my baby. Evander has not yet moved. He is a lump of weight upon my chest.

"Svetlana, are you all right?"

My child's head rests below my chin. His complexion is pale, his expression peaceful. I kiss his soft hair, breathe in his baby-boy scent.

He stirs. His little heart beats strong upon my chest.

He pushes up. Gazes at me with a look of joy.

"Mommy," he says.

The FBI woman talks into her phone, calling for backup.

I sit up.

Evander hugs me. I feel as if Andrew is there, too, with his arms around us, holding us together.

"We're okay," I say. "We're okay."

Fran kneels in front of us and ruffles Evander's hair. "So this is little Andrew."

"He is Evander," I say.

Fran's chin quivers when he smiles. "I'd recognize those eyes anywhere." He stands, then scans the surrounding area. "What the hell just happened?"

David has let us go.

I can feel it.

I just know it.

We are free from confinement.

Energy has transformed.

From one thing into another.

Planets have shifted.
Stars aligned.
We are free to go.
And about this I am very happy.
But I also know that everything in life is temporary.

Russia smells like Russia.

Like snow and birches and damp soil.

I wake up every morning and know exactly where I am.

I'm not in America anymore. Not in Kirksberg or Ashbury Falls.

I'm in Tula with Evander, with my sister, Helena, and her husband, Ivan, and their daughter, Alexandria.

The FBI gave us a free ride out of the U.S. with a special escort. After the incident in the park (which the government deemed a strange weather occurrence), Fran told them about my history—my parents' history with the KGB, that is—and the government was more than happy to pay for our tickets abroad. When the plane touched down, I woke from a restless sleep and heard Andrew's voice again. He said, "Good, Sveta. Good."

A few days before the Kirksberg UFO Festival, Andrew's voice had visited Fran as well. It came to him in a dream. "Andrew told me you needed me in Kirksberg," he said. "It was like he was standing right next to me. I couldn't see him there, but I felt him, his presence. I thought about it for days. I couldn't ignore it."

Thank goodness he didn't.

Fran emails every couple of weeks. He has promised to provide me with updates on the case. Not that there ever are any. The family disappeared the day of the Kirksberg Festival. Abandoned their homes. Left their jobs.

A search of their residences revealed nothing. No files, notes, journals. No letters, unusual objects, space dust.

NASA won't let the FBI anywhere near the offices of Starbright International.

Every morning, I teach Evander and Alexander their letters and numbers and colors, the ordinary things an adult teaches a child, but I do so in both English and Russian. Because who knows where our lives may take us? Together we gaze at the night sky. We have no expensive telescopes, but we can see Uncle Jimmy's home in Orion's Belt, and at the right time of year, Jupiter and Callisto come into view. That's my favorite time, when I know my husband can see us.

Helena doesn't believe my story, and I don't blame her. She thinks I suffer some kind of stress disorder, and maybe I do. My husband has died. I was kidnapped. My own family tried to take my child. Whenever I tell her we must make the most of our time together, she thinks it is some American motto. Some apple-pie positiveness.

She's wrong.

David let us go. About this, I am sure. He let us go because he's not worried. Earth, as he said, is not that large. One day, when Evander has matured, David will descend from the clouds like a god and tell us it's time to come back. To go home. To be with the Jovians once again.

They will groom him for a leadership role so he can begin to influence the worldview, raise a family, and start a new generation of humans—if they haven't used his skin cells to do that already.

I don't know what I'll do when that happens. I hope my husband and Uncle Jimmy will guide us.

For now, I get what I want.

Evander gets me, and I get Evander.

He is my child. I am his mother. Our bond is forever.

He will grow up knowing the power of a mother's love.

And one day, when he's able to understand, when he's grown big and strong and even more marvelous than he is now, I'll tell him the truth about who he is.

That he is both human and Jovian.

And that they will be coming for us.

ACKNOWLEDGMENTS

First and foremost, I want to thank my family: Joe and Sienna, Mom, Dad, and Jen. You've all been there in both small and large ways, celebrating my little achievements, holding me above water when I felt like I was sinking, making it all possible. I love you very much. This book has been a long time coming, and as I think back to the first creative writing workshop I enrolled in at the age of twenty, I realize how many people have helped me along the way. Professors Boyers and Goldensohn, you hooked me on this thing called literature and there was no turning back. E. M. Forster and Lucy Honeychurch, you provided the spark that set me aflame. Amy Hempel and Meg Wolitzer, what an honor and a privilege it was to learn from you both; to this day I recall advice you gave me and your inspiration to last a lifetime. Thank you to Jay Fraser and Jennifer Violette Na for reminding me why I do it; and to Anne Slater, Ann Snow Cosgrove, Uncle Henry, Aunt Theresa, and my mother-in-law, Carol Catanzarite, for early support and letting me know it was okay to dream big. Thank you to my beta readers, Paula Radell, John Remington, Laura Mahal, and Jen

Eyre—I literally could not have done this without your invaluable feedback. Thank you also to all of my proofers, among them Karen Fullerton. To my good friend and fellow wordsmith, Tricia LaRochelle—we are in this together, lady! Finally, thanks to my editors, Elizabeth Bruce, John Matthew Fox, and Rachel Randall for being amazing at what you do.